DEATH at CROOKED CRE

"...I've read a few murder m_____
have been as cleverly crafted with as many red herrings thrown in
as Death at Crooked Creek by Mary Ann Cherry. This is superbly
written with a plot that takes you on twists and turns you don't
expect and leaves you guessing or, even better, makes you think
you know "whodunit" before the actual reveal. I loved the artistic
setting of the story and the fact that the author, an artist of note
herself, was able to inject her knowledge into the story naturally
and without artifice...I cannot pay this author any higher
compliment than to say, I want to read more about Jessie
O'Bourne's crime-solving adventures....I can only hope there are
more on the way. A highly recommended read."

- Grant Leishman for Readers' Favorite

"...Death at Crooked Creek is a well written mystery with a touch
of romance. I loved how she made the people come to life through
their distinct personalities, making them seem like the person next
door...I enjoyed this book and looked forward to reading more
every time I had to set it down."

 - Peggy Jo Wipf for Readers' Favorite

"...Author Mary Ann Cherry has written an intriguing art mystery
story in Death at Crooked Creek.... I enjoyed how convoluted and
complicated the story was—a fascinating read!"

 - Deborah Lloyd for Readers' Favorite

DEATH at CROOKED CREEK

by

Mary Ann Cherry

DEDICATION

This book is dedicated to my sons and daughters, who are the light of my life, and to their wonderful spouses. I am so lucky my children chose well. It is also dedicated to my grandchildren and future great-grandchildren. Enjoy!

DISCLAIMER

This book is a work of fiction. Graehl Frames, from the Kalispell, Montana area, and Ten Spoon Winery near Missoula, Montana, are real businesses with wonderful products, but the characters, incidents and dialogue in the novel are drawn from the author's imagination and should not be construed as real. Any resemblance to actual events or living persons is entirely coincidental with the exception of Cheri Cappello, a contemporary living artist, and Emily Carr, an actual Canadian artist and writer (now deceased). I also briefly mention Georgina Goodlander, a lovely artist friend who is the Willard Art Council's Visual Arts Director here in Idaho Falls, and who graciously allowed me to use her name. Thanks, Georgina!

Emily Carr (December 13, 1871 – March 2, 1945) was one of the first painters in Canada to adopt a Modernist and Post-Impressionist painting style. Carr was inspired by the Indigenous people of the Pacific Northwest Coast. Events in this novel regarding Carr paintings are fictitious. A bit of a rebel spirit, she is supposedly one of the first women to ride a horse without doing so side-saddle.

Cheri Cappello is an exceptionally gifted artist who creates the type of Native American reproductions portrayed in this story. Thank you, Cheri, for allowing me to give you a fictitious personality in my mystery novel. I certainly had fun doing so, and I think that if Jessie were a real person, you two would be great friends.

Copyright © 2018 by Mary Ann Cherry

Death at Crooked Creek

by Mary Ann Cherry

PROLOGUE

September - Nielson's farm near Crooked Creek, Montana

Adele Nielson stood with her hands on her hips and gave her father her best teenage stink-eye. *Is he the most stubborn man on the planet? He's as bullheaded as that monstrous Angus in Fergusen's back paddock.*

Berg Nielson avoided her gaze. He sat in his favorite chair, his normally bronzed face as pale as white bread and his eyes rheumy. He looked bone-weary. Adele knew the chemo had stomped the stuffing out of him. *Thank God he's through with the barrage of treatments,* she thought. According to the oncologist, the chemo had been superbly successful. Even so, Doc warned her Berg would feel as useful as an old work boot for several weeks—one with no laces, holes in the sole, and shredded lining.

She stiffened her spine and prepared to do battle. Adele knew that to grow a successful crop come spring, winter wheat should be planted at least six weeks before the ground froze. Eight weeks was even better. Worn out as he was, her dad was nonetheless determined he could do the planting himself.

"You know you aren't up to it. Not yet." She gave him a stern look. "Besides, Jeff Benson came over yesterday and loaded the planter with seed. The John Deere's all ready to go, and my evening shift at work doesn't start 'til six. I have the whole day. I can at least get the north field planted."

She looked at her watch and frowned. She'd better get started. Even with the entire day to plant, she'd be late to work if she

1

didn't hop to it. She didn't want to stop planting mid-field. Adele loved her job at the library—her first real after-school job—but the world wouldn't stop spinning if people waited fifteen minutes to check out a Louise Penny or Dan Brown novel. Of course, Mrs. Lehman, that gossipy old biddy, might feel out of sorts if her interlibrary loan had come in and Adele wasn't behind the desk the second the hour hand hit six so she could pick it up. For some reason, she seemed to keep track of Adele's shifts and came in only when she knew Adele would be working the desk. *The woman is curious about Dad.* Adele gave a shudder. But, she was in her early sixties, about the same age as Berg, and since Adele's mother, Vi, passed away, the Lehman woman always inquired about Berg's health. *Oh, well. It doesn't bear thinking about.*

Adele twisted a lock of her shoulder-length brown hair and gave her dad a look that would wither steel. "And tomorrow's Saturday. I have all weekend to do winter wheat."

Without further discussion, she walked to the entryway closet and pulled out his coveralls, holding them against her body to judge the size. She realized with a wince how long it had been since she'd fully pulled her own weight on the farm—so long that her own coveralls no longer fit. Grimacing, she gave Berg's large coveralls a critical glance. While she was nowhere near her dad's breadth, she *was* tall. And hippy. Maybe she could manage with them for a day. It would save her jeans. Every time she worked in the barn or drove the old John Deere, she managed to wipe oil on her jeans.

Hmmmm. Dominic was more her size. Maybe she should go up to her brother's old bedroom and borrow some work clothes. Goodness knows, he won't need them back until he comes home from his deployment. Still, she hated to just help herself to his things.

Her dad gave her a critical look. "You'll be swimming in those, Addy." Then he stared out the window at the unseeded fields with a wistful expression. "You sure you can do it? You don't mind?"

"I don't mind," she insisted. "It'll be fun." Smiling to herself, she realized she meant it. In fact, she felt a little skip in her step at the thought of having something substantial she could help with, instead of sitting by helplessly and worrying about her Dad's health. She gave the heavy coveralls a shake. "And these'll do fine."

"Okay, okay. But not unless you sit and have a good breakfast before you start."

She wasn't hungry, but she hesitated. She knew he didn't feel up to cooking for himself. And he still didn't have his appetite back. He'd skip eating unless she made him a meal and watched him chow down.

"That's a great idea. I'm hungry as heck for bacon and eggs. But I'm only fixing them if you'll eat, too." She draped the coveralls over the back of a chair, went to the kitchen and took a frying pan off the hanging pot rack. Humming, Adele bustled around the cheerful room, pulling a loaf of sourdough from the wooden bread box and setting out ingredients for French toast, scrambled eggs and bacon. Soon, the mouthwatering smell of frying bacon made her glad she'd decided to postpone the fieldwork and cook. She plopped the French toast into another pan, and while it sizzled, she quickly packed drinks and snacks into a cooler to take along in the tractor.

Half an hour later, she sat at the kitchen table across from her father. He looked better. The hot breakfast was a good idea. They argued too much lately—especially about her choice of boyfriends—and sharing a companionable breakfast took the edge off the irritation they sometimes felt toward each other.

She tried to cut him some slack, knowing the chemo made him cranky as an old grizzly, but he seemed to be mighty opinionated about college. About girls who married too young. About jobs. The boredom of the snack shop job she'd tried before landing the position at the library proved he was right about *that* job. College *was* a good idea. She shivered inwardly. Not marriage. Not at nineteen. She wasn't ready, even though at first it had sounded like fun to have her own place. If she ever did get married, she hoped it would be because she couldn't be happy without one specific man. *A man*. Not a boy. And right now, she was pretty sure she was the only adult in her relationship even though her boyfriend had four years on her. And the worst thing was that he had some screwed-up values. Very screwed-up. She stood and began clearing the table.

When her father got sick, she'd grown up a little—actually, a lot—learning how easy it was to *want* to take care of someone you loved, but how hard it was to *do* it. *It must be even harder to take care of kids*, she mused. She didn't want to give her dad the satisfaction of telling him he'd been right all along, though. Grinning, she guessed it all broke down to wanting to argue for the sake of stating her own mind, letting him know she was all grown up. Making her own decisions.

"What are you smiling at, girl? Thinking of that damn boyfriend, I'll bet. That engagement ring the kid offered you had a diamond about the size of a pinhead. You know what that fellow has most of, don'tcha?"

"No, but I'll bet you're going to tell me," she said in a combative tone, egging him on. She chewed her bottom lip. *Heck, that brought a little color to his cheeks. I need to remember he's been sick. Stomp on my tongue a little. Besides, he's a lot older than my friend's folks. Old enough to be my grandpa instead of my dad. Man, Dom and I must have been the classic afterthoughts.*

"Bull. That man is full of it. Pure bull. Never heard the like." He guffawed, the laugh ending in a short cough. "Why, he's more full of bull than old Johnson's big Aberdeen Angus. And he's too old for you, that's for sure."

Adele put the last plate in the dishwasher and grabbed the coveralls, slipping the baggy legs over her jeans. It was a bit nippy out and the heater in the cab of the tractor wasn't working. She reached into the hall closet again to take one of Berg's blue knit caps off the shelf.

"You could be right, Dad." Tucking her hair under the hat, she grabbed the cooler, pecked the surprised man on the cheek and headed out the door. "Love you!" she called over her shoulder.

Partway to the tractor she heard the door to the house open and Berg call after her, "I love you too, Addy!"

* * *

4

"Ugh." She'd forgotten how mind-numbingly boring seeding could be. Row after row after row at five miles an hour. How could she have thought it might be fun? It was getting towards eleven when she began obsessing about lunch. Even though she'd munched all the snacks from the cooler, her stomach rumbled like an approaching train. The music pounding through the cab helped the boredom but didn't do squat for the hunger pangs. She wished she'd packed more in the cooler. *Was there at least one of those cardboard-tasting granola bars left?* Continuing her slow pace down the row, she reached an arm over, flipped open the small insulated bag and rifled through wrappers and napkins. An apple core. A plastic fork.

After her fingers found and grabbed the last peanut butter and honey bar, she straightened. There was a distant pop and something sharp stung the side of her neck. She slapped her hand at it. A gasp erupted from her throat when she saw that her fingers were crimson with blood from a wound on her neck. A spider web crack had blossomed across the front windshield. The John Deere lurched across the field as she wiped the back of her neck in horror. She twisted around and saw a neat round hole in the back window.

A bullet. It must've just grazed me.

Her head swung around, her eyes scanning the field. Nothing. She pulled the tractor to a stop and put it in park. Then she looked toward the far ridge. Next to a parked pickup, someone stood there holding a rifle.

"What the heck? What's he—"

As Adele saw the man raise the rifle to take aim again, she stiffened in horror. She threw herself to the floor a fraction of a second too late.

* * *

Out at the highway, the shooter lowered the rifle. "Oh, God! No, no, no. Not Addy."

He swore aloud in disgust and disbelief. Just as the girl began to dive for cover—just as he squeezed off the second shot—he'd realized it wasn't Berg. Damn! She'd been wearing her dad's knit cap. *Damn, damn, damn, damn, damn!*

He let the rifle drop to the ground and covered his face with his hands. He squinted his eyes shut, seeing the bullet plowing its way through that lovely face in his mind's eye. That sweet, beautiful girl. His stomach roiled. He couldn't let himself vomit. *DNA*, he thought. *If you can get it from hair, you can sure get DNA from someone's lost lunch.*

"Addy . . . Oh, Addy. You stupid kid." Anger made his voice unrecognizable even to himself.

He should have planned better. His stomach threatened to erupt. He ejected the shell casing and put it into his pocket. Then, looking frantically around, he spotted the first empty casing. He grabbed it and picked up the rifle. He ran to his pickup, jumped in and stomped on the gas. He had to get out of there. As he headed over the hill, his eyes filled, making it difficult to see the road. Without bothering to wipe the tears away, he headed toward town. Reason reasserted itself. *Don't be stupid. Follow the original plan*, he thought. He hit the gas. When he got to town, he'd stop in at the gas station on the other side of Main. Then get a cup of coffee from the diner. Make it easy for people to remember just what time he'd stopped by. To place himself in town.

His mind churned into overdrive.

"Think, you idiot!" he bellowed aloud. "Think!"

He forced himself to be calm...to concentrate. He would have killed her later. Or maybe not. But he wasn't prepared to deal with it so soon. And now, his plan had to be revamped. Totally revamped. Worse than that. Could he salvage any small part of the plan at all?

His upset stomach threatened to ruin his focus. Glancing at the passenger seat, he saw the fast food sack from his morning run through the Quik Stop. At the time, he thought he could eat, but he'd been so nervous he hadn't swallowed more than a bite. His stomach did another heave. He pulled the pickup over and stopped on the edge of the gravel road. He snatched the bag and opened it to be met with the nauseating odor of a greasy breakfast burrito.

"Oh, God," he groaned. He leaned over the paper sack and retched.

Chapter One

Following March - Crooked Creek Resort

Jessie O'Bourne brushed her red hair back from her face, pulled on her knit gloves and gathered her strength. Then she grabbed the handle of the unwieldy hand-truck and dragged it backward. The handcart loaded with paintings threatened to spill as she waded through six-inch deep snow to the service entrance of the majestic Crooked Creek Lodge. The Hawk, her beloved motor home, sat double-parked as close as she'd been able to manage, with her orange tom wailing like a tortured soul in the cat carrier while she unloaded. She couldn't chance Jack getting loose—and lost—while she took trip after trip into the building.

Unlike the well-lit, welcoming front entrance of the hotel where she'd checked in, the artists' parking area remained unplowed. Numerous tracks through the snow testified that many artists had already slogged through the deep snow to carry their paintings and display panels into their reserved rooms—rooms where each painter or sculptor would exhibit for the four days of the annual Crooked Creek Art Expo.

"Why the heck didn't they plow and shovel back here?" Jessie grumbled aloud. *With the snow still coming down, whoever responsible for snow removal must plan to wait until ALL the heavy white stuff quit falling.* Under her breath, she muttered several of Arvid's favorite four-letter words. Her Norwegian friend, Detective Sergeant Arvid Abrahmsen, from the Sage Bluff,

Montana, Sheriff's Office, had some choice expletives he liked to blame on the Swedes.

"Drek," Jessie said aloud, trying out another choice Arvidism. Then her heel caught the edge of the buried sidewalk, and she lost her grip on the hand-truck handle. She stumbled, overcompensated for the weight of the cumbersome cart, and tumbled backward into the dirty wet snow, her behind settling squishily into the slush just as she heard the door behind her open with a loud squeak. She swore again.

"Let me help you." The voice was amused and deeply masculine.

She reached a hand up, expecting to be helped from her ignominious position. Instead, the owner of the rich baritone waded casually toward her, grabbed the handle of the pushcart full of paintings, yanked the whole shebang easily up and over the curb and, as Jessie turned her head to watch, disappeared with it through the propped-open door of the hotel. Then he stuck his head out the door and said, "Can't have those beautiful paintings left in the falling snow…might ruin the liners on the frames. Better get up and find something to wipe 'em off with."

Jessie sat, feeling the cold wet moisture seep into her jeans.

"Thanks," she muttered belatedly. He was already gone. She heaved herself up and slogged through the door. The blasted man was right about the frames, though. Each of her expensive custom frames had a brushed-gold metallic liner. Most of the art was wrapped in bubble wrap, but the two pieces on the outside were brand new and she'd decided not to take time to wrap them just to go twenty feet. Their burnished liners would need to be wiped immediately to prevent water spots. She pulled several tissues out of her coat pocket and did just that. She pulled the cart down the wide hotel hallway to the Yellowstone Room, where her work would hang during the show. While the other participating artists exhibited their work in main floor hotel rooms emptied of beds and furniture for the duration of the show, a large portion of the coveted convention room was allotted to Jessie's work.

'The Yellowstone' was a centrally located room with space originally reserved for Georgina Goodlander, a local watercolor painter. Goodlander, pregnant with her first child, had been invited as the featured guest artist, but a week before the show, she'd delivered a dangerously premature baby boy in the Billings hospital. The infant remained in the hospital's neonatal care unit, while his mother stayed in the Motor Lodge next to the facility. Georgina—Georgy to Jessie, who'd known her since high school—had begged Jessie to take her place when the panicked show committee asked her to recommend someone to fill in as the guest artist. After much persuasion, Jessie had agreed.

After a scary situation the previous year in Sage Bluff where she'd nearly been shot by a dangerous, unscrupulous woman, then a hectic barrage of show after show, she'd been looking forward to a break at her home in Santa Fe, time to paint, relax a bit, and take stock of her life. Instead, she'd packed as many paintings as she had on hand and driven back to Montana. In addition to setting up a display of her work, the tasks of doing several oil painting demonstrations, teaching a one-day workshop, and giving a short talk now fell to Jessie.

The Yellowstone Room would be manned by a volunteer from the Creek's Edge Museum. Jessie wouldn't have to handle sales of her own paintings, or even do the repetitive "meet and greet" of visitors to the display space. The museum would handle all of that, since their knick-knacks, small sculptures, tee-shirts, and books about Montana and Montana artists would also be shown in the convention room. Two of Jessie's larger landscapes would be transported to the Creek's Edge Museum and hung there.

Unlocking the door to the Yellowstone Room for about the tenth time, she pushed it open and tiredly stacked the paintings from the hand-truck against the wall. Pleased, she saw that about a dozen four-by-eight-foot art display panels had been delivered. Her paintings would be hung on these. She looked at her watch. There was no time to set them up and hang the work now. There was a meeting covering the rules and schedule of the show due to start in about thirty minutes. Grimacing, she decided she'd better make an appearance.

She felt the back of her jeans. Soaked. Locking the door to the room, she hurried back to the Hawk and chattered to Jack as she pulled onto the main road and drove to the designated artists' parking lot. It was also unplowed, and Jessie groaned as she pulled

9

her RV into a large space at the back of the lot and imagined the walk back to the lodge.

"Just wait two seconds, Butter Tub," she said, "and I'll let you loose."

"Yeeowwwwr!" He scrabbled against the door of the carrier, sticking his pink nose through the wire of the door and making feline sounds of impatience. "Nik, nik, nik!"

"Yeah, I know. Poor thing. You're sooo abused," she crooned to the orange tom in a faux sympathetic tone as she let him out of the carrier. He wound around her legs, rumbling his gratitude. Jessie gave his back a few quick strokes, then yanked a T-shirt, sweater, and her favorite pair of blingy jeans out of a drawer and added them to a rapidly filling suitcase. Grinning, she thought how she'd have scorned the sequined pockets a year earlier. That was before seeing how Monette, a southern belle in jeans decorated so heavily on the rear pockets that Jessie dubbed them "stoplight jeans", captivated every male in the room with the sway of that sexy billboard.

Blast Monette. Blast Russell, she thought, her grin turning upside down as she remembered how susceptible her old flame in Sage Bluff had been to Monette's transparent flirting. *And blast Grant, too.*

"Dritt," she said aloud in Arvid's Norwegian. *Grant was the worst.* Her mind wandered back to Sage Bluff and her encounter with Grant the year before. He'd let her think he was free and clear, but an unmentioned wife answered his phone when Jessie called his Boston number. Before that little incident, she'd had high hopes for a relationship with six-two—and gorgeous—Grant Kennedy. With her in Santa Fe most of the year and him in Boston, it would have been a difficult, long-distance relationship. Boston to Santa Fe. She sighed. Assigned to the art theft division of the FBI, Grant was knowledgeable about art. Unlike Russell, he appreciated her work. And her. Jessie's thoughts turned back to the time they'd spent together in Sage Bluff the previous year. His sense of humor was part of his attraction. He'd made her laugh, as well as feel special.

But not special enough to be the "other woman", she thought grimly. *That louse.*

10

"You're the only male I like right now, Jack Boy," she told him, reaching down again to chuck him under the chin and scratch behind one ragged ear. He stood, feet apart, tail up, squinting his eyes in catly bliss. After the artists' meeting, she'd haul him and all his paraphernalia to the hotel. "I've got to go, Bud," she said, giving his fur one more quick ruffling. "No clawing on the sofa. No carousing. No pulling open the cupboards or shredding the toilet paper. Back in a few."

Locking the door of the Hawk, she stepped out into the softly falling snow, the white flakes coming down big and thick as though God, Jesus, and Saint Peter pelted each other with feather pillows in wild abandon. It seemed like a long way to the hotel from the Hawk. And it was cold. However, she was fairly sure her pipes wouldn't freeze. After all, it was March.

Springtime in Big Sky Country. Almost.

The short-lived spring storm had whipped through Montana, swatting down thoughts of spring with a vengeance, but the weather hadn't turned very cold. She drew the hood of her coat close around her face, hurried across the parking lot into the hotel, stomped her boots on the mat inside the door, and took the elevator to the fifth floor.

With no water available to the Hawk, the lodge would be "home sweet home" during the show. Stepping through the door to room 510, she checked her watch and realized she was running late. She hurriedly stripped, wound her long, red hair on top of her head with a tie, and hopped into the shower, letting the hot water pelt her skin.

It was Heaven. Stepping out and drying off with a fluffy towel from a heated towel rack, she looked appreciatively around the spacious room. Every inch of it oozed western decor, from the running horse design on the duvet to the expensively framed wildlife paintings on the wall.

She snuggled her bare toes into the fluffy white sheepskin rug at the end of the bed while she pulled her hair free of its tie. Jessie yanked on underwear, then slipped on her favorite tee. Deep blue, it was covered with an image of Edvard Munch's *The Scream*. Finger combing her hair, she decided it would have to do, even

11

though the steam from the shower had blessed its natural curl with an annoying finger-in-the-light-socket frizz.

In five minutes, she was dressed and heading out the door to what she expected would be a deadly dull meeting. She pushed the button to summon the elevator, and heard it ascend, chiming at each floor. She tapped her foot, willing the elevator to hurry. As the doors slid silently open at her floor, and she stepped into the empty chamber, Jessie caught sight of her hair in the mirrored surface of the back of the chamber. She grimaced at the tangle of curly waist-length auburn hair.

I wonder how the heck you say "scary mess" in Norwegian.

She silently mimicked the screaming face on the front of her shirt until the elevator doors began to slide open at the first floor.

Chapter Two

The mood in the conference room resembled Belgium in 1815—the Battle of Waterloo—instead of the Crooked Creek Art Expo meeting of artists and show organizers. The general meeting usually explained procedures, policies, and new activities to the attending artists.

Jessie stared up at the rustic lodgepole pine beams towering two stories high and the log walls decorated with western art and artifacts, and then swung her gaze to the many familiar faces. Professional artists attend many of the same shows across the country, so the art community is normally like a big, happy family of painters and sculptors. Not today. The immense rock fireplace blazed with welcome heat, but the feeling in the room couldn't be chillier. The expressions on the artists' faces ranged from icy to irritated.

Max Watson, the short overweight show director with a Napoleon complex, was on his feet shouting in the direction of Camille Johnson's shoulder. Camille, a statuesque blond woman of about forty, looked down at him with a disgusted expression. She pointed her index finger at Max.

"Listen, you need to deliver more than lip service. Last year, your board promised better advertising. Instead, it's worse than ever. Were there any full-page promotions in any of the national art magazines?" Max opened his mouth to respond, but Camille cut him off. "No. The magazines containing those non-existent ads were supposed to be distributed on various airlines months ago. Months ago. It was lucky that many of us bought our own ads. We did *our* part to promote the show. Your committee didn't do *theirs*."

The little man puffed out his chest and sputtered as, all around the room, artists added their raised voices to Camille's.

"Yeah! You tell him, Camille," shouted a man sitting in the last chair of an outer row. Jessie knew him well. It was Glen Heath, one of her favorite wildlife sculptors. A beefy six-foot-four, he was bald on top with a monkish ring of salt and pepper hair pulled into a thin ponytail. Its length drizzled half-heartedly down his back to obscure part of the Harley logo on his black leather vest. Spotting an empty chair behind him, she made her way toward it and sat.

It had been at least a year since she'd last seen Glen. His work seemed more suited to high-end galleries than a hotel show, where each artist displayed work in a reserved room. It had been some time since Jessie herself had participated in the hotel art shows. Selling her art through galleries was simpler, and more in keeping with her now exorbitant prices. Even though she no longer had a showroom, she always sent a painting to the Crooked Creek annual auction. She appreciated that each year a different charity received a percentage of the auction profits.

"You promised at least three television spots to pump it up the week before the show," a woman hollered as Camille dropped back into her chair. "I never saw even one!"

"Yeah, yeah, I know. Calm down. It's not our fault." Max slapped a manila folder against his knee. "When the board decided that local advertising was a better way to go, we scheduled those TV spots. I'm not sure what happened, but the channel canceled two at the last minute. But we still have time to get the last one in. They say we just need to get an artist to Channel 8 at seven tomorrow morning and—"

Then Max Watson spotted her. He grasped at a change of subject like a man dying in the desert lunged for a bottle of water.

"Hey, there's Jessie! Everyone, say hello to our guest artist, Jessie O'Bourne. Let's give her a big Montana welcome." With a relieved expression, he began to clap until the artists joined in and

14

then announced loudly, "She'd be perfect—just perfect to do the interview."

Jessie half stood and raised her hand to halt the applause. "I appreciate the great welcome, Max. Everyone," she said, nodding her head at the crowd. "I'm honored to be here. Sorry I'm late, but please don't let me interrupt the discussion."

"Good to see you, Jessie," Glen said warmly as he looked over his shoulder, smiled at her, then gave her a wink. "Dibs on a hug later. Welcome to the madhouse." Then he turned back and raised his voice. "Getting back to the subject at hand, I agree with Camille. Even with a good television interview, it might be too little, too late. People need advance notice to plan to attend, especially during the winter, and with the high price of our auction tickets."

Another voice growled from the back of the room. "You bet. And the ticket price was raised this year."

Since she wasn't a regular exhibitor at the Expo, most of the meeting discussion didn't pertain to her, and Jessie began to daydream as the complaints swirled around her like the swarming of gnats. In front of her, Glen stretched his long legs into the aisle as he slouched down in his seat and locked his hands together under his ponytail as though settling in for a nap. His position gave Jessie a prime view of the top of his shiny head, the overhead light bouncing off the pasty white circle. She stared. Glen's head became a tiny, empty, round canvas. In her mind, she painted a small robin's nest on that bare space, the wiry hairs surrounding the spot becoming woven twigs encircling three blue eggs. Mama Robin perched on the small branches, head cocked to the side, her beady, dark eyes looking proudly into the nest.

Jessie's hand lifted involuntarily, the thumb and index finger pinched together almost as though holding a brush. She grinned inwardly as her imaginary bird painting morphed into a hatching dinosaur egg, the leathery predator peeking out at the new world with wondering, wide eyes.

"Tyrannosaurus," she muttered. "T-rex."

"What," asked the woman on her right. "You talking to me?"

"Sorry. No. Just daydreaming out loud." She was tired. What was she thinking? She liked Glen. *He's a big sweetheart. So what*

15

if he's sworn off visits to a barber? She shook her head to clear her thoughts, but her gaze drifted back to Glen's gleaming bald head. The artist to Jessie's right stood, then edged past Jessie and headed off toward the restrooms.

Another irate sounding man stood, and Jessie twisted her gaze away from that perfect round circle.

"Well," the angry man said. "My beef is that most of my collectors are from out of town—actually, out of state—and they tell me they never received any "save the date" postcard or invitation this year. In the past, they received an elegant, personal invitation from the show committee. You know, snail mail. With an actual postage stamp," he added sarcastically. "Something they hold in their hand. Stick to the fridge. Good thing I mailed my own invitations. Hell, I always do, or they wouldn't fly in and park those private jets at the airport." He crossed his arms and widened his stance. "These folks are long standing show supporters. They spend big bucks at the auction. They stay here at the lodge. They attend the seminars. The least they can expect is an invite and info from y'all running this dog-and-pony show." He gave a sorrowful shake of his head and sat. "A blinking dog-and-pony show," he muttered again in a low tone.

Max's face flushed. He pulled a handkerchief from his pocket and wiped sweat from his forehead that Jessie suspected had little to do with his proximity to the burning logs in the fireplace. "Please. Please. Just settle down. We're doing everything we can—"

"The hell you are!" A tall thin man yelled, his hand cutting through the air in a gesture of dismissal.

Max ignored the interruption. "We're trying something new this year. More social networking." He drew himself up to his full five-foot-five, his small potbelly refusing to go along for the ride and drooping dejectedly over his belt. "Why, my assistant, Evan, and I have been on the computer for a couple hours every morning for two months, inviting new—and old—clients to the show. We're using our Facebook and Twitter presence." He flashed a nervous smile. "I think the digital approach is working great. And every online post or email contained an e-mailable invitation specially designed by Fox Tail Graphics. Saved us a ton on postage."

"Oh great," Camille bellowed, again jumping to her feet. "A high visibility magazine ad that would reach thousands of potential customers replaced by tweets. Seriously? Free tweets? So where did the ad money go?"

"Listen," Max said, puffing out his chest and focusing intently on the bottom of Camille's chin. "Our graphic design was very expensive. Our website alone cost $20,000 to produce and maintain through the year."

"How can that be," whined a small, thin woman. "You gave us each a password and asked us to maintain our own pages. Once the initial website was up, surely there wasn't much need or cost for its maintenance. A little help now and then for the computer dinosaurs, maybe?"

"That would be about half of you, Arlene," Max said. "Our web designer spent a lot of time helping those who just aren't computer literate. We had to pay him for the time spent working on that."

Several artists looked sheepish, Jessie noticed. But one dark-haired man standing at the side of the room stared toward the committee at the front of the room with such hatred in his eyes that she almost shivered. She followed his gaze, uncertain which person had been the target of that look—a look of pure disgust and anger. She thought the bullseye had been drawn on the young assistant, Evan Hanson.

That's strange. Evan is just a gopher. He only does what Max suggests. The glaring man stood stiffly, clenching and unclenching his fists. Then, as quickly as it had come, the look was replaced by a calm expression.

I didn't imagine it, Jessie thought. *He's so all-fired angry, he nearly smokes.* There had to be more of a story here than just poor management of the art show. She studied him. She didn't think she'd seen him on the art show circuit before. He was easy on the eye, with a bad-boy edginess. Tall, dressed in a western shirt and nicely fitting blue jeans, he had the sort of easy grace and sex appeal that reminded Jessie of Russell. It wasn't intentional in Russell's case. It seeped from his pores without the clueless man

17

even realizing it. But this guy . . .she suspected this guy was a whole different animal. *Sure of himself. Arrogant. Who is he?*

Then she knew. He was the stranger who'd hauled her paintings through the service door and left her sitting on her tuckus in the snow. She looked at him again, and as if he felt her gaze, he turned and looked directly at her, giving her a lazy, sardonic grin and a little salute. Jessie felt her face flush and knew her freckles were probably glowing red as stoplights. She swung her gaze back to the speaker at the front of the room.

Several minutes later, she was contemplating leaning over to tap Glen and ask about the man, but as she lifted her finger to tap his shoulder, the sculptor heaved his impressive bulk to a standing position and cleared his throat. "I'm going to say it again. You've done diddly to get the customers in, and you aren't taking good care of the artists who pay for each show room, either. Our fees are your bread and butter money—it's where the cash comes from for promoting and running the show. We don't begrudge you your percentage for running the expo but do it right. When I got here this morning, the parking lot wasn't plowed. I waded through the snow, hauling my sculptures on moving dollies that I could barely haul through the drifts. If you think customers are going to try to park in that mess you got another think coming. They'll turn around and go home." He plopped back down.

"I'll get a snow plow in early tomorrow morning. And we have a large banner printed that hangs on a portable billboard. The snow held us up. After the plowing, we'll bring the billboard to the hotel and get it set up." He chewed on his bottom lip. "It'll be a great ad. Real visible. You'll see." He looked down at his notes. "And I'd be happy to send each artist a detailed list of where the money was distributed," Max mumbled into the microphone. Then his eyes brightened. "I see the restaurant has the urn of coffee and snacks they promised us ready at the back of the room. Let's all grab a cup while we calm down, and then we'll cover the rest of the agenda."

Glen stood and stretched, then stepped out of the aisle and reached for Jessie, giving her a bear hug that lifted her off her feet. He whirled her in a circle, then plunked her down.

"Like I said, it's good to see you, Jess." He gave a belly laugh. "When are you coming on that motorcycle ride with me? You know, you promised to check out my new touring bike at the show down in Albuquerque, but I never saw hide nor hair of you after that."

"Great to see you too, you big mauler. Maybe sometime this week." After exchanging a few more pleasantries with the sculptor, Jessie meandered over to grab a cup of coffee. After quick hugs and greetings from numerous artists while everyone stormed the refreshment table, she sat down several minutes later with two peanut butter cookies and a steaming cup of decaf.

Max was introducing a dowdy, gray-haired woman. "This is our volunteer coordinator, Judith Miller." When she stood, hands were immediately raised all over the room.

Camille spoke first. "I see there's no hospitality room this year." She sighed with Oscar-winning drama. "Is it too much to ask for a coffee pot and cookies in a spare room where artists can grab a quick snack? Do we have to buy coffee at the Creek's Edge Restaurant? It's always packed. Most of us can't be away from our show rooms that long. Especially since our rooms are supposed to be open eleven hours a day."

Jessie groaned inwardly. On the way to the meeting she'd passed the restaurant near the hotel lobby and noticed the waiting line snaked out the door and around the corner.

"Yeah. And I practically had to dig through the couch cushions this year to put together enough cash to come. Coffee in that fancy place here is expensive," another man complained. Jessie looked toward the voice. It belonged to a good looking, muscular man who leaned nonchalantly against one of the lodge pole pine beams. His rich brown hair fell over his forehead in a studiedly casual look. A salon cut, Jessie decided. She also noticed he was very well-dressed for someone claiming to be financially challenged. His decorative cowboy boots were of exotic leather— probably Lucchese brand ostrich—and real pricey. About $600 a pop, Jessie knew. He wore a silky western shirt and kerchief, and a belt with a large silver buckle. But, she mused, many artists "dress for success" at the shows. It's a known paradox. You have to look successful before anyone wants to buy art from you. And, as Jessie

19

knew—with her own closet holding several western jackets, including one with fringe and beading that she purchased in a weak moment—looking successful isn't cheap.

"Me, too," said a voice in the back of the crowd. People all around the room nodded their heads in agreement. Murmured complaints about the poor economy and lousy art sales reached Jessie's ears.

One man swore he'd raided his eight-year-old's piggy bank for gas money. And the least he could expect after paying the high show fee was a place to get free coffee.

"Camille, that isn't correct," Judith Miller announced, giving Camille the fish eye. "We do have a hospitality room. Number 108. It was simply omitted from the printed list because we were uncertain which room the hotel would allow us to use. Our volunteers will serve beverages throughout the show, and a continental breakfast each morning. Please feel free to bring any high rollers into the hospitality room and give them a coffee and some of Millie's fabulous coffee cake and—"

The volunteer coordinator was interrupted by a rousing cheer. Jessie smiled. Artists were the same everywhere. She knew they loved the camaraderie of the show hospitality rooms as much as the free coffee and snacks. Comparing notes about galleries and art shows over a hot cup of morning coffee was part of the fun.

Judith Miller continued, telling the assembled group she had tucked one free lunch voucher from the on-site restaurant into each artist's welcome packet. Soon, with the artists slightly placated, the discussion turned to concerns such as the show schedule and parking.

Jessie, finally feeling warm, shrugged out of her jacket and slung it over the back of her chair. She watched. Listened. Wondered what kind of rodeo she'd gotten herself roped into. After all the grumbling, she was glad she'd pulled the Hawk into the correct parking area after unloading, even though it meant slogging through the snow to the hotel. The parking issue always got the show committees riled up. One artist in every crowd grabbed a prime spot near one of the entry doors and left his vehicle there throughout a show. That meant one less parking spot for a potential customer. The Crooked Creek Show Committee threatened to have the vehicle towed if any artist's vehicle was found in those primo spots. And rightly so, Jessie thought, yawning.

The meeting limped on and on. Her stomach rumbled, even after she'd eaten both cookies. Dinnertime was long past, and she hated eating alone. If only Arvid and Esther had arrived, she'd have asked them to go for a late dinner. But, Esther wasn't slated to play the piano until the next evening at the V.I.P. reception. They'd probably get to Crooked Creek early the next afternoon. Her stomach complained again. In her head, Jessie did a mental cupboard search, trying to remember what edibles were back at the Hawk. *Crackers.* She squirmed in her chair. *Some brie in the refrigerator.* She squirmed again. The blasted blingy jeans she'd talked herself into buying rubbed just a bit at the waistline. Maybe she was better off skipping dinner tonight.

She gave herself a mental shake and sighed. Glancing again at Glen's bald head, she pictured it as an ornate clock face with Roman numerals.

Damn, I'm just so exhausted.

Looking out the floor to ceiling window, she saw it was getting dark as pitch.

I wished I'd moved Jack to the hotel room before coming to this battleground. It had taken some silver-tongued persuasion on her part to get permission from the hotel manager, Bob Newton, to bring her beloved tomcat. Newton's concession to allow Jack in her room was the only reason she'd given in to Georgina's pleading that she take her place at such short notice.

She shoved an annoying curl back from her forehead and wondered idly how her friend's baby was doing. Declan, Georgy had named him. What a fun name. An intense longing washed over her, and her damned biological clock started buzzing. It was bad enough when it used to tick like Big Ben, but now it had taken to sounding like an alarm clock full of hornets. Glaring at Glen's bald spot she saw both the hour and minute hand on the imaginary clock now stuttering at eleven. Then she pictured it as the top of a hornet nest, the angry insects buzzing out of the top. She waved her hand involuntarily, thinking about colors. Maybe cadmium orange and

21

Payne's grey, mixed with a little ultramarine blue for richness for the wasps. She hated to use straight black. It was such a dead color.

"I just don't like black," she muttered. The woman next to her whispered back, "Excuse me?" in an annoyed tone.

Jessie threw her an apologetic look and mimed, "Sorry." Then she realized it was Barbara Bardon, the huge, gaudily dressed, African-American scratch-board artist. She had taken the seat vacated by the earlier occupant. Wincing, Jessie remembered how sensitive the woman was about what she called 'bigoted redneck idiots'. "I was thinking about a painting," she whispered. "A wasp nest."

Jessie's eyes flitted involuntarily to Glen's big bald dome, and Barbara glanced over curiously. Her lips formed an "O". Then she flashed Jessie a wicked smile. She wagged her finger at Jessie, but her wide shoulders began to shake as she silently chuckled.

Jessie heard a soft, muted "ping" from her cell phone and reached into her pocket to pull it out. It was a text from Georgina asking if she'd arrived at the show. Jessie typed a quick "Got here fine—no worries. Get some rest and enjoy that baby!" Then she turned the phone off and shoved it back into her pocket. Relaxing, Jessie thought about her friend and the new baby. She'd never seen one that tiny. Maybe on her way home from the show she'd get a chance to go visit Georgina and take a peek at the newborn.

Lately, whenever she thought of children, her thoughts drifted to her talented nephew, K.D., who was now nearly seven. After Jessie's brother, Kevin, had died, Russell had married Kevin's pregnant girlfriend and taken on the job of being a father to his best friend's child. Anger filled Jessie's mind as she thought again about the hurt of discovering her brother had left behind a wonderful little boy and nobody had told her. Not Russell, not her own father. She felt her eyes begin to fill. The little boy could already draw as well as most adults. She wondered if she'd ever get to teach him to paint. She explained to Russell how important learning drawing and painting skills was for a child with that amount of raw talent. *Nearly impossible to get through to Russell.* She'd given it her best shot, but Russell didn't understand. *Actually*, she admitted to herself, *he didn't want to.*

Lost in her reverie, her head snapped up as the current speaker, a heavyset woman with bluish hair, clapped her hands to get everyone's attention and announced loudly, "Don't forget to go to the "Curl Up and Dye" salon and get your free haircut. Remember, this year's sponsored charity makes wigs for cancer patients and most of you promised to get your hair cut and donate it to the cause." She gave a little wave. "Goodnight all!"

As everyone began to leave, artists nodded and smiled at Jessie as they passed by. Some gave her a quick hug. Evan, the young show assistant, stopped to welcome her. Good looking and slightly built, the young man exuded the charm of a practiced salesman. He tossed overdone, flattering phrases her direction the way boys lobbed pebbles into a pond. As he exhausted his repertoire and turned away, a twenty-something blond woman dressed in jeans and a flowing tunic waylaid him by grasping his arm and holding up a laptop.

"When I was registering at the Expo desk, I saw this on the table," Jessie heard her say. "There were quite a few people around, but nobody was watching the art registration desk." The woman patted the zippered case she carried. "I figured you wouldn't want sticky fingers to walk off with this baby." She giggled. "Heck, Evan. I was tempted myself."

Evan gave her a look of appreciation.

"Geez, thanks, Karen. I guess I forgot it there when I was helping with the artist check-ins. I keep all my notes and schedules on my laptop. I'd be lost without it."

"If anyone took mine I'd go into cardiac arrest. I'm watching a couple stocks and don't want to miss my entry point."

"Entry point? You mean time to buy?"

"That's right, Sugar. No time to chat. I need to check them right away. See ya." The woman scurried away.

"That's Karen Sutherland," Evan said. "Nearly everyone calls her 'Ticker' because she's always spouting stock quotes. I have no idea when that gal has the time to paint, she's so hung up on the stock market. Does well with it, too."

Jessie looked after the retreating figure. "I can understand the appeal," she said. "There are a few stocks I keep an eye on. Not obsessively, but I like to know if I'm losing my shirt. Unfortunately, I find it as addictive as gambling."

Evan gave her a lop-sided smile. "Me too. Maybe someday, when my ship comes in, I'll pick up a few." He gave Jessie a two-fingered salute. "See ya. Let me know if you need anything."

Jessie was almost out the door when someone called her name. She swiveled and looked inquiringly at the blue-haired woman. It was the woman who'd been speaking about haircuts. With teeth big and white like the pickets of a newly painted fence, she smiled at Jessie. "Georgina Goodlander was going to get her hair snipped right short, Miss O'Bourne. I'm sure since you took her place as our honored guest, you'll be glad to set a good example and get that gorgeous red hair of yours 'clipped for the cause', as we like to say." She grinned and repeated, "Clipped for the cause." She enunciated each syllable as though it was a mantra and looked at Jessie with firm determination in her pale blue eyes. "Right short," she repeated.

Jessie groaned inwardly.

"Um, we'll see. I'll think about it, but right now I have to go rescue a cat."

"Oh, it will only take a minute or two to tell you all about our Locks for Ladies program." She waved a brochure in Jessie's direction, peering at Jessie's hair with an almost predatory gaze.

Trapped like a rat, Jessie thought. *But like Dad always says, sometimes you just have to grin and bear it. And time is both the cheapest and most valuable thing you can give people.*

"Of course," she said graciously. She read the name tag on the woman's patterned blouse. "I'd be happy to hear all about it, Mrs. Jackson."

The pickets gleamed again. "Just call me Maureen, dear."

With a sense of foreboding, Jessie sat.

Chapter Three

Artists' parking lot

In the bedroom of the Hawk, Jack laid his ears back. Something moved in the underbelly of the motorhome. Jumping from the bed onto the inside access hatch to the storage area—the door Jessie jokingly called her "laundry chute to the Hawk's basement"—Jack sniffed. Opening his mouth slightly, the big tom expelled his breath in short huffs. He made a chuffing sound. Then, with his tongue slightly protruding he uttered a low growl.

More thumps came from below.

Curious, the mouser scratched at the hatch, using all the weight of his twenty-two pounds and pulling at the carpet-covered piece of plywood with claws as sharp as fishhooks. The carpet covered plywood lifted an inch or two and thumped back into place. Immediately, a loud shuffling sound came from below as something slithered backwards away from the hatch area. Then the tom heard the banging of the exterior door to the storage area and the crunch of running feet on snow. He latched claws into the carpeted lid once more, popping it up an inch before it dropped. His sensitive nose caught the smell of something metallic.

A ridge of fur along his spine lifted into stiff spikes. From deep in his chest, the cat emitted a low growl.

Then he hissed.

Chapter Four

Artists' parking lot

Reaching the Hawk, Jessie pulled open the door and shut it firmly behind her. She wiped her boots on the mat. Not wanting to track snow any further into the motorhome, she called her furry sidekick and waited for him to come trotting out from his favorite spot at the foot of her bed. He didn't come.

He's pouting, she thought. Mrs. Jackson had droned on and on about the Locks for Ladies program. Then, after Jessie finally agreed to get her hair trimmed, not cut short, but trimmed, and Mrs. Jackson went in search of new blood, Jessie'd gone to the cafe and wolfed down a bowl of clam chowder.

"Ja-aack," she crooned softly. "Time to go."

The cat didn't appear. Jessie scraped her feet on the mat and took the bag of cat treats from the nearest cupboard. She shook it. That never failed to make him show.

"C'mon Jack."

Still no cat.

Darnit, I'm gonna have to go find the big baby.

She stomped back to the bedroom and found him perched on the interior access hatch to the storage area, peering intently downward. When she wasn't hauling paintings, she kept a laundry basket in the space under the hatch and dropped dirty clothes straight into it. So handy. After having just emptied the space,

Jessie knew there was no mouse in there, but Jack sure looked like "game on".

"Nothing in there, Big Guy. NO mice. No nothing. I hauled everything into the hotel. All that's left to go is one blubber tub cat and all his stuff." She grabbed him and began to lift. Jack growled and spread his paws, digging his claws more firmly into the carpet covering the hatch.

Jessie tugged. A hiss like air whooshing from a punctured tire erupted from the cat. She let go.

"Oh for Pete's sake, you big baby," Jessie said in surprise. "Let's go!" She reached down and stroked his head, talking to him in a soothing voice. "You'll love the hotel room. It's got cat food. It's warm. It's going to get chilly in the Hawk."

The cat began to purr slightly and relax, kneading the carpet. Jessie grabbed the advantage—and the tom—then straightened up.

"Gotcha!"

Making her way back to the front door, she skirted a roll of bubble wrap, a stack of blank canvasses, an extra pair of boots, and her travel easel. She'd have to come back and get the litter box from the bathroom area, but there was no time to tidy up. She still had paintings to hang.

Jessie exited the motorhome with her arms full of cat. Trudging past the back of the motorhome, she caught her jacket sleeve on the edge of the storage compartment door. It was hanging slightly open. Hadn't she closed that when she drove over to park in the artists' lot? *I'm getting sloppy*, she thought. She walked over, still clutching Jack firmly to her chest, lifted her foot and pushed the door firmly closed.

* * *

Back at the hotel, having yowled and complained during the elevator ride, Jack now explored the room, tail up and waving like a king's pennant. His Highness was pleased. The tom acted especially delighted with the large sheepskin rug. He pushed his head and shoulders under it, forming a cat cave, then burrowed the rest of his bulk into the space until all that showed was the twitching tip of an orange tail. Jessie kneeled down and scratched

27

her fingers on the rug about eight inches from where she calculated Jack's paws to be. He lunged. She moved her hand and repeated the cat and mouse game until his entire tail disappeared under the rug and he barreled out the other side, jumping in a quick circle to face her with a wide stance that showed her he was ready to rumble. The fur on his back and tail stood at attention. His yellow reptilian eyes were wild and his lower lip had snagged on one tooth.

"You handsome devil," Jessie said, flopping on her back on the sheepskin rug, laughing. Jack walked over to peer into her eyes, then walked stiff-legged off in a huff. She pulled herself off the floor, pulled her coat back on, and left him to his explorations.

On her way to retrieve Jack's litter box and another small suitcase case from the Hawk, she bumped into Max Watson waiting for the elevator. He held out his hand and shook hers firmly, puffing his chest out in a 'Bantam rooster' affectation. It reminded Jessie of the strutting antics of the little chickens she'd seen at a neighbor's farm when she was a child. Max's hair, nearly buzz cut, with the longest section combed to a bit of a point at the midpoint of his forehead, unfortunately reinforced the impression of "rooster".

"We're honored that you agreed to be our guest artist, Jessie." He nodded, rooster tail bobbing.

"Thanks. I'm glad to be here," Jessie agreed with a smile, making the requisite small talk.

"You're doing a landscape painting demonstration Saturday, right?"

"Yes. A creek-side scene, I think." Then she thought of the fields full of cattle she'd seen on the way to Crooked Creek. There'd been so many calves. Cute little things. Maybe she'd change her mind and do something with cows. "Actually, I haven't decided," she said. "I've been thinking about what to say on the Channel 8 interview and planning tomorrow morning's workshop on composition and color harmony." The elevator pinged as it reached the ground floor.

The rooster tail bobbed again. "People are looking forward to that, too. Sixteen students, right?"

28

Jessie nodded agreement. "There may be several more. Perhaps as many as twenty. I looked at the space when I arrived. There are four locals who want to attend, but until I saw the room allocated for the class, I didn't dare add them to the list. It looks like there's plenty of room, so Evan phoned them and offered them a space in the workshop. Even if all of them show up, I'm sure it's fine." She had printed extra workshop folders and information sheets before leaving Santa Fe, just in case.

"Wish I had time to take it myself." He looked thoughtful. "Mind if I drop by for a few minutes if I get a chance and take a few photos or videotape part of the class? It would be good publicity." Max tapped his foot impatiently while waiting for the elevator door to slide open. As they stepped inside he said, "Say, have you seen Evan? He told me he was going to meet you in the parking lot and help move that painting, but I haven't seen him since. I need to ask him if he's scheduled the snow plow tomorrow. No sense duplicating efforts."

"No, I haven't seen him. I did meet him after the meeting. He welcomed me to the Expo. But I have no idea why he'd want to meet me in the parking lot. And what painting are you talking about?" The elevator gave a lurch, and Jessie grabbed the handrail on the wall.

Watson looked at her with a puzzled expression. "Well, he said you sent him a text, saying you needed some help hauling another big painting from your motorhome before you arranged the work on your panels. He was going out to meet you in parking lot B. Didn't he show up?"

"Oh, no. You must have misunderstood him. I never sent Evan any text. And I've already hauled in every piece of my work." She frowned. "It must have been a different artist." She pulled her phone from her pocket and glanced at it. "No. There's nothing in my messages from Evan."

Max groaned theatrically. "That young fellow is decent at his job, but always gets the artists mixed up. Some poor woman is probably waiting for him to show up and he has the name wrong." The elevator groaned to a stop. "I try and try to mentor him. I keep telling him, 'Evan, you're the type of person who needs to write things down.'"

"Hmmm." Jessie murmured, thinking of Evan's laptop and his comment that he kept detailed notes on it.

"Oh, well," Max grumbled. "I always say if you want something done, you should do it yourself. That's why I'm the show director. An excellent show director. I know all the ins and outs of each person's job." He puffed his chest out once more, becoming somewhat deflated when he noticed Jessie's lack of interest. Again, he reminded Jessie of old Boomer the rooster, puffing his chest out and crowing for the ladies—the ladies who ignored him and wandered off in search of chicken feed. "Say," Max asked, "Did the committee supply enough show panels to hang your work?"

Jessie nodded. "Plenty."

"Good. Good. Good." Watson rubbed his hands together in satisfaction. Then he shrugged. "Well, I guess Evan will eventually figure out who needed the help."

The elevator door opened. Evan stood there with hands on hips and an impatient look on his face.

"Ah, speak of the devil. Here he is now."

"Did you need something, Max?" Evan asked. "I was just coming down to double-check with you before I headed home."

"No, but I just told Jessie here that you were out in the snow looking for her." He looked at Evan with an annoyed expression. "She didn't text you for help. You've confused her with another artist."

Evan gave a long-suffering sigh. He gave Jessie a puzzled look and he held up his phone. "No, I didn't. I have Jessie's text right here. I was just going out the door when Sophie snagged me to help haul a heavy box. I sent Benny out to help with the painting." He looked at Jessie. "Sophie's in a wheelchair. She's a great painter, but getting her display set up is a challenge for her." He smiled. "I'm assuming Benny lent you a hand?"

"That's the odd thing," Jessie said, hands on hips. "I really never sent a text asking for help. And I haven't seen Benny. In fact, I don't even know which guy he is."

Evan gave Jessie a look she suspected he reserved for total idiots. "Benny is one of our volunteers," he explained. "And you must have forgotten about the text you sent," he said, pointing to his phone. "It was just an hour ago."

She grimaced in annoyance. "May I see that, please?" Jessie held her hand out expectantly.

Evan looked puzzled, but he slid his finger across the screen of his phone and then gave it to her. "See?" He pointed. "That one right there."

Jessie stared at the screen. In the list of recent messages was one marked 'from Jessie'. She read: "Evan, please give me some muscle at the motorhome. I have one huge piece to haul in and could use a hand. I'll meet you at the artists' parking lot. Back left corner in about half an hour. Thanks.'

"Well, how weird is that?" She handed the phone back to the young man. "But it isn't from me. My number has a New Mexico prefix."

Max's gaze swiveled to the younger man. "Oh, of course it does. Do we have another artist here named Jessie?"

"I don't think so." Evan looked thoughtful. "No, I'm sure we don't."

"Heck, I wonder what happened." Max looked perplexed, then grimaced. "Well, some artist is going to be annoyed at our lack of response."

"Can't be helped. I told Benny he could go home after he carried the painting in for Jessie," Evan said. "Guess when she wasn't at the motorhome, he high-tailed it before the snow got any deeper. And before we thought of something else for him to do. He's been watching the weather and road reports."

Max said. "He should have called to ask if he should wait for her."

"Yeah, Benny's a decent sort, but he isn't the brightest bulb on the Christmas tree. And living out in the country like he does, his roads do get treacherous." He frowned and tilted his head as if considering something, then swiped his finger across the screen of his phone. "Think I'll text him right now and make sure he got home." He glanced at Jessie. "He has a couple dogs he treats like babies. Poor guy's been worried all day that the power might've gone out at his cabin and the pooches would be home alone and cold."

31

Jessie smiled at the men. "Yeah, I get that. I just slogged through the snow to haul Jack, my big tomcat, back to the room where he'd be warm. Guess I'd better go back for the rest of the things we'll need for the night."

"He's not picking up," Evan said in a worried tone. "Jessie, if he's still out at your motorhome he'll be turning into a popsicle. Just tell him he can go home, will you?"

"Will do." Jessie gave them a little wave and headed down the hall.

* * *

Pushing open the heavy door and stepping outside, she was amazed at how much new snow had fallen. The cars parked near the exit, out of the wind, were white mounds of varying sizes and shapes. When Jessie trudged out of the shelter of the building, she realized gusting wind had blown the snow into drifts and the light poles were coated with sticky white. The vans and vehicles in the artists' parking lot hadn't fared as well as those near the lodge. They were coated with a crust of moisture that was beginning to freeze.

By the time she reached the Hawk, she was cold, cranky, and wishing she was home in the Santa Fe heat. She wiped her jacket sleeve repeatedly across the door so that she could see where to stick the cold metal key into the half-frozen lock. *Brrrrr.* She hoped the Hawk's pipes didn't freeze. Then she remembered there was supposed to be a power outlet on the nearby pole. She grabbed a long extension cord from the storage under the dinette bench, and went out to slog through the snow, eventually locating an outlet and plugging in the electrical system of the Hawk. She gave a mental fist pump and went back inside to get organized. At least she'd have better light while she gathered her things.

"Ugh," she said aloud, as she headed to the back of the Hawk to retrieve the litter box and small bag of litter. She grabbed her make-up bag from the tiny bathroom. Juggling everything, determined not to make yet another trip, she opened the door and trudged back to the lodge only to find she was locked out. A sign near the door said, 'after ten, use room key'. As she turned to set things down so she could find her keycard, she heard an ominous whooshing sound from the roof. A white avalanche caught Jessie on the head and chest and tumbled her backward into the drifted snow.

She lay there on her back, spouting as many of Arvid's Norwegian swear words as she could recall, ending with a good old American 'Goddammit'. Then she began to laugh, and as her laugh dwindled to a hiccup, she became aware of someone else's deep laughter—laughter that had a throaty, male sound.

Chapter Five

Jessie stared at the huge gloved hand that was reaching down to help her up. Standing over her was the same man who'd left her sitting on her tush in the snow earlier that day. He wore a midnight blue down jacket. The gloves were the nylon snowmobile type. For a split second, she contemplated yanking hard on that big hand— pulling its owner down into the snow. At the warning look in his sparkling blue eyes, almost as though he'd read her mind, she thought better of it. She allowed him to grasp her hand and help her to her feet. A sharp pain in her back almost made her gasp. She'd twisted awkwardly when she fell. Inwardly, she grimaced, knowing she'd likely be sore as heck when she taught her workshop the following day.

"No cart of artwork this time?" His eyes met hers in amusement. Then he noticed her pained expression and asked in a serious tone, "You okay?"

She nodded. Swallowing her embarrassment and ignoring the throbbing pain in her lower back, she brushed the snow from her jacket and jeans, tossed back the jacket hood and shook flakes out of her long hair. She blinked her eyes to flutter snow from her lashes.

"Yeah. Thanks." Then, remembering how he'd rescued her artwork that morning, then left her sitting in the snow, she said in a sarcastic tone, "And no paintings to damage this time. I'm a lucky gal. Only my pride is hurt."

It was his turn to look embarrassed.

34

"Ah, well. Like the old adage, pride goeth before a fall," he said with a grin. "In your case it came afterward. My fault. I was on the run before the meeting. Sorry for leaving you in the snow."

Jessie stared at him. The midnight blue bulk of his chest against the yellow light streaming from the glass of the hotel door was interesting. Without thinking, she leaned slightly forward and stared. It would make a nice study. She loved to work with back-lighting.

He looked puzzled, then turned his head to look over his shoulder. By the time his gaze swung back to Jessie, she had shaken herself back to the moment and was speaking.

"Oh, it's fine. You were right about the metallic liners on the frames. I wiped them off—no spots, thank goodness. Those frames are gorgeous, a little pricey but worth the money. Much better to rescue them first. I'm easier to clean up." She smiled and waved her hand in a dismissive gesture.

He grinned. "I must have seemed pretty rude," he said. "I'm Tate Kamaka. To make up for it, I'll treat you to hot cocoa from the Creek's Edge Restaurant. Nothing better for soothing that wounded pride than a mug of the best hot chocolate you've ever had." Glancing around, he found the shoulder bag and litter box, both half-buried in the snow, and pulled them free. "I'll carry these to the elevator for you. You can drop them at your room while I go order our cocoa."

He smiled broadly, causing Jessie to stare at him in surprise. The blasted man was devilishly handsome when he smiled, and Jessie suspected that 'devilish' was exactly the right adjective for this man. *Probably hit the nail splat on the head with that one*, she thought. There was something about him that gave her a slightly uneasy feeling. An edginess. A feeling that there was more to him than he showed. In looks, he did remind her of Russell, but this man seemed...well, she couldn't quite put a word to it. Then she thought, *Sexier. Russell is sexy but doesn't realize it. This guy knows he's attractive, and maybe uses that to his advantage, the big, smart alec. Hot. And maybe dangerous? Hmmm. A big loud warning bell went off in her head. Well, she was swearing off men right now, so he wasn't going to get her motor revved up. Damn men,* she thought.

She raised her chin and looked into those twinkling eyes. Aloud, she said smoothly, "Name's Jessie O'Bourne." Then she continued, "Surely the restaurant's closed by now."

She saw him looking at the litter box curiously, and she turned a chuckle into a quick little cough and put up a palm toward him. "And really, that's not necessary. I can carry my own things." Jessie grabbed the edge of the box and tugged it away from him, then picked up the small bag of litter.

"The restaurant's open for another hour. I'm sure they'll take pity on us and give us the goods," he said, letting her have the lightweight box, but not relinquishing his hold on her larger bag. "What is that thing anyway?"

"This," she said with a dramatic gesture and tone, "is His Royal Highness, Jack Dempsey's, litter box." She smirked at him.

"Dempsey—"

"My cat. He's a big orange tom named after Jack Dempsey— aka the Manassa Mauler—a boxer from the 1920s. One of Dempsey's boxing matches was the first to pull in a million-dollar purse. Dad was too young to have seen them, but he researched the boxing matches, so he and Gramps had something to gab about." She cocked her head. "Jack's a fighter, a cocky little brute. He's definitely the King in our household. At least *Jack* thinks he's royalty."

Tate pulled a face, waving his gloved hands in the air as though flicking feline germs off right and left.

"What you're saying," he said with a grimace, "is that I was holding a nasty litter box against my best down jacket. I didn't realize what it was. Blech." Tate brushed off his jacket with an exaggerated sweep of his hands, held her make-up bag out to her, and crossed his arms over his chest. "In that case," he said, in a dramatic, haughty tone, "You, Snow maiden of the Crooked Creek Court, are granted the privilege of toting the royal potty pan."

Jessie couldn't help it. She took the bag, slung it over her shoulder and burst out laughing. Soon his baritone joined her. Then he swept the door open and waved her in with a flourish.

"After you, m'Lady." He looked at her, his eyes sparkling with mischief.

He looked appealing. Beguiling. Overconfident.

36

Oh well, Jessie thought. She held the litter pan, which was actually brand new, with elaborate majesty as she walked—chin up, head held high—through the door. She opened her mouth to say she'd take a rain check. Instead, she heard herself say, "Cocoa it is."

But what she thought was *'splat'!*.

Chapter Six

Up in the hotel bathroom, Jessie pulled the brush through her hair in swift, angry strokes, addressing her own reflection in the mirror.

Idiot! Where's your common sense? With your stellar bad luck with men you had the stupidity to say yes to hot chocolate with a total stranger? A totally arrogant, much too appealing stranger?

She yanked harder.

"Oh, yes, I'd love a hot chocolate, Tate," she mimicked to her reflection. Jack wound around her ankles and she looked down to tell the cat, "I'm a glutton for punishment, Butter Tub. That man just oozes trouble." She turned again to the looking glass and mouthed "Stupid, stupid."

She yanked off wet jeans for the second time that day, inspected them and draped them over the towel rod. They'd be dry by morning, but at this rate, if there wasn't a laundry service at the lodge she was going to have to find a laundromat. Pulling the last blingy pair from her suitcase, she finished dressing by slipping her feet into her sexy black leather boots, the pair with the uncomfortably high heels, slipping into a black cashmere pullover sweater, and spritzing herself with her favorite perfume. She drew a tube of lip gloss across her bottom lip and smacked her lips together.

"I know, I know," she told Jack. "I'm such a hypocrite. But if I'm going to dive back into the pool I might as well make a splash."

He looked up at her with slanted eyes. She leaned over to gently run her hand from the top of his head to his haunches, repeating the motion several times.

"Don't worry, Jack. If he doesn't like cats, we don't like him." Her eye fell on the open suitcase. She crossed to it, took out her Nikon camera and 9mm pistol, and locked both in the small hotel room safe before she picked up her purse.

But, of course the man does offer chocolate. A man who bribes you with chocolate is either very bad or very good. She suspected the man she was going down to meet was a bit of both. She lifted her foot and flexed the leather boot. The cocoa and company had better be worth wearing these killers.

* * *

Ten minutes later, Jessie sighed as she took her second sip of the Crooked Creek Lodge special dark cocoa. The decadent brew, heaped with whipped cream, appeared at the table in tall mugs with the lodge emblem embossed on the side. It was served with a plate of honey and maple flavored "Dutch stroopwafels", a round cookie baked with an embossed waffle pattern and filled with a gooey thick caramel.

Total heaven. In fact, she expected an angelic chorus to sing *"Hallelujah"* any minute. Definitely worth wearing the killer boots.

Tate gestured toward a glossy catalog he'd placed on the table by his plate. "I was looking through the auction listings and artist biographies while I waited. Your studio is in Santa Fe, it says, but you're originally from Montana?" Tate picked up a cookie, took a healthy bite, and chewed while he looked expectantly at Jessie.

"Yeah. I'm ninety-nine percent redneck Montanan. I was raised in Sage Bluff and went to art school in France, but Santa Fe seems to be a good market for my work. I'm not even sure how I wound up there, to tell the truth. It just happened." Jessie looked at the dark windows of the restaurant. She knew why she moved to Santa Fe. It was because she hadn't felt anyone wanted her to come home. She hadn't realized that it was because her family wanted her to succeed and they thought that wouldn't happen if she came

39

back to Sage Bluff. The rural area didn't offer enough opportunity in the art world.

There is success...and then there is happiness. As always, she wondered if she'd made good choices. She'd missed her family. And she'd missed the last two years of her mother's life. She lifted the mug and sipped without tasting.

Tate looked at her with a quizzical expression. "You ever think of moving back to Montana?"

"Yeah. At least once a day." Jessie wasn't going to elaborate, but then said. "It's a long story." She gave him a pinched look. "More like a soap opera," she muttered glumly. "I have a talented nephew in Sage Bluff. His name is K.D. I'd love to stay more involved with him. He's my brother Kevin's son, but Kevin died before the little boy was born. And his mother died soon after."

Tate's deep brown eyes again stared into hers, and he said nothing. Then he seemed to come to a decision. "If you'd like to talk about it, I don't mind soap operas. We knights of the Crooked Creek Court make good listeners. Must be from all the suffering we endure wearing that heavy armor." He waited for her to continue.

She gave him a grin. "Russell, my brother's best friend, knew Kevin's fiancé, Trish, was expecting. When Kevin died, Russell married her immediately after the funeral. Then Trish passed away, too, and Russell has been raising K. D." She bit into a stroopwafel and chewed, thinking she shouldn't have burdened Tate with the story. "I warned you it was like a soap opera."

She didn't tell Tate that Russell was an old flame—or how devastated she'd been when he married—or that her mother passed away two weeks after Kevin and Trish. Her father had been a mess for more than a year. Now, he was happily remarried.

"It wasn't until last year that Dad and I knew for certain that the little boy was Kevin's." She took a sip of rich cocoa and put down her mug. "Dad suspected. Now, he looks so much like my brother did at that age, there was no way Russell could hide it any longer. Like I said, it's a long story." She gestured toward her drink. "Too long for hot chocolate. It would be nice to be able to teach K.D. good drawing and painting basics. He's remarkable. So much talent, and he eats and breathes sketching and painting."

Tate made a sympathetic sound. Then his face brightened. "Maybe the long story can wait until we go to dinner during the Expo."

Russell's face came unbidden into Jessie's thoughts. He had proposed. But he only wanted to marry her if she'd give up painting and come home to stay. Not travel or take her work to art shows and galleries. Her answer had been no. Sighing deeply, she bit into a cookie and gave a slight sound of appreciation. "We'll see. Anyway, that little nephew of mine is the only reason I'd consider moving back to rural Montana. I love it here, but it's too far from the galleries and shows I need to deliver work to. Shipping prices are unreasonable. Plus, there's a lot to be said for flying the flag, making the effort to talk to gallery owners and customers in person."

"Yes, I agree." He gave her a serious look. "And I won't ask any more personal questions tonight, either."

"I will," Jessie deadpanned, "It's my turn."

Tate laughed and made a gun with his thumb and index finger. "Shoot."

She rubbed her palms together as though in anticipation. "Let the inquisition begin. First, what do you paint?"

"I don't. I draw. I'm a pencil artist. Graphite drawings and sketches." He broke the last cookie in two and put half on her saucer by her mug.

She grinned. "I spend time sketching as well. I keep a journal with a bit of writing, but mostly drawings of people done from memory."

"I'd like to see it sometime."

Jessie smiled, but knew that wouldn't happen. The journal was too personal. If he asked more pointedly in future, she'd make an excuse. Besides, when she went back to her room, she would add his portrait to the pages.

"Sometimes I like to work in pen and ink. And I love the looseness of a good charcoal portrait," Tate said. "Color stumps me. I'm a bit color blind."

"Ah." She nodded. "But how can person be 'a bit' color blind? Isn't it either-or?" She stirred the remaining whipped cream

41

topping into the dark brown liquid. "Do you have red-green issues? I know that's the most common type for men."

"Color blindness varies dramatically from case to case. I can see, for instance, that your hair is a fascinating shade of red." He reached toward a long curl dangling over her shoulder. "They say that sometimes you can 'feel' color," he teased. "I think I'd be able to see the exact shade if I could just touch——"

Before his hand could reach Jessie's lock of hair, a fragile-appearing elderly gentleman in a red and black-checked wool jacket interrupted Tate's sentence. A compact medical oxygen canister was attached to a belt around his waist, and a thin air hose wound a figure eight from the canister to the man's nostrils. He leaned precariously on a cane and listed toward their table. "Are you from Crooked Creek, young man? You a veteran? You look military."

A fleeting look of surprise passed over Tate's face as he drew his hand back from Jessie's hair and gazed at the elderly man. "Hello, sir. I'm…."

The old gent spoke over Tate's words. Jessie suspected that he was hard of hearing. She wondered what Tate had been about to say.

"You just got that look about you. That look of the military man. Now, I'm a Korean War veteran. Not many of us left. Lot more of us than there are of World War II vets, but we're getting thinned out like old pine trees in a forest fire. I gotta drag my oxygen pack with me everywhere I go. But by damn, I get the word out about the wars, so the young people of today don't forget. They should know about the sacrifices we old codgers made. I give out pamphlets about the wars." He gazed unseeingly out the window. "There've been too many wars, and there'll be others, human nature being the beast it is. You been to the Korean War Memorial in Washington D.C.? Best memorial there."

"Yes," Tate said. "I agree. It is the best memorial there." He looked at Jessie, who gave a slight shake of her head to indicate she had not seen it. "It's made of sculpted figures who represent a platoon on patrol moving through Korean terrain. You feel as if you are among them. It's very moving." He looked up at the old fellow and cleared his throat. "I've never been in the service myself."

The old man watched Tate's lips moving but gave no sign he'd heard what was said.

"I call this oxy pack 'Jim', after a friend of mine. When the Red Chinese attacked at Chosin Reservoir, he saved my life. Then he was wounded. I carried him for hours. But I didn't mind. Jim was my friend, you see. We went to school together in Crooked Creek. James Jefferson Montgomery, his name was." Again, his rheumy eyes took on a far-away look. "Most folks don't know that over fifty thousand Americans were killed over there. And nearly eight thousand American military men are still missing just from the Korean War. Lost souls." He shook his head. "It's hard for those families to wonder—to never know—where their loved one wound up—how he died. The older you get, the more you think about the past. Friends and family—dead or alive—they all help make you who you are."

Jessie made a murmuring sound of assent. Tate nodded respectfully.

The old man leaned heavily on his cane with his left hand, and waved his leathery, heavily-veined right hand toward Jessie. "What's your name, gal?" She started to speak, but he talked over her reply, making her even more certain of his lack of hearing. "When I came home, I married Jim's girl. She was a beauty like you. Not a carrot top like yourself. Brunette, she was. Hair almost black. I felt guilty for years that I wound up with Shanna."

He shook his head. "And when I wasn't feeling guilty, I sure wished he'd been the one to come home and marry that ornery woman." He cackled at the look of surprise on Tate and Jessie's faces. "Well, we had a good long life together. She's probably up there with Jim now, complaining about how I was always late to dinner. Always smoked my smelly pipe." He cleared his throat. "Here's one of my pamphlets." He pulled out a thin folded brochure from his jacket pocket and laid it on the table. "Korea's often called 'the forgotten war'. Remember how important the military men were. Will be again, too, you know. Like I said, human nature's a beast. A ravening beast." He looked at Tate. "We

43

need military men like yourself. Keep our country safe. You young people enjoy the cocoa and conversation."

He turned and began a slow shuffle toward the door. Jessie rose and caught up with him, and to the old man's surprise, she gave him a quick hug and a swift kiss on the cheek. The man's eyes filled and his face split into a huge smile. "Bye, girl." He looked back at Tate and gave a short salute. "Sure glad she ain't a brunette. Dark-haired gals are trouble."

The cafe hostess smiled at Jessie as the old man left the restaurant. "That's the Gingerbread Man. Thanks for making his day."

"The Gingerbread Man?" Jessie asked quizzically.

"Uh huh. When I was a little girl, his wife used to make gingerbread cookies to hand out each Halloween. Then she got cancer, God bless her. Every year since she died, Mr. Helland has carved small wooden gingerbread men—dozens of them—to pass out to every kid who stops at their farmhouse to trick or treat." She tore a customer's bill from a pad on the counter. "My kids hang ours on the Christmas tree. They don't even know Mr. Helland has a name other than 'the Gingerbread Man'."

"What a neat story," Jessie said. "I'll bet they're real keepsakes. Something they'll pass to their own kids someday." Kids, she thought. The ticking of Old Ben, as Jessie called her biological clock, thudded in her chest. She waved her hand as though to shoo a bluebottle fly.

"The poor soul was hale and hearty just a few months ago," the hostess said. "Sure is sad to see how fast an older guy like that can go downhill. I hate to see him so frail. Reminds me to go see my dad, I guess. It's high time." She gave Jessie a wistful smile and nod as she passed, walking to a nearby booth crammed full of twenty-somethings dressed to kill and laughing uproariously. The hostess placed the bill on the table and every young man in the booth suddenly noticed something interesting through the window, their glances sliding surreptitiously back at the bill, hoping someone else would pick it up.

"Let's all chip in," a female voice suggested. Her idea was greeted with the enthusiasm Jack gave a newly opened can of salmon.

Jessie had just reseated herself across from Tate when Max came strolling to their table. "Hey there." He turned a glum face toward Jessie. "Enjoying the signature cocoa, I see. I could eat a million of those maple cookies." His mouth turned down. "Say, did Benny ever track you down, Jessie? I called his cell half a dozen times. It went right to voicemail, so I tried his land-line and he still never picked up. I'm worried he never made it home with the roads so terrible. I was hoping he'd finally connected with you. His dogs are out there by themselves and if he thought there was even a slim chance he could make it home to take care of them, he'd try the bad roads."

"No, sorry. I haven't seen him. Well, like I said before, I have no idea what he looks like. But he hasn't come and introduced himself."

"Hmmm. Well, if he does, please tell him to call me, will you?"

"I'll do that, Max. But I'd sure like to know who used my name on that text."

"You and me both." He looked at Tate and held out his hand. His expression had a look of intensity as he glanced at Max. "Tate, isn't it?"

Tate nodded unenthusiastically.

"One of our new artists this year. You do western themed graphite drawings, don't you? A lot of rodeo pieces?"

To Jessie's surprise, Tate gave him a look of dislike and hesitated a few seconds before grasping Max's hand to shake. *And he was squeezing hard. Really hard,* Jessie thought, as she noticed Max's wince. *Interesting. Wonder what that's about.*

Max let go and cautiously wiggled his fingers.

"Yes, that's right," Tate told him. "Western themed, but not rodeo. Mostly just running horses and ranch scenes. Cattle dogs, cattle and sheep drives, that kind of thing."

"Well, I'll be down to your display room tomorrow to check out your work. Welcome to the Art Expo. We're glad to add a good pencil artist to the roster. We try to keep variety in the show. There seem to be oil painters around every corner," He looked at Jessie in horror. "Oh, sorry. What I meant to say is that we have quite a few oil painters, but not as many sculptors or good pencil artists." He nodded to Tate dismissively and then told Jessie. "Don't forget to ask Benny to call if he shows up, Jessie." He gave her a little salute. "Thanks." Max turned and walked toward the door.

"What's this about a fake text?" Tate asked, then held his palm up in a stop gesture. "Just a sec." Before Jessie could answer, he waved to their waitress as she was hurrying past. "Hit us again, will you? Another round of cocoa."

Jessie squirmed a little, picturing an army of calories with miniscule faces and crablike pincers, all laughing in crablike giggles about the snug waistband on her blingy wranglers. Inwardly, she rolled her eyes and scheduled some time on the treadmill. She explained about the text Max received—a text supposedly from Jessie—that asked him to come out to her motor home and help her with a large painting. And how Evan had passed the chore on to Benny.

"That's odd," Tate mused. "Wonder who benefitted from that?" His face was serious. "Something had to be gained."

"Gained?" Jessie pushed her empty mug to the side. "Why do you say 'benefitted'?"

"Well, someone tried to send Evan on a wild goose chase out to the parking lot, don't you think? Even if it *is* dark and snowy and they were doing it as a joke, that isn't enough of an inconvenience to be funny. It would take so much time to pull off the fake text that it wouldn't be worth the effort."

"Yes, I see what you mean." An uneasy feeling settled over Jessie. *Why send Evan out to the Hawk? Why to my vehicle? Why not someone else's?*

"And you were parked out in the far lot? The artists' lot?"

"Yeah. But I've been out to the Hawk—" Sorry," she explained, seeing the puzzled look on his face, "The Hawk is what I call my motorhome. It's a Jayco Greyhawk. I'm one of those obnoxious people who names everything."

Tate grinned. "I like it."

"Anyway," Jessie continued, "Benny wasn't waiting there. And now that it's gotten dark and the snow's been coming down so fast and heavy, I'll bet a person couldn't see any footprints showing he'd ever been there."

"Yeah, you're right. I was going to suggest Max should just check the parking lot for whatever Benny drives, but I guess with all the vehicles looking like snow mounds that isn't an option." He gave Jessie a grin. "Unless a person knows exactly the space where their own vehicle is parked folks aren't even finding their own. Besides, when he saw how bad the roads were getting, he probably hightailed it home." He shook his head. "The poor guy is probably sitting in a snow bank somewhere if he tried to drive home in this mess."

The waitress returned with two more steaming mugs of hot chocolate and another plate of stroopwafels. They smelled heavenly. This time, Jessie was sure she heard a distant *"Hallelujah"*.

Over their second cup of cocoa Tate asked Jessie questions about the past year's art shows. As she opened her mouth to inquire about his experiences with the art market, he changed the subject, wondering aloud about possible attendance at the show after the unseasonable snowfall.

"Actually," Jessie said, "Sometimes traffic is better when the weather is awful. Nobody wants to be outside. They're looking for something to do indoors."

"Doesn't matter," Tate insisted. "The weatherman claims it'll quit snowing overnight."

"I don't have a lot of faith in weathermen," Jessie laughed, thinking of Old Koot in Sage Bluff. "They're wrong as often as they're right."

"Just watch. The sun will dazzle us tomorrow. The art rooms will be full of customers."

Jessie snorted. "You dreamer, you. Probably full of lookie-loos and tire-kickers." Then she thought better of her gloomy prediction. "I'll be teaching a workshop tomorrow. But I'll stop in and see your work later. I plan to make the rounds of all the art rooms."

"What about your own display? You going to duck out? You won't pick up any sales by being a slacker," he said in an ominous tone.

"Nah, I'm being spoiled. My work is marketed by the show committee, and with the commission they're taking, I don't mind letting them do the work selling it."

"How high a commission?"

"Forty-five percent."

Tate whistled. "That seems pretty steep considering you bailed them out by filling in as guest artist."

"Oh, well." She bit a stroopwafel. "I'm happy to take part. And after the show—weather willing—I plan to stay on a week."

"What for? Do you have family in the area?"

"No. I'm hoping to paint on location with a friend who lives a few miles outside of town. Jan has a couple horses and we want to take an overnight trip into an area where there's an old cabin by a lake. It should be fun. And, she has a mule registered in the annual Mule Race on Thursday." She smiled. "I don't want to miss that."

"Mule races?" Tate smiled.

"Yes. I've never been to one before, but I hear they're a lot of fun. Jan is riding a mixed breed called Penelope. It's named after an old prospector's mule—a mule that had a creek named after her."

"Hey, that sounds like a blast. And it sounds like a redneck painters' holiday, all right. You never hear of anything like that back home. The more I see of the West, the more I love it."

"Where's home, Tate?"

"Hawaii. I've lived on several of the islands. Most recently I've been staying with an old buddy on Maui. It's rocky. Very rocky. Maui isn't what you normally think of when you think 'Hawaii'. Most people think about sandy beaches and sun. Oh, we have beaches, but not like the long sandy beaches on the Big Island. And depending on what part of the island you're on, it can rain hardly at all, or pour buckets. Now, here's one difference between Montana and Hawaii. The first time I came to town was last year at this time. I came to visit the show, not to exhibit. There wasn't any snow then, but most of the highway was under construction. So they'd taken the snow markers down. This year when I drove in, there were all these eight-foot-high poles along the road to show the snowplow driver where in heck the road was. I had to ask the hotel desk clerk what they were." He gave an endearing grin. "Now, we have cattle ranches in Hawaii, too. Parker Ranch in Waimea valley is one of the largest spreads in the entire U.S. and the owner raises cattle in waist high grass. Instead of snow markers, we have tsunami warning posts. They show how high the water level could be in an area after an earthquake."

Jessie laughed. "That sounds really strange. I'd like to see that."

"I know you paint a lot outdoors. You should take a trip to Hawaii sometime, to paint something totally new."

"Maybe someday. Dad recently went to Oahu on a honeymoon. He married a nice woman after Mom passed away. After looking at his photos, I was envious of the tropical scenery he'd seen. I have to admit I thought about heading over there to paint the very next morning. What I'd love to do is to see pineapples growing, hit the coffee plantations. Maybe paint on a beach, just for fun."

"You should try your hand at snorkeling. Put on a bikini and take a swim in the ocean." His eyes glinted as he looked at her.

Jessie saw the appraising look on Tate's face and felt herself flush. She knew if she looked in the mirror that her face would be crimson...and peppered with freckles as it always got when she was embarrassed. *Crap. Would she never grow out of blushing?* She stared at him. For just a moment she became lost in his eyes, dark ocean blue with pupils as dark as obsidian. The look he gave her reminded her of someone. Not the color of Tate's eyes, but the intensity of his gaze. *Who was it?* Then she knew.

Oh, dritt. She had hoped her thoughts of Grant Kennedy had sunk into the quicksand of the past. She stared at Tate, evaluating. His features were nothing like Grant's. It was his posture and attitude. Remembering Grant's lie about being unmarried, and how she'd fallen for it, reminded Jessie that perhaps she was better off staying away from men in general. *All men.* She was fine on her own. *No males. Well, just Jack.*

"It does sound like fun," she said, her voice cool. "But on that note, I think I'll head back to my room. Nice to visit with you, Tate. I'll probably see you sometime during the show. If not, have a successful one."

His expression was puzzled.

49

"Wait, Jessie. I wanted to mention that after the reception tomorrow night, the band will still be playing for an hour over by Buck's Bar. Poolside. It's a small pub near the hotel's convention area. Why don't you plan to hit my display room about nine? I'll show you my sketches and you can rave about my work? You can tell me 'Oh, it's wonderful, blah, blah, blah. Wow, you've never seen such talent.' Then we can go over to Buck's, dance a bit and you can compliment me on my dancing." He grinned engagingly and winked. "How about it?"

"My, my. Not at all sure of yourself, are you? I do hate to see men with such low self-esteem."

Tate smiled broadly at her. But even through the humorous banter, she could see that his smile had a feral quality. A dangerous edge, hiding like a knife in a leather sheath. The old man who'd come to their table had probably sensed the same thing. Tate was capable, self-confident, and ready to do battle. A little shiver went up her spine. Her hand came up and her fingers flexed, in the way she did at the studio before picking up a brush. She could almost grasp that aura as something palpable. *I'd like to paint him . . . capture that 'ready to fight' expression. Military, the old guy had stated firmly, and Jessie saw it clear as crystal. Military. And hiding something,* she thought. *I wonder what...*

"What do you say, Jessie?"

"We'll see." She put away the imaginary brushes. "I have a friend who's playing the piano during the reception. We may go out to dinner afterward." Jessie stood and walked toward the door, feeling his gaze on her across the length of the restaurant.

What I say, she thought, *is that men who bribe you with chocolate and whipped cream are not to be trusted.* But, it had been quite some time since she'd felt so attractive. Desirable. Not since she'd seen Grant in Sage Bluff. A wave of loneliness washed over her. Tate was fun. And his attentiveness and gift of blarney were not to be sneezed at. *Hmph.* She snorted inwardly, then admitted to herself that his interest in her was flattering. She glanced over and saw Tate's reflection in the large window at the exit. He was still watching her.

Yes, not to be sneezed at. Well, I might at least give it a couple coughs. Or at least a hiccup.

Back in her room, Jack sprawled across the bed, snoozing, tail twitching, as Jessie pulled on her pajamas, then retrieved her journal from the suitcase and picked up a pencil. She began the sketch of Tate—rendering his intense eyes, the square jaw, the straight posture. Her fingers danced across the paper creating swift, sure strokes, each stroke as important as a single note in a musical composition. Twenty minutes later, she picked up a gum eraser and rubbed out part of the jaw, then attacked the likeness again with fervor. Finished, she picked up the journal and held it at arm's length. She squinted at the drawing, narrowing her eyes until she saw masses of light and dark instead of detail. Her eyes widened, and in a fit of temper, she tore the page out, crumpled it to the size of a golf ball and pitched it toward the small wastebasket. Jack raised his head, twitched his tail and yawned.

She looked at the fresh page of the journal, sharpened the pencil and began drawing again, this time capturing the sleeping tomcat. Her gaze swung from the paper to Jack's feline form and back again as she worked, using the side of the pencil to create soft fur. A feeling of calm seeped into her. She sharpened the point several times, muttering as she worked.

"Snooze on, Lazybones. This is going to be a detailed sketch of your Highness."

The ruined drawing that lay crumpled on the floor was perfect. But it wasn't Tate. And although Tate resembled Russell, it didn't look like Russell, either. It was that heel. That liar. That louse.

It was Grant Kennedy.

Chapter Seven

Nielson's farm - October, previous year

Berg Nielson stared numbly at the sheet of paper. A week after Addy's funeral, he'd begun receiving notes—first sent by mail, then slipped under the door or left on the stoop weighted down with a rock. The message was always the same. 'I'm coming for you next, old man.' This note had said 'soon', instead of 'next'.

Soon. Berg worried about what to do, turning the issue over and over in his mind like fast moving water pushing a pebble downstream.

Finally, he went to his gun safe and pulled out a shotgun. He loaded it and leaned it in the corner of the entryway.

Coming for me soon, huh? Well, it can't be soon enough. And I'll be ready for you, you goddamned bastard. You must be quite the young punk, if you think I'm an old man. Berg gave a snort.

He opened the drawer in the television stand and shoved the new note angrily in with the rest. Then he dropped heavily into the worn recliner and gazed blankly out the window. First Addy. Then these god-awful notes. He wondered if he should even bother to call Jacob down at the Sheriff's Office this time. The poor snot-nosed young dope didn't seem able—or willing—to do anything about Berg's troubles. When Berg had called him the previous fall to report that Potter kid shooting at his outbuildings, Jacob had just made excuses for the young man.

So what if he's a tad slow? He should at least be spoken to about the dangers of shooting into folk's farmyards.

Then there'd been the contemptuous look in the young deputy's eyes when Berg took the last warning note to the Sheriff's Office.

Berg scowled, remembering. *Perhaps,* he thought morosely, *Jacob Cramer thinks I'm fabricating the threatening notes myself to get a little attention.* He wondered if the deputy was professional about keeping folks' personal business private. He'd heard rumors that he wasn't. Probably blabbing about the notes down at the local bar. Something in the old man twisted at the thought. If I go again, I'll demand to see Sheriff Fischer.

He drummed his fingers on the arm of the recliner and thought about Addy's death.

Accident, my eye.

Her death hadn't been caused by some stupid poacher not paying attention to his aim, like Jacob kept insisting. Someone afraid to come forward. No. It was something dark. Something unfathomable. He could feel it slithering toward him. Like one of those big rattlesnakes he sometimes surprised in the loose haystack when he pitch-forked hay to the cows. Darn things had even been slithering into the loose hay in the barn.

Standing, he went to the small tole-painted table near the phone and reached into the drawer to pull out the thick phone book. Thumbing through the yellow pages, Berg found the listing he was searching for and called to make an appointment with Richie Christofferson, his lawyer, for that afternoon. *Richard Christofferson,* he reminded himself. Dang it anyhow. He still thought of him as a little boy. *Youngster's still wet behind the ears,* he thought. *Probably why he had an appointment slot open so soon.* Of course, everyone under fifty looked like a youngster to him these days. Berg gave a snort of dry laughter. And surely even Richie could handle drawing up a new will. That settled, he reached into the drawer and pulled out paper and a pen.

Thank God, it was re-enlistment time for Dom. Regretting what he was about to do, he was going to write his son for advice, and if nothing helpful came to mind—he'd ask him to come home instead of signing his re-enlistment papers. He hesitated a moment,

53

then began writing. The letter was short and to the point. Berg went back to the drawer and removed several of the most recent notes, enclosing them with the note to Dominic, sealing the envelope and adding postage.

"I'm a weak man," he grumbled aloud. His head drooped, his chin lowering to rest almost against his chest. "Weak. And after that damn cancer, feeling way too old for sixty-four."

He walked down the long lane to the mailbox at the driveway entrance, inserted the letter and put the flag up to let the rural carrier know the mailbox held outgoing mail. His worried deep blue eyes scanned the road to the south, then his gaze went back to the north, as he recalled one note that had been dropped into the mailbox while he was in town for his last doctor's visit. Once he retrieved the mail on his way home, he discovered the note inserted in the center of his favorite gun magazine. Reaching into the box, Berg pulled his letter to Dom back out and held it in one hand, tapping the edge of the envelope on his other palm. Leaving anything important in his box wasn't a good idea. When he got back to the house, he opened the door to the Chevy and tossed the envelope onto the seat of his pickup. He went into the house to grab his keys. Thirty minutes later, he dropped the letter addressed to his son's military APO in the outgoing slot at the Crooked Creek Post Office and then headed to Christofferson's office.

* * *

When Berg returned home two hours later, a small cooler sat on the front porch. The damn kid had been there again. Berg let his head drop to his chest. Maybe, just maybe, he'd misjudged the boy. He was sure taking Addy's death hard. And doing his damnedest to make sure Berg ate. He opened the cooler and grunted.

Hmpph. The boy had outdone himself this time. Chicken dinner, a big tub of mashed potatoes, and four ears of sweet corn, wrapped in foil. Enough for several meals. He popped the lid back on and stood looking at the cooler for several minutes, then kicked it with his booted foot and stomped through the front door. A few minutes later, he opened the door and stared down. He stooped,

54

hauled the large cooler inside and hefted it onto the kitchen counter with a grunt. Sighing, he lifted the lid and unwrapped a large foil-wrapped blob. The heady aroma of fried chicken wafted out. Berg inhaled deeply, drawing the scent into his lungs.

"Ah, what the Hell," he muttered. He reached into the foil packet and pulled out a crisp, golden-brown drumstick.

As he chewed, he thought about the kid. Maybe he'd give him a call. Addy had liked him. He wasn't much in the way of muscle. Some brains though, maybe. And hadn't he said he owned a night-vision trail camera? One of those infrared gizmos that took pictures of animals in the dark? Maybe he'd see if he could borrow it and set it up near the front door. Wouldn't it be something if next time the lunatic dropped by to leave a threatening note, he could catch him on camera? Red-handed by infrared. Holding the drumstick at arms' length like a pistol, Berg said aloud, "Pow! Gotcha!" Then he smiled at the thought, lifted the chicken to his mouth, finished it, and threw the bone into the trash.

He opened the cupboard door and grabbed a plate. Then he peered into the cooler, lifted an ear of corn onto the plate and pulled a chicken breast out of the foil package, adding it to his bounty. He topped it off with a softball-sized dollop of mashed potatoes. Shoving the dinner into the microwave, he stood waiting for the timer to ding.

Glancing into the living room, he saw the shotgun he'd loaded and propped in the corner nearest the door. He snorted.

That pimple-faced Jacob Cramer. By God, he isn't a bit of help.

After meeting with Christofferson, he'd gone yet again to the Sheriff's Office and shown Cramer the newest note. He frowned, remembering that, like the last time he went in, the young Deputy had made him feel like a silly old man. Probably figured anyone over fifty was ready for the scrap heap. *Sometimes*, he thought, with another look at the Remington 12 gauge, *you just need to handle things yourself.* He scratched at the neck of his wool shirt collar with a leathery finger. Deep in thought when the timer dinged, he jumped like he'd been stuck with a pin.

"Berg," he said aloud, shaking his head at his own jumpiness, "You really are a silly old codger."

Chapter Eight

The tinkling alarm on Jessie's phone sounded much too early the next morning. She groaned and looked across the bed into yellow reptilian eyes. "Jack," she muttered aloud, "Six is such an ungodly hour it should have to repent. And I'll bet you plan to sleep all day." She swept a finger across the phone screen to set it for "snooze" and put the cell phone carefully on the night stand by the bed.

Maybe ten more minutes would be okay. She'd thought she'd have to hustle through her morning shower and makeup, then drive to Channel 8, but instead, the reporter wanted to conduct the interview in the Yellowstone room where Jessie's paintings were hung. The interview shouldn't take long and she could go right to the conference room to teach her one-day workshop on color and composition.

Jack grumbled, then suddenly jumped onto the night stand, peered down at the phone and shoved it with a paw, knocking it onto the carpeted floor.

"Jack!" Jessie leaped from the bed and grabbed the phone, swiping her finger across the screen and then dismissing the alarm. She shook her finger at the tom. "You little bugger. That's an expensive phone, Fat Boy."

He squinted his eyes, giving the feline face a smug expression. Then he jumped from the night stand and sauntered over to his bowl, glancing back at her. *You're out of bed. Feed me.*

"So. I'm nothing more than cat staff, and don't think I don't know it. I also know where the treat bag is, and you, Mister, do not have opposable thumbs," Jessie told him, tossing him a dirty look. She shuffled over to get the bag of kibble, poured a cup in his dish and then hit the shower. While she shampooed and soaped, she thought about the first talk she planned to present on color. Some students had trouble understanding that red and orange weren't always hot colors. Blue and green weren't cold. It was all relative. Color must be judged by the hues throughout the painting, especially those in proximity.

She remembered telling one student in her first class that adding white "cooled" a color as well as lightened it. She'd been chattering on for ten minutes about her thoughts on color, intensity and color complements, until the poor guy just looked at her blankly and said. "Huh?" He hadn't absorbed any of it. He was still at the beginner stage in learning color, but he drew extremely well. "I just don't get it," he'd said. "Maybe I can't do this."

Jessie smiled ruefully in the shower, while the blissfully hot water drenched her hair and ran down her back. She'd learned more in that workshop than her students. Patience for starters. She learned to take it slow. Everyone has individual strengths and weaknesses, and each student is at a different level of understanding. You can't toss them painting tips it took you years to learn like they were clay pigeons at a skeet range.

Jessie hurriedly dried her hair, dressed, dabbed on minimal make-up and picked up Jack. She hugged him close and gave him a squeeze, expecting a loud protest. Instead, he rubbed his cheek against hers and gave a rumbling purr.

"See you later, Butter Tub. And don't terrorize the maid." She set him on the bed, scratched behind his rag tag ear, grabbed her room key and stepped through the door. She had just enough time to grab a bite of breakfast.

* * *

"What the heck?" Jessie said aloud, her toe colliding with a small hard object in the doorway.

57

She pulled the hotel door shut behind her and looked down at a tiny, toy tractor about four inches long. She reached down and scooped it up. It was cute as a button. A replica John Deere. She tapped it with her fingernail. *Metal. You don't see metal toys much anymore. Some poor kid is probably bawling about losing his favorite plaything.*

She slipped it into the bag with her workshop handouts and headed to the stairwell, anxious to find some breakfast. At the lobby check-in desk, a slim young man held a phone tight between his hunched shoulder and cheek, clicking away on his computer keyboard with nimble fingers, accepting a reservation. He glanced at Jessie and mouthed, "be with you as soon as I can". She nodded and looked around the lobby with interest while she waited. One wall boasted an enormous oil painting of running pronghorn antelope. Their bodies were rendered with sure brush strokes that gave the two-dimensional animals a feeling of fluid movement. Blue-gray sage and prairie grass lent texture and color. The painting flooded Jessie's mind with memories of summer trips with her granddad, trips during which he lugged his heavy old-fashioned camera, 400 mm lens and tripod, and she carried his bag of film. She'd peppered him with questions, but he'd never lost patience with his little granddaughter. She leaned in to peer at the corner of the work, trying to read the signature, but without success. And with her closer scrutiny came a slight feeling of disappointment. It was a print. A good reproduction on canvas, but a print, not an original.

Under the artwork was a glass display case containing finds from a dinosaur dig in rural Montana. An impressive triceratops femur lay surrounded by smaller finds, teeth, claws and other fossilized remains. The signage read 'replicas of fossils found near Jordan, Montana." *Prints of fine art, copies of old bones. Not much is real anymore.*

"Can I help you?" The desk clerk asked. "Sorry for the wait. The phone hasn't stopped all morning."

Jessie walked over and set the small tractor on the counter.

"I found this in the hall outside my door. I'm on the fifth floor."

58

"Hey, thanks." He picked it up and examined it. "It's cute. Think they sell these at the Farm and Ranch store. Hopefully, someone will realize it's missing before they check out." He set it on the counter. "Our lost and found cupboard is well stocked with all kinds of weird things people leave. By the time they get fifty miles out of town, they don't feel like backtracking to get them. I think I'll just leave it here on the counter. Then it can't be missed." The phone rang again, and he reached for it with an exasperated expression, but he spoke cheerily into the receiver. "Crooked Creek Resort," he sing-songed. "How can I help you?" He mouthed a "thank-you" at her as she began to walk away.

She tossed him a short wave before rounding the corner. Turning, she bumped solidly into a body that seemed to fill the hall.

"Hey, Jess, take it easy."

The big man standing at the end of the short line into the Creek's Edge Restaurant turned and took her arm, steadying her. It was Glen. He wore a black vest, but today, it wasn't a Harley Davidson, it was Ranch Wear suede. Gone was the look of the motorcycle boots and bald head of the day before. Today, Glen looked like the ultimate western cowboy, except for the pony tail hanging down his back. He'd paired the vest with a stonewashed denim shirt with western detailing, a cerulean blue paisley silk kerchief, cowboy boots, and a black cowboy hat with a braided horse-hair band. The hat and cowboy boots added a good six inches to his already towering height.

Jessie stepped back. "I'm so sorry...Hope I didn't hurt you," she teased. She winked at him, her eye-level somewhere in the middle of his chest. "I know how delicate you are."

He snorted, looking down at her.

"Yeah. I'm feelin' a bit weepy after the pain of the impact. Probably got a broken rib or three." He thumped his chest. "Big pain right here."

Now Jessie snorted. Same old Glen.

"Have you been waiting in line long? The restaurant looks packed," Jessie said, giving him a smile. "Hope I can at least get in to grab some coffee. I have to go do the Channel 8 interview before my workshop starts."

"Coffee? That's not going to do it for you, if you're teaching. Teaching is ex-haust-ing." He drew the word out into three long syllables. "Join us for breakfast, why don't you?"

"Who's 'us'?" Jessie asked.

"Oh," he stepped slightly to the side. "Camille and I are sharing a table, so we can get in and out before Armageddon. We've been waiting about twenty minutes, but everyone's dawdling over their coffee. The hostess just told us they were opening the back room to add more seating, though."

Camille peered around him, saw Jessie and gave her a brilliant smile.

Jessie had looked up at Glen. Now she looked up—and up—at Camille. She smiled hesitantly at them, feeling very small. Diminutive. Weensy. Except for her appetite. She was famished.

"Yes, do," Camille said warmly. "It's great to see you." She cocked her head toward the beckoning hostess. "Super, they've got us a booth. Come sit with us and fill us in on art sales in your neck of the woods."

"I would love to." Her stomach gave a loud rumble. Jessie winced in embarrassment. "In fact, it's unanimous."

Glen took Jessie's arm and steered her ahead of him into the cafe.

The hostess led them through the bustling restaurant to the back room, and to a table already set with silverware and a pitcher of ice water. She leaned over to raise the window blinds as Jessie slid onto an elegant tapestry seat. Practically tossing the menus at them, she recited the breakfast specials as fast as an experienced auctioneer at a cattle auction, turned and rushed in the other direction. Glen yelled after her. "Three coffees, please!"

"Sure thing, hon!" The waitress didn't turn around but gave him a little finger wave.

Jessie glanced out the window. The promised advertising banner had arrived. *How odd,* Jessie thought. The sign was supposed to hang on a portable billboard. Instead, a behemoth of a John Deere tractor was parked outside, draped with the Crooked Creek Expo banner proclaiming, "Art Show Today!" *Well, heck. Not really the classiest way to advertise, but maybe it gets the job done. After all, this is farm country.*

Then, Jessie looked again. The front window of the tractor was a spiderweb of cracks. Raised on a farm in rural Montana, she was familiar with farm machinery. The green monster outside was the same model as the toy she'd just turned in at the desk. *What a weird coincidence.*

The waitress returned to plunk coffee mugs on the table, along with a tall thermal carafe. Ginger, as her name tag proclaimed, poured each of them a steaming cup, looked at Glen pointedly and said, "More where that came from, darlin'," before hurrying off again.

Jessie was raising her mug to sip, when from the booth behind them she heard a woman's strident voice ask, "Isn't that Berg Nielson's tractor? The one Adele was driving when some idiot shot her? You know, honey... last fall?"

The cup stopped halfway to Jessie's lips. Along with every diner within earshot, she turned her head to stare out the window at the John Deere.

* * *

Later, with the interview over, Jessie stood in front of the conference room looking at twenty-one eager faces. Organized on the front table were several stacks of printed information, colored folders with pockets, small notebooks, white index cards, pencils and blank name tags. Artists stood beside tripod easels or sat in chairs with table easels placed in front of them.

"Please sign and wear your name tags, so I know your name. I'm handing out blank paper. Please take good notes," she said calmly. "Next year—and the next—read through the notes from this class. I throw a lot of information at you—too much to absorb in one workshop if you're a beginner—but a year from now, you'll have painted more and with that experience, will understand more. If some things we talk about in this class don't quite gel, by then, those concepts might jump out, clear as day.

"Painting well takes lots of practice. Take other classes. Most painters absorb just a bit from every workshop." She pinched the tips of her thumb and index finger together. "Sometimes what they learn isn't from the teacher. It's from a student painting next to them."

She picked up the stack of colored folders and began handing one to each person. "To become a good painter, you have to paint as much as you can. Every day if possible. A thousand paintings." She thought of Russell, her old flame, and his lack of enthusiasm for her art. He had deemed it a waste of time. "Even if some don't turn out, it's never a waste of time. One sheet I'm passing out covers the steps of self-critique. Be your own harshest critic and your own loudest cheerleader. You must be both. Don't let friends or relatives bring you down with a critical comment. Don't let them pat you on the back so much that you think you've gotten as good as you need to be."

She picked up a stack of color-wheels. "Stretch yourself. Try new things. Rejoice in each new painting skill, no matter how small." She walked around the room, passing a color wheel and name tag to each student as she spoke. "Remember," she said, as she handed the sheet to an older man whose face beamed with enthusiasm, "half the fun is doing something you enjoy." The next student, a heavyset woman in a blue apron, smiled at her and mouthed her thanks.

"Let's get started. We'll begin by evaluating each person's reference photos. Did everyone bring a couple?" Hands reached into bags and painting boxes and people began pulling out their chosen photographs, mostly scenery. "Your painting is only going to be as good as your references and your planning. We'll start with deciding *why* you want to paint it. If you don't know, it's a good bet your viewer won't have a clue. The key is to have one idea for one painting. If you get only one thing out of today's class, that's the one to remember."

She reached for her artist's apron, a cream-colored adjustable cover-up that sported a vintage Arbuckle Coffee advertisement and three large front pockets, and slipped it on, pulling the ties behind her back and securing them. "After we look at the reference photos, I'm going to explain how I use this blasted color wheel." She picked it up from a nearby table and held it up. "It isn't exactly as they're meant to be used, but it works great. I wish someone had explained it to me the first year I picked up a brush. It would have saved me tons of time."

..*

Three hours later, Jessie stood at the easel applying two wide brush strokes of oil paint side by side. One was a pale yellow-green and the other a washed-out pink. She'd had a question from one of the advanced students about how to make a "lost edge", a transition where the outline of an object blurred into its neighbor's.

"See the difference?" She looked around the room at nodding heads. "Do you notice that although they are different colors, the edge of the main object," she pointed to the area, "and the edge of the object right next to it," again she pointed to the area, making a slight circular motion encompassing both areas with her hand, "are the same value, the same relative lightness or darkness? Now, squint your eyes." Twenty-one students immediately looked nearsighted.

"When you squint, the line between them blurs and disappears. That's called a 'lost edge'. To make our work more realistic, we need some looser areas. Our eyes don't see the world in a 'cut and paste' look with immaculate, crisp edges. The only place our eyes focus crisp and sharp is on one area at a time. The peripheral vision is always blurrier. Softer."

She made another stroke. "Beginners, don't stew over this, but please write it down. When you visit galleries or art shows, try to identify such soft edges in other people's paintings."

As she lifted the paintbrush and stepped back so that the students could gather around the easel and look more closely, the door opened and a teen-aged girl in a well-worn hooded sweatshirt strolled in. She gave Jessie a smile full of braces.

Waving a fistful of papers, she said, "Excuse me. Max and Mrs. Jackson said I should drop these off now, before you broke for lunch, you know? The Curl Up and Dye has signed forms from most of the workshop participants. Mona down at the salon said her five gals would cut these guys' hair over the lunch hour. Work 'em in, like, so you workshop folks can get the haircuts, like, done slam-bam, you know?" She gave the stack of papers to the woman

63

at the first desk. "Pass 'em back, will ya?" She handed Jessie one with a little flourish. Inwardly, Jessie groaned.

"Thanks."

Jessie remembered now that Maureen Jackson was the blue-haired woman, the woman that coerced her into getting her hair cut. Unless they made bluish wigs, the aggressive Mrs. Jackson probably had the only safe head of hair in town. Jessie frowned and automatically reached back to slide her hand down her long ponytail. How short had she promised? It had taken her years to grow it this long.

"Oh, and I have a message from Evan Hansen. "He told me to ask you if you'd ever seen Benny?" The girl smacked gum between her words. "The last time anyone saw him was when he was heading out to your trailer house. His dogs went over to the neighbor's house, because he never went home last night. And, like, the neighbor says Benny loves those dogs. He'd never, you know, leave them to fend for themselves. I love animals, don't you? My dad doesn't want me to have a dog. He says they're smelly, but I don't care. I love' em all. I'm earning money to pay for vet bills. He says if I can do that . . .maybe, just maybe, I can have one."

"Yes, I do love animals and no, I have not seen Benny. But remind Evan that I don't know what Benny looks like, so I could have passed him in the lobby and not realized it." *And my Hawk is not a trailer house. It is a motorhome*, she grumbled inwardly. Frowning, Jessie realized she was feeling downright cranky over the idea of getting her hair cut. Well, heck, it *was* just hair. She smiled at the girl, who dazzled her with a wide silver one in return. "Thanks for delivering the haircut forms. I'm sure Benny will turn up."

"I hope so. Benny's a nice guy. He's going to give me a puppy next spring if his spaniel has a new litter. Spaniels are kind of stupid compared to like, border collies, but they're lovable. Oh, and Mrs. Jackson said she needed your hair cut awesome short. They need red hair. I can't remember why. But it's got to be red, and your hair is flaming."

Dritt.

Chapter Nine

Curl Up and Dye - March

Snip.

Jessie almost whimpered. In the mirror, she watched the first tendril of her auburn hair drop toward the linoleum floor. She grimaced but gave the spectators a thumbs-up gesture. A cheer went up behind her, encouragement shouted from the other artists waiting their turn to donate hair to the "Locks for Ladies" cancer program. They hooted and yelled when the beautician took a second big snip. And the third. All of the enthusiastic bodies waiting their turn were students in the "composition and color harmony" workshop Jessie was teaching that day. And every artist in the class had volunteered to get their hair "cut for the cause", taking their lunch break to get it done. Jessie gave permission for her hair, nearly down to her waist in the signature look she'd had for the past few years, to be shortened to shoulder-length, but she'd had to steel herself to volunteer. *Hope it's not ugly as sin*, she mused.

Mrs. Jackson had explained to Jessie that every year the Crooked Creek Art Show and Auction chose a different charity to receive a small percentage of the overall profits. The hair sheared during today's "Cutathon" would be woven into free wigs for women and girls who'd lost their hair after chemotherapy.

Sniffing, Jessie wrinkled her nose. *Phew*. The beauty shop had the standard salon odor, a sulfurous smell of permanent solution. It reminded her of the rotten egg stench that filled the air near the geysers at Yellowstone Park. *Ick.* The beauty shop was decorated—overly decorated—in Peptol Bismol pink. Framed photos of the beauticians' families stood on small shelves near their work stations—all framed in pink plastic frames. The plastic chairs were pink. The Formica counters were pink. Jessie pictured the blow driers, hairbrushes, combs and curlers rocketing into the sky like Old Faithful in a pink plume of cosmetic paraphernalia. She grinned.

The beautician, Mona, beamed back at her. Jessie figured the stylist thought she was being friendly—a good sport about getting her hair cut. The doll-like woman wore a lavender smock made of fabric printed with scissor and comb images festooned with googly eyes and smiles. She clomped around Jessie's chair on high platform sandals that added four inches to her tiny frame, and undoubtedly caused aching arches by the end of a day. She chewed and smacked gum as she mumbled encouraging words, alternately smiling into the mirror at Jessie, then scowling darkly at the back of Jessie's head, yanking the red tresses and muttering to herself about thick hair. Mona's own hair had a streak of purple. Jessie wondered briefly if the color changed according to the stylist's mood, like a mood ring.

She glanced at the beauty shop clock, impatient to get sheared and get going. She'd driven the Hawk, and because of the motor home's length, she'd parked in the slushy alley at the shop manager's suggestion. It was an illegal parking spot. And she'd left Jack loose in the Hawk. She made a face, thinking of the ingenious cat, hoping he wasn't trying to open the kitchen cupboard with the weak latch. Or digging with his claws at the carpeted storage area hatch that fascinated him so much lately. She winced as Mona accidentally yanked a small tendril. "Ow. Will this take much longer?"

"Sorry. Nah. I'm nearly done already. And don't you worry, darlin'." She tugged one curly hank into submission and snipped. "It'll be real cute. Cute, cute, cute. I've got big plans for this here hair. Since I volunteered to cut all day, Locks for Ladies promised me that some red hair could be earmarked special for my niece,

66

Camilla. Poor baby was a redhead, but she got cancer and now she don't have a lick of hair left on her bald little bean."

"Awww . . ." Jessie's sighed sympathetically, "Poor little thing."

"Little smooth head reminds me of one of those Great Northern beans they make ham 'n bean soup outta. You ever make that?" She peered around Jessie's head and met her deep blue, concerned eyes in the mirror. "I love that stuff, especially with some bacon bits in it. It don't like me much. Anyhow, she used to be a little spitfire, too, but that damn leukemia took the starch right out of her. Like lettin' the air out of a balloon." The beautician gestured to a photo taped to the edge of the mirror. It showed two little girls in their Sunday best, looking directly at the camera. One had a smiling face framed by two long red pigtails, the other child wore a sober expression and a green knit cap. "They're twins." She tapped a painted fingernail on the child in the cap. "That's Cami. Her momma and I are hoping a wig will give her a lift, bless her heart."

"I hope so, too." Jessie stared at the photo while her hair was lifted, yanked and trimmed. The little girl's eyes showed a tired look with a hint of sadness. Dark shadows hung under eyes that looked too large for the small face. For the first time since she'd lowered herself into the salon chair, Jessie felt happy to be getting her hair cut. "You tell Cami I had it cut special for her." Squirming, she adjusted herself more comfortably in the vinyl chair, and met Mona's eyes in the mirror. "You can take several more inches if it helps."

"Too late. I got the length and shape set. Don't worry. It's plenty." Snip. "You got thick hair." Snip. "Gorgeous stuff, too."

"Thanks."

"I hope the wig program makes some money." The beautician waved her pink scissors in the air, snapping the blades together, making Jessie think of lobster claws. "The haircuts are free today, you know. We're doing them for the publicity. Been written up in the paper. But anyone who wants can add a buck or two to the donation pot." She grinned and gestured to a plastic wig form with a big slot cut in the top of the head. "If you want, you can put some right in old 'Mabel' there," she said. "Besides the donations, the

67

charity gets five percent of the art show profits. Whatever people pay for an auction piece, thirty percent goes to the promoter and five percent goes right to Locks for Ladies, Brandy told me."

"Brandy?"

"She's head of the charity's board of directors. And she's worried. Last year the show supported the Creekside Humane Society. They didn't make much."

"Really? That surprises me. Was it a bad show?" Jessie winced as Mona worked, her mind more on the twinges to her scalp than on the small talk.

"Sure didn't look like a bad show. Everybody I know who likes animals tried to buy at least a tiny piece. Everybody in town knew part of the money was going to fund a big spay and neuter program." She muttered to herself and lifted a piece of Jessie's hair from each side of her head, judging the length. "And last year, the charity was supposed to get ten percent, not just five, like the cancer fund this year. Turns out profits were so poor, the Humane Society didn't get enough money to do much."

Jessie stared at her hair in the mirror, glaring at the reflection. She was going to *reeeaally* hate this haircut. Then what Mona had just said registered. Last year, Jessie hadn't attended the show, but she'd sent a huge oil painting to their auction—one of her best paintings of the Glacier Park area. She'd specified that her share of the selling price, sixty percent, should be donated to the Creekside Humane Society. *Hmmmm.* She didn't recall getting a thank you note from the CHS group. She'd received a note from the show committee, though, telling her that her piece had had sold for five figures. Fifty-two thousand, if she remembered correctly. She did some mental math, figuring her 60 percent at over thirty thousand dollars.

Where had that money gone?

She bit her lip and glanced at Mona from the corner of her eye.

"Brandy told you this? That can't be right. Where did she hear that?"

"Put your head down. I'm checking to make sure I got it even." Snip. "Put your head up now. Turn to the right." Snip. "Well, that's easy. Brandy's married to the director of the Humane

68

Society. Cliff, his name is. They make such a nice couple. I style her hair. Well, I can't say I style her hair. Brandy hasn't changed her hairdo in years. Do you notice that some folks aren't brave enough to try anything new? Now, I change mine every couple of months. I'm so gray. But I can be any color I want and let me tell you, darlin', gray ain't it."

As Mona spoke, she untied the cover-up protecting Jessie's green t-shirt, shook the loose hair from it and tossed it into a nearby hamper. One of the other beauticians' swept Jessie's hair from the floor and tipped it quickly into a plastic container marked "Locks for Ladies".

Mona then grabbed the back of the swivel chair and turned it toward the mirror, fluffing Jessie's bangs with a flourish.

"Looks good. Thanks, darlin'. You're a peach." Mona beckoned to the woman next in line. "Next."

Jessie stood, still too stunned at Brandy's comments to look in the mirror and check out her new style. "What's Brandy's last name?"

"Morrison." Mona was already tying the cords of a clean cover-up into a bow at the back of the next customer's neck.

"Thanks." Jessie rifled through her handbag, pulled out a couple of twenty-dollar bills and stuffed them into the donation slot on the wig form. She yanked a pen and a small notepad from her purse and wrote 'Brandy and Cliff Morrison' on the top sheet. She would talk to Max Watson and ask for the skinny on last year's auction. Then find and speak to the Morrisons. If the money from her donated painting never got to the Creekside Humane Society, she wanted to find out why the hell not.

* * *

Jessie stepped out of the beauty shop into the Montana sunshine feeling five pounds lighter. Her hair was short! Short! Well, still shoulder length, but shorter than she'd worn it in years. And the day was gorgeous. The sunshine flecked the disappearing bits of snow with dazzling sparkles of metallic gold and was quickly turning the unseasonable white fluff to slush. She was glad of the

69

waterproofing on her boots as she sloshed through the chilly puddles to the end of the block and squished down the alley.

When Mona removed the cape covering Jessie's clothing, loose hair had slipped down the neck of her T-shirt and it itched like a son-of-a-gun. After she turned the corner and was heading down the alley out of sight of public view, she grabbed the hem of her shirt, pulled it away from her body and shook the loose fabric vigorously. Snips of hair dumped out into the slush.

Yech.

She'd have to change in the motorhome. Looking ahead, she saw Jack through the windshield of the Hawk, sitting on the dash watching for her. He stood and jumped down when she reached the motorhome, and she knew he'd be lurking behind the door, hoping to slip out. He was tired of being cooped up. When they got back to the hotel she'd remember to take her cat leash in with her, so she could take him for a nice long walk this evening. Otherwise every time she went in or out, or the maid came in to tidy the room, he'd try to pull a disappearing act.

She shoved her key in the lock, opened the door a crack and carefully squeezed through, expecting to have to push the cat backward.

"Ha," she said, inching through and slamming the door behind her. Then she deflated when she realized Jack was nowhere in sight. Jessie found him in the compact bedroom of the Hawk, sitting on the hatch of the storage compartment, slanty-eyed and inscrutable.

"Hey, Good Lookin'," she quipped. "You're slipping. Or are you just too lazy to want out?"

She stepped into the adjoining cherrywood bathroom and carefully peeled off the itchy shirt, folding it inside out to corral the loose hair. Then she held a washcloth under the faucet and sponge-bathed. Much better. Looking in the mirror, she closed her eyes in horror. Then brushed her hair. Hard. Her once waist-length hair now swung just below her shoulders. Jessie sighed, turned, and stepped back into the bedroom. From a built-in drawer, she pulled out a charcoal grey knit tunic and slipped it over her head. Portraying Michelangelo's famous image of God and Adam

70

touching index fingers, it was emblazoned with the text: *Sistine Chapel, La Capella Sistina Roma Anno Domini MDXII.*

Jack still sat on the laundry chute hatch. "C'mon, Big Guy, you're not getting down there. What's with you and that storage hatch, anyhow? C'mon, now. I'm in a hurry. I've got a class to finish this afternoon." Jessie lifted Jack down from the storage hatch and dumped him unceremoniously into the outer room of the Hawk and shut the sliding bedroom door. A paw immediately reached under the crack of the door, and slipped left and right, searching for something—anything—to stick a claw into.

Jessie shook her head at Jack's determination, then picked up the hairy T-shirt. She lifted the hatch cover wide open before she remembered there was no longer a clothes' hamper in the storage area. The shirt fell from her hand, and her screams filled the Hawk. Open eyes stared up at her from a face that looked unquestionably dead.

Chapter Ten

Crooked Creek Sheriff's Office

"No. I've never seen him before. Ever. Not in my lifetime," Jessie said frostily, her eyes fixed on the steely blue ones of the middle-aged, uniformed officer. Everything about him seemed unyielding—even his hair, clipped into a short buzz cut. "I don't know what else I can tell you, Sheriff Fischer."

"But you say that the night you arrived, Evan Hanson received," He glanced unnecessarily at his notes, "… a text message from you—"

"No. That is not what I said," Jessie interrupted. "I said he received a text that *seemed* to be from me, but absolutely was *not* from me."

"…asking him to come out to your motorhome. Instead, he sent someone named Benny." Fischer gave her a steely-eyed look. "Well, little lady. The hell of it is that this poor Benny shows up dead in your RV, with you driving him all over town. Robbery wasn't a motive. His wallet was in his pocket, still holding his cash, credit cards and driver's license."

Jessie disliked his condescending tone. She *really* disliked being called "little lady". She returned his look without flinching. "Yes. So you tell me. But the message …was not from my number. It was only worded to sound as though it came from me."

"Why do you think someone would do that, Miss O'Bourne? Why do you think someone wanted to kill poor old Benny? And why stuff him in *your* RV?"

Jessie hung her head tiredly. She'd been sitting in the same chair for two hours. Two hours getting nowhere. At least the Sergeant had allowed her to call Max and tell him what happened. The afternoon workshop session on painting composition had to be canceled or postponed. She'd also asked him to call Arvid Abramsen, requesting that he come to the Sheriff's Office as soon as he arrived. Under Jessie's chair, Jack flexed his claws in and out of the carpet in annoyance. The huge orange tom was hungry and had been muttering periodically.

Six months, she thought. It was about six months ago that she and Jack had sat in almost the same pose in Russell's office at the Sheriff's Office in Sage Bluff, the day she'd given Arvid her statement about finding Amber Reynolds dying in her dad's hayfield. The difference was that Arvid had been pleasant. She had an awful suspicion that the man in front of her thought she was involved in this death or had something to hide.

Fischer continued to drone on, but Jessie was lost in thought, thinking of her dad. Of Russell. Of Arvid. Of Sage Bluff. Homesickness washed over her like an ocean wave over empty beach. God help her, she was homesick. How she wished her Dad was here. Dan O'Bourne was huge. He made everyone she met seem small by comparison.

Wasn't she too old to want her father to fix things? She stared down at her knee, eyes filling.

Oh, no. She was NOT going to cry.

She willed herself to concentrate on the blue of her jeans. *Denim. A mix of ultramarine blue, a bit of burnt umber and white.* Her fingers flexed. Fischer said something—loud—and she looked up, meeting his inquiring brown eyes.

"What do you have to say about that, Miss O'Bourne?"

Yes, a touch of burnt umber. "Er, sorry?"

"Miss O'Bourne? Are you with me here?" His eyes narrowed.

"Um …can I make another call?" Maybe Arvid was in Crooked Creek but Max hadn't gotten through to him. Arvid was

73

an electronic dinosaur and his cell phone was truly archaic. One of those flip things. He compensated by not carrying it very often.

"YeowRrrr." Jack thrummed grouchily, yawning wide, showing a mouthful of needle-like teeth. He got up to pace restlessly around Sergeant Fischer's office, prowling from desk to filing cabinet and circling the Sergeant's chair. When he got close enough to sniff Fischer's pant leg, the man visibly cringed.

Geez, Jessie thought. The man dislikes cats. Or is afraid of cats. Maybe both.

She reached down and tapped her fingers on the floor. "C'mere, Baby. C'mon, Jack. Leave Sheriff Fischer alone."

Jack gave Fischer's boot a last sniff, wrinkled his nose and chuffed, before wandering back to check out Jessie's fingers with his usual hope that cat treats might appear from mid-air. Finding none, he leaped onto her lap, put a paw on her shoulder and stared soulfully into her face.

"I asked why Evan would send Benny out to help you instead of going himself."

"And as I have told you several times, I do not know. I have no idea. Ask Evan Hanson. Ask Max Watson." She threw up her hands, startling Jack. "You could talk to the art show committee. Anybody who knew him. But I can't help you."

"Oh, be assured we will be speaking to everyone at the lodge, Miss O'Bourne. And in the meantime, your motorhome will have to be confiscated for evidence gathering. We need to go over it with a fine-toothed comb for fingerprints, and anything else we can find."

"Can't you just check out the storage area and give it back?"

"Nope. 'Fraid not."

"How long?" Jessie asked solemnly. Then she wondered how she could ever drive it again. Would she always see Benny's dead eyes staring up at her from the storage area? She cleared her throat, again analyzing the the denim color of her slacks—mentally adding just the tip of a palette knife of cobalt—and held back a sob. "How long do you need to keep it?"

"Well," Sergeant Fischer said, leaning back in his oak desk chair, hands laced behind his head. "That pretty much depends on what we find. I can't give you a specific date when you'll get it back."

"I see." Jessie took mental inventory of what she had in the hotel room, and what was in the Hawk. "I suppose I can't retrieve personal belongings?"

"Sorry, no. At least you have your credit cards and cash, since you had the ladies' travel wallet in your pocket. After all, it's a murder investigation. It's to your advantage as well as ours that we check the interior of the motorhome before anything else is removed. Rule out that the victim had been inside before his death." He gave her a skeptical look. "We won't find Benny's fingerprints inside, will we?"

"I'm sure not." Jessie's thoughts churned as she reviewed the checklist. Clothes? Paint? Canvases? Cat items? Leash? Crap, she thought. The hell with Arvid's Norwegian swear words. I've got to have a damn leash.

"Well, I think we've covered about all we can for now. You realize that often the person who reports a body is the same person who placed it there?" He gave her a two-fingered salute. "Don't leave town."

The absurdity of that struck Jessie, and she almost grinned. "I can't leave town. Not only do I have an art show to help with, and a workshop to teach, but you've taken my only means of transportation."

"Uh huh. I need to check the team's progress at the resort parking lot. See if they've found anything in the area you said you were parked. I mean before you left for the beauty shop." Sergeant Fischer stood and retrieved his jacket from the back of his chair. "Do you need a lift back to the hotel?"

"Yes," Jessie said.

The desk phone buzzed. Fischer picked it up with an abrupt, "Yes?"

He listened, then said brusquely, "Send him in."

"Seems your champion has arrived, Miss O'Bourne. An old acquaintance?" He rubbed his chin with his hand and looked unhappy.

Jessie brightened at the sound of a knock on the door, which was pushed open even before Fischer called a gruff, "Come in."

Arvid's large frame filled the doorway. Jessie relaxed with relief, letting out a breath she hadn't realized she'd been holding. If she couldn't have her father available for moral support, Arvid was a wonderful second best. Along with his air of self-confidence he wore a flannel-lined denim jacket over a blue plaid woolen shirt— a blue that made his eyes seem the intensity of a summer sky. His salt and pepper hair was tousled, as though he'd been running his meaty fingers through the mop in agitation. He glanced at Jessie in concern, then nodded to her.

Fischer stepped forward and held out his hand to the big Norwegian. Grasping the Sergeant's hand, Arvid gave it a brief pump before saying, "Good to meet you, Detective Sergeant. Name's Arvid Abrahmsen. Jessie's an old friend of mine, and my wife's. I'm with the Sage Bluff Sheriff's Office. Whole thing sounds like a can of worms without a fishing pole in sight, don't it?" Then he looked at Jessie. "I dropped Esther at the check-in desk and hustled my behind over here. You can fill me in on the ride back to the hotel, okay?" He looked at Fischer. "You must be about done with her for now?"

"Yeah, I guess so," Fischer said grudgingly.

"But you got the Hawk?" Arvid gave him a questioning look.

"What hawk?" Fischer asked. "What are you talking about?"

"Huh. Sorry. I mean the motorhome. Jessie's Greyhawk. You confiscate it to run forensics?"

"Oh. Yes. We certainly did." Fischer's tone was self-important. "But we're a small community. We use the State Police for lab work like that. And they're always backlogged. We'll have it for at least a week."

"A week? Good god, they ought to be able to finish with it before that."

Jessie gave Arvid a warning look. He grunted, then reached into a shirt pocket and handed Fischer a card.

"Well. Alrighty then. Here's my info. We'd appreciate it if you'd keep us informed as to your progress and time frame for getting Miss O'Bourne's vehicle back."

"Yeah. Our time frame is: we'll be done when we're done. No special courtesies just because you and I are in the same profession."

76

Arvid gave him a look that could curdle milk. "Didn't ask for any. You give her a receipt for the motorhome and the contents?" At Fischer's nod, Arvid glanced at Jessie and reached out to take Jack, hugged the tom to his massive chest and scratched under his chin, working his fingers to the tom's cheek and behind an ear. Jack purred. Arvid smiled and handed the rumbling cat back to her. "You ready to head back to the hotel?"

"Sure." Then she reconsidered. "Actually, can we hit a pet store first? I need a couple things for the beast."

"Wait a minute," Fischer said. Jessie turned. The Sergeant had slipped on a pair of shades that reflected Jessie's face in the lenses. "You don't know who took the art show banner off the signpost and hung it on the tractor instead, do you, Miss O'Bourne?"

"What? The big banner about the show? No, I have no idea. Why on earth do you want to know?"

"Never mind. That's not your concern." He waved his hand imperiously at her as though shooing away a fly. "You can go for now. I'll be in touch."

Jessie gave an annoyed huff. Without realizing it in her irritation, she'd tightened her hold on Jack, who rumbled his displeasure. His reptilian yellow eyes narrowed.

"You're squeezing the life out of that cat," Arvid grabbed Jessie's elbow and almost pulled her through the door.

As they walked down the hall, Arvid whispered. "Don't say nothin'."

When they were further down the hall, Jessie said, "Isn't he just the...the most obnoxious...the most self-important man you've ever met?"

"Yeah, he's sure got a stick up... uh, he's . . .," Arvid scratched his head. "Hmm. Well...he's just trying to do his job, Jess."

"Hmph. Well, I don't like him. I am *so* not going to sketch his portrait in my journal."

Arvid gave her a skeptical look. He was well aware Jessie kept a notebook with a quick pencil portrait of nearly everyone she knew included within the pages. Grinning, he changed the subject. "I 'spose even your cat food is locked in the Hawk? There might be a clue in it, you know," he teased. "It'd make a good book." He rolled his hand as though introducing a guest speaker at a podium. "Introducing Sheriff Fischer, author of *The Clue in the Kibble*," he said in a low, dramatic tone.

Jessie snickered.

"So, are we making the pet store run for cat food?" Arvid glanced at Jack, then back at Jessie with a grin. "He looks like he could live on his layer of blubber for a week, Jess."

Jack gave a guttural thrum.

"No. Jack's kibble was one of the first things I carried into the hotel room." Jessie sighed. "But I do need a cat harness. Jack's is still in the Hawk because I forgot to take it into the hotel. He's already sick of being cooped up. He's being a real pain about trying to get out when the maid comes to clean the room. I don't want to lose him. I'm going to take him for walks while we're stuck staying in the lodge."

Arvid's chuckle echoed down the corridor. "I can't wait to see that. I'm gonna have to borrow Esther's new phone and make a video."

"Oh, sure. I can see you doing that. First, you'd have to ask Esther how to turn it on. Then, you'd be on the phone calling tech support for at least an hour—maybe two—before you could figure out the video app," she chortled. "Esther would think you were having an affair with someone named Habib."

"Say, now." Arvid shook his finger at her. "Didn't I just rescue your tuckus from the possibility of the hoosegow?"

"Huh," Jessie grunted, mimicking one of Arvid's most pertinent sayings. "Not hardly."

"Yeowr," Jack echoed.

Chapter Eleven

Downtown Crooked Creek

"So, someone sent the show assistant an email, pretending to be you, asking for help? That's weird."

Arvid slowed to a stop as the light turned yellow, then red. He tapped his finger impatiently on the wheel of the pickup. They'd stopped at the pet store, bought Jack a flashy blue cat harness that included a leash and a bag of cat treats, and were heading back toward the lodge.

"Yeah. Actually, a text."

"You know how electronically challenged I am. A text is on your phone, right? And it uses your phone number or a computer account in your name somehow, right?"

"Yes. Most use a phone number. So, whoever sent it had to go to all the trouble to create a fake account with my name, then send the text." Jessie smoothed the hair on Jack's back, realizing the gesture was more calming to herself than to the big tom. He was used to riding. Loved it, in fact. "But they must have used a burner phone. A throwaway."

"Geez. Then it was definitely intentional. No way that could be some computer gremlin."

"Not a chance."

"Fischer don't seem like the kind of guy to be careless. I don't think he and me are gonna be best buds, but that ain't important. He'll check on the text. You got any ideas on who might be annoyed enough at you to pull that stunt?"

79

"At me? No. I don't think it has anything to do with me, Arvid. I think my Hawk was just a handy spot to hide the body."

"Hope that's all there is to it. Hey, look. Let's pull in and have a bite." He put on his blinker, drove past a shop advertising custom-made saddles and pulled immediately into the only empty parking space in front of an eatery whose sign read 'Hank's Diner and Dogs'. "Getting a parking place right here in front." He made a thumbs-up gesture. "Must be good old fate. Diner and Dogs. Bet they got chili dogs. I haven't had a crumb to eat since we left Sage Bluff."

Jessie looked dubiously at the cafe. "Well…" Her stomach was roiling. But she knew she should eat. Some food would perk her up if she could keep it down.

"Oh, for Pete's sake, Jess. Be a sport. I'm riding on empty here."

"Oh, alright. Sheesh. I'm not sure I can eat anything, I'm so keyed up."

"Sure you can. A burger and a piece of pie will fix you right up. Guess I'd better call Esther and see if I need to bring her back a sandwich or maybe order and go pick her up while they make our food. I didn't even think of it. Heck, I must be a thoughtless hunk of no good husband." He pulled his cell phone from his pocket and began to dial.

"Oh, I doubt that. I know how often Esther says you bring home flowers and such."

"Well, yeah, but that's out of guilt because I'm always doing some dumb little thing she gets all fired up about." He held the phone to his ear. He wiggled his eyebrows at Jessie. "Keeps the peace." He turned his attention to the phone.

"Hi, honey. I can pick you up, so you can have lunch with Jessie and me. We're stopping for a chili dog. We can fill you in on what's happening while we eat. I'm starving here."

Jessie heard mumbling in the background, and Arvid shook his head back and forth, then up and down, waiting for his turn to speak. Then he swiped the phone to off and put it back in his jacket pocket.

"Well, what did she say?"

"Huh," Arvid grunted. "First, she said, 'Chili dogs, oh gross'. And then she said, 'I knew you'd stop and eat without me, you big Norwegian lug'. And earlier, when I told her you found a dead body in the Hawk, she said a word I didn't even know she knew. Came right outta her sweet mouth." He shook his head. "She's going to order a chicken salad from the restaurant at the lodge. Can you imagine ordering a salad instead of eating chili dogs with us?"

Jessie smiled, and with that simple action, felt her spirits lift. How the refined and elegant Esther and the huge crusty Norwegian Sheriff's Deputy had managed to meet on common ground and marry was a mystery. She began to chuckle. "Oh, Arvid, you don't even know if they have them."

"Ya, sure they will. Say, is Jack going to be okay in the truck while we eat? I'll lower my window a tad."

"He'll be fine." Jack looked up at her tom. One of his fangs was snagged, overlapping his lip, but he was doing his best to look snooty. He'd caught the word "truck" and the intention to leave him in the vehicle. "He doesn't mind being left in a vehicle when the weather is this cool. In fact, he likes to lay on the dash and growl at passers-by."

"That is the damnedest cat I've ever seen." He reached toward Jack's lip. "Poor big ole Jack. Let me help you, Bud."

"Don't try it, Arvid," Jessie said quickly. "He'll bite."

"Huh." He drew his hand back as Jack's eyes narrowed to slits. "Well, that looks dang uncomfortable."

"He's okay. I'll crack the window on my side, but we have to lock the doors. I don't want anyone stealing my handsome boy. And he knows how to open the old truck door at Dad's, so we have to make sure this is locked tight."

Arvid guffawed as he and Jessie got out and she insisted on locking the pickup doors before walking to the restaurant entrance.

"After you," he said, as he pushed open the door and they looked around the sparkling interior of a small, but cheerful, cafe. The walls were sunshine yellow. The floor was black and white checked linoleum—well-scrubbed and well-worn—probably installed about 1950. Several cowboy hats hung on a rack near the door and above the rack hung an ad covered with shamrocks touting an Irish Festival in Butte.

COME DOWN TO BUTTE FOR ST. PATTY'S DAY AND FIND YOUR IRISH ROOTS! HAVE A GREEN BEER, AN IRISH WHISKY, AND LISTEN TO SOME PIPES AND DRUMS. ENTER THE RAFFLE FOR THE REMINGTON MODEL 870 WINGMASTER SHOTGUN—ALL PROCEEDS BENEFIT OUR BUTTE FIRE STATION

The room was a weird mix of art deco meets rustic western with a few St. Patrick's Day decorations tossed in. The smell of frying burgers made Jessie's mouth water. But every table and booth was full. Arvid began to turn and exit in disappointment.

A pint-sized waitress with legs slim as a shore-bird's, and slightly knock-kneed, came barreling over and barked at him in a drill-sergeant's booming voice, "Wait a sec, wait a sec. We'll have a booth open in a tic." Jessie and Arvid hesitated. She stood and wrung her hands, muttering, "Let me see. Let's see, now." Then she focused on her target with missile-like precision.

"Frank!" She yelled toward a glum, slump-shouldered, wispy-haired man in a threadbare red woolen shirt. "You been sitting over that same cup of coffee for an hour. Move your butt over to the counter and give these nice folks your booth."

"Aw, Beth Marie," came his whiny voice. "Not again."

"I mean it. Get a move on, and I'll refill your cup and pop a piece of pie in the microwave for you. Add some real whippin' cream, even." She made a shooing motion at him. "Whippin' cream," she coaxed in a sultry voice. "You go on, now."

Frank, now looking remarkably cheery for someone being evicted from his space, rose, strode to the counter and slid onto a tall stool. "I want the Dutch apple this time, Beth." He grabbed a white napkin from a chrome dispenser, pulled a fork from a container of clean utensils, placed them to his left, and waited expectantly.

"C'mon," the bossy little woman directed Arvid and Jessie. She swished a rag over the table and waved them into the now empty booth, "I'm Beth Marie, and I'll be your server. Set yourselves down and I'll be there in a whipstitch. Coffee?"

"Yes, please," Jessie replied. Arvid nodded and held up two fingers.

"Cream or sugar?"

"Black is fine."

"Cream and sugar. I need my calories." Arvid gave her an impish smile as he slid into the booth.

Over the table hung a bone-white bison skull. Someone had taped shamrocks over the eye holes and under the macabre head, a stained poster covered with hearts proclaimed, 'Have a Happy Valentine's Day'. The edge of a faded Christmas border peeked out from under the Valentine wishes. Jessie downgraded her first impression of the cafe from 'immaculate' to 'clean enough to eat in'.

Beth Marie turned on a heel and swept through the small cafe, returning with a pot full to the brim, filling the hapless Frank's coffee cup in drive-by fashion with one hand and plunking a thick wedge of plated pie in front of him with the other. As she hurried around the counter toward their booth, she tucked a couple menus under her arm and snagged two mugs. Jessie stared at her in wordless wonder.

"Here you go." She placed two menus on the table. "Our special today is cream of chicken soup with a grilled cheese sandwich on sourdough. The soup is good for what ails you. It's got chunks of chicken, onion, garlic and a dab of fresh rosemary. Don't ask about bread 'cause it don't come on nothin' but sourdough. We have two pies—coconut cream or Dutch apple. Fresh today. I put the half and half for your coffee there on the lazy Susan with the napkins. Back in a flash." And off she went.

"I swear that little woman leaves a trail of smoke," Arvid said admiringly. "She's like a super power."

Jessie smiled and tried not to snicker. She was looking at the menu.

"What the...?" Arvid was crestfallen. There were no chili dogs on the menu. No bratwurst. No hot dogs. But in a corner of the menu was a photo of a fat yellow lab with a chihuahua standing between his legs. In bold red letters, it stated 'If you don't want to share the cafe with our dogs, there is outdoor seating in the back of Hank's Diner and Dogs. Please let us know if you plan to eat outside.'

Jessie and Arvid looked at each other. Arvid raised an eyebrow. Then they looked around and spotted a old, gray-muzzled dog stretched out flat under the back table, legs twitching in sleep. Curled up near the chin of the larger dog was the chihuahua.

"Guess I'll have the special. And two pieces of pie. One of each."

Beth Marie had materialized like a wraith. "Good choice. How about you, Miss?"

"Make it two specials. But only one piece of pie for me. I'll have the coconut cream."

* * *

Half an hour later, Arvid patted his ample stomach. "Alice's Cafe back in Sage Bluff makes just a mite better Dutch apple pie, but this was more than passable. Good coffee, too." He put down his fork. "How'd you like the coconut cream?"

"To die for." Jessie's fork stopped an inch from her mouth. "Oh, what an awful choice of words." She put a hand on her forehead, shoving the red curls back. "Arvid, what am I going to do? Surely Fischer doesn't think I had anything to do with that dead man." A tear slid down her cheek. "Poor, poor Benny. I'm never going to open that hatch again without seeing his face staring up at me." She swallowed hard. "My God. Those staring eyes. It was awful."

"Hang in there. No time to fall apart, Jess." Arvid patted her hand and looked glum. "How dark was it?"

"How dark was what? In the Hawk's storage space?"

"Nah. How dark was it outside when Evan Hansen sent Benny out to the Hawk?"

"Oh. I see what you're getting at. It was getting late…dark enough that someone might mistake him for Evan. Heck, in the winter jackets everyone wore, he could have been mistaken for anyone. And where I was parked, it was dark as pitch. The pole lights weren't working in that part of the parking lot." She paused. "It was really annoying because I had to run the electric cord from the Hawk to the special electrical outlet on the pole. I have a flashlight app on my phone and I was thinking about getting the phone out and using it. Anyway, when I went to haul in some things for Jack, I could barely see my way back to the motorhome."

"It's gotta be a given that Evan was the actual target, Jessie. Someone better warn him. That is, if Fischer hasn't already put the fear of God into him. Whoever sent that email to lure him out to the parking lot must've known you were parked in the far corner where it would be easy to hide. Very dark. Very isolated. I wonder if the street light was intentionally damaged." He drummed his fingers on the table. "Ya. Someone has it in for Evan Hansen."

"I agree." She chased a small piece of pie around the plate with her fork. "You sound as if you know him."

"I do. I met him last year when Esther played piano here at the show. She does it nearly every year. I don't know him well, but he seems like a nice enough young fellow. He's been studying marketing. Does all of the show promotion."

"That reminds me, Arvid." Jessie told him about the painting she'd donated to the auction the previous year, and about the rumor that the money hadn't reached the Humane Society as promised.

"You want me to go with you when you tackle Max Watson about that?"

"Of course not." She waved a hand dismissively. "I'm a big girl. I'll put on my pointy-toed cowgirl boots and go broach the subject. But I'll fill you in when I find some answers."

"You have any idea who bought your painting?"

"No. But I think I can find out. I'll locate and speak to the person who had the winning bid and make certain the sale went through. If it didn't, the painting should have been returned to me."

Arvid nodded, slouching back against the booth seat and taking a sip of coffee. "Say, why do you suppose Sergeant Fischer wanted to know about the banner on the tractor?"

"No clue. I thought that was weird, too." Then Jessie went on to tell him about the tiny reproduction she'd found in the hall that morning. "It was the cutest thing. A toy exactly like the big one parked out in the lot. Isn't that a coincidence?"

Arvid sat up straight. "I don't believe in coincidences, Jess. Fischer asking about the tractor while he was interviewing you about a dead body in the Hawk. And now you're saying there was a replica of the same tractor outside your hotel room door." He

85

looked at his untouched coconut cream pie and frowned. Then he put it into a white Styrofoam 'to go' box the waitress had left. "Nup. I don't like it. And I don't think it's just happenstance."

"Well, thanks for making me feel oh-so-much better."

"Sorry. I just think it's weird." He looked contrite. Then he eyed the go box. "Hey, I got this piece of pie to go, but I think I'll have it now. You want half?"

"Sure," Jessie said quickly. At Arvid's crestfallen expression she grinned. "Just kidding. *Now*, I feel better."

He shook his head at her in mock disgust, but his eyes brightened as he opened the white box. "Wish they'd had huckleberry or rhubarb. Just the wrong time of year. Now, a rhubarb-custard pie is hard to beat." He aimed a fork at Jessie. "Did you know that rhubarb originated in China in about 2700 BC? It showed up in America between 1790-1800. It even has some medicinal qualities."

Smiling, Jessie pointed her own fork at Arvid. "Nobody but you would bother to research pie filling, Arvid. And you know that Esther is going to ask you how many pieces you had."

"I got a good response to that. I'm gonna say, 'Esther, that info is on a need to know basis'. And then if she grumbles, I'll promise to start watching my diet on the first of next month."

Jessie grinned and shook her finger at him. "April Fool's Day, huh?"

Arvid nodded. "You're welcome to borrow that phrase whenever you want. I'm generous that way."

The little waitress was back with the coffee pot. "Want a hotter?"

Both Arvid and Jessie took an inch.

"I heard you say 'rhubarb'. I always got some in the freezer. Come back next Wednesday and double-crust rhubarb pie'll be the special on the menu." She buzzed off like her feet were on fire.

Arvid scowled. He wouldn't be in town long enough.

Picking up her coffee mug, Jessie took a healthy swig. She did feel better. Eating had been smart. Gazing outside she saw Jack, actually the back half of Jack, hind feet and tail-end pressed against the glass, in the window of Arvid's truck. She knew immediately that his head and front feet were at the level of the door handle.

The little bugger's trying to get out.

She was on her feet in an instant, jogging toward the door.

"What the heck?" Arvid rose to follow but Beth Marie stepped in front of him with the bill.

Jessie reached the truck just as the door popped slightly open and a jubilant Jack squeezed through and stepped out onto the sidewalk, tail up and a self-satisfied feline expression on his face. He lifted his head and sniffed, then turned toward the deli two doors down and lifted one large paw to begin his survey of Crooked Creek.

"Oh, no you don't, Houdini. You could get lost or hit by a car." She scooped him up and reached into the truck for the new cat harness.

Chapter Twelve

Previous December, Fort Stewart Army Base, Georgia

Dominic read the letter, scowling. The anonymous letters to Berg must have started soon after Addy's funeral nearly three months ago. Why hadn't his Dad given him a heads-up earlier? *Probably too proud.* But the timing couldn't be better. It was right at the deadline date when he could either re-enlist or take an honorable discharge. If he didn't re-up, his last day would be the middle of next week. December 15th. Then he remembered that he had two weeks of leave coming. Maybe he could book a flight out in the next couple of days if he turned in that leave. The Army would even owe him a bit of money. *I could be home before Christmas, maybe cook Dad a turkey.* He rubbed his chin in thought, in his mind smelling the rich aroma he associated with Christmas—the baking bird, pumpkin pie, a freshly cut evergreen tree. He sighed. Only him and the old man this Christmas. It wouldn't seem like much of a holiday with his mother and Addy both gone, but he could make it as normal as possible. He folded the note and put it into the pocket of his fatigues.

He sighed. He'd better just get out of the military. He'd joined for two reasons. First, because he thought every man should take his turn serving his country. Second, so he could take advantage of the student loan repayment program. Taking classes to earn the Agricultural Business degree from Montana State had been expensive. Worth it, though. His mother had been the bookkeeper for the ranch. After she passed away, his Dad always messed up the books. It went from bad to worse after he was diagnosed with cancer. The place started going downhill. Addy tried to do what she could. Dom couldn't imagine how hard it must be now without her. The poor old man had no family at home to help and, proud as Berg was, Dom knew he wouldn't call on friends and neighbors even if things got to be too much for him on the farm. Dom cursed under his breath. With the advent of the threatening notes, he was more certain than ever that his sister's death was no accident. His eyes filled, and he wiped a sleeve across his face.

Why would anyone want to kill his sweet kid sister? And how come the Sheriff wasn't doing more to find the bastard who did it?

Worry gnawed at his gut. He chewed his lip. Tomorrow he'd take his dad's letter to a friend in the military police. The guy was clever and might have some good ideas on how to go about finding the bastard threatening his old man. Dom could work on that. He clenched his fist. He'd love to get his hands on the culprit. And at least now, when he went home, he'd feel like more of an asset than just another pair of hands. Dammit, his dad might even listen to some of his ideas on how to improve the ranch. Yes. He'd book a flight as soon as possible. Dom smiled at the thought.

"Guess what, Freeman?" He directed the question at his Army buddy, Harris Freeman, a round-faced, dark-haired man stretched out on his bunk reading a manual. They'd joined at the same time when the recruiter came to Crooked Creek.

"You're a surprise a minute, Nielson. Now, how am I supposed to guess what in hell you're up to?" The man gave Dom a crooked grin. "Just enlighten me, wouldja?" He slapped the manual down on his bunk.

"I'm going home, man. Taking the rest of my leave and opting out."

"You're kidding, right?" The other man sat bolt upright. "Who's gonna stick around and wipe my nose?" He gave an elaborate sniff. "You know I'm dying of boredom here. That's why I left you everything in my will, Nielson. All my wordly possessions."

Dominic laughed. "Yeah, sure. I left you mine, too, remember? All twenty bucks and my extra skivvies." The friends had written fast, tongue in cheek wills when they thought they were being mobilized a second time to Afghanistan—a mobilization that never materialized.

"Geez, Nielson." Freeman stood and stared in incredulity. "You're serious. I thought we were in it together for the long haul when we joined up." Freeman stood and stretched. "Four years. Until all our student loans were covered. You sure you know what you're doing?"

Dominic thought of the letter resting in his pocket. With some wacko harassing the old man, he needed to get back to Crooked Creek. He had a feeling of urgency. If he explained the situation, his commanding officer might help expedite his separation from the Army.

"Most of my loans are covered. Near enough, anyhow." He pulled the letter back out of his pocket and handed it to Freeman with a frown. "It doesn't matter. There's some trouble at home."

Freeman read quickly, his lips tightening as he read. When he finished he looked at Dom, worry evident in his gaze. "Well, Holy Ned. This is the craziest thing I've ever heard of. First your sister was shot by some nut case, and now somebody's writing such crap to an old guy like your dad." He handed the letter back to Dom with a serious expression on his face. "I signed my reenlistment papers yesterday. My leave has been planned for months, but it doesn't start until the end of January. Sounds like your Dad thinks he might get a bit of help from Addy's boyfriend. That's a great idea, if he actually set up that trail camera. Once I get there and catch up a bit with my family, I'll swing over and check in with you. See if you need my help."

"Sure. You do that. But I hope I have it handled by then. I'll head to the Sheriff's Office first, find out what they've been doing to look into it. Dad doesn't have any faith in the younger deputy, Jacob. That's the guy he's been showing the notes to. The one he calls the 'lazy, ignorant, disrespectful cowpie of a kid' in the letter." Dom and Freeman both grinned. Then Dom sobered. "But I always thought old stiff-necked Fischer might be a decent man in a pinch."

"Yeah, me too. Remember when he caught us with the six-packs after graduation? He was cool to just confiscate the beer and not rat us out to the folks. He was a straight shooter."

"Hey, he probably downed free beer after work every day for three months." Dom chuckled. "I think I'll bypass cowpie Jacob and go see Sheriff Fischer as soon as I've had a few minutes to visit with Dad. See what the Sheriff thinks we can do to help catch this creep." He gave Freeman a thoughtful look. "I've been thinking I might sign on as a volunteer deputy once I get processed out of the Army. It depends on whether I can get a job right away. I'm not sure what I can do around Crooked Creek with a business degree." He smiled. "Once I start pulling in a few bucks, I might call Tabatha Williams and see if she's still single."

"Aw, shut up, will ya, Dom?" Freeman snarled. "I'm starting to regret signing that re-up form."

Chapter Thirteen

Crooked Creek Lodge - March

Arvid drove slowly into the entrance of the lodge, eyeballing the tractor parked next to the hotel driveway. The art show banner stretched from the front of the John Deere to the back, covering the entire side. "Wonder what happened to the windshield," he said. "You know, that looks like a bullet hole in the back window."

"Yes. And at the restaurant this morning I overheard someone say a girl was shot in it. It was late when I had cocoa in the restaurant. It wasn't there then, so someone brought it in after I went back to the room," Jessie replied.

"Interesting. I'm just dang curious about why Fischer asked about it."

Jessie shrugged. "Me, too. But, I don't have a clue."

Arvid pulled into the unloading area by the lodge entrance and stopped, letting the engine idle.

"I'll drop you off, then go find a spot to park. No sense looking for a rental car until tomorrow."

"No, I have to be here at the hotel all evening, anyway, so I wouldn't be driving one. Thanks for everything, Arvid." Jessie lifted Jack, now decked out in his cat harness, got out and walked around the truck. She set him on the sidewalk, the loop of the blue leash wrapped around her hand.

Arvid rolled his window down. "Say, Jess. If Esther isn't in our room—it's room 212—why don't you call her cell and meet her by those tables near the piano? She's looking forward to seeing you, and I'll be there in a couple minutes."

"That'd be great. But I've got a few things to do first. Give me at least half an hour. I need to contact Max and find out what he's arranged about continuing—or canceling—the workshop. And I want to speak to him about last year's auction." The cat had flopped onto his back and was rolling on the now dry concrete.

"Okay." He gestured to Jack and blew a raspberry through pursed lips. "Look at him. You're dreamin' if you think that cat is gonna walk on that leash. Poop. I knew that harness was a waste of money. You'll probably have to just sort of drag him along." He made a rolling motion with his hand.

Jessie gave him a dirty look. "Nobody's dragging my cat around. He not only walks fine with his harness on, but he has better manners than that brute of yours. Not that I don't love that big brute." Arvid's enormous Neapolitan mastiff, Bass, had saved Jessie's life six months earlier. The dog had been trained to recognize only Norwegian commands, and Jessie was forced to commit a list of terms to memory in order to manage the huge animal. She continued, "Jack doesn't slobber, and he understands English. Jack is, um…refined."

"Ha." He snickered at the thought of the rag-tag ear and the tooth that frequently hung over the cat's lip. "Refined." He slapped his knee. "Not hardly. And I'd like to see you get Jack to follow any commands at all. That cat don't take orders. In fact, I think that feline gives 'em."

"Oh, yeah? Listen and learn, Arvid. Listen and learn." Jessie turned to the tom, who was now standing, looking curiously around. "Let's go, Big Guy." In an undertone to Jack she said, "Treats." Then in a louder, commanding voice she said, "Inside, Jack. Let's go, Butter Tub." Jack strode purposely toward the door of the lodge, tail up.

Jessie glanced over her shoulder at Arvid and waggled her fingers in a wave.

He shook his head in amazement. "I don't think that's really a cat," he muttered aloud. He stepped on the gas and pulled away from the lodge, his rich chuckle filling the cab.

93

* * *

The door slid open with a swish as Jessie and Jack strolled into the lobby. The Art Expo had an info desk set up and people stood in line to buy western T-shirts, posters, and tickets to the special events. The crowd contained people dressed in everything from casual jeans and T-shirts to elaborately fringed and beaded contemporary western chic leather jackets, cowboy hats, and fancy boots.

Jessie and the cat skirted the crowd and were heading toward the elevator when a woman waiting in the long line at the hotel check-in counter touched her on the shoulder.

"Excuse me. Are you familiar with this show?"

"Yes," Jessie said. "Did you have a question?"

"Can you tell me what's worth attending? And are any of the events free?"

"Sure." Jessie explained, "Browsing through the showrooms costs absolutely nothing. It's free for the duration of the show, all three days. But some events—such as seminars, talks, a quick-draw, buffet style dinner and the main auction—do cost something. Tickets purchased individually at the door are more expensive, so most patrons purchase an all-inclusive ticket. That ticket lets you in to all the activities, and you also get a bidding number for the auctions on Friday and Saturday night."

The woman, her shiny salt and pepper hair swinging to her shoulders, reached down to pet Jack. Before Jessie could say "he bites", the lady's hand touched the orange head. Jack immediately began purring softly, squinting his eyes in ecstasy.

"You lovely, well-behaved boy," she crooned, pursing her lips at the tom. "Look at handsome little you and your classy harness." Then she straightened, pushed her hair behind one ear, and smiled at Jessie. "What a sweetie. I imagine you can tell that I have cats." She glanced back at the busy check-in desk, then said, "So, getting back to the art show—what about the quick-draw? I heard several people say they wanted to go. How does it work?" She laughed. "I'm assuming it isn't a pistol contest."

Jessie chuckled dutifully. "No, it isn't. Before the Saturday night auction, visitors can watch fifteen artists each create a work

94

of art in only an hour, starting with a blank canvas. Servers wander the crowds, passing out tasty hors d'oeuvres, wine and elegant small desserts. People seem to really enjoy it. When the hour ends, the new pieces are auctioned off at the start of the main auction."

"Oh, I'm definitely going to watch that. Are you?"

Jack, the traitor, was rubbing against the woman's leg. The woman wore lovely black trousers in an expensive looking fabric. Jessie winced as she saw several orange hairs attach themselves to the cloth like Velcro to flannel.

"Actually, I'm going to be painting in the quick-draw."

"Oh, wonderful," the woman said with enthusiasm. "I'll come and watch." Then she frowned. "I came to town to handle some business this afternoon, but some of it has to wait until Monday. Luckily, I was able to get a reservation here. What a pleasant surprise to find an art show going on. I thought I'd have nothing to do between meetings." She held out a delicate, well-manicured hand that sported expensive looking turquoise rings and a wide silver cuff bracelet. "I'm Anna Farraday."

Jessie looked into the woman's warm brown eyes and reached out to grasp Anna Farraday's hand, wishing her own were soft and baby-smooth instead of sandpaper rough, and her nails not so utilitarian, with the stain of ultramarine blue oil paint under several fingernails even after repeated scrubbing.

"Nice to meet you. Welcome to the show. I'm Jessie O'Bourne. At two o'clock tomorrow afternoon I'll be doing an oil painting demonstration in the area next to where the musicians will be playing."

"Oh, I'd love to watch that. What will you paint?"

"I'm not sure yet. If I can find a model, it will be a portrait. But I suspect I'll be painting a landscape from photo references. Maybe something with a few cows." She gestured toward the art show information table. "You can pick up a schedule of events over there."

"Thanks."

"Next." The clerk at the hotel check-in desk beckoned.

Anna Farraday turned slightly toward the counter, but before stepping over to check in, she cocked her head to the side and said, "So nice to meet you, Jessie. And your sweet cat."

95

Jessie nodded, trying to keep a straight face. "Let's go, sweet thing," she told Jack, giving a slight tug at his harness. They headed to the elevator where she saw a man waiting, leaning on the "up" button. Not wanting to take a chance on Jack's leash becoming tangled in the door, she picked him up and gathered the excess cord as she waited for the elevator car. "Sweet. That woman called you 'sweet'." She threw back her head and laughter bubbled forth. She heard the elevator mechanism started with a rumble and a slight ding signaled the car was on its way downward. The light above the door indicated it had started from the top level. Jessie was stroking Jack's soft fur when she realized the man waiting was Evan Hansen. His haggard face and hollow eyes gave evidence that he'd heard about his friend Benny's murder.

"I'm so sorry about Benny," Jessie murmured. "It's awful. Is there anything I can do?"

"No." Evan shook his head. "I should never have sent him out to the parking lot. I wasn't thinking." His face twisted as though in pain.

"You certainly had no way of knowing he'd be attacked, Evan. It isn't your fault."

"Oh, that's where you're wrong, Miss O'Bourne. Jessie. It was my fault alright." He punched the button again and again, then held his finger on it. "My fault entirely. It hadn't occurred to me...," He turned and looked at Jessie, his eyes haunted. "I don't know why the text was made to look like it came from you. I guess just to get me out to the farthest, darkest corner of the parking lot. I'm really, really, sorry about that. If you'd gone out too, you could have been hurt."

"But...who...?" Jack squirmed, and Jessie put him down, snugging the leash close to her body so he couldn't get near the elevator door. "What's going on? You obviously think someone wanted to kill you, not Benny." She peered closely at his face. "Why?"

The door to the elevator opened, Evan stepped in and turned to face her, a ravaged expression on his face. He held the door open with one hand, and with the other he raked fingers through his hair. "Maybe I do. But I can't prove anything. And you're b-b-better off knowing nothing." He was beginning to stutter.

"Then you need to talk to the Sheriff."

Evan hung his head. "I...I'm on my way there as soon as I get my jacket. To speak to Sheriff Fischer again. But I d-d-doubt it will do any good. Take the next one Jessie. Don't be seen talking to me." The elevator doors slid shut. Jessie realized that while they spoke, but before she could step aboard, Evan had pressed the "door close" button.

How rude. And how odd.

Jessie stood staring, perplexed, at the closed doors, listening to the "ding" as the lift hit the various floors. Finally, it came back down, and after several passengers disembarked, she and Jack stepped in. Once they exited at the fifth floor, she set him down on the carpet and Jack trotted by her side in dog-like fashion. When she reached room 510, she gawked. In front of her door was another toy replica of the large tractor parked in front of the hotel. She picked it up and turned it over in her hand, looking at it in puzzlement. It matched the one she'd turned in at the hotel desk except part of the tractor cab had been painted with splotchy red.

It doesn't look as cute with the nasty blobs of red paint, she thought. Finally, she unlocked her door, stepped over an envelope that had been slipped under the door, and set the toy on the walnut dresser.

As she stooped to pick up the missive, a swift orange paw swiped it sideways, sending it through the crack under the closet door. The cat gave a guttural sound of satisfaction, then yowled piteously to remind her that he had been a model of decorum and it was now time such good behavior should be rewarded, hopefully with salmon nuggets. Jessie removed Jack's harness before rummaging in the box of cat paraphernalia to pull out treats. She pitched several to him, smiling as he pounced on each.

Then she opened the closet door and reached for the white envelope. As she picked it up she saw a second one on the floor at the back of the small space. She grabbed it as well and glared at Jack. "You wily little bugger. You've been intercepting my hotel notes. I think that's mail fraud." Jack flipped the last piece of kibble into the air and pounced again.

Jessie sank heavily onto the bed and opened the envelope that must have arrived first. It was a single sheet of thin paper covered in large black print. "What the heck?" she said aloud. "It's like a bad fortune cookie." The block letters stated:

MIND YOUR OWN BUSINESS
IF YOU WANT TO LIVE

Puzzled, Jessie turned it over and looked for a signature. Nothing. "This has to be some sort of joke. But it isn't funny," she told the tom, glancing down at him. "You do stick your nose in everything." Jack slanted his reptilian eyes at her. She relented. "Well, okay, me too. We're both snoopy. But nobody here knows that. It's just plain weird."

She tossed the note aside and slid her finger under the flap of the second envelope.

Definitely not a joke.

The enclosed note said;

THE GIRL ON THE TRACTOR DIED FAST. SOMETHING MORE UNPLEASANT WILL HAPPEN TO YOU IF YOU DON'T STAY AWAY FROM SHERIFF FISCHER.

Jessie sat stunned, her mouth slightly open. She looked from the note in her hand to the toy tractor, with its ominous splotch of red. She again stared down at the blunt note with the nasty warning.

I'll bet the first note has been here since sometime in the night—the same time the tractor must have been left at the door. She remembered the woman in the restaurant booth talking about a girl named Adele who got shot while in a tractor. *And the Sheriff asked about the big tractor...it must be connected to the toys dropped at my door. But why on earth threaten ME, for God's sake?*

Goosebumps rose along her forearms and Jessie felt chilled. She rubbed her arms with the palms of her hands and glanced around the room cautiously. It looked normal. The room was tidy. Welcoming. Beautifully appointed. The same rich bedspread covered the bed. The room held the same luxuriously thick sheepskin rug she had oohed and aahed over the night before. A coffee pot rested on a tray filled with packets of regular and decaf grounds. A clear baggie held creamer, stirring sticks, and sugar packets.

Nothing had changed.

Jessie had told housekeeping they could keep work to a minimum on her room, since she'd be staying nearly a week. The maid had been in with new towels, but the woman hadn't vacuumed, or she'd have found the first note that Jack must've flipped under the closet door and she'd have picked it up and set it on the desk.

From her seat on the bed, Jessie stared at her reflection in the mirror over the walnut burl dresser. Her eyes were huge in a face as pale as cream except where freckles scattered across her face like confetti. As usual, her auburn hair, albeit shorter than normal, was a tangle of unruly curls. On her casual gray tunic, the image of Michelangelo's famous touching fingers looked accusing, as though the two pointed at each other in condemnation. She reached down and picked up the cat, hugging him close to her chest and pressing her face into his fur. She shuddered.

"You know what, Jack? I really hate room 510."

Chapter Fourteen

Poolside, Crooked Creek Lodge

"My gosh, Jessie. You cut your hair. Let me look at you." Esther circled Jessie, staring in amazement. "It's cute. So much shorter, but very cleverly cut." The slender woman's white blond hair sported her usual short spiky "do" and she towered over Jessie. Always elegant, Esther was wearing a flowing red skirt and one of what Jessie considered Esther's signature tops—a long silky tunic with a pattern of treble and bass clef notes. She wore strappy red heels that added an extra three inches to her already tall frame. After visiting with Glen and Camille, and now Esther and Arvid, Jessie, at 5'7", was beginning to feel like a munchkin. Maybe she needed some stacked heel cowboy boots to go with her western outfits.

"Yeah," she said, "Most of the artists got their hair cut for a charity the art show is sponsoring this year."

Arvid looked startled. He peered at Jessie as though he were nearsighted. "Geez, you sure did. It's shorter. I didn't notice."

Esther and Jessie exchanged amused glances.

"Yes. It's a couple feet shorter. It was down to her waist." Esther grimaced good-naturedly. "Do you mean to tell me that you just lunched with Jessie and never noticed? I should save my money by not going to the beauty shop if a change this drastic doesn't register with you, you big blind goof. I could save up for that baby grand piano I want." Her gaze took on a dreamy quality. "Maybe not a Steinway, but still...a good one."

"Aw, Esther, you know I notice everything about you, Sweetheart." He gave her a mock leer.

"Hmph," she muttered. She put her hands on her hips. "It's a good thing you have other redeeming qualities, or I'd simply have to trade you in for a couple twenty-five-year-olds." She sat back down, a tablet of lined musical composition paper in front of her. She was seldom without it, saying she never knew when an idea might hit.

"Arvid has redeeming qualities?" Jessie laughed and took the seat across from Esther. "And more than one?" she teased, looking at him. "What's top of the list?"

Esther looked thoughtful. "Well...There's um..." She flipped the pencil she was holding end over end, finally setting it down on the music score she'd been composing. "And hmmm. Well, uh." She snapped her fingers. "The man makes a mean omelet. The best ever."

"That's it?" blustered Arvid. "A mean omelet? That's all you can think of?" Then he glimpsed the look of sheer devilment in Esther's beautiful ice-blue eyes. "See if you get any more of my specialty Sunday eggs." He looked at Jessie and crooked a thumb at Esther. "She likes my baked trout, too. That reminds me. I need to check on the fishing regs. I talked to Glen Heath a few minutes ago and he said yesterday he spotted a huge rainbow trout in the riffles over in Bobcat Creek. I'm going to—"

Jessie was done with small talk. She laid her hand over his, causing him to look at her in surprise. Her eyes were serious pools of deep blue. "Arvid. I know you're anxious to get in some fly fishing. But something came up that I need to run by you and Esther before we discuss trout. I haven't even made an appointment with Max over the issue of last year's painting proceeds." She took in a deep breath and was horrified to hear her voice catch as she continued. "You know the toy tractor I found by the door to my room? Well, there was another one waiting for me when we came back from lunch...and it was splotched with red and came accompanied by a bizarre note. A threatening note."

She placed the toy tractor and the two envelopes in front of him. While he opened them and read, glancing up at her in alarm when he came to the part about the girl dying on the tractor, she told Esther about the toys, the text message that lured Benny out to the parking lot, finding his body in the Hawk and the interview with Sheriff Fischer. She also mentioned Evan's odd comments and her suspicion that he knew something.

"There's no sense worrying about fingerprints, I suppose. I handled both letters and envelopes, and it looks like Jack gnawed on the corner of the first one while he was batting it around. It must have been slipped under the door sometime during the night, and Jack managed to push it under the crack of the closet door out of sight. He loves to play with paper. I found it just a few minutes ago." Then Jessie told them about the conversation she remembered overhearing in the lodge restaurant that morning—the discussion about a woman being shot in the tractor that now supported the big advertising banner.

"Well, I'll be damned. And Sheriff Fischer was asking you what you knew about the big John Deere outside." Checking his watch, he said, "Like I said before, I don't believe in coincidences. Get your coat, Jess. Let's head back down to the Sheriff's Office and talk to Fischer right now."

"I should...," Jessie began. She had wanted to stop by the Yellowstone Room and see how the display looked before the opening reception and ask if the museum staff manning it that evening had any questions. She looked at her watch. Well, she'd given them the prices and info on each of her paintings. She could simply assume they knew what they were doing, but before she went to the reception, she needed to shower, dress and do her hair. As guest artist, she wanted to at least look nice. She put a hand to her mouth. But the notes rattled her. She gave herself a mental shake.

Calm down. As she often did when overstressed, she took a deep breath and began silently reciting the colors on her studio palette to herself.

Ultramarine blue. Cobalt. Burnt umber. Burnt sienna. Cadmium orange. She put her hand down and flexed her fingers. Yellow ochre. Cadmium yellow pale ...

"Nah," Arvid said. "No matter what you were going to say, it can wait. We're going to find out why Fischer was asking about the behemoth of a tractor out there and find out anything and everything about this girl who was killed in one. He's gotta know something. We'll plop the fish back in his creel."

Jessie stared at him.

"You know. Toss the ball back in his court." He smirked. "I like to give the old clichés a bit of fisherman's panache. And when we come back, we'll brainstorm."

Esther started to stand and put her sweater on.

"Where do you think you're going?" Arvid asked.

"I'm coming with you."

"Nup," Arvid said. "You've got rehearsal in about fifteen minutes. We'll fill you in when we get back."

"But—" Esther looked crestfallen.

"No, he's right. There's no need for all of us to go. I don't have a vehicle, or I could go by myself."

"Oh, sure." Arvid's tone was sarcastic. "Someone just got murdered. The body got dumped in the Hawk. You're getting threatening letters. But you think you can handle it by your lonesome?" He gave her a mock disgusted look.

"Well," Jessie said in a small voice. "I'd rather have help. That's why I brought the notes to you. But I'm fine." She knew by the tremor in her voice that she wasn't fine, though. She wasn't good. She wasn't even fair.

Blast it, she thought. *I don't even think it's just room 510.*

She looked out at the slushy landscape and the snow— yesterday a gorgeous, sparkling white—now a filthy sludge from the mud churned up by vehicle tires.

I just flat out hate Crooked Creek. And tractors. I really hate tractors.

Chapter Fifteen

Fort Stewart Army Base, Georgia - Previous December

Harris Freeman watched his buddy as Dom scribbled a list of what he needed to do—and in what order—to expedite leaving the service.

Dom always was an organized S.O.B., he thought. His ducks aren't just in a row. They waddle military style in a precision line-up. Hell, his goddamn ducks salute.

Harris figured Dom got that quality from his mother, Vi, who'd been an accountant until she retired—a financial whiz. He also knew, since their farms were on adjoining properties and his own mom went to Vi Nielson for advice, that Dom's folks had invested beaucoup bucks while she was still working. Her investments were the reason the Nielson farm always had new equipment. New outbuildings. Hmmm. Yeah, the continual list writing probably came from Dom's mother's influence. Watching the pencil swipe furiously back and forth, he studied Dom. Then he rubbed his chin as he thought about the notes Berg Nielson had received. There was no guile in Dominic Nielson. He wasn't stupid. But he was naive, unlikely to see the rot in other people because he was such an upfront guy himself. It would be hard for Dom to think Adele's death could be anything other than accidental, and hard for him to find the louse writing the notes. Freeman shut his eyes in deep thought. Somehow, they were connected. Had to be.

The note campaign Dom told him about—because that's how he'd sum it up, a targeted 'campaign' to drive Berg Nielson over the deep end—was diabolical. The threats seemed designed to make old Berg ever more wary, and they'd built in intensity until Berg was no doubt paranoid as a schizophrenic. "Tell someone about your product or service at least ten times and escalate the message, and soon they begin to believe it" was a standard phrase in the marketing classes Harris had taken before enlisting.

He didn't have a lot of sympathy for Berg Nielson. He'd never much liked the straight-laced old grouch. But his insides twisted whenever he thought of Addy's death. It took a cold-blooded killer to shoot the beautiful teen. After the violent deaths he'd seen during his stint in Iraq the idea of killing—especially killing for no reason—made him ill. It must've been a sick bastard that killed that sweet kid. And what for? So far as he could see, no reason at all. Hell. Maybe it *was* accidental.

Freeman yawned and stretched. His body ached. Man, he hated hiking. They'd hiked miles and miles the past three days. He pulled off his boots and flexed his toes, eliciting an involuntary grunt. Yeah, his dogs were sore and his ankle stiff as a rusty gate hinge. He rubbed his throbbing feet and looked around at the concrete block walls. Glancing over at Dom—still scribbling away at his endless lists—he thought how nice it would be if he were the one heading home for good. Wouldn't he just love to settle down with a good paying job on the outside, something in advertising, instead of looking at these ugly grey walls another eighteen months. Maybe after he got out he'd use the GI bill and go back to school. After he graduated he'd get a loan and start his own company. Yeah. *Crooked Creek Marketing.* Nah, too dull. Something with more snap. He'd ask his stepbrother for some ideas. The big lug had imagination oozing out of his pores.

"Hey, Nielson. You said you hadn't told your dad yet that you were coming home. Why don't you *surprise* him? My step-brother, Wheels, is staying at the house right now. Remember him? Goes to all kinds of art shows. We used to only see him during the big show in March. Especially after his dad died. Then he showed up out of the blue for a visit. He stayed on after Mom went to the nursing home. Maybe he could pick you up at the airport and drop you off at the farm."

"Naw. That would be too much of an imposition." Dom tapped the pencil point on the notepad.

"Heck, he'd be glad to get away from the place for a few hours. Wheels was on the go all the time before Mom started failing. He kept in touch with her, though." *Bummed a lot of money off her.* "Then he got sick. He was visiting at our place— recuperating from some kind of god-awful stomach surgery— when she had the stroke. Mom said he'd been painting the entire inside of the house and doing some machinery repairs. He likes machinery. The only thing is, he isn't much of a farmer. And I swear the poor clod doesn't know the cows from the bulls." Harris gave a short laugh.

"Who's been taking care of the ranch then?"

"You know how nice the Christofferson brothers are?"

Dom nodded.

"We've been having them take care of the fields and Angus herd ever since Pop died. They don't charge us much. Just take a small percentage when hay or cattle sell."

"Yeah. I remember. There were three brothers. The youngest one, Richard, is Dad's lawyer." Dom ground his pencil in a small sharpener and inspected the point. On his list he wrote 'get an appointment with Richie Christofferson and write a new will'. "If I recall, Chet and Merle stayed on the farm."

"That's right. They're our go-to guys. We might not trust Wheels with the ranch, but he can certainly drive to Billings and pick you up from the airport. He might like a little gas money. He has a lot of expensive hobbies."

"Well, I could have him pick me up if he'd let me pay him. I don't like to be beholden. The drive to the airport would be tiring for dad. So I guess if Wheels doesn't want to pick me up, I'll rent a car." Dom looked thoughtfully down at his notes.

Harris smiled. *Quack, quack.* he thought. He suspected Dom was checking that row of ducks to see if 'check on car rentals' was scribbled on the list.

Dom looked up. "Maybe I can talk to your step-brother after my plans are solid. When I get home, Dad's got an old truck I can

106

use until I find myself a junker." Dom looked at his list and added a note. 'Ask Dad if the truck still runs.'

Harris looked over Dom's shoulder at the lengthening list and smiled. In his mind's eye, he saw the row of ducks standing at attention—orange feet with the heels clicked firmly together, yellow bills pointing forward, each with a wing raised in salute.

"You know what I think?" Harris asked.

Dom grunted.

"I think this loony toon is more dangerous than you think. And you're too damn gullible and trusting."

"No. I'm not that trusting, Harris," Dom said in a low tone. "This situation doesn't feel right. Not right at all. I think the bastard who's writing dad these notes might be the same person who killed Addy." He looked down at his list. "I just can't figure out who—or why." He looked up and the two men locked eyes. "But when I do, I'm going to get him."

"I'm at least twice as intelligent as you, you know."

Dom looked up then. "You don't say."

"I think you need some help with the crazy note writer. Tell you what. If you haven't found out who it is by next month, and gone to the Sheriff, I'll put in for leave and come give you a hand." Harris grabbed Dom's notebook and tore a page out of the back. Then he snatched the pencil from Dom's hand. "And I have an idea."

"Hey," Dom protested.

"Okay. You know who's smarter than both of us put together?"

Dom immediately threw out a name.

"Yep. That's who I'd pick too. He's a good buddy. We should run this by him and ask him to investigate. I'll have him look at the note your dad sent if you'll leave it with me. He always said he wanted to see Montana. I'll tell him we can't pay him a nickel, but if he'll come and investigate we'll show him a good time."

"Harris, someone killed my sister." Dom's eyes were dark and serious. "There's a chance someone truly means to harm Dad—and once I get home, maybe me, too. Both of you might be taking a risk if you come out to Crooked Creek and try to help."

107

"So, it could be a dangerous job and we can't give him hazardous duty pay." He grinned. "I know what we can do. If he agrees to come and investigate, we'll each leave him twenty bucks in our wills. Or our entire estate." He chortled. "Oh wait. That *is* my entire estate. Hell, I vote we add him to our wills anyway. He'll know it's a joke.

"You're such a drama queen," Dom chuckled. "Agreed. But only if you let me write the will. I can actually spell and it's my paper and my pencil. And Harris?"

"Yeah?"

"This will is serious business. It's no joke."

Harris slowly held out the sheet of notepaper and dropped the pencil into Dom's waiting hand.

"Okay. No joke. Done."

"Done. I'll buy the beer."

Chapter Sixteen

Crooked Creek Sheriff's Office

Sheriff Fischer turned the small tractor around and around in his big hands, inspecting it. Then he plunked it down on a stack of papers. Even if Jessie and Arvid had not handled it, the miniscule John Deere would give up no fingerprints. It was too bumpy with the mechanics of the real machine duplicated in miniature but without working parts.

"I don't like it," Fischer said in his gravelly voice. "You breeze into town, find a body in your motorhome, claim you've gotten threatening notes, but don't mention them before our interview today. Now, you say someone is leaving toy tractors outside your hotel door. Miss O'Bourne, your story seems…" He cleared his throat, the sound reminding Jessie of the low growl Arvid's dog, Bass, could produce if provoked. "…far-fetched." He leaned back in his oak desk chair and glowered at her, the front legs of the chair leaving the ground as he tipped way back, arms crossed over his chest. "Weren't you raised in Sage Bluff and didn't Arvid say you were there last summer? That's only a couple hours from here. You also had work in last year's art auction, so you had plenty of reason to meet Benny. You sure you didn't know him before you came to town?"

Jessie glowered at Fischer. "He was a total stranger to me. My work was shipped to the auction last year. I didn't attend. And I have no reason to want to come to Crooked Creek and kill anyone.

Or cause any other sort of trouble and, believe me, I have enough to do without making up stories just for your entertainment."

Jessie could feel her fiery temper begin to boil over. Pressure built behind her eyes until she felt she could scream in frustration. Then she felt Arvid's foot nudge her ankle. She knew the gentle nudge was meant as a reminder to cool her hot, red-headed temper.

"Sheriff Fischer is just doing his job," Arvid said. "And you have to admit the toy tractors are weird."

"Maybe someone else was supposed to be in room 510," Jessie said in a cool tone. "Maybe the notes and toy tractors aren't actually meant for me." She frowned. "I mean, how could they be? I hadn't even heard about this poor girl being shot. And you said it was likely a hunting accident, Sheriff?"

Arvid arched an eyebrow. He was staring at the sheriff with a deeply skeptical expression. Sheriff Fischer had indeed said it was written off as a hunting accident. "You don't think it was an accident, do you, Sheriff Fischer? I took a look at the tractor. There were two bullet holes in the back window. Now, a person might write off one shot as an accident. But not two."

"Oh, hell." He dropped the chair legs to the hardwood floor with a thump. "No, I don't think it was an accident. And the idea was mentioned that it might have been a vandal, but that doesn't hold water."

"A vandal?" Arvid raised his eyebrows.

"Yeah. We've had someone shooting holes in machinery and mailboxes this past year. Heck, some of the good old boys get soused and pop off a few rounds at other folks' machinery. That could have been an explanation if the machine had just been left there, but the ignition was still turned on. She wasn't just sitting there eating her lunch or taking a break." He sighed heavily, the expulsion of air like a bellows. "And even though your story is just about as cuckoo as they come, I tend to think you're telling the truth." He paused. "I think Adele Nielson was murdered. The poor little gal. The family had a run of real bad luck lately." His expression was dark. "I asked you about the big tractor the art show is using to display the sign, because Evan Hansen, the assistant art show director, called me about it. He was fuming. He had no idea who put it out in front of the lodge. I called around and nobody gave permission for it to be hauled in from the farm, nor did the art show ask to use it. The Nielson's lawyer was spitting mad that someone helped themselves to it. It was still in driving condition. But whoever moved it had possession of the key."

"Why would someone bring it in to town?" Jessie asked. "Especially during the snow we've been having."

"I think somebody placed it there as a huge reminder of Adele Nielson's death. A threatening message, I think, like the paper messages and little toy John Deere tractors that you've been getting. I just don't know who the threat is intended to frighten. I suspect, but I don't know. I feel certain that if you ask for a room change, you won't receive any more of these little gifts." He plunked the tractor down on his desk. "I have to ask you not to leave town. But it's just a formality. And because the State forensic guy is dragging his feet on getting your motorhome checked out."

"What if there is a real threat to Jessie? Some nut case who assumes she knew all about the girl who died and is trying to scare her."

Sheriff Fischer scratched the back of his neck and then ran a hand over his forehead, squeezing his brows together, causing a furrow between his eyes. "I'd sure be surprised if there's a real threat to Miss O'Bourne, but of course we would try our best to protect her, even though I'm short-handed at the moment." He looked at Jessie. "I think it was someone from Crooked Creek who killed Adele. If you've been telling me the truth, I think you're actually safe. I'll come down and see if I can discover if someone else had been, or was supposed to be, in room 510."

"What can you tell us about the girl's case, Sheriff?" Jessie asked. "It doesn't sound like the Sheriff's Office has made much headway. And you said the family has had a run of bad luck. Is there any reason someone in the family might have brought the tractor to town?

"You know, as a Sheriff, I'm in the business of asking questions, not volunteering information. You can probably find the whole sordid story online, Miss O'Bourne." He turned to Arvid. "God, what isn't on the internet these days?"

111

"Yeah." Arvid gave a low chuckle. "Every time I get on the computer, I'm afraid I'll find a YouTube video of me pulling on my socks or brushing my teeth."

Fischer smiled, the relaxation of his features making him look almost boyish. Jessie peered intently at him, then raised her hand and made a slight movement as though making a brush stroke. In her mind, a portrait of the man behind the Sheriff's badge began to appear—the shape of the head, the shadow under the chin, the heavy-lidded, exhausted eyes. Then, as quickly as his features had relaxed, they stiffened again into his professional persona. Jessie hand dropped to her lap, but she continued to stare, still imagining his portrait flowing onto a non-existent canvas.

Fischer stared back for several seconds, then looked questioningly at Arvid.

Arvid made a dismissive gesture with his hand, then rolled his eyes. "She's fine. Absent minded. Happens all the time," he muttered. He cleared his throat loudly.

"Oh. Are we done?" Jessie asked with a slight shake of her head. "I really have to get back."

"Yeah, I guess so," Fischer said. "As I said, I don't really think you're involved except by being in the wrong place at the wrong time. But I've been wrong before."

"You aren't wrong, Sheriff." Jessie brushed a stray curl away from her face.

"Well, switch to a different room. Stay in touch. Don't leave town. And Miss O'Bourne..."

"Yes?" Jessie swiveled to face him.

Sheriff Fischer looked sheepish. "Thanks for not bringing the cat."

Jessie grinned. "You're welcome. And call me Jessie." She stood, turned and walked through the door.

As Arvid stood and stepped toward the door, Sheriff Fischer put out a hand out to stop him. He gave Arvid a serious look. "I didn't want to discuss it in front of Miss O'Bourne, but, could you come back to the office after you drop Miss O'Bourne off and discuss the possibility of collaborating with the Sage Bluff Sheriff's Office on this recent murder? I do think it's linked to

112

Adele Nielson's death. And like I said before, I am god-awful short-handed here."

Arvid looked surprised. Then he glanced at the clock. "Can't do it tonight, or I'll miss my wife's piano performance at the art show. We can't do any collaborating until you talk to the Sheriff in Sage Bluff. That would be Russell Bonham. I'll probably give him a call anyway, let him know what's happened. Jessie O'Bourne is a family friend. I'd be glad to come and brainstorm first thing in the morning. But why do you think Benny's murder is linked to that older case?"

Fischer gave Arvid a meaningful look. "Because after the girl was killed, her father received threatening notes exactly like those received by your friend. I didn't want to scare her but keep an eagle eye on Miss O'Bourne." He shook his head warningly. "An eagle eye."

"I certainly will, Sheriff Fischer." Arvid gave him a serious look. "So, her father got threats, huh? Did he get these weird little tractors?"

"No, but the notes were similar. I'll fill you in tomorrow." He cocked his head. "I'll call the head honcho in Sage Bluff and discuss the collaboration. It's protocol. And the name is Brian."

"All right. See you in the morning. And call me Arvid."

As he turned to go, Fischer asked, "That's an interesting name. Swedish?"

"Nup," Arvid grumbled. "No. It is not." He yanked his ball cap over his short salt and pepper hair and stomped out after Jessie. As the door shut behind him he groused. "Huh. Swedish. As if."

Jessie, halfway down the hallway, turned and waited for Arvid to catch up. "I thought you were right behind me." She frowned. "Well. Don't you look grumpy? Did he think of something annoying to ask?"

"Ya. And you know, I got a birthday next month. I saw these T-shirts on ebay that say, 'Made in America from Norwegian Parts'. Ask Esther to get me a couple, wouldja?"

Jessie laughed. "Okay. I will. And I saw one that said, 'Awesome Norse Viking'."

"Hmmph." Arvid growled. Then he bobbed his head in the affirmative and grinned. "Yeah, maybe. Black. Extra extra-large."

113

Chapter Seventeen

Crooked Creek Lodge

"I'm so sorry, Miss O'Bourne. We don't have a single empty room available until Monday." The young male clerk looked flustered. "Is there something wrong with your accommodations? We'd be happy to do all we can to rectify the situation."

"No, the room is wonderful, but ..." Jessie looked at him helplessly, then glanced at Esther and Arvid, who waited nearby. Then she leaned over and whispered to the clerk. "I seem to be getting notes slipped under my door. Notes that are obviously meant for someone else. Notes," she paused, "that aren't very nice."

He leaned conspiratorially in to hear her. "Oh. Oh, no. Do you know who they are for? Or who they are from?"

"No. No, I don't. But they are quite upsetting."

A flush of pink rose up his neck and he met her eyes, his tongue sweeping over his lips nervously. His glance swept down to her breasts and quickly back to her face. "Ah. That kind of note. I am so very sorry. Can you just throw them out without reading them?"

"I...Uh. Well, I don't think they're not the kind of note *you're* thinking—" Jessie was interrupted by Esther's cool voice.

"Never mind," she said. "My husband and I will change rooms with her. We're in 212. Arvid and Esther Abrahmsen. Switch the names on the room invoices and we're all set."

114

Esther took Jessie by the arm and led her away from the desk to where Arvid stood, staring into the display case of dinosaur fossils. "Look at the size of this tooth." He peered into the exhibit and began reading the label. "Did you know the first T. Rex ever discovered was found in Montana? Garfield County in 1902."

Both women ignored him.

"That's a sweet offer," Jessie said to Esther in a no-nonsense tone, "but I most certainly will not take your room." She shook her head. "I'll be fine. In fact, I even have my 9mm pistol in the room safe. Thank God I took it in with me before Benny was killed and the Hawk was confiscated. It isn't as though I'm helpless."

"One of these suckers would rip a man right in two," Arvid said. "Man-eaters." He looked at the two women squaring off over the hotel room issue. "Yep. Man eaters."

Esther glared at Jessie, who met her gaze with equally determined blue eyes.

"Oh, don't be stubborn, Jess." Pointing at Arvid, Esther asked, "Would you feel safer with your pistol? Or would you feel safer with this big lug who also comes with his own gun. Imagine that. I'm so lucky. It's a twofer." She put her hands on her hips. "Let me tell you, I'd bet on my husband hands down and he'll be in the room to protect me from anything that comes my way. *You* are taking our room."

"But—," Jessie began.

Turning to look at the women, Arvid said, "No buts. Esther's right. We'll switch. No argument." Then he grinned at Esther, put his arm around her waist, and kissed her lightly on the cheek. "Let's go move rooms." Then he scowled. "Don't s'pose we have time to grab dinner. But they'll have hors d' oeuvres at the reception and if we're still hungry, we can eat something more substantial afterward."

"Maybe we should wait and switch the rooms after the reception. Both Esther and I need to change clothes for the evening reception, and Esther can't be late, since she's the pianist."

"Nah, we'll hurry," Arvid insisted. His expression hardened. "Fischer was real serious when he told me to keep an eye on you. I don't think it should wait. We'll meet you at 510 in about fifteen minutes with our suitcases and one of those rolling carts and help you haul your bags and the big beasty boy down to 212."

As they walked away, he gestured back at the display case and told Esther. "We should take a weekend trip with the motorhome over to one of these dinosaur digs…see some real fossils. Hey, I can take my fly rods and get in some fishing. Grilled trout for dinner under the open sky." He waved his hand breezily in the air. He leered at her. "It'll be real romantic."

Esther looked over her shoulder at Jessie and rolled her eyes dramatically. Then she grinned.

Chapter Eighteen

Previous December, Billings Airport

Dom Nielson slung his khaki green canvas duffel bag over his shoulder and looked up and down the road. The plane had been delayed forty-five minutes because of weather, and he was worried that Wheels had given up on him.

Surely Wheels would've checked the flight schedule and been aware of the delay.

He looked at his phone. No messages. He set his bag down on the icy pavement and wrapped his arms around himself, shivering in the military jacket suitable for Georgia weather, not winter in Montana. Ten minutes later, his teeth began to chatter, and he went into the terminal to wait. Another fifteen minutes passed, and he went back out into the cold, looking down the road. He hoped his ride wasn't sitting in the ditch between Crooked Creek and Billings. Pulling out his phone, he was about to punch in Wheels' number when a GMC Yukon barreled up. The tires of the SUV tossed slush onto the sidewalk as it swerved in and parked at the curb. Dom jumped back, but then got a look at the driver in the cab and smiled. He tucked the phone into a pocket and lifted his duffel.

The driver's window slid down. "Hey soldier, need a lift?" Wheels grinned at Dom. "Or were you waiting for someone better looking and long-legged?"

"I was, but I guess you'll have to do," Dom quipped. "I'd almost given up on you. Pictured you stuck in the ditch."

In reply, Wheels just gave a grunt.

After Dom stowed his bag in the back, he jumped into the front passenger seat and extended his hand. His own was dwarfed by a huge paw encased in a brown suede winter glove. Wheels was massive, his head was broad, his face round and tan. His hair was covered by a knit hat and the hood of his brown down jacket. Under the jacket he wore heavy-weight brown Carhart coveralls. The effect was of a humongous brown creature.

I'm getting a lift from Bigfoot, Dom thought, smiling slightly.

Thinking back, he realized he'd only met Wheels a couple of times. He was almost a generation older than Dom and Harris, who'd been high-school friends as well as army buddies. Dom calculated in his head. Wheels must've been at least seventeen when Tom Freeman remarried. Harris was born when the Freemans were old enough to be grandparents.

"Thanks, man. I really appreciate your picking me up," he told the big man. "Sorry you had to wait. I was afraid I was going to be bumped until tomorrow morning because of this storm. How're the roads?"

"Nasty. Very nasty. Calling them roads is a misuse of the English language," Wheels joked. "The plows are out. We should make it okay on the freeway, but I don't think your dad's lane has been cleared. I might have to just drop you at the driveway entrance. I'm sorry. I know you wanted to surprise your dad, but it's going to be so late by the time I drop you off that I took the liberty of calling him to let him know you were coming home, and we were on the road. Told him he might want to just go to bed and leave the door unlocked for you. Well, actually, I had to leave the message on his answering machine. He was probably in the john." He glanced at Dom. "You strong enough to haul that little bag up the lane? Didn't the Army build up any muscles in those scrawny arms? Haw, haw." His guffaws echoed in the cab like backfire from a Mack truck.

Dom laughed, too. Taking a bit of good-natured teasing was a small price to pay for a ride home. And he'd made it before Christmas, too. Three days before. There'd still be time to find a

118

tree and bring a little Christmas into the old farmhouse. "That's okay, Wheels. You're right. It'll be midnight before we get there. It wouldn't be a good idea to surprise an old man in the middle of the night, anyway." *Lucky stiff is probably already in bed*, Dom thought. "Harris applied for leave, by the way. He said to tell you and his mom hello, and that he'd call when he knew his schedule."

Wheels nodded and grinned. "Be good to see the little piss-ant."

Heading out of Billings toward Crooked Creek, the visibility became poor. Dom stared into the mesmerizing flakes hitting the windshield, white against the black of the unending asphalt. He yawned. After several minutes of small talk, his eyelids drooped.

"Sorry,Wheels. My body's still on Georgia Time. Put the radio on if you need something to keep you awake, would you? Give me a yell when we get close to home. I have to catch a few winks."

"Will do. Man, it's miserable driving in this crappy snow." He peered through the windshield. "I'm going to follow this semi as long as I can. He can probably see the road better'n us. At least he's blazing us a trail."

* * *

The wind blew the snow into knee-high drifts across the yard as Berg Nielson hurried through the door, slammed it behind him and piled his armload of wood near the fireplace. He hung his jacket in the hall closet, put his fogged glasses on the sideboard, then dropped an apple log onto the fire, prodding the embers to life with the poker. He sniffed. It smelled wonderful. After pruning one of the Haralson apple trees several years before, he'd let the branches dry, then salvaged every inch of the dense, aromatic wood. Still, he wished he'd listened to Addy and installed a gas fireplace in the living room and put more insulation in the attic. As cheerful as the fire was, it didn't do a good job of keeping the place warm. Slipping a flannel shirt jacket on over his sweatshirt, he lowered himself into his armchair, then sat watching the hypnotic flames. In the corner of the room, a small light blinked unnoticed on the rarely used answering machine.

119

Maybe he should turn the thermostat up now, get the house nice and warm in case the power failed. Berg scowled. The utility bills had been atrocious. It wasn't that he couldn't afford it. It was the principle of it. The power companies were getting too big. Greedy bastards. He shivered. Grumbling under his breath, he got up, dialed the heat up a notch and heard the furnace kick on.

Money down the drain.

He went to the kitchen and put a kettle of water on to boil for instant cocoa. While the water heated, he methodically checked the windows and doors. He'd gotten another threatening note that morning. This one was the worst yet. He'd given up on that young lout, Jacob, down at the Sheriff's Office. Today, Berg had breezed right in and demanded to see Sheriff Fischer instead. As he'd suspected, the little snot hadn't told Fischer about any of the previous threats. Sheriff Fischer asked him to bring all of the notes to his office before noon. Berg heaved a big sigh, remembering the relief he'd felt when he realized the Sheriff had taken him seriously.

Peering out the last window, he could see the snow still coming down like gangbusters. When he was out getting wood from the pile, he saw that the driveway was already filling with drifts. Tomorrow he'd plow it out with the big Ford, the one with the snow blade. And he'd write Dom to let him know it would sure be nice to see his son, but he didn't need to rush home just to protect his old man. His stomach churned, though, thinking of the last note.

Old. After the cancer and then losing Addy, I'm just feeling so damn old. But I'm not so feeble I can't protect myself a bit, though. I wonder if that demon who's been writing these goddamned notes would be crazy enough to come after me on a night like this.

He glanced over at the shotgun propped in the corner of the room. Maybe he should replace the birdshot shells with buckshot, but at close range there wasn't much difference in the damage either would do. Deep in thought when the teakettle whistled, he jerked in his armchair as though an explosion had rocked the house. He walked into the kitchen, dumped a packet of instant chocolate into a mug and shakily added hot water. As he brought the empty mug back to the sink a while later, the lights flickered and went out.

* * *

"Wake up, Dom. We're just about at your dad's driveway." He reached over and gave Dom's arm a shove. "Hey, wake up, will ya? I don't want to stop more than a minute. Got to backtrack and see how bad my own driveway is. I plowed before I left, but it's been coming down so hard I might have to walk in and plow out the drifts again before driving in."

"I'm awake." Dom yawned and straightened. He looked blearily around. He checked his watch. Nearly midnight. The snow still fell in fat flakes and was driven sideways by a sharp wind. It was going to be a white Christmas. A very white Christmas, by the look of it. "I surely do thank you. Much appreciated."

Wheels came to a stop, letting the motor idle while Dom retrieved his duffel and shut the back door. Dom glanced at the driveway, trying to judge the depth of the snow by the light from the open vehicle door. "Yeah, it would be stupid to try the driveway. It looks pretty bad."

"You going to be okay getting to the house?" Wheels smirked. "I've heard of people getting lost in their own yard when it's as nasty as this."

"Nuts. I could walk in with my eyes closed. No problem."

"See ya, then." He gave Dom a sloppy salute.

After Wheels drove away, Dom saw that no light came from the house. Maybe the power was out. Shouldering his duffel, he started down the long snowy driveway, instinct, as much as visibility guiding him toward the house. He was thankful for the boots on his feet, but he sure could have used the old-fashioned long-johns he wore while working the farm when he was a kid. The wind slammed biting snow crystals into his face. He trudged on, in some places through knee-high drifts. As he neared the front porch, he slipped and nearly dropped the heavy bag. The house was pitch black. His dad probably went to bed hours ago. Dom tried to turn the door knob and it didn't budge. Locked. Either Berg had locked it out of habit or hadn't gotten Wheels' message.

121

He considered knocking but hated to wake the old man. If the window of his old bedroom still had the funky catch, he could climb through and surprise his dad in the morning.

Wading past the front porch and heading to the side window, he dragged one hand against the house to keep his bearings. At his old bedroom window, he set the bag on the ground and worked the window up just enough to slip through before it refused to budge. He lifted the bag with his left hand and was reaching out to push it into the room before he shinnied through the space. Then he saw a slight flicker of movement on the other side. There was a blast of noise. Splinters of wood and shards of glass exploded outward. Fire burned through his side. He screamed in agony as he fell backward into a featherbed of fluffy cold.

Shot. I've been shot.

The thought registered a millisecond before his head made impact with something hard under the snow.

He didn't hear the sound of glass tinkling onto the interior hardwood floor as it was brushed from the sill or see the light of a flashlight bobbing crazily in the window opening.

Berg said in a choked voice, "What's the matter with you anyway, harassing an old man, breaking into my house? God, oh God! All those notes and threats. And if you're the one that shot my baby girl, I'm glad you're flat out down in the snow, you scum." His voice ended in a strangled hiccup. "If you're still alive, I should shoot you again, dammit. By God, I would too, if I hadn't called the Sheriff as soon as I heard you rattling the door."

Berg left the window. He hurried through the house, slamming the door behind him with a crash before making his way around the house to the still body. "Well, let's see who the hell you are and if you're still breathin'." He swung the flashlight toward the ground.

Dom came to as the flashlight beam hit him in the face and his father began to scream. He tried to speak, but it came out as an unintelligible gurgle. Then the dark wrapped around him like a heavy   quilt.

Chapter Nineteen

Sage Bluff Sheriff's Office, present day

Sheriff Russell Bonham picked up the phone, eyes widening in surprise when he heard Arvid's voice at the other end. "Hey, Russell."

"Hey, yourself. What's up? You never call when you have time off. I figured you'd be hip deep in some trout stream by now while Esther pounded the piano keys."

"Yeah, yeah. Rub it in." A wistful note crept into Arvid's voice. "Maybe later. I'm calling from our hotel room. Esther's getting all duded up for the reception. Listen, expect a call from a guy named Fischer. Sheriff Brian Fischer. From here in Crooked Creek. He's gonna ask you if he can borrow me for a bit and I want you to give him the go-ahead."

"Oh, yeah? What are you, a library book, Arvid? Must be one of those big illustrated comics." Russell chuckled at his own joke. They both knew that Arvid was more qualified than Russell to have the Sage Bluff Sheriff's position, but the big man liked being what he called 'semi-retired'.

"Very funny," Arvid said in a long-suffering tone. "You'll want to loan me out because it has to do with Jessie."

"Jessie?"

"Ya. You know, the redhead you won't admit has you tied in knots? The one you should've put a ring on last summer. The big arteest. The one who—"

"Oh, can it. I know which Jessie. What's going on?" His stomach clenched. If the Sheriff there needs outside help to handle a case, it can't be good.

Arvid filled him in, finishing with, "And then each note comes with this goofy little toy tractor and—"

"What the hell? A toy? Are you kidding?"

"Dead serious." Arvid explained.

"That's macabre. There's not a thing going on here in Sage Bluff right now. Baker can fill in for me. In fact, she'll be delighted. I'm coming up to Crooked Creek."

"Yeah. I thought you might. Well, listen. Fischer will call. I just wanted to make sure you said yes. And let me give you a head's up. With this big art show in town there's no available lodging. There probably isn't space in an RV park either, because Jessie checked earlier. When Fischer calls, ask him where you can park a motorhome."

"A motorhome? I can't afford to rent a motorhome."

"Uh huh. I know. I'll let you borrow my baby. There's a spare key in the drawer of my office. Maybe Fischer'll let you park it at his house or something. Or behind the Sheriff's Office. Don't mess it up. Don't scratch it. Don't slop your coffee on the carpet. And—"

"Okay, okay. I get it." Russell thought a minute, drumming his fingers on the desk. "Wow. You don't let anyone borrow that. Are you sure?" Arvid polished and pampered his motorhome like a teenager with his first car. He'd won a horse trailer in a contest the year before and used it as the down payment for the fancy motorhome he and Esther took on numerous fishing trips and jaunts to music festivals.

Arvid was silent. Then he said. "Ya. I'm sure. Because it's for Jessie, Russ. She won't admit it, but she's scared. I think it will help that we traded rooms, but we just don't know that yet. And she's stewing about the Hawk. I'll take her out tomorrow to rent a reliable vehicle. Something with four-wheel-drive."

"Good idea."

"Maybe you and I can find some clues Fischer hasn't run across yet. It worries me that nobody has been able to solve the girl's murder. Fischer seems like a decent sort. Smart. Tough. But

124

he's discovered nada. And now here's this new murder, with the body crammed into Jessie's Hawk. There's also something he hasn't told me yet about the girl's family." He sighed audibly. "Something in the way he talked makes me suspect there isn't a family left."

"That sounds ominous."

"Yeah." Arvid heaved another audible sigh. "Well. I'll find out tomorrow."

"Keep me posted."

"I will. Let me know when you hit town."

Russell ended the call and sat staring into space. Arvid was right on every level. He kicked himself in the behind five times a day for not following Jessie when she left town the previous summer. He'd asked her to marry him, and she'd said no. But looking back on it, he guessed it was a pretty piss poor proposal. One he knew blew like a balloon with a hole in it.

Nah. Like the Hindenburg. It was that bad.

He'd been heading out the door to follow Jessie and get down on one knee—do it right—when a bad accident call came in.

By the time the wreckage of the Taurus and the Honda were cleared up, people toted off to the hospital and the accident reports filled out, Jessie was miles and miles out of reach. And so was the impulse of heading off into the sunset after her. He didn't even know which way she'd headed. His head knew it was for the best. But his heart was filled with sorrow. And now he felt the pressure of worry that she could be in trouble. Serious trouble.

He looked at his watch. Baker was out on a call at Simpson's place again. It was the last house considered city limits. Just another barking dog complaint. He couldn't understand why people got dogs if they didn't want to pay any attention to them. Dogs, cats, kids. A lot of folks shouldn't have kids. You needed a license to drive a car, but you can have all these poor kids that don't come with an instruction manual.

He thought about K.D.. His buddy Kevin, K.D.'s biological dad, would have been a fabulous father.

I hope I can measure up. He sighed. *Well, no matter what, he's my son, now.*

And his son was never going to feel neglected. Russell wanted a wife who planned to stay home and be a great mother to K.D.. He rubbed his hand across the stubble on his chin. Why, why, why does that maddening Jessie have to travel? He'd loved her ever since she was fifteen and she stopped seeming like a kid sister. But all she wanted to do was paint. When she didn't have a brush in her hand, she was daydreaming about what to paint next. Or she was mesmerized by the view out the window. The color of the sky. The shape of someone's head. The slant of light coming through window blinds.

Aw, heck, Jessie. K.D. and I aren't playing second string to your damn art. We just must not be suited for each other.

A niggle of worry hit him. Then fear for her. He slammed his palm down on the desk. He buzzed the secretary. Instead of waiting until morning, he'd leave tonight.

"Is Baker back yet, Nora?" He grimaced at her answer. "Not yet, huh? How about Lenny?"

He drew a circle on a small open place on his desk blotter. The rest of the space was covered by small drawings and crayon renderings K.D. had created. Each one had a quirky style. They were elaborate and three-dimensional. *The kid's a genius like Jess.* Russell colored in his circle. Then he gave it a small head and antennae. *Pathetic,* he thought. Then he heard Nora come back on the line to tell him Lenny just got in. Russell drew circular squiggles like penmanship practice.

"Good. I can't wait for Baker to get back. Something's come up in Crooked Creek and we're going to collaborate with their office. I'm packing and heading up there. Tell Lenny I'm out of here, and I'll call him somewhere on the road when I stop to get gas. Send any calls to him until Baker returns. Change Arvid's designation from 'on leave' to 'on loan'." Russell smirked. "Yeah, Nora … like a library book."

He called his babysitter and let her know he'd be swinging by to pick K.D. up soon. I'll have to drop him at Dan O'Bourne's for a few days. Dan'll probably be thrilled.

Then he looked up the number for the Crooked Creek Sheriff's Office and called to inform Fischer that he planned to attend the morning meeting with Arvid. As Russell spoke, he

126

realized that the odd note he'd heard in Fischer's voice was relief. And Fischer did indeed know where Russell could park a motorhome. He promised to pull in a favor from an R.V. dealer in town who would let Russell park free of charge near their sales office. He'd have an electrical hook up, water, wi-fi and T.V. The whole enchilada. Russell jotted down the address and asked Fischer if he'd have the owner of the dealership meet him there at 8:30. That allowed three hours to get organized, pack and drive to Crooked Creek.

Russell pulled a ring of keys from his desk drawer, snagged his jacket from the coat rack, locked his door, and headed down to Arvid's office. He grinned. He was going to borrow the big Norwegian's baby. His grin widened. And he was going to see Jessie.

Chapter Twenty

Previous December - Nielson's Farm

"Freezing," Dom muttered aloud. He was so cold, clammy, but his left side was hot. It was burning up. Waves of pain rippled through his body. He lay in the snow, light flakes dropping with feathery touches onto his face, and took stock. His memory swept back. "Bullet wound," he whispered. The duffel probably saved his life. Then he remembered his dad screaming and Dom tried to rise. It was dark except off to the right, where he saw a beacon of yellow light, a flashlight on the ground beside his father. Berg was on his back in the snow, the man's breath coming in rasps, his hand on his chest.

"Dad!" Dom crawled to him, the numbing pain in his left thigh and forearm making it a spider-like sideways motion.

"Son," Berg gasped. "Sorry. So sorry." In a quavering whisper he said. "My heart, I think. Thought you were—"

"Don't try to talk. I'll get help." Dom's voice had a bubbling sound. "I'll . . . I'll call first. 911. Then I'll get you into the house out of the cold." Fumbling in the right pocket of his jacket, his fingers found his cell and he pulled it out and turned it on with stiff fingers. He punched in the numbers. When he heard the dispatcher's voice Dom bellowed into the phone, his voice as authoritative as when he'd given orders to medics in Afghanistan.

"Two men down at Nielson's farm. One accidental gunshot. One heart attack. 209 South Wildcat Road. Need the ambulance. Stat."

The phone fell from his fingers, and as it dropped he began to feel disoriented. Light-headed.

I'm going into shock, he thought, *or dying. I've got to get Dad out of the cold, before I'm completely useless.* With determination, he bent over Berg. With his right arm, he pulled his father into a sitting position. Then he positioned himself behind him.

"God, give me strength," he muttered. Could he lift him? Berg was such a big man. Or had been before the cancer withered him from his healthy weight to nearly skin and bone. *Please God.* He positioned the flashlight so that the glow lit the side of the house. He circled his father's torso with his right arm, pushed his own nearly useless left arm under his Dad's armpit and clasped his hands together. In a superhuman effort, he lifted, grunting with the struggle, and pulled his dad to the side of the house. Heaving and swearing, he pushed Berg's weight through the open window and dropped him, none too gently, to the floor of the dark bedroom.

Then he turned, grabbed the flashlight and tossed it into the room toward where he remembered his childhood bed had stood. A soft thump was his reward. The flashlight had landed on the bed. He hadn't broken it. As he struggled through the window and into the bedroom of his youth he felt the blood flowing down his leg, and inside his jacket. *No time to worry about it now. I have to get dad into a warm area.*

Dom grabbed the flashlight from the bed and, with his stronger right arm, dragged Berg through the door into the hallway where it was warmer. He took the patchwork quilt from the bed, draped it over his father, tucked it snug to the man's body and closed the bedroom door to shut out the cold. By the light of the flashlight, he staggered to the bathroom to find aspirin and a small cup, which he filled with water. Going back down the hall, he held Berg's head while his father swallowed the pill.

"I've got to leave you and fix myself up a bit, Dad...I ...I love you."

His father made an unintelligible response.

Dom made his way slowly down the hallway to the kitchen and was peering into the broom closet with the flashlight when the lights blazed. Power was restored.

Hanging from a peg was the roll of duct tape he hoped would save his life. He unzipped his jeans, and pulled them off, grimacing at the gaping wounds. Yanking the beginning of the roll with his teeth, he unwound a long strip of duct tape and used it to secure a makeshift dressing comprised of kitchen towels around his thigh. Then he took off his jacket and shirt and did the same with his lower arm and the holes in his side.

The room was beginning to swim. Willing himself to stay standing, he found the coveralls Berg always hung at the back door and slipped them on as best he could. Blessed be that his dad was such a big man. The coveralls slid right over the fat dressings. He was now in battle mode, and instinctively he knew it was going to be a close fight. Too close. Unless the ambulance could get into the yard, Berg would probably die. Perhaps he would, too. He could feel death looking down at him like a big hound, salivating. His legs felt weak. His vision swam. But the ambulance couldn't get down the drive unless Dom plowed the way.

"Battle mode," he said aloud. He grabbed the keys to the big Ford from their usual place—a wooden rack shaped like a big key, hanging on the wall. Then he opened the back door and staggered out, slamming the door behind him. When he reached the garage, he steeled himself. If the big Ford didn't have the plow blade attached, he was toast. And so was Berg. If the side door was locked, it was the end. He hadn't thought to grab that key from the hook, and he didn't have the strength to lift the big overhead door. Or to go back for the key. He wobbled his way to the side door, leaning heavily against the side of the building as he went. Turning the knob, he pushed weakly at the door and panicked when it didn't open. It can't be locked. He leaned his weight against it as he pushed, and he stumbled forward as the door opened. He flipped on the light, and almost wept with relief. The F150 sported the heavy-duty snow plow attachment and was ready to go.

Thank you, God.

Dom pushed the button to open the automatic door. He staggered to the pickup, his left leg nearly useless. He opened the door and reached in to grab the steering wheel, using his right arm to leverage his weight onto the seat. Fumbling, he shoved the key in the ignition, started the engine and stomped on the gas. The big pickup lurched out of the garage. He was in business.

Ten minutes later half the long drive was plowed. He could feel the pickup pulling to the right, but he no longer had enough strength to swivel the wheel to correct it. Or to step on the gas pedal. The truck ground to a halt. Dom's coveralls were sodden with blood. In his mind, the big dog advanced, jaws opening, snarling.

We're losing, Dad. We're not going to make it. I'm sorry. I'm so sorry.

Then, in the glare of the headlights, he saw the outline of a big man in a winter parka and boots, coming down the plowed side of the drive toward the pickup. The man held a gun and zigzagged from side to side as though making himself a difficult target. Red and blue lights flashed at the end of the lane. *Two vehicles*, Dom thought. And in the distance came the sound of more approaching sirens.

The man had reached within fifteen feet of the truck. "This is the County Sheriff. Step out of the truck." Dom registered that the man was screaming the command, but within the enclosure of the cab he heard a different sound.

The deep guttural growl of a hound.

The man came closer. Then the pickup door was wrenched open and Sheriff Fischer reached in to pull Dom from the cab as easily as if he were a child. Two EMTs appeared and lay Dom gently on a stretcher and began to cover him with blankets. They lifted the gurney as Dom whispered, "Hall of the house ... Dad ... his heart."

Sheriff Fischer nodded. "We'll get him, Dom. Don't you worry. You did good, kid. Real good." Fischer's mouth was set in a grim line.

Dom felt his eyes drifting shut, felt his heartbeat slow. Again, he heard the growl. The jaws clamped down.

Chapter Twenty-one

Jessie was settled into a mirror image of her original hotel room. Jack was not pleased. After examining the new space from corner to corner, he now lay half under the bed, his large orange rump and twitching tail protruding. Jessie prodded the round behind with the toe of her stockinged foot and heard a healthy hiss.

"You poor baby. You miss the Hawk with your own space, the toys, and the cat door, don't you?"

Jessie had a small hatch installed in the door of the Hawk for Jack, but she only unlocked it when they parked at one of her usual locations for plein-air painting. Several of her old friends, all who now lived in different states, owned property in picturesque rural areas of Wyoming, Colorado and Arizona. They made it a point to keep their friendship alive by inviting her to come at least once a year to paint. It was fun to take the Hawk—which served as a studio on wheels—and park next to a stream or small fishing pond, or right on site at one of their ranches.

Glumly, she wondered how long it would take to erase the image of Benny's face—especially the milky eyes—looking up at her from the storage area of the Hawk. She shuddered.

Could the threatening notes have something to do with his murder? Sheriff Fischer isn't telling all he knows.

Deep in thought, she twisted a lock of red hair around her finger, wincing as she realized how much shorter that curl was than before the cut. *Yes, Fischer is definitely hiding something. I'll do some searching on good old Google...see if there was more to the story of Adele Nielson's shooting on the tractor. But first I'd better get dressed.*

Pulling a sea-green silk shirt and a black velvet skirt from the closet, she dressed in a rush, adding an old Indian pawn squash blossom necklace, Navajo pearl earrings, and a long black vest of buttery suede to the ensemble. She loved the fun western cowboy chic style that was standard wear at western art shows. Giving Jack a little rub with her toe before pulling on black round-toed boots, she stepped to the full-length mirror and gave herself what her mother used to call the old once-over. She ran the brush through her hair once more and fastened a turquoise boot bracelet over each boot.

Reaching into the box of Jack's paraphernalia, she took out the bag of kibble, giving it a healthy shake. As the first few bits clattered noisily into Jack's bowl, he quickly backed out from under the bed. Jessie ruffled his fur and told him what a wonderful, handsome fellow he was, then checked the clock. Twenty minutes to spare. She had time for a bit of quick research.

Opening her laptop, Jessie put in the hotel wi-fi code and typed Adele Nielson's name into the search bar. Immediately, news articles from three Montana papers popped up. She scanned the list. A headline caught her eye that screamed *Double Tragedy at Crooked Creek*. Jessie tensed. The article began:

Only months after 19-year-old Adele Nielson was shot while seeding winter wheat in one of the family's fields, death again visited the Nielson family. During the recent snowstorm, Dominic Nielson returned home unexpectedly in the middle of the night from Fort Stewart Army Base in Georgia. Berg Nielson did not answer his son's knock on the door, so Dominic, rather than wake his father, attempted to climb in his old bedroom window and was shot by his father as an intruder. Sheriff Fischer of the Crooked Creek Sheriff's Office said that Berg had been receiving threatening notes since the death of his daughter, and those threats had recently escalated.

"Omigod! Threatening notes!" The words burst from Jessie's mouth. Then she looked at the screen and read on.

> Upon realizing he had shot his son, Berg went into cardiac arrest and Dominic, though gravely wounded, called 911. When Sheriff Fischer and the volunteer medical personnel arrived, they discovered Dominic slumped over the steering wheel of a truck. The truck had a wide affixed blade used to clear snow. Evidently, Dominic was trying to plow out the driveway, so that the emergency crew could get in to assist his father and himself. Berg had unfortunately succumbed. Dominic was transported to St. Vincent's Hospital, but did not regain consciousness.

Jessie gasped. *How awful. And the poor old man began getting those threatening notes right after his daughter died. This has to be linked to the toy tractors and notes I was getting. But why me? It must be mistaken identity and they're meant for someone else.*

She closed her laptop. Minutes ticked by as Jessie sat, thinking of the Nielson family. Gone. The entire family. She got up and looked out her window. In the lighted hotel entrance, she saw the enormous tractor. It was an innocuous looking machine until you thought about the back window—the bullet holes, the girl who died in the cab. Now, it looked malevolent. Beastly.

Jack's soft padding went unnoticed until a paw snaked out and claws hooked onto the turquoise boot bracelet. Jessie gave a start.

"Hey! Watch it." She carefully unsnagged the orange paw and scratched behind his ears. "I'm getting maudlin, Jack." She looked at the clock on the dresser. "And I need to go." Jessie pulled a catnip mouse—one that emitted a high-pitched squeak—out of the bag of cat paraphernalia and tossed it onto the rug. Jack pounced on it and looked at Jessie expectantly. She threw it once more, then opened the door to go.

"See you later, Butter Tub."

Chapter Twenty-two

Expo Reception

Jessie picked a chicken teriyaki skewer and a brie-stuffed mushroom cap from the tray as the server offered the assortment of hors d'oeuvres. She popped the small mushroom into her mouth and looked around the room as she chewed appreciatively. Right now, a classical guitarist was playing, but soon it would be Esther's turn to entertain the crowd. She spotted Esther arranging her sheet music at the piano near the bar area. Jessie moved toward the baby grand, snagging several more canapes as she went and accepting a glass of white wine from a smiling steward.

Max Watson might be cheap with his advertising budget and mailing costs, but he puts on a nice event for the art enthusiasts.

Wonder where he is.

She scanned the reception area. Everywhere she looked were art enthusiasts dressed in their western best. Tables of various heights draped in elegant black cloths were dotted across the room. Some were high and only large enough to set down several glasses while the guests stood to chat. Others were low, round and wide, large enough to seat six or more people while they enjoyed their canapes and wine. Jessie spotted Max across the room, but before she could head in his direction, a gallery dealer strode purposefully toward him and tapped him on the shoulder. The woman was waving her hands in the air as she spoke. Even from a distance Jessie could see her agitation.

135

Someone isn't happy, Jessie thought. Well, I'm not happy with Max either. Not if he shorted last year's charity.

She made a mental note to ask for an appointment. She still hadn't spoken to him about the proceeds from her donated landscape of the previous year. Using a toothpick, she stabbed a small piece of pineapple and put it in her mouth. It would be smart to find out what else had been consigned to the event and how high the winning bids were before she asked about a possible discrepancy in the funds. Maybe there were other auction lots that should have sold in the five-figure range. She bit into a chocolate covered strawberry, then took a sip of wine. *Mmmm.* Both were excellent. But she suspected Arvid would want to go out for dinner when Esther was finished playing, so she'd chosen only a few hors d'oeuvres from the tray when the server stopped to tempt her.

She munched a celery stick as she wondered where she could get a copy of last year's auction catalog. Surely someone working the show committee table would have a couple.

Placing her empty plate on one of the rolling carts supplied for that purpose, she meandered through the crowd, stopping to say hello to old friends, on her way to the ticket desk.

"Hey, Jessie." Glen Heath stepped in front of her and greeted her with a Cheshire cat grin. Wearing a suede vest over a deep green, heavily embroidered western silk shirt and caiman boots, the sculptor looked every inch successful and self-assured. Then he met Jessie's eyes. "Esther told me you were singing tonight. I'm delighted to hear it." He took a healthy sip from the delicate wine glass he held in his broad hand. "I haven't heard you belt out a song since the time we were both," he gulped, "at the show in Carefree. Carefree, Arizona." He waved his wine glass around, the liquid creating its own little whirlpool. "At that little karaoke bar. Wasn't that on the corner of Easy Street? Man, what wouldn't I give to be on Easy Street for real," he slurred, "And then *I'd* be delighted."

Delighted was obviously his word of the day, Jessie mused. "Um ....no...I'm not singing. I don't know where she got that idea."

Glen waved his wine glass again. "I'm going to find Max and tell Max that you'll be deeeelighted to sing." He drawled his word

136

of the day, and started to turn away from Jessie, but just then Camille joined them, putting her free hand on his arm. She was dressed in a calf-length white leather dress, with cut fringe trailing down one side seam, a necklace comprised of several loops of turquoise beads with matching hoop earrings, and a wide silver bracelet. The high heels on her tooled boots brought her eye to eye with Glen. She looked magnificent.

In fact, Jessie thought, she looks downright intimidating. She gives me a bad case of the frumps.

"I think someone should have had dinner before he had, oh, about four or five glasses of wine, don't you?" Camille tugged him toward a nearby table and placed her own heaping plate of hors d'oeuvres in front of him. "C'mon, Glen. Come and sit with me and eat a bite." She pursed her lips at him, then glanced over reassuringly at Jessie as she told him, "You're not going to coerce Jessie to sing. Eat. Then you'll have a cup of coffee, or I'm going to tell Max that *you'll* sing."

Glen looked stricken. "Aw, Camille. You know I can't carry a tune. If I could carry a tune, I'd be delighted to sing." He looked at the plate and his eyes widened in appreciation. "Oh look, chicken." Then he frowned. "Every blamed art show serves the same chicken on a stick." He looked accusingly at Jessie. "Do you think this is the same chicken? God, that had to be a huge chicken. And why aren't you singing?"

"Sorry, Jessie," Camille said ruefully, looking down at Jessie.

"It's okay," Jessie said. She looked at the wine in her hand, and then at Glen. Resolutely, she placed her own half-empty glass on the nearest dish trolley. It was great wine, too. "Farm Dog Red" from the Ten Spoon Winery in Missoula, Montana, according to the bartender. "I didn't get time to eat either. And Glen knows that I sing at a lot of the shows." Jessie gave him a stern look. "But not tonight."

"You owe me a motorcycle ride," Glen grumbled between bites. "Wait and see. It'll be—"

"Yeah, yeah," Camille said, rolling her eyes. "It'll be *so* delightful." She looked at Jessie. "You looked like a woman on a mission when I saw Glen waylay you. Were you ducking out of the reception?"

137

"No. I was just going to talk to the workers at the ticket desk, then come and listen to Esther play. It'll be so different from her usual music. I heard they asked her to do a mix of jazz and country western. Can you imagine Esther doing country western?"

"Oh, please." She chuckled. "No, I really can't. I'll have to hear that to believe it. Now, Beethoven I could believe." She shook her finger at Glen, who looked about to speak. "Eat," she commanded. "But if Esther is doing country western, you know it'll be good. And I heard they booked an incredible guitarist to play with her."

"It sounds like fun."

"It is." Camille looked at Jessie with a thoughtful expression. "I know you've sent work to the auction in the past, but isn't this the first time you've come to the show in person and displayed in a room? I hate to tell you that this is the night nobody—well *almost* nobody—sells art. We're all down here listening to the music and schmoozing potential buyers. Then, when the rooms open tomorrow, here they come."

"We hope so anyhow, right?" Jessie asked.

Camille smiled. "Oh, they do. You'll see."

"Get along little dogies," Glen supplied, waving a non-existent lariat over his head. "Head 'em on in."

"What were you going to ask the show committee about?" Camille asked.

"I wondered if they could find a catalog from last year's auction. I had a piece in it and couldn't recall how much it sold for. I was just curious."

"Heck, I have an old catalog up in my room. And it has all the winning bids listed. I always bring the previous year's catalog, so I can compare current prices on similar work. At every auction I write down the winning bids, and the no-sales that don't meet the reserve, or lowest minimum, price. I like to know where the art market is headed, don't you?"

"Yes, exactly." Jessie didn't want to voice any suspicions she couldn't back up with facts. "Do you mind if I borrow it? I can return it before tomorrow night's auction."

Camille nodded. "Sure, no problem. I'm staying in my display room, 145, right down the hall. Let's walk over and get it now."

Glen started to rise and Camille pushed down on his shoulder, effectively re-seating him. "Sit," she commanded. "Eat. We'll be back in five minutes and we'll bring coffee."

As Jessie and Camille walked off, he was muttering about pushy women and chewing the chicken off a teriyaki skewer.

..*

"Don't think too badly of Glen," Camille said, as they entered her hotel room. "We've been friends for over ten years and I tend to look out for him a bit at shows. It's nothing romantic." She hesitated. "At first, I wanted it to be. I gave up that idea when I realized how much he drinks. He's his own worst enemy when he hits the booze, and it's been worse lately. He's been grumpy at the last two shows. Maybe he's depressed. It's sure hard to figure out."

"Have you asked him what's wrong?"

"Yeah, I have. One day he said his fingers are getting arthritic. He claims he isn't kicking out the large body of work he used to, and pain in his fingers and thumb is affecting his sculpting." Camille shrugged her shoulders. "I can't see a big difference in his new sculptures, but he says *he* can. He swears that because of his stiff fingers, the quality of his work is sliding downhill fast."

"But he's so young. He's only in his late forties, isn't he?"

"Yeah, but he worries he has rheumatoid arthritis. It's an inherited disease and his mother has it. But the big goof won't go to the doctor and get it confirmed. Maybe it's just stiffness from pressing the wax or clay he uses. It's hard on fingers and hands, that repetitive motion."

"I'm so sorry." Jessie automatically flexed her fingers, thinking how scary any loss of fine motor control would be to an artist. Not as terrifying as loss of vision, perhaps, but frightening nevertheless. "That's awful."

Camille nodded. "Yes, but then the next day, he's in high spirits and says he's going to get himself a new studio. A big space where he can sculpt monumental pieces—life-sized horses and such. He has some wonderful, well-heeled clients." She met Jessie's gaze. "I'm talking people with their own planes and lots of cash. Old money. New money. They treat him like family. You'd

139

be surprised how much traveling he's done just this year. Some of the clients fly him to their ranches to take reference photos or meet the bull or horse he's supposed to sculpt. It's crazy." She shook her head, making the blond curls shimmer.

Jessie was immediately lost in the color and movement. *What a great portrait study Camille would make.* She closed her eyes, imagining the play of light. She'd pose her on a vividly colored chair near a window, letting the effect of backlighting warm the edges of Camille's—.

"You okay?" Camille was staring at Jessie with a worried expression.

"Oh, sure. Sorry. I…uh…I was just thinking Glen must be doing very well with his sculpting."

"But you know how Glen is. He hasn't saved much money over his career. He accepts all the plane rides and the down payments. Then he blows the money. Now he's worried he won't be able to fulfill commissions because he needs a huge space to work on some of the large pieces. And, what if the arthritis flares up?"

Jessie gave her a sympathetic glance. "Scary. I'm not sure what I'd do if I couldn't paint. It must be frightening for him to think about not being able to take a piece of clay and make something wonderful."

"Yes. I know it is."

"But if he hasn't saved enough for retirement or emergencies, where does he think he'll get the funds to build a huge studio?" Jessie heard the words coming out of her mouth and would have loved to recall them. It wasn't any of her business, but she continued. "And if he's worried about his health, why does he want to take on more debt?"

Camille threw out her hands. "Exactly. When I ask him he just glowers at me. Or, typical Glen, he laughs and says, 'It'll work out fine. I have a plan.' Sometimes he mimics George Peppard from that old '80s TV series, you know, *The A Team*, who says, 'I love it when a plan comes together.'" Camille gave a good impression of Glen pretending to chomp on a cigar while he gave the old tag line. "But serious, logical ideas? A decent business plan?" She shook her head again. "It just isn't in his make-up. Sometimes I think half the artists I know are dreamers. Smart, creative, but without good heads for business. Have you ever noticed that some of the best artists seem to sell well, but they aren't good marketers? If they were, they'd be household names." Then Camille looked at Jessie, and her face reddened. "Present company excepted."

Jessie laughed, but dropped the subject and looked around the room. Camille's art was scratch-board, sketches created with an engraving technique in which the artist uses a pointed tool to scratch through a black ink surface to reveal white or colored paper below. After making the initial sketch, Camille used acrylics to add lifelike color to her delicate renderings.

Her pieces were displayed on floor to ceiling black panels that covered three walls of the room. Right now, none of her display lights were turned on to illuminate the artwork. Jessie would come back in the morning take a better look. She had long admired her friend's art and would love to own a piece. A small wall in her Santa Fe home practically cried out for one of the artist's tiny bird pieces. *Maybe a hummingbird.*

Even if her display lights had been on, it would have been difficult to maneuver around the queen-sized rollaway bed, which took up the free space in the small hotel room. Regular hotel furniture—desk, table, chairs, regular bed—had been removed to allow visitors to go through the rooms and look at the art. Artists who didn't want to pay for an extra room for sleeping nearly always opted to bring their own sleeping bags, or use the economical rollaway beds supplied by the hotel that staff folded up and stored each morning.

The tall blonde squatted down and rummaged through the open suitcase on the bed. "Here's the catalog." She stood and handed it to Jessie. "Let's go back to the table and take the big dope a jumbo cup of coffee. We can sit and go through the auction listings while he sobers up a little."

"Fine with me."

They stepped out into the hall. Camille mentioned, "There were some surprises in the winning bids, and one or two things at the end of the auction never made it into the print catalog."

"Really? Why not?"

"Just added too late, I suppose. Late donations to help support the charity, maybe. I wrote the titles and description down. It seems like that happens nearly every year. At least here it seems to. And they never sell well that late in the evening. All the good buyers have gone, not realizing there are more lots at the end. I call them bargain basement pieces."

Interesting, Jessie thought. Donated paintings whose proceeds don't reach the charity, and add-ons that don't show up in the auction catalog.

* * *

Ten minutes later, Glen sported a wide, whipped-cream mustache and loudly sipped a mocha grande. "You coming to my art-room in the morning to see my new pieces, Jessie? If they plow the roads, we'll take a cold ride. Cold, but mighty fun."

"I'd love to come and see your work," Jessie replied. "But we'll see about the ride. Sounds pretty chilly to me." She sat down beside Camille.

Camille pointed out artwork in the previous year's catalog that had brought more than double the price estimated. She lamented over a few pieces she'd wanted to bid on, but the price had rocketed upward past her budget. "Here's your Glacier Park landscape." She pointed to an image titled, *View from Going to the Sun Road.* "It was gorgeous. Of course, I didn't even try to bid on it. Bidding was fierce. It was a three-way contest between a local collector, Max Watson, and a collector from Boston." She consulted her notes. "It went for $32,500."

"That's what I was told, except I didn't know Max bid on it," Jessie said. "Those proceeds were supposed to go to the Humane Society."

"Yes, I know. See here?" She pointed to an abbreviation she'd added next to the painting. "I added 'DN' next to the price on those pieces that Max announced were full donations to the Creekside Humane Society. Some buyers with big bucks purchased pieces simply to help fund a spay-neuter program and support a new addition to their facility. At one point, a husband and wife didn't realize they were bidding against each other." She waved her hand

142

in the air. "It was a riot. Anyway, some of those pieces sold for double their normal value. They shouldn't have put yours so far back in the auction or it might have brought even more. Max said his idea was that it would keep buyers in their seats until the end of the auction, but the crowd was pretty thin by then. Personally, I think he was hoping for that. I think he wanted it himself and hoped it would go low since it was at the end. The local collector dropped out early on, but the guy from Boston was more determined than Max and had a bigger wallet." Camille chuckled. "He also bought a small piece added to the end of the auction. Now *that* made Max livid. I was watching his face when he was deciding whether to raise his paddle. He was apoplectic."

Jessie smiled. Over the loudspeaker, she heard Max announcing Esther's stint at the piano. It was time to go over and listen to her friend's performance.

Glen had finally focused on the conversation and gave a belly laugh. "Max was spitting mad when he was outbid. The same buyer from Boston bought one of my small ones. A horse and rider piece." He rubbed his chin. "What was that guy's name? Some president's name. Man, I can see him standing there with that pleased look on his face. He comes nearly every year. Big man, almost my height. Sandy blonde hair, slightly crooked nose."

"Sexy," Camille threw in. "Very hunky."

Jessie stared at them. It surely couldn't be. From Boston? Big, light haired and with a cute little crook to his nose. She felt heat suffuse her face. That louse.

Then Glen took another slurp of mocha grande. "Johnson. Big buyer. Nice fellow, too."

Jessie felt herself relax. She stood. "I'm going to go over and stand closer to the piano. Esther's ready to play."

Camille nodded at Jessie. "Keep the catalog until tomorrow." Then she looked at Glen. "No, it wasn't Johnson. It was—"

"No, no, don't tell me." Glen snapped his fingers. "That coffee is clearing my mind. I've got it. Two presidents. He's named after not one, but two, of our fearless leaders."

From the other end of the room, Esther and the guitarist pounded into an instrumental version of Carrie Underwood's

"Before He Cheats" with just a hint of sultry background murmuring from Esther to replace the vocal portion.

She's good, Jessie thought. *And what a choice of music.* She could relate to the lyrics. Jessie sighed. At least nothing but a dinner date really happened between that louse and herself, but she had been hopeful she'd finally found a soul mate—until she discovered he was married. *Drek.* Jessie knew whose name Glen was going to say before he said it. Then Glen's earlier words registered. And he comes nearly every year? *He'd better not show his face, the liar. He had a huge nerve to buy my Glacier Park painting.*

"The guy's name is Grant Kennedy," Glen announced triumphantly.

Jessie threw Glen a dark look. She was seething. If she didn't do something she felt as though she'd burst into flame.

"Hey." He reared back. "What's that look for? I didn't do anything."

"No, you didn't." Jessie picked up his wine glass and downed the remains in one gulp. "But I'm going to."

Glen and Camille gaped at her.

"What? What're you going to do, Jess?" Glen grumbled looking at his empty glass.

Camille followed Jessie's gaze and understanding dawned. She smiled broadly. "Ha! She's going to sing."

"Hey," Glen called after Jessie as she stormed toward Esther and the baby grand. "I bet it'll be delightful."

* * *

Arvid was lounging by the piano, beaming at Esther while her fingers flew over the keys. She was lost in the music. He was sure she'd forgotten he was there, but he was in a forgiving mood. For him, not much beat listening to his wife at the piano, doing what she did so well. Well, maybe listening to Esther and Jessie together. They filled a room with soul. Or maybe listening to Esther and Jessie while munching on more of those stuffed mushrooms. He looked at his small empty plate, then gazed hopefully around to see if there were any more servers in the vicinity.

Huh, here comes Jessie. And that gal looks mad as a Swede with his beard caught in the mailbox. Cripes. Wonder what's up?

The last note of the song reverberated through the sound system as Jessie stormed up. She nodded to the guitarist, then gave Esther a look that Esther interpreted immediately. Her lovely smile took in Jessie's stormy expression, but instead of questioning her, she reached into a satchel and pulled out a folder of music.

"Music's good for what ails you," she murmured. "Want to belt out some songs?"

* * *

When Russell walked in, Jessie was wailing out a Reba McIntyre song, stomping a booted foot that sported a dangling turquoise bangle, her green silk blouse open at the neck, and her black velvet skirt swirling around shapely legs. Esther, Jessie, and the grinning guitarist were rocking the reception. The crowd was rowdy, loud, and bordered on disorderly. Some of the men waved cowboy hats in the air and many of Jessie's artist friends yelled, "Go, Jess!"

Leaning against a pillar near the piano, Arvid stood tapping a foot and popping cherry tomatoes into his mouth from a paper napkin. He saw Russell and beckoned him over.

"Hey, Russell. Where's K.D.?"

"I decided not to bring him. I dropped him at his grandpa's and asked Janice Dahlgren to fill in if Dan needs her." He didn't look at Arvid. His eyes were trained on the red-head wailing into the microphone. Then he looked around the room. "Sure glad I decided not to bring him, K.D.. Half the room looks soused."

"Nup," Arvid said gruffly, "Most of them are just having a good time, Russell. I think it's too bad you left your son home. As much as K.D. likes to draw, the boy would have been in his element going through the art rooms. Man, he would have loved it. But maybe next year, huh?" Then he noticed the mesmerized look on Russell's face as his gaze fell on Jessie.

She became a different person when she sang. The music took hold of her as thoroughly as the colors on her artist's palette and

145

the feel of a brush in her hand. Arvid waved a beefy hand holding a teriyaki skewer at the piano where Esther pounded the keys with the impact of gunfire, and Jessie, head thrown back, eyes closed, filled the room with her rich, throaty voice. "So, what do you think?"

"Omigod," Russell said. "I just can't believe it." He looked at Arvid and gave him a stricken look. "Jessie cut her hair."

Chapter Twenty-three

Tate sat in room 160 and looked at the numerical list of art-work. He pulled a drawing from one of the boxes, unwound the bubble-wrap, flipped it over and checked the back.

Nothing.

He tried the next one.

Zip. Blast it.

Why did his sister offer to dream up titles for each one if she wasn't going to put a corresponding number on the back when she made up the list? At least the display was up. The lights looked good. The panels looked like he knew what he was doing.

Thank God for rental services.

Walking down the hall after getting dinner, he noticed that some of the artists were already open for business. Evidently, they'd invited special customers and opened their show rooms, even though the schedule listed the Expo opening as ten the next morning. Well, he was learning the ropes.

Some great music came from the reception area. He stood by the open double doors and listed for a few minutes. Man, some gal had an amazing pair of pipes. He dragged himself away. He didn't have time to listen if he was going to pull off this art show. The room had to look professional. He needed access to the artists' hospitality room and hoped to meet as many artists as possible. Get them to talk to him.

Worried, he looked at the boxes lined up by the wall. They were full of framed sketches. He wondered if the work he'd

147

brought would fool anyone. *Would they think he was good enough to be here?* Then he shook his head. *I always wanted to give it a try, but that didn't matter. It isn't the point. Selling art is not your plan, my man. Keep your eye on the goal.*

He checked his watch. 7:50. He didn't really expect Jessie O'Bourne to show up at nine. But wouldn't it be nice if she did? If she took him up on his offer of dancing at Buck's Pub? Just in case, he'd better pull this together pronto. He wished he'd worked on it during the afternoon.

He opened another box and examined another sketch.

Not bad.

The loose drawing was a good likeness of the appaloosa mare he'd had in high school. Snowdrop. What a neat horse she'd been. Staring at the piece, he became lost in thought, his mind dragging his heart back to the past, to the feel of the horse beneath him, the smell of lilacs at the edge of the horse paddock. Then he took one of the labels and carefully printed a title in neat block letters. How should he price it?

Maybe I'll mark it sold. Keep the damn thing.

He examined the frame. It sure wasn't like the expensive ones Jessie O'Bourne had on her work, but passable. The frame shop had given him a break on the price since he needed fifteen of the same molding. They'd framed them, boxed them and shipped them. Most of the time, he'd drawn on a paper with a rough "deckled" or uncut edge. The frame shop had mounted each sketch on a backing of dark grey matboard, letting the rough edges show. He liked the finished product. All he'd had to do was slap over two thousand dollars on his credit card.

Ouch.

He grinned, looking at the drawing. This one was Patterson's Barn.

Hoo-boy. It made him think of Louise Patterson and the senior prom. He looked at the list.

Yep. Number five.

He was getting the hang of this. Picking up a metal hanger that slipped over the top edge of the carpet-covered display panel, he hung the drawing, then neatly printed the price label and mounted it on the panel with a small piece of Velcro. It looked damn good. Maybe he'd even sell some.

Wouldn't it be crazy if he broke even on this lunatic plan?

Every hotel room in town was full because of the western art show, so it was lucky there was a last-minute space in the show and he could get a rollaway bed and sleep in the room. He turned on his display lights to make sure all of the bulbs lit.

Well, I'd better get busy.

* * *

While he was squatting on the floor unwrapping the last eight sketches, Tate heard a tentative knock on the door. He checked his watch and smiled. *Nine.* He stood and stretched, rubbed the small of his back, and swung the door open. Jessie stood there, positively glowing. She gave him a little wave. Tate grinned.

"Greetings, M'Lady O'Bourne of Crooked Creek." He bowed theatrically. Then he noticed she was accompanied by a tall elegant woman with close-cropped white hair. A woman who looked amused. Behind the woman were two men—one enormous bruiser who smiled broadly and one younger, slightly shorter man whose face wore a gloomy expression.

"Ah. I see you've brought your entourage as well."

"We came by to check out your work and then we're off for a late dinner. Care to come along?" Jessie's eyes twinkled.

Tate stood back and invited them in. Jessie made quick introductions and looked around the room.

"Well, you slug. You aren't even finished setting up yet." She picked up a wrapped drawing and began removing the bubble wrap. When it was unwrapped, she looked at the drawing of a small girl sitting on a swing, holding a long-haired cat. "This is lovely. You have a great flair for pencil work. I like the way you used the side of your pencil here to soften the shading on the little girl's face, but elsewhere the strokes of graphite are as crisp and expressive as brush strokes."

She beamed at Tate. "I'll come and look at everything tomorrow." She leaned the drawing against a display panel. Esther

149

and Arvid were admiring the few pieces already hung. Russell was standing near the open doorway.

"Don't you want to come and eat before you hang the rest?" Jessie asked. "You said last night that the band would be playing at Buck's pub by the pool, and Arvid said the restaurant has a special—chicken-fried steak. We thought we'd get our food to go and take it out to a table, so we can listen to the music."

Tate looked at Jessie, then at the scowl that deepened on her friend Russell's face. He thought about the chicken-fried steak, mashed potatoes and gravy he'd had only a couple hours earlier. He'd topped it off with an enormous piece of New York cheesecake with the best raspberry topping he'd ever tasted. Glancing again at the thundercloud countenance of Russell's face, Tate felt the devil of mischief tap him on the shoulder. A big sharp rap.

"Sure," he said heartily, slapping Russell on the back. "Nice to meet you. Let's do it." He reached up and turned off the strip of display lights. He draped an arm around Jessie. "Maybe tomorrow you can give me some pointers on spiffing up my display, Lady O'Bourne." He grinned at Arvid and Esther. "Man, I'm starved, aren't you?"

Chapter Twenty-four

Crooked Creek Sheriff's Office, next morning

"No, there weren't any toy tractors left with Berg Nielson's threatening notes," Sheriff Fischer said in a matter of fact tone. "But there is a similarity between his and those left at the hotel." He placed one of the threats Berg Nielson had received next to one left at Jessie's hotel door. "Most people think printing isn't distinctive but they're wrong. Look at these." He held his thumb and index finger a pinch apart. "People tend to print their letters about the same height every time. They use the same slight slant. Subtle, but definitely there if you know what to look for."

"Ya. The sad thing is, you gotta compare it something you can connect with a name, if you want to catch who's doing it," Arvid said, peering at the two sheets. Fischer laid another threatening note next to the one Jessie had received. Then another. Soon, there were about ten more threatening missives lined up on the oak desk. There was a definite look about them. And Jessie's two notes looked like they were printed by the same hand as the rest.

"He was persistent, wasn't he?" Russell asked in a disgusted tone. "You promote the idea that you're going to come and kill the old man, just drive him crazy with worry. Then paranoia finally does the dirty job for the killer. What a devilish plan on top of shooting the daughter. I'm assuming you feel that her death was no accident?"

Fischer nodded. "No accident."

"And why didn't he know his son was on the way home?" Arvid looked sad. "A whole family. Gone."

"The neighbor—he goes by the nickname 'Wheels'," Fischer said making air quotes, "told us that originally Dominic wanted to surprise his dad for Christmas. Anyhow, Wheels agreed to pick him up at the airport. He said he was glad to do it, just to help a member of the armed forces. When the weather turned so sour, he called Berg to let him know he'd be dropping Dominic off, but it would be really late because of the horrible roads. The call must have come in when Berg was outside doing chores. We don't think the old man noticed there was a message on the machine."

Russell and Arvid looked expectantly at Fischer. Fischer was working his jaw.

"But, you've got something don't you?" Arvid finally asked.

"A video."

"A video?" Arvid and Russell spoke at once.

"Don't get excited. All it shows is boots. Goddamn boots. Someone is walking up to the front door at night, and we have the infrared video of someone's boots. It's from one of those trail cams that capture photos of wildlife at night. They take infrared pictures—short videos, actually—when movement triggers the mechanism. Adele's boyfriend suggested it to Berg and set it up for him so that it was unobtrusive. I suspect Berg was curious, and after the kid set it to take pictures of the front door, Berg picked it up but didn't put it back at quite the correct angle. All we got was a movie of the perp's feet. And we wouldn't even have those if the boyfriend hadn't called us about it after Berg and Dom died. We had to dig around in the snow to find it."

"And what's the boyfriend's name?" Arvid took out a small notebook and a stub of a chewed pencil. Russell pulled up the note program on his phone.

"Evan Hanson."

Arvid and Russell stared. An hour earlier they'd written Evan Hanson's name down for another reason. He was the one who was supposed to be in Jessie's room.

"This isn't good," Arvid said. "Especially not for Evan Hanson."

152

"Nope. It isn't." Fischer tapped his pencil on the desk. "When I found out Evan Hanson was originally booked into the hotel room where the threatening notes were left, you could have blown me away like dandelion fuzz. Someone must know he brought us the video and whoever that is, they wrongly suspect that he knows more than he does."

"So. Jessie must be right. Benny was killed accidentally. In the dark corner of that parking lot, with the snow coming down, he could easily have been mistaken for Evan. I'll bet the killer was expecting Evan, not his cousin." Arvid grumbled. "Can we see the trail cam footage?"

Fifteen minutes later, after watching Evan's video twice, Russell asked Arvid. "Can you get a handle on how big the feet are?"

Arvid shook his head.

"I can't either. There isn't anything to judge the size against." He looked toward Fischer. "The boots are also pretty nondescript. Everybody around here probably has a pair like that." He leaned back in his chair, then leaned forward, rolling his shoulders and stretching the kinks out of his back. Then he told Fischer. "You know, we had a murder case last summer in Sage Bluff, and Jessie was more help than anybody on the payroll. She's observant."

Fischer gawked. "Miss O'Bourne? You aren't suggesting that we let a civilian look at it, are you? I really wouldn't be in favor of that."

"Huh," Arvid grunted. "Well, Russell's right. She looks at things differently. She's a lot more observant. Might be a help."

"I agree," Russell said. "But I hate to get Jess involved in this case."

"Absolutely not," Fischer agreed. "I wouldn't even consider showing this to anyone not on the case. And now that she's moved to a different room, I'm certain she'll be okay."

Arvid shrugged. "We hope so."

"Who inherits the Nielson's ranch?" Russell asked, changing the subject.

"It's still up in the air," Fischer said. "Berg Nielson was dead when the paramedics found him. Dom was still alive but died shortly thereafter. He would have been next in line. And he had a

153

will. A sorry excuse of a will, actually, but according to the lawyer for the estate it is a viable will. It was a handwritten sheet we found in his wallet, and it left everything to a buddy from Fort Stewart Army Base."

"Interesting." Arvid scribbled down the name of the base. "So why haven't they contacted him after all this time? And what's his name?"

"His name is Harris Freeman. He's Wheels' stepbrother. But here's where it gets interesting. He's been AWOL since early January."

"AWOL?" Russell asked.

"Poop, he's missing?" Arvid shook his head and he and Russell turned to Fischer.

"The brother of the guy who gave Dom a ride?" Russell asked. "That's some coincidence."

"He's a stepbrother." Fischer said. "Yeah. It's a hell of a coincidence."

"I don't like it."

"Dom and Harris Freeman signed up together," Fischer continued. "Good friends. All we know is that Harris was granted leave and left base to come home. The MPs located a motel in Hinesville where he stayed overnight. The bed hadn't been slept in. His suitcase was left behind."

"Why Hinesville? Is that near an airport?"

"He had a bus ticket from Hinesville to Savannah. According to what I was told, the bus drops the soldiers right at the airport. Needless to say, the ticket wasn't used."

"Any leads to the kid's whereabouts?" Arvid asked.

"Not really. The motel desk clerk said he happened to be outside taking a smoking break, when he saw a guy he thought might have been Harris get in a black vehicle. Couldn't give a make or model. Couldn't even swear that it had been Harris Freeman. But there's been no sign of him since."

"Oh, this gets curiouser and curiouser," Russell intoned. "I wouldn't call it going AWOL if you disappear and don't take anything with you. I don't think this sounds too good for Harris Freeman."

"Nup. Me either," Arvid said. "No other clues?"

"Well, there was an odd thing in his motel room. A flier. Get this. It was a flier advertising the Crooked Creek Art Expo. The one going on right now."

"Good God," Arvid barked.

"I know. His stepbrother, Wheels, participates in this show. He's a sculptor. We asked if he'd sent it to Harris. He says no. And they picked up good prints off it. We checked Glen's prints just to be sure. Not a match. In fact, no match on the fingerprints anywhere in the system except for those of Harris Freeman."

"So, Glen's in the clear. Who inherits Berg Nielson's place if Harris is found dead? Glen Heath—uh, Wheels, I guess you call him?"

"No. Freeman's mom, I suppose. She's in a nursing home here." Fischer went to the coffee pot, poured a cup, and took it back to his desk. "Her husband was a good friend of mine. I visit once a week to tell her there's no news. God, I hate to go. It's heartbreaking."

"Yeah, that's gotta be hard." Russell said.

"So, where was Wheels when his stepbrother went missing?" Arvid asked. "Sometimes family ties come unraveled when money comes into the mix. Especially with step-siblings."

"Wheels was here in town. Solid alibi." Fischer did not look happy.

"How about when Adele Nielson was shot on the tractor?" Arvid poised his pencil over his notebook. "And during the months when Berg was receiving the threatening notes?"

"We checked that out upside down, inside out, and backwards. When Adele was shot, he was at a motorcycle rally in California. It was verified by numerous bikers. No way he could have shot the girl. He was in town during the delivery of a couple notes, but not most of them. He never got to town until the end of November, and he came to lay around and recuperate from gallbladder surgery. We verified his surgery and his whereabouts in mid-November. He was flat on his back in a hospital in New Orleans. Then, shortly after he came home, his stepmother had a stroke and she went into the nursing home. What I don't like is that he left the message on Berg's answering machine, supposedly saying he was bringing Dom home. Now, Berg never listened to it. We don't know why.

155

Maybe he was outside. Maybe he was in the john. But," Fischer paused for effect. "Even if he'd tried to listen to it, the message was so garbled he wouldn't have understood a thing."

Russell looked at Fischer inquiringly.

"Did Wheels have an explanation for that?" Russell asked.

"Not really. He said his best guess was that because of the storm and being too far out of cell tower range, the message didn't go through well. And it does happen."

"Think he was harassing the old man and garbled the cell message on purpose?"

Fischer shrugged. "You never know."

"How about that trailcam video," Arvid asked. "You think those boots might be Wheels'?

"I doubt it. Wheels wears nothing but cowboy boots. Big, maybe size twelve, twelve and a half."

"Yeah. The ones in the video are work boots, not cowboy boots." Arvid stuck out a foot. "Probably bigger than mine."

Russell laughed. "Bigger? I doubt it."

Arvid gave him a dirty look.

Russell ignored him. "Who else might benefit with the family gone from Nielson's ranch?"

"Well," Fischer scratched his head. "There's a rancher nearby who wants to add property to his spread. Nielson's acreage adjoins his property, so it'd be perfect. If whoever inherits isn't planning to run the ranch for cattle or use the land for crops like it's seeded in now, they might sell to the guy. His name is Collin Bingham. Nielson's place has good outbuildings too. Bingham needs a better barn and a good hay shed. But it's a stretch. He'd have no way of knowing whether the heir would actually sell him the land, or the entire ranch, or even if he could get a loan big enough to buy it."

"Huh," Arvid grunted in agreement. "If it's like Sage Bluff, a lot of farmers and ranchers are 'land poor'. They have so much money tied up in their land that it's a stretch to purchase decent farm machinery, let alone a nice home for the missus. Things go begging while they tally up more and more property trying to make a living off wheat and alfalfa. And cattle."

"Yeah, it's the same here. Feel free to go pick Bingham's brain if you want. He's an interesting fellow anyhow. I told him to think on the issue a bit last time I was there. Maybe he's come up with some theories or ideas since then."

"So, you asked this local guy his ideas, but you don't want to bring Jessie in to look at the video? What's sauce for the goose is sauce for the gander."

Fischer had the grace to look embarrassed. "Well, yes, but he's local. And he knew Berg Nielson well. They were friends."

"Did Berg Nielson tell Bingham about the threats? And if he was interested in the land, is it possible he might actually be the shooter? And be the one behind the notes? You say he lives close by. He probably had opportunity."

"I might have thought so earlier, but not after Miss O'Bourne received the notes outside her door. It just doesn't seem like something Bingham would pull together. My guess is it's someone closer to Evan Hanson. Someone associated with the art show, or who knows the Hanson family. What gets me is how they knew which room Evan would be in? Even though he was moved, the only reason he was moved was so Miss O'Bourne could have the room with her cat. It's one of the few designated as 'pet friendly'."

"Ours was too," Arvid said. "Esther and I gave her our room, because there wasn't any other vacancy. So, Jessie and the beast are in there now. And for Pete's sake, call her Jessie." He waved his hand in the air. "I can't even figure out who you're talking about with this 'Miss O'Bourne' this and 'Miss O'Bourne' that."

"You and Esther are staying in her old room now, Arvid?" Fischer looked concerned. "Be very, very careful. Aren't you worried about your wife there alone?"

"Nah, not much. She was determined we'd switch with Jessie. Jessie can take care of herself okay, but my Esther is a force to be reckoned with. She helped nab one of the guilty parties last year during that murder case in Sage Bluff. Broke his kneecap with a cast iron frying pan." He shook his head, wincing. "BAM! Down went the skillet and that kneecap made a sound like a firecracker. Cool as a cucumber, Esther was. Not a wince. Not the slightest bit remorseful or sympathetic. Let me tell you, the fellow was no good, but my own knees ached for a week just witnessing that, and I trembled in fear for a month every time she picked up that skillet to fry the morning bacon."

Russell chuckled.

Fischer looked skeptical. "Well, be careful anyhow."

Arvid nodded, and he and Russell rose and began slipping on their jackets. "You still have Jessie's Hawk in your lot, don't you?" Russell asked.

"Yes, but I have good news. I think we can release her motorhome tomorrow, so perhaps she won't need to rent an interim vehicle. The forensics technician is coming this afternoon. I'll call her by ten tomorrow morning and let her know for certain." Fischer rose and shook each man's hand. "Sure appreciate the collaboration on this." As Russell and Arvid turned to go, the Sheriff held up his hand in a stop gesture. "Just a second." He scribbled on the back of one of his business cards and handed it to Russell. "Here's the address for Collin Bingham. Let me know if he gives you anything worthwhile."

"Will do." Russell tucked the card in his pocket.

"Oh. And watch out for his dog. He's got a big monster of a hound."

Arvid nodded, tossing Fischer a sloppy salute.

..*

Russell looked at Arvid after they'd exited the Sheriff's Office and rounded the corner of the hallway. "Guess you've got the hound thing covered, huh, Arvid? I mean, you're the one with experience with big dogs." Russell snorted in amusement. "They don't come any bigger than that Mastiff of yours."

"Poop." Arvid snickered. "Fischer was afraid of Jack. *Jack.* Can you imagine? That hound he claims is so fierce is probably the size of a Chihuahua."

"Hope it isn't a Chihuahua. Take it from me. They'd just as soon gnaw your ankle as look at you." Russell tapped his fingers and thumb together rapidly like biting teeth and grinned. "They're the worst."

Chapter Twenty-five

Forensic Investigator, Monte Taggart, stood in the beautifully appointed, tidy kitchen of the Hawk looking around appreciatively. He liked the solid cherry cabinets and the cheerful Native American motif of the dinette set. A lovely small painting of peonies was screwed—he peered closely—yes, actually screwed, to the wall. *Hmm. Guess it keeps it from shifting if the road is rough.* He stepped forward, his large bootie-covered shoes making a scuffling sound like boots through dry leaves.

Unfortunate that the motorhome was too large to pull into the garage at the Sheriff's Office, he thought. In an ideal world, even small towns would have a secure, climate-controlled facility, not this podunk outdoor shelter more suitable for storing hay.

Actually, from the shreds he'd noticed here and there, he realized someone *still* stored hay in the shelter during the winter.

As Taggart worked, he spoke into a small hand-held recorder used to document his findings during each evidence recovery job. Too bad he'd found no obvious clues that anyone except the owner had been inside the Greyhawk. Although he'd lifted numerous fingerprints, all the fingerprints probably belonged to the same woman. It would take a few days to go through it all. One thing was certain. Unless the lady who owned the motorhome was stronger than most women, she wouldn't have had enough strength

159

to shove the body into that storage unit. Not without help. And not without disturbing more of the snow near the vehicle.

Monte swabbed the inside of the door handle and steering wheel of the vehicle, and then decided to do both seat-belt buckles. The swabs would be checked for DNA. Maybe the victim had never been inside the interior areas of the motorhome, but he prided himself on being thorough. The storage area of the big vehicle had probably just been a convenient place to stash the body. By the police report, it was suspected that he'd been killed in the parking lot, not the well-appointed motorhome.

Poor bugger, he thought, imagining the victim crammed into the storage area like a bundle of old cloth. *Poor, poor bugger.*

He peered down at the pet entrance installed in the door of the Jayco Greyhawk. Cat, or small dog, he figured, judging by the few nuggets remaining in the bowl of pet food. He unlocked the pet door and pushed the vinyl flap back and forth. It was too small for a person to slide through. He spoke again into his recorder. Stepping out of the Greyhawk, he turned and pulled the outer door firmly closed. Having processed both the interior and exterior of the assigned vehicle, he removed his booties and gloves, then strode toward his van with a light step, humming to himself as he walked. He slid behind the wheel of his trusty van, made a note of the time in his notebook—padding the expended time by forty-five minutes—and grinned.

A good day's work for a good day's pay.

* * *

At dusk, a masked intruder walked under and around the Hawk. The raccoon's curious nose sniffed the tires. It stood on its hind feet, nose twitching, testing the air. When it reached the step to the door, it clambered up the steps and sniffed again. Then it stuck its head through the pet door Monte Taggart had neglected to lock. The marauder swiveled its head, peering cautiously around. Something smelled delicious. With dexterous paws the coon pulled at cupboards not properly closed by the investigator, unwound paper towels, and hit the jackpot when it discovered a full bag of cat food under the kitchen sink. Dragging the sack out and chewing

160

through the heavy paper to liberate the kibble was a task of mere minutes. Soon, after devouring half a bag of seafood medley, it pushed its way back out the pet hatch and ambled away, leaving the remains to the shadow that followed the raccoon's nightly rounds.

A second animal scurried up the steps.

Chapter Twenty-six

Bingham Farm

Arvid and Russell turned at the Bingham mailbox. It was shaped like an enormous shotgun shell and had, ironically, been the unfortunate target of some target shooting. It was peppered with holes that were beginning to get an edge of rust. Arvid grinned. "You gotta love Montanans, Russell. They come up with the craziest rural mailboxes."

"I still like yours better. Pretty hard to beat a Viking ship being attacked by a sea serpent."

"Esther gets most of the credit for that idea," Arvid replied, "but ja, it's hard to beat."

The pickup rumbled down the heavily graveled lane, bordered on each side by a rail fence with rough pine poles, both weathered to grey. Arvid avoided the worst of the puddles left by the melting snow. The fence around the rambling farmhouse had been painted white. On top of several posts perched bluebird houses waiting for new occupants.

As they pulled up to the house, a large brown dog barreled around the corner of the building, sending up an alarm of deep-chested whoofs. It stopped near the porch and continued its throaty bellows. The dog's wide stance showed off a massive chest. It was a beefy, heavily-muscled animal ready to rumble.

"Fischer wasn't kidding," Russell said. "That dog must be some kind of Rhodesian ridgeback mix."

"Ja. It's huge. I'm thinking maybe part bullmastiff and part Mount Rushmore." Arvid watched the dog, trying to judge its threat level and shook his head. "We're not getting out until the Binghams open the door. They can't miss hearing that dog's racket. And Russ," he continued, "when we *do* get out, don't shut your pickup door until they get that animal under control. We might have to jump back into the truck." They sat inside the pickup and looked toward the white house, waiting to see if the dog's alarm would bring the owners.

In a few seconds, the door swung open and two people stepped out onto the narrow porch. They were well-matched. The woman was short, heavy hipped and blocky, dressed in worn, capacious blue jeans. Her husband was short and square, put together as solidly as a concrete roadblock. Both had short grey hair. They were a couple built in the generation of heavy battleships—solid and dependable and as ready for combat as the dog.

They gazed at Arvid and Russell with unfriendly eyes but were courteous enough to call the dog. The big animal turned feverishly around in a circle several times but then turned and trotted to the woman's side. It licked her hand and she laid a soothing hand on its head.

Russell and Arvid exited the vehicle, stood by their open doors, and nodded to the couple.

"Morning," Arvid said. "I'm Detective Sergeant Arvid Abrahmsen and this is Sheriff Russell Bonham. We're from Sage Bluff and are collaborating with the Crooked Creek Sheriff's Office for a spell."

Russell nodded with a, "Hello."

"Sheriff Fischer asked us to come out and visit with you." Arvid continued, "Is this a good time?"

The woman's expression softened.

"Good a time as any, I guess," Bingham growled, but his eyes held less animosity. "Fischer sent you, huh? Then you might as well come in."

Arvid and Russell shut the pickup doors and turned. As Russell took the first step toward the house, the dog bared his teeth and started toward him, chest low to the ground, menace erupting into snarls.

Both men took a step back, their hands gripping their pickup door handles. As they retreated, the dog paused, head thrust forward. His growls held a note of inquiry. Should I eat them? Or let them live?

"Hank! Come!" The answer came with the woman's sharp command. The dog turned, moved to her side and sat. His tongue lolled, giving him a friendly clown-like expression. A huge tail thumped a dull percussion on the wooden porch. "He won't bite. Not most folk, anyhow." She turned and opened the door. "Coffee's on. Just made a batch of cookies."

* * *

"Nah," Bingham said in answer to Russell's question. "I can't think of anybody who'd want to kill that sweet Adele. Or harass Berg Nielson, neither. He was a nice old guy. Sure glad he's dead, though."

Russell and Arvid's eyes met in surprise. Then Arvid's gaze met Collin Bingham's. The man was serious.

"Oh, Collin. You know how bad that sounds." Felicia Bingham stood and reached for the coffee pot, stepping to the table and filling the men's mugs. She opened the refrigerator, withdrew a carton of half and half and placed it by her husband's hand. "He means because Berg shot his boy. Ain't nobody'd want to live through that. The memory would be a living death."

Collin nodded. He doctored his coffee, sent an inquiring glance around the table and when nobody else wanted cream, he got up and returned the carton to the refrigerator.

"It would plumb do me in," he said gruffly. "Hard enough for old Berg to live through Addy's death. He worried whoever shot her was after him instead. Thought it was a case of mistaken identity. I wondered if the guilt over Addy might kill him. Then it went from bad to worse when the boy came home, and Berg shot him by accident." He stirred his coffee and looked down into the mocha brew. "God, what a horrible thing."

"Do you think he was right? I mean, that the shooter didn't expect it to be Adele?" Russell took a chocolate-chip cookie from the plate Felicia held out, murmuring his thanks. "Who might have wanted to shoot Berg Nielson?

"Been through all this with the Sheriff." Collin shook his head. "Poor Fischer means well. He sure wants to figure it out." He sighed. "Never heard of any hard feelings. And all the Nielson's had was the acreage. The land. Nobody but Addy and Dom would have inherited it. And I don't think the kids would sell. Not unless it was a desperate situation. Especially not that little Addy. That girl loved the farm. So, the killer still wouldn't get the property."

"It just makes no sense," Felicia said. "Addy was a pretty little thing. She always had a boy or two hanging around. My guess is some teenaged boy shot her in a jealous rage. But then, neither situation covers the notes Berg started getting." She wiped an eye. "And he hadn't told us about them. We heard about them only after he died."

"How about this new death, Felicia?" Arvid bit into a cookie and chewed thoughtfully. "Can you think of anyone who would have wanted to hurt Benny Potter?"

"Hmmph." Felicia pursed her mouth.

"He wasn't one of our favorite people," Collin Bingham said. He broke off half his cookie, reached down and fed it to Hank, who swallowed it in a gulp and looked expectantly up at his master hoping for another windfall. "He wasn't allowed on our property. I don't have any idea who killed him, but I'm not shedding tears."

"He tried to shoot our Hank," Felicia said. "I was making bread and had my hands full of flour. I washed my hands in a hurry, thinking maybe it was the UPS guy, but it took me so long to get to the door that Benny must have thought nobody was home. I was drying my hands when I heard the truck leave—you know, tires on gravel. So, I looked out the window to see who I'd missed. Benny's truck was already by the mailbox." She tapped her index finger on the table. "When he pulled out onto the highway, damned if he didn't stop." She tapped again. "I thought, 'what the heck is Benny stopping at our mailbox for? Then I saw him roll down the window of that old truck, poke a rifle out and aim. I don't know why I was so sure he was aiming at the dog, but I opened the door

165

and screamed, and Hank ran toward the porch, or he'd have gotten him for sure. When he saw me, he hit the gas and barreled away helter-skelter. He was going so fast he fish-tailed."

"Felicia is sure it was Benny." He took a sip of coffee. "I wasn't home, or I'd have hopped in the pickup and chased him down. I did catch him in town the next day and told him never to set foot on our property again unless he wanted a load of buckshot up his britches."

"Interesting," Arvid said. "What did he say?"

"Claimed it wasn't him. Said he hadn't even used his pickup that day and—"

Felicia jumped in. "But it *was* that rust bucket he drives. I recognized it."

Hank laid his broad head on Felicia's lap and looked at her with soulful deep-brown eyes.

"Yes, the nasty bastard tried to shoot my boy, didn't he?" She baby-talked to the huge beast.

"Were other folks' animals shot around here about that time, by any chance?" Russell directed the question to Collin.

"Not any that we know of, but Benny was always shooting at birds. Any birds. Songbirds, woodpeckers. Things you don't eat. Hunting is one thing. People who hunt eat the meat. But Benny drove around in that truck and used about anything for target practice. I don't hold with that. And lots of people had their grain bins, mailboxes, and outbuildings peppered with holes. Most likely teenagers with not enough to do, shooting holes in anything that looks easy to hit just out of boredom. But one of the neighbors said they thought it might be Benny."

"Why had Benny stopped at your place that day?"

"Don't know," Collin said. "Don't rightly care. Probably wanted to borrow something. I was so mad I forgot to ask. Just told him to stay the hell off our property."

"Huh," Arvid grunted. "Anything else you know that might be helpful?"

"Well." Felicia stood and got Hank a dog treat from a cookie jar on the counter. "Can't imagine it's important but I heard at the beauty shop that he was trying to find homes for his dogs."

"Do you know why?" Russell asked.

"Just heard he was finding homes for them. That's all I know. It was odd, because even if he tried to shoot Hank, his own dogs were like his babies. He truly loved those animals."

Arvid stood and nodded to Collin, then to Felicia. "Thanks so much for your time, and the coffee and cookies, Ma'am." Halfway to the door, he turned. "Say, do you happen to know who wound up with the dogs?"

"Yeah," Bingham replied. "The minister over at Crooked Creek Lutheran took them. Pastor Anderson. Not sure if she kept 'em or found someone in the congregation who gave 'em a home."

"Glad someone's taking care of them. Thank you again," Arvid said. "If something else occurs to you, please give us a call." He put a business card on the table.

Bingham picked up the card and read, "Piano lessons for reasonable rates? Tunes for tots?"

Arvid snatched it back and rummaged in his pocket. "Nup. That one's my wife's." His hand came out empty. He patted his shirt pocket, finding nothing. "Russ?"

Russell placed a card on the table and grinned at the couple.

As the door to the pickup shut on Russell's side, he burst out laughing. "Tunes for tots!"

"Hmmph." Arvid growled. He pointed the pickup down the lane and stepped on the gas.

* * *

Halfway back to Crooked Creek, Arvid said, "You know how I feel about my dogs."

"Yeah. You'd let 'em gnaw off your right hand if they were hungry. And I know what you're getting at."

"Let's hear it, then."

"Benny was planning on going somewhere. Someplace where he couldn't take his dogs. A plane trip or something," Russell suggested.

"It's what I think, too." Arvid slowed for a pheasant rooster that ran across the road and disappeared into the ditch."

"And if Benny was going somewhere, it might be because he was scared...thought he should get out of town."

167

"Could be he thought he was on the killer's list." Russell rubbed the back of his neck.

"All speculation," Arvid said. "Here's a different scenario. It strikes me there might be a reason he stopped at the end of the lane to take a pot-shot at Hank. Bet it's about the same distance from the road to a moving tractor in a field."

Russell gave him his full attention. "Yeah, probably a similar distance."

"Uh huh," Arvid said, hands tightening on the wheel, "Maybe old Benny was practicing."

Chapter Twenty-seven

Previous January - Motel near Savannah, Georgia

Harris Freeman tucked his airline ticket home into his wallet. He'd hitched a ride to Savannah with a buddy, planning to take the bus to Atlanta and fly to Billings from there. *Guess I'll have to rent a car now, since Wheels says he can't pick me up.* He looked out the window at the empty parking lot.

Nobody yet.

He picked up the small notebook he'd been using since he'd heard about Dom's death. *It's like I inherited Dom's penchant for list writing. Hell, maybe I inherited all his saluting ducks, too,* he thought, *as well as the Nielson ranch. And what am I gonna do with that place until I get out of the Army?* Then he thought about the Christofferson brothers. *If he sold a few acres, he could afford to pay someone to keep the place up for the next eighteen months of his military commitment. Then, he'd go home and see if he had the stuffing to be a rancher. Maybe the Christofferson brothers. They were already doing most of the work at his mom's place. Lately they'd said they'd prefer to have a contract for the work, since they were dealing with Harris and no longer with Althea, who they knew best. Probably because their lawyer brother thought they needed to do things more by the book.*

He thumbed through his notebook, glancing at the meticulous scribblings until he found a blank page. Picking up the motel pen, he noted the cost of the bus ticket. Then he pulled his phone out and re-checked the next day's flight schedule to make certain the bus would get him to the airport in plenty of time.

After that, he called Christofferson's law office and made an appointment for the day after his expected arrival in Crooked Creek. He noted that in his small journal as well. He'd already faxed the law office copies of the wills he and Dom had written, dated and signed—the wills written almost in jest when both expected to be deployed to Afghanistan. Harris had already signed every paper he could possibly sign—even without stepping foot in Crooked Creek. Richard Christofferson was good that way, experienced and thorough. Berg Nielson's ranch belonged to Harris now—lock, stock and barrel. He rubbed his chin, thinking. Becoming an unexpected landowner didn't make him feel any happier. It had come at too high a price. The newspaper article Christofferson had sent him told a downright gruesome story.

Poor Dom.

Harris pulled another piece of paper out of his pocket and took a photo of it with his phone, texting that to Christofferson's office with a brief explanation. It was better than sending an email, because his phone could send a handwritten signature with the note. He signed the phone screen. Then he opened his suitcase and pulled the threatening note he'd received in the mail—the one that had come with the art show flier—and photographed that with the intention of sending it to Christofferson as well. Strange how ominous just a few words could be. *Stay away or die.*

"Not that I plan on dying anytime soon," he muttered aloud. "But going back to Crooked Creek feels like heading for a battle-zone and not knowing who the enemy is."

He sat on the bed, the cheap mattress squeaking under his weight. Adele's shooting, the harassing notes that made Berg so paranoid he'd shot Dom on his homecoming...both had to be tied to someone wanting the Nielson place, he reasoned. And now, with the receipt of the note in the mail, he knew he'd become the next target. When he got back to Crooked Creek he was going straight to the Sheriff's Office. See if they could figure out what was going on.

Harris dropped the notebook into his suitcase and tossed the pen onto the rickety motel desk. Then he stuffed the threatening

170

note and his phone back into his pocket without realizing he had neglected to hit send.

A horn beeped out in the parking lot and Harris opened the door, a chill breeze blasting in. He waved a hand at the black vehicle. Then he ducked back inside, grabbed a jacket and stepped out, locking the motel door behind him.

He hurried to the black SUV and wrenched open the door. "Oh, I didn't expect *you*," he exclaimed. "Good to see you though, man. It's been a while."

The driver gave him a wide smile. "Last minute change. Hop in. I'm just the delivery boy. Got a contract here for you …something about taking care of your ranch for Althea. What a great deal. I'm going to get paid for bringing it all the way here."

"Really? A contract? And they paid your airfare to fly down? That's really strange. I hope they don't expect me to reimburse them. We've always done the agreement with just a handshake before."

The driver just looked at him with a blank expression and gave a shrug.

"Well, let me put it in the room first, then." He went back to the motel room and pitched it onto the bed. Then he returned to the SUV, stepped on the running board and jumped into the passenger seat. He yanked the seatbelt over his lap and spoke as he clicked it into place. "Colder than Montana out there, today. Just heard the weatherman say it was only thirty-one. Brr. So, where's my brother? Where are we headed?"

Chapter Twenty-eight

Crooked Creek Sheriff's Office

"Jacob, take these keys, jog over to the lot and bring the O'Bourne woman's motorhome back here. I told the fellows from Sage Bluff that I'd give her a call this morning. Too bad there isn't anyone in the area that does crime scene clean up, but she strikes me as a pretty tough little gal. She may as well pick it up and get at it."

"Will do, Sheriff." A look of elation crossed the young man's face.

"And be careful." Fischer gave him a stern look. "You ever drive anything that big before? If you haven't, I'll go get it myself."

"I can do it, Sheriff. Heck, they don't get any bigger than my dad's combine. It weighs seven and a half tons and has a 35-foot header. I'm an expert with that big sucker. I've been driving it since I was fifteen." He paused, thinking. "Maybe since I was fourteen. No. No, I guess I was a bit older than that. I was a freshman. You've gotta remove the header before you can take it on the road, and over by Hansen's there's that narrow bridge. You can't take the combine over that even with the header off. When we need to switch fields, I have to backtrack all the way over to—"

"Just go get it, will you?" Fischer said, rolling his eyes. "And since you're such an expert, I expect you to get it here in one piece. To hear Jessie O'Bourne talk about that motorhome, you'd think it was her first-born kid."

"Sure." Jacob looked crestfallen. "I can do that."

Fischer looked out the window as the young officer jogged past the building at a fast clip. His heart ached for the kid. He'd learned a hard lesson when Berg Nielson died. Jacob hadn't taken the old man seriously when he'd come in with the first few threatening notes. It was a grave error. Now, the kid was trying so hard to make up for it that he made a lot of stupid mistakes. Fischer shook his head sadly. It was another lesson for the kid to learn that no matter how hard you try it's just human to make mistakes.

And guilt is the worst. You can cope with fear. You can get over loss. But guilt never seems to go away. Yeah, he thought, thinking of poor choices he'd made during his early years. Guilt saps a lot of the joy out of life.

*   *   *

Jacob unlocked the driver's door of the Hawk and jumped into the seat, stretching out his long legs and flexing his fingers in anticipation as he put the key into the ignition. He put his hands on the wheel, and a big smile split his face.

He'd get it back in record time. In one piece. With no scratches. *Perfecto.* Who did Fischer think he was talking to, some amateur? He snorted, hit the gas and pulled out of the shelter and turned right onto the gravel road that cut through the rest stop parking lot and tied into Pump Station Road—the fast way back to the Sheriff's Office.

"Oh yeah. Short cut," he said aloud. Then he mimed talking into a microphone. "Here comes Jacob in the big fancy bomber. Give him some room, ladies and gentlemen." Then he sniffed. "Man, someone must've hit a skunk. I got a big whiff."

"Peeeyew," he gagged. "Whooee, that's nasty!"

He rubbed his nose as he edged into the turn leading into the rest stop and passed the area for trucker's parking. Behind him he heard a sound like sliding pebbles and he glanced quickly over his shoulder. *Crap.* Spilled dog food or something was rolling around on the kitchen hardwood floor. *The place is a mess. And Fischer worried about ME messing it up. That's rich.*

An odd hissing sound seemed to emanate from the rear of the vehicle as Jacob drove slowly by several parked cars. He sniffed again. Then he spasmed in his seat. Quickly, he again glanced over his shoulder and his eyes bulged. A furry body eased out from under the dinette and flipped its black and white body so that its hindquarters faced Jacob. The fluffy tail stood up and waved like a beauty queen on a parade float. As the little animal backed in Jacob's direction, swaying with the swerving of the vehicle, it squirted copious amounts of fluid to the left and right.

"Shit!" The motorhome swerved, glancing off the back fender of a Toyota and taking the tailgate off a beat-up blue pickup.

Jacob froze at the steering wheel. He couldn't take his eyes off the business end of the skunk, now atomizing the entire interior of the motorhome. His throat burned. His eyes stung like he'd been pepper sprayed. Gagging, he jerked his foot off the gas and covered his mouth with his hands. The Hawk swerved into the grassy area of the rest stop, digging its tires into the moist sod, scattering screaming visitors. Jacob clawed frantically at his eyes. The tail of the motorhome caromed off the concrete corner of the tourist information sign touting local dinosaur digs, mashing the back end of the vehicle. Then it lurched to a stop with the nose of the Hawk butted against the women's restroom door.

Jacob exploded from the cab in a dive and rolled onto the grassy lot. Behind him, a furry body scrambled out of the open door and ambled fluidly off, the black and white fur rippling like waves on a lake as it scurried away, accompanied by wave after wave of putrid scent.

"Oh, man." The voice was a twangy whine. A burly trucker stood over Jacob, slapping his cap against his thigh. "I been drivin' long haul a lot of years, and I seen a lot of accidents. But I ain't seen nothing like that flippin' beauty. Whooooeee. Deputy, from the stink of it and the mashed-up back end, I think your insurance company is just gonna total that baby out."

174

The sound of frantic pounding and yelling came from the ladies' restroom. "Hey! What kind of stunt is this? Hey, let us out!"

"And if you didn't smell so bad and you wasn't a cop, I'd whomp you a good one. I'm hauling this load on a tight deadline. And I can't leave now. You know why?" He scowled down at Jacob. "You know why I can't make deadline? Because my old lady's stuck in the can, that's why. She's gonna be madder than a wolverine with a migraine."

Jacob groaned.

Chapter Twenty-nine

March - Crooked Creek Art Expo

Glen was gesturing toward the largest sculpture in his display room and grinning at his potential client. "It's the best one I've ever done," he said, "And definitely one of my personal favorites."

His customer, a man dressed in a blue Hawaiian shirt with a swordfish pattern, bent down to peer at the detail in the long pack-train bronze. A rider astride a muscled horse led three pack horses laden with panniers, one with elk antlers piled atop the supplies and wrapped meat.

"Where did you get the idea for this one, Glen?" He straightened up and fingered the price tag.

"Up in the Kalispell area, near the Canadian border...we had a pretty good hunt that year." Glen looked closely at his price tag and then told the man, "I can come down a thousand for you, Butch, since you're a repeat buyer. One of my favorite clients. Make it about fifteen thousand five hundred." He looked expectantly at the man, who stroked his chin and seemed to consider the price.

Jessie sat in Glen's small easy chair while he and the man exchanged good-hearted banter. She thumbed through a motorcycle magazine on Glen's end table. My gosh. Glen was worse than her dentist. Why have such an old magazine? She looked at the issue date. It was two years old. One article on antique Harley Davidson motorcycles made her open her eyes wide. She'd had no idea they were worth so much money. As much as her Greyhawk. Thinking of the Hawk, she scowled.

When am I going to get it back?

She pulled her attention back to the big sculptor and his customer.

"It's a done deal, then," Glen was telling the man. "Fifteen even and you pay the shipping, Butch." He slapped the smaller man on the back. "You drive a hard bargain. But I appreciate you, man."

Butch beamed. His eyes had the gleam of a man who looked in the mirror and imagined a killer negotiator looking back.

"Oh, that's exciting," Jessie said, putting the magazine down and standing to give the man a wide smile. "Where are you going to put your new piece?"

"This one's going in my corporate office, I think." He looked at Jessie with appreciation. "Or perhaps the cabin in Vail." He held out his hand to shake Jessie's. "You're the guest artist, aren't you? Jessie O'Bourne? I just bought one of your wildlife paintings—the 20 x 40 of the mule deer coming down the game trail. I may hang it above this sculpture of Glen's."

"I'm delighted," Jessie said cheerfully, "and pleased it will be in such great company. Glen's sculptures are fabulous."

After a few minutes of small talk, Butch left, and Glen grabbed Jessie by the arm. "He was an early appointment," Glen said. "He wanted first pick before the show opened. Shall we lock the room, and take our ride? They plowed this morning and with the sunshine we're getting today we shouldn't have any trouble. I'm anxious to show you my new bike. Once you try the Harley you're going to want one, Jess," he said in a voice booming with confidence. "You flat out won't be able to resist." He glanced at the magazine Jessie had put down. "See anything you can't live without? There are some valuable bikes in that collector's issue. Pricey. I'd have to sell a bunch of these big pieces to buy the one I'd like to own."

Jessie laughed, thinking of a couple pages of bikes with price tags more like those of second homes for wealthy clientele. "I'll take your word for it. I don't know a thing about motorcycles. This is going to be my first experience on anything with two wheels. Well, except my old Schwinn."

Glen steered her through the door and locked it. "Well, you're in for a treat, and since I just made a wonderful sale, the cinnamon rolls and coffee are on me. There's a place here in town, the Black Cow Coffee Shop, that has the best pastries you ever tasted." He gave her a leering smile. "I'll warn you, I'm going to be your favorite person after this. Wait and see. Our first date, Jessie. When I feed a gal, I call it a date."

Jessie threw back her head and laughed, "I've been there." Then she shook her finger at him. "Oh, a date, huh? You must think I'm a pretty cheap date, mister. A cinnamon roll? No, I don't call it a date unless I get fed steak. Or prime rib." She grinned to let him know she was teasing. "I'll bet you were the kind of teenager who took your date to the Gas 'n' Go on Saturday night and bought her a piece of beef jerky and day-old nachos with easy cheese."

"Nah. I sprung for a coke, too. What do you think I am? Cheap?"

In the parking lot, Glen handed her a helmet. "Here, put this on. See if you can cram all that red hair in there." He put on his own helmet. "And wait until you see these cinnamon rolls. They're as wide as a dinner plate. You won't be dissing my dating skills. Besides, I'm not *that* out of practice."

Jessie got on the bike, then put on the helmet and wrapped her arms as far as she could around Glen's middle. As they sped down the street she hung on and said a few Norwegian gems under her breath. But after several blocks, she was having a blast. If it was this much fun to go 32 miles an hour in town, what it would be like out on the open road? *Exhilarating*, she thought. Then she saw a small spatter spread across the faceplate of her helmet. *And buggy.* Especially in mid-summer when some of the grasshoppers in Montana seemed the size of small birds. Glen cut a corner on the next block and hit the gas. Jessie began to feel exposed on the Harley.

Motorcycles are notoriously bad in an accident. Deadly.

She wanted something nice and big to drive—aka safer—for trips to rural places where she could paint outdoors. In Sage Bluff, she used an old Ford truck she'd driven in high school. It was perfect. And she liked having a vehicle that allowed her to take Jack along. Maybe when she went to choose her loaner, she'd give something larger a try. Maybe an F350 pickup.

They ground to a halt at a stoplight, next to exactly the kind of pickup she had in mind. It was a large blue Ford F350 that loomed over the Glen's cycle. Jessie grinned. It was almost like she'd conjured up the big vehicle. The Harley rumbled underneath her as Jessie stared at the behemoth next to them. Involuntarily, she took one hand from Glen's waist and flexed her fingers. In her mind, she mixed ultramarine and a touch of cobalt—colors she figured would achieve the blue color of that mirror-like polish. Her hand made a tentative stroke with an imaginary brush.

Glen gave a whoop and twisted the throttle. The bike lurched forward, jarring Jessie back into the present. She hurriedly put her hand back on his waist. As they passed the pickup, Glen tossed the driver a wave.

By the time they pulled up in front of The Black Cow Coffee Shop, Jessie was daydreaming about what color pickup she'd rent. *Cherry red*, she thought. *Cadmium. Maybe with a glint of metallic.*

* * *

"Oh, Lordy," Jessie exclaimed as the chubby waitress set the cinnamon roll down in front of her. She looked up at the server. "I can tell you right now I'm going to need a take-out box."

"Most folks do," the waitress said with a knowing look. Then she looked at Glen.

"Nope. No box here. I might even eat her extra half," he said.

The waitress nodded and hurried off.

Jessie took a sip of coffee, then cut the roll in two, pushing one half to the side of the plate and slathering the other with butter. She cut off a piece and popped it into her mouth. "Yum. You were right. Best rolls ever, except for those my friend Shelly bakes." She bit into another piece, savoring the cinnamon and raisin center thoughtfully. "Hmmm. A close tie, but Shelly wears the crown— queen of any kind of sweet roll. Of course, I give her extra credit because she and her husband own a couple of my paintings." Her

179

mouth turned down, remembering that she'd helped the couple find their daughter's killer the year before.

"That doesn't count. You have to judge on the sweet roll alone." He seemed to register Jessie's thoughtful expression. "What are you thinking? You look sort of down. Are you getting soured like me? Sick of selling work you poured your whole heart into to people with so much money they don't bother to count it? Seems like every time I sell a sculpture it's to someone who packs it away in their collection and barely thinks about it afterward."

"No. I wasn't thinking that." Jessie answered. She pushed thoughts of the dead Reynolds girl away and tried to smile. "I'm always tickled to sell my work, whether it's a large expensive showpiece or a little 8 x 10." She frowned at Glen. "Don't you think it's obvious they love your work when they decide to buy? I don't expect to be the only one whose work they appreciate. You're a wonderful sculptor. People buy your pieces because they're so good. Destined to be collector's items or family heirlooms."

"Hmph." Glen frowned back at her. "Thanks, but it gets my goat. Like this guy who just bought the pack train sculpture. He won't remember he even owns it once he puts it in his corporate office. He's only there a few weeks out of the year. Hell, he probably thinks I'm like a clerk at the dollar store. My price tags are peanuts to people like that. You and I both know he could have afforded to pay full price. It costs a fortune to cast something that big in bronze."

Jessie made murmuring sounds of agreement. She did indeed know how expensive it was to cast a bronze. "I do know. Framing a large painting costs quite a bit but not like casting a bronze sculpture. Especially a big one."

"Two grand. I came down two grand because he wants to feel like a fabulous negotiator. It makes him feel important. And that's the only time that jerk ever buys." He took a bite of roll. "Ah well. I needed the money."

"I understand what you're saying. But personally, I don't mind giving people a bit of a break. Especially if they've bought artwork from me before."

180

"Well, not me." He scowled. "I'm tired of not getting top dollar for my work. After all, I won't be able to sculpt forever. There's too much repetitive motion with sculpting and I'm getting older." He gave her a fake leer. "I'm not TOO old, you understand." Then his expression became serious. "But arthritis is starting to give me problems with my hands." He flexed his fingers. "And the continual modeling of the wax is causing carpal tunnel."

"That's too bad." Giving Glen a sympathetic look, Jessie took a last bite of her roll, then put the other half in the go box. "That has to be a huge worry. Have you been to a doctor? They can do a lot with carpal tunnel problems even with exercises alone."

Glen avoided her gaze. "Uh huh. I'm not worried. Somehow, I just have a feeling my ship is about to come in. And it's going to be a super tanker." He made a fist pump. Then he chuckled, gave her a warm smile and picked up the check as he got to his feet. "Let's head back. We don't want to miss that boat. Just in case it docked while I was showing you such a good time. With my extreme dating skills and all that."

Jessie rolled her eyes and stood, picking up her go box.

"Besides," Glen continued. "I heard about the cops messing up your motorhome. That's tough luck. How about we stop off at the Harley place and see if you can rent a bike? Ten to one they have a couple they use for exactly that."

Jessie laughed. "No, thanks! If I decide I need a rental, I've got my eye on a pickup."

Glen blew her a raspberry.

Chapter Thirty

Arvid held the phone to his ear, listening to Sheriff Fischer explain about the motorhome. He turned his head to the side and choked back a laugh. Esther looked at him with inquiring eyes.

"Nup." Arvid choked out. "Jessie must have her phone off. She wanted to set up supplies—you know, paint and canvas—for her painting demo before she came down to pick up the motorhome." Arvid looked at his watch. "Yep. She asked me to bring her down. And it does sound like news you should break in person, not over the phone. I imagine there's paperwork involved." He listened. "Hmmm. I've never had that experience, either. I'm not exactly sure what the protocol is. But we were planning to head your way in about twenty minutes." More mumbling from the phone and then Arvid said firmly. "Oh, no you don't. Uh uh. Not me."

He felt sorry for Fischer. But not sorry enough to be the one who told Jessie about her beloved Hawk. "I'm not going to do your dirty work." He grimaced and looked at Esther. "I doubt it. But if you think the situation could use a woman's touch, ask her yourself." He held the cell phone out to Esther and doubled over. "It's Fischer," he grunted.

"This is Esther Abrahmsen. How are you this fine day, Sheriff Fischer?" She glanced at Arvid in alarm. He was now holding his stomach and wheezing. "Oh, not good. I'm so sorry. Hmmm. Yes …skunked. Totaled? Ah…I see." Her eyes twinkled as she

182

murmured into the phone in a soothing, sympathetic and cultured tone. "Nooo. I'm so sorry to hear about that. Jessie will be devastated. Absolutely devastated...I see. You want me to warn her and soften the blow?"

She waggled her finger at Arvid and waved her hand in front of her face as though fanning away fumes. Then she stuck her tongue out and pulled a stinky face, pretending to hold her nose before speaking into the cellphone, still in her dulcet tones. "Wild horses, Sheriff Fischer." She straightened her spine and scowled. "I'm sure you know the cliché. The proverbial wild horses, bison bulls and red devils couldn't coerce me to do your dirty work. Pull up those big boy boxers and tell Jessie yourself." Then she added sweetly. "Have a wonderful day." She handed Arvid his cellphone. "The nerve of that coward."

Arvid grabbed her around her waist and pulled her to him in a bear hug. He dropped a kiss on the top of her head. "That's my girl."

* * *

Arvid glanced sideways at Jessie, sitting in the passenger seat of his pickup and looking pleased to be on the way to pick up her Hawk.

Man, I should probably warn her, he thought. *A teenager with his first car has nothing on the way she feels about that motorhome.*

"Uh, you know, there seemed to be something sort of iffy about you picking up the Hawk today when I talked to Fischer. Maybe it isn't quite ready. I'll help you find a good rental if that's the case."

"Nah. He said it was good to go when I talked to him this morning. But thanks anyhow, Arvid."

"But you know, things happen."

"They'd better not happen," Jessie snapped. "The Sheriff's Office should be done with it by now. I need the Hawk. Half my wardrobe is in the closet."

"I'm just sayin'. If for any reason you do need a rental, maybe you can...uh...find a good pickup or something to tide you over.

183

Er...until you have things figured out." He scratched the back of his head, near the band of his blue ballcap.

Jessie looked at him with suspicion. "There's something you aren't saying. Spit it out, Arvid."

"Ah," he said, pulling into a parking place in front of the Sheriff's Office. "Look at this. Are we lucky or what? A space right in front." He pushed open the door of his pickup, hurriedly locked it and began striding with purposeful steps toward the entrance, his long legs covering ground like a long-distance runner.

When Jessie caught up to him he'd already knocked quickly on Sheriff Fischer's door and was shoving it open. She followed him in and saw Sheriff Fischer standing behind his desk, a look of resignation on his craggy face.

Fischer cleared his throat. "Uh. Yes, hello, Miss O'Bourne," he began. He looked over at Arvid. Arvid's face was impassive and he gave a slight shake of his head. Fischer met Jessie's eyes and said gruffly, "There's...well. An unfortunate problem has come up regarding your motorhome."

"Oh, really?" Jessie glanced from Sheriff Fischer to Arvid. She noted the look on Arvid's face. Then she realized the Sheriff was standing as uncomfortably in his own office as though he'd been visiting for the first time. Apprehension skittered up her spine like a fat spider on a fragile web.

"Omigosh." She felt her knees go weak. "Did you find evidence the killer had been inside the Hawk after all?"

"No." Fischer raised his eyebrows. He held a palm up in a gesture of denial. "No. Nothing leads us to believe that—" He was interrupted by a series of sharp raps that rattled the office door. "Who is it?" he barked.

The door swung inward and Jacob stepped in. His face was pale. His jaw was clenched. Then he looked around the room, met the Sheriff's surprised gaze, nodded at Arvid and then at Jessie.

He spoke directly to her. "I'm Deputy Williams. Jacob Williams." He cleared his throat. "I should be the one to talk to you." His gaze swung to meet Fischer's. "Uh, you know, there've been times when I was clowning around a bit and you would tell me to grow the hell...er...sorry...to grow up. I figured now was as good a time as any." He shifted his weight from foot to foot. Then

184

his glance focused on Jessie again. "Well, here's the thing, Miss O'Bourne. I've been driving combine since I was nigh as tall as dad's waist, so I sure thought I wouldn't have a lick of trouble with your motorhome. Combines are huge suckers. I mean they're really huge and—"

Sheriff Fischer made a rolling motion with his hand, urging Jacob to move the story along.

Jessie's eyes glazed over. She was standing close to the young man and a singularly unpleasant and quite recognizable smell was wafting from his direction. She coughed and backed several paces toward Arvid.

"It was over at the field near one of the rest stops, you know? The motorhome, I mean. It's not near as big as a combine, and the Sheriff here, well he told me to go get it and ...

* * *

Fifteen minutes later, Jessie opened the door to the Hawk and peered cautiously in. She withdrew her head immediately and staggered back. Arvid leaned over, hands on his knees. "Hooooeee. The stench just hits you like a wave, don't it?"

"Omigod! It's hideous. I don't see how anyone could salvage a blessed thing out of it." She pinched her nose with the fingers of one hand. She turned to Arvid, snatching the cap off his head, and swatting him hard on the shoulder with it, complaining nasally. "Why didn't you warn me, you big lumbering Norsky goof?"

"Aw, Jessie. I figured you'd know soon enough." He straightened and grabbed his cap. "That's assaulting an officer, you know."

"Well, you're out of your jurisdiction, so it doesn't count."

"Huh." He grunted, then rubbed his shoulder as though she'd conked him with a boulder as big as Billings. "Guess I deserved that. Anyway, getting back to the Hawk, I agree. The insurance agent for the county that Fischer called will have to take a look, but even if they can find someone willing to clean it—and even if those folks do a super job—I think there'll still be times it'll stink. Especially in any sort of humidity. Rain. Snow. Using the shower.

There just isn't a good way to remove the smell from carpet or even wood paneling. And a mechanic has to give estimates on repairs, too."

"Yeah." Jessie looked at the Hawk and her expression darkened. "I'm going to have to rent something. I'll need something big enough to haul paintings in as soon as this show is over." She threw up her hands in disgust. "Arvid, I can't even think about it right now. I'd like to just pull my hair out, I'm so annoyed. But I've got to get back for the demo. Can we go?"

"Sure." He slapped his cap back on and gave the Hawk a thoughtful look. "You know, the insurance agent may just total it out. I can't imagine there are many people willing to clean a mess like that. Add that to the damage caused when the kid bounced it into the concrete pillar. Yup. I think the Hawk's a goner."

"We'll see, I guess."

"What would you buy in its place?" He held open the pickup door for her.

After he slid into the driver's seat, she said, "Something similar to the Hawk. Maybe exactly the same thing. It's like a rolling art studio. It holds all the supplies for plein-air painting, handles hauling the framed work to and from galleries and shows and is just as comfortable as a hotel room. It's been a great investment. Now I wonder if I'll be able to get past the memory of finding Benny in the laundry chute. That memory is worse than this smell."

"Yep. I hear you." Arvid snapped his seat belt closed. "Well, let's get back. You too upset to do your demo?"

"I'll be okay once I get started. After the first few brush strokes I can't think of anything but my painting. It centers me. It'll be fine."

She thought about what Sheriff Fischer said about the young man who wrecked the Hawk. "I'm probably in a lot better shape than poor young Jacob. Imagine how guilty he must feel. First, not taking that old man seriously, and now being responsible for damaging such an expensive vehicle. At least Sheriff Fischer seems understanding."

"Uh huh. Mostly because the kid came in and told you about it himself. That took guts," Arvid said, glancing in his rear-view mirror before pulling out into the street. "Haw. I'll bet Jacob thought he was the biggest dog in the yard when he got to drive the Hawk. Can you imagine looking back into the motorhome and seeing that black and white tail end working its way toward you?" Arvid gave a slight chuckle.

Jessie glared at him. Her precious Hawk was a mess. *Ruined.* And was he snickering?

Arvid's breath came out in a whoosh and he guffawed. Jessie couldn't help it. Her lips curved in a smile. She pictured the southwest tones of her motorhome interior. The rich hues of sunset and red rock. The cherrywood cupboards and paneling. Jacob feeling on top of the world driving such elegance. And then, backing down the center of the main living space came a waving black and white tail. She gave a giggle.

"And then trapping those poor women in the restroom," Arvid hooted. "I wonder if the kid has a girlfriend. There isn't enough men's cologne in the store to cover that stench. He's gonna smell for a week." A huge belly laugh erupted from the big man and Arvid shook his head and smacked the dash with the palm of his hand. "Haw haw!"

Jessie grimaced. Then grinned. Then she gave a snort of laughter, and soon her shoulders began to shake.

Chapter Thirty-one

Crooked Creek Art Expo - Demo

Standing in front of her easel, poised to begin her demo, Jessie's stomach ached from laughing. She gave the waiting audience a wide smile. This afternoon, she wore a painting apron with an Arbuckle coffee logo and her hair was pulled up into a short pony tail. Her painting palette was organized, tubes of paint and a small jar of thinner at the ready. Her brushes were set out.

Instead of working from photo references as originally planned, Jessie had opted to invite Lissa, one of the teenage volunteers—a waif-like girl with dark hair—to sit for a portrait. She adjusted the light near the model's chair, angling it to brighten one side of the face and throw the other side of the face into dramatic shadow. She brushed the girl's hair to the side, away from her forehead and brows. Then she stepped back to the easel.

Jessie twirled one red curl around and around a finger, squinting at the lovely picture the girl presented. There was a glow of reflected light—a beautiful note of color—under Lissa's chin, bounced from a red scarf draped casually over her shoulder. Lissa's bone structure was delicate and her skin tones were...*hmm*. She'd begin with yellow ochre, cadmium red light, and a bit of burnt sienna and white. Of course, first she'd block in the masses of deep shadow on the left side of Lissa's face. Gold and silver hoops marched the length of the ear facing the light, and on the ear in shadow, a cross-shaped earring glinted, drooping from a silver wire. The girl had beautiful eyes. A bit sorrowful.

The teen years are never all sunshine and roses, Jessie thought. *Teenage angst. I wouldn't go back to being sixteen unless someone put a million bucks in my name in an interest-bearing offshore account. Maybe two million.*

Jessie scowled, wondering what a new Greyhawk motorhome cost.

Heck, I can't think about that now.

Lissa glanced nervously at Jessie, and Jessie gave her a thumbs-up gesture and what she hoped was a reassuring smile. As though captured in a series of snapshots, the girl began to metamorphose in Jessie's mind to simply a mass of darks and lights, colors, and hard and soft edges. She looked down at her palette, images of Lissa's face and form solidifying in her mind's eye, and picked up a brush, swiping it into the paint.

Max Watson stood on a small platform near the covered pool. He held a microphone, tapping it on the side with the tip of his index finger. The mic complained and whistled like a hot teakettle. He adjusted the volume and tapped again, seeming happier with the subsequent lighter screeching *phweet* of the microphone. He went into his spiel.

"Are we having fun yet?" This was met by clapping and several yeehaws. "I'd like to introduce our guest artist, Jessie O'Bourne, who put on her cowgirl boots and stepped in for Georgina Goodlander. Today, she'll be painting a two-hour portrait study titled "Lissa in Red". Jessie will take several short breaks during the demo to give her model time to stretch. During those short breaks, she'll be glad to answer any questions. Our servers will make the rounds with wine and the best hors d'oeuvres this side of the Mississippi while Jessie works her magic." He waved his arm toward a long counter. "There's also a no-host bar."

Sporadic clapping emphasized his words.

"After the demo, feel free to stick around and visit with the artist. You can see more of Jessie's work in the Crooked Creek Museum's display room." This brought more clapping. Max placed the microphone in the stand on his small platform and stepped down. "You need anything, Jessie?" he asked as he approached her demo area.

189

She continued to glance at Lissa, then back to the canvas, broad strokes of her brush blocking in the cheek area on the rapidly developing portrait. She picked up a soft rag, wiped her brush and used it to pick up a glob of burnt umber. "I think a little ultramarine blue," she murmured. "Just a squinch. It'll add richer depth to the darks." She picked up a palette knife and dabbed a dot of blue into the umber mix, then used the flat side to mix the two colors.

"No," Max said, watching the process. "I mean, do you need a bottle of water or something?"

Jessie spared him a look. "Oh. That was you asking, Max? Hey, sorry. I would love a big go-cup of coffee. Strong. Thanks."

"Black?"

"Well, you get a richer dark if you mix the burnt umber and the ultramarine blue. Black is so harsh." She turned back to her work, making a curving stroke with the brush that gave a three-dimensional feel to the cheek.

Max gawked. "Jessie, you want cream in the coffee?"

"Geez no, sorry." She focused on him with an effort and smiled. "I just want coffee in my coffee. I'm Norwegian. We like it strong. Thank you."

"Got it. Dark and strong. No cream." Max watched the movement of the brush flick back and forth, up and down. In several swipes, the delicate cheekbone was sculpted, the orbital area of the eye took shape. He gave a slight shake of his head and turned to walk toward the lodge restaurant.

The sound of Evan Hanson's voice came over the mic at the other end of the room as he introduced Esther on the piano. A piano arpeggio rippled across the room and then Esther's voice said, "This next one is something new for me. It's a western piece I wrote especially for the Expo. I hope you enjoy it."

Jessie began to hum, her brush picking up speed with the fast-paced music.

* * *

She had answered numerous questions during the first break and was waiting for Lissa to return from the ladies' room. Someone

190

paused by the table and a well-manicured hand reached out to pick up a workshop brochure. "Anna Farraday. Remember me? We met at the check in desk when I first arrived. You were with your handsome cat."

"Of course. I remember. How nice of you to come and watch."

"I am thoroughly enjoying it, Jessie." She gestured to the portrait. "The likeness evolved so quickly. You nailed it. And with another hour to go I can't imagine what you even need to do to finish it."

"Oh, believe me, there's still plenty to do."

"I'll be interested to see it progress. I wondered if you'd be interested in coming to Anchorage this fall? I'm on a chamber of commerce board there and we're always looking for interesting classes for both locals and tourists. We've done writing classes, floral classes, astronomy classes—Northern lights and all that, you know—maybe it's time for you to teach one of your workshops in the Land of the Midnight Sun."

Jessie smiled. "I just might be interested. The flier you picked up has my contact information. We can visit more about particulars later. Please feel free to call me."

"I'll plan on it." As she left, a heavy-set man in western garb approached Jessie's easel. His stomach preceded him like the cow-catcher on an old time locomotive. He nodded to Jessie. "Hello." The man tipped his cowboy hat, then bent over from the waist to peer closely at the portrait of Lissa, resting his hands on his knees.

A server held out a tray to Jessie and she shook her head. Maybe after the demo she'd find something to nibble on. She sipped her coffee, glancing around at the milling crowd. Everyone seemed to be having fun.

Near the no host bar, Jessie spotted a familiar figure. It was the elderly man with the portable oxygen pack who'd been in the restaurant when she and Tate went out for cocoa. "The Gingerbread Man", the cafe hostess had called him. He was working his way through the crowd, carrying a small stack of his fliers. He stepped into one of the art rooms and disappeared.

"Say there." The big man who'd been examining the portrait took off his hat and reached out to shake Jessie's hand. "Really

191

like what you got going on here. Especially the fact that this here is a picture of the prettiest gal in town."

Jessie looked at him inquiringly.

"Lissa's my granddaughter," he explained. "I'd like to buy the finished portrait for her mama."

"Oh, how nice. I can't process the sale myself. My demos during the show will be sold by the museum staff in their gallery room. I donated the proceeds of the demos to their youth scholarship program."

"How much are they going to charge?"

Jessie hesitated. "I don't think they're asking too much. But I would go let them know now that you want it, Mr. ….?"

"Huffman. Gary Huffman. I appreciate it. Her mama's had a hard time of it lately. It'll lift her spirits."

"Grandpa!" Lissa was back and hugged Huffman around the waist. He gave her a squeeze, dropping a light kiss on the top of her head.

"Hey there, Beautiful Girl. I'm picking up this portrait for your mama when it's done. Get yourself back over there now, and let this young lady finish it." He made a shooing motion. "And your mama is doing much better today, Lissa. Real good." Lissa smiled broadly, then glided over to the seat and flopped into the chair with a more relaxed set to her body than she'd exhibited during the first painting session. Jessie rearranged the scarf so that it was approximately in the original position.

Almost perfect. Close enough, anyhow. Something had changed in the girl's eyes, too. Now, Lissa's lovely eyes had a happy sparkle. So that's it, Jessie thought. Not boy trouble or mean girls. A sick mother.

Jessie grabbed her brush, wanting to capture that happy expression on the girl's face before the end of the hour. Any mother would prefer her current cheerful expression to the gloomier one she'd shown earlier. Jessie again hummed under her breath while she worked. The brush danced quickly across the canvas and Jessie squinted twice at her model before making each brushstroke on the painting.

Finally, she began adding background, mostly neutral colors. A dull orange against the black hair in the portrait, with the color

192

complement of the bluish highlights on the girl's lovely mass of hair, added snap. *Hmmm.* It seemed too crisp. Jessie took a clean dry brush and lightly dragged it across part of the edge where the hair met the background. She wiped her brush on a rag and made another swipe at the crisp edge. Staring at the portrait now, not the model, she continued to work. It was her favorite part of painting—the time when every stroke seemed to have a life of its own.

She softened the outline of Lissa's hair, blending it to fade into the background. She softened the earlobe with the side of her little finger, then swiped the same finger, dull orange paint and all, across a harsh edge on the red scarf, melding the red with the dark color of Lissa's deep navy shirt. It added a softness. The scarf was no longer a single element competing with the face, but melded with the shirt, even picking up a bit of color from the background. It had become part of the whole package. Jessie hummed louder.

Glancing at her model, Jessie looked back at the painting and placed highlights in the pupils of the eyes and on the edge of the lower eyelid, then just a fleck of light on the metallic cross peeping out of the shadowed area. After wiping her brush, she lightly picked up some cadmium red on the tip and added a short stroke of soft red at the side of the nose, where the skin was always a warmer tone, then strengthened the reflected red highlight under the chin.

Jessie looked at her watch. Then in the lower right corner she signed the painting *Lissa in Red, demo, Jessie O'Bourne,* just as the two-hour buzzer sounded.

Max's voice announced, "That's the demo for today, folks. Now, don't forget that we have over fifty rooms of art, folks. Fifty rooms," he said again emphatically. "Something for everyone. And I hope to see you all tonight at Friday's quick-draw and auction."

Dropping her current brush into the jar of turpentine, Jessie wiped her hands on a rag. Her model stood and stretched. Around the easel, clapping began, and Jessie heard several whoops from Lissa's proud granddad. She smiled and gave the crowd a small, self-conscious wave. In her mind, she was still elaborating on bits of the portrait. A heightened awareness of shape, color and light made everything and everyone in the room seem crisp. Full of detail.

Across the room, she saw the Gingerbread Man come out of another art room in a shuffling, stooped gait. He looked up as though sensing her stare and met her gaze over thick glasses.

How strange.

Just for a second, he'd looked so much younger, so different, that she hadn't thought it was the same man she'd met. She raised her hand as though to shape the contours of his face with a loaded brush. She blinked and shook her head slightly.

Don't be daft. Yes, of course it's him—the elderly veteran.

He was slowly coming toward her.

Chapter Thirty-two

Billings Airport

Grant Kennedy peered out the airplane window as he felt the thump of the jet's wheels hitting the runway. Because of his delayed flight from Salt Lake City, he'd had to reschedule his flight to Montana. Once he disembarked, he planned to rent a car and make his way to Crooked Creek. Car? *Heck. I'd better see if I can rent something bigger and with four-wheel drive if the weather is still as lousy as the last report I heard.* Winter storm warning with winds and drifting snow. *In March?* He stared at his watch. *Blast! I'm sure to miss the opening reception if the roads are bad, but at least I'll be there in time for Friday evening's show and auction.*

He pulled his paperback, *"Hundreds and Thousands—the Journals of Emily Carr"*, from the seat pocket in front of him and tucked it into his briefcase along with the file he'd put together on Carr's artwork. The briefcase also held the auction catalog he'd requested from the director of the Crooked Creek Art Auction. What a lucky break that he'd called his Italian friend Vincenzo. Knowing Grant's obsession with old masters, "Vince" informed him that an estate lawyer he knew had consigned a small Carr painting to the upcoming auction at the request of a client. It might be within Grant's budget.

Grant read through the catalog on the flight and found no lot number for an Emily Carr painting. After double-checking every page, he frowned. Could it have been consigned too late for the piece to get into the printed catalog? The recent press releases and national magazine coverage hadn't mention a Carr painting, either. The painting would sell below value without publicity. Collectors of her work would not have the opportunity to bid on it.

The painting was 12 x 18 inches and of similar palette and style to *Autumn in France*, a piece that Carr painted in 1911. Grant had seen that particular piece in the National Gallery of Canada. He'd gone to Ottowa on the trail of a stolen Franz Hals as part of his job with the FBI Art Theft Division. The case came to an abrupt close when the tiny Hals painting was located by Dutch police. Since he was already nearby, Grant hadn't been able to resist a quick tour of the striking National Gallery, a gorgeous architectural creation of granite and glass.

Although, he had to admit, the gargantuan spider sculpture guarding the facility, *Maman* by Louise Bourgeois, did little more than give him the creeps. Goosebumps raised on his arms. Thirty feet of stainless steel and bronze spider, including marble eggs in a suspended sac was enough to give anyone night frights. *Brrr.* He had to remember to tell Jessie about it when he saw her at the show. He grinned from ear to ear, causing his seatmate to look at him quizzically.

Man, I'm so lucky that Jessie was invited to fill in for the show's original guest artist. I should go to Vegas after I'm done in Crooked Creek. Pleasurable expectation ran though him. He hummed under his breath.

Thank god for Arvid. After Jessie told the Sage Bluff Detective that she'd tried to call Grant and gotten a "wife's voice" on the answering machine, the big Norwegian had mulled it over for several weeks. Finally, Arvid had casually called Grant one morning to "say howdy". Grant answered the phone, plunked down on a wicker chair on the veranda of his Boston condo when he realized it was Arvid, and they'd visited for ten minutes about what was happening in Sage Bluff.

Then Arvid said abruptly. "We're pretty fond of Jessie. I got the feeling you were, too," Arvid said. "We don't want her hurt, Grant. You told her you were single, but are you actually married?" Getting Grant's immediate denial, Arvid told him that Jessie tried to return one of Grant's calls and reached a woman. A woman who identified herself as Mrs. Grant Kennedy. "Jessie said she didn't leave a message," Arvid told him, "But she was mad as a wet cat when she told Esther and me about it."

As they spoke, Grant realized his jealous ex-wife, Patricia, must have visited his condo while Grant was in Sage Bluff and had been there when Jessie phoned. She'd also changed the message on his answering machine—evidently hoping to ward off any female callers. He played the phony answering machine message over and over, boiling with frustration and annoyance. Her sultry message on the machine made it sound as though they were not only still married, but happy as a beagle with two tails.

Damn the woman. Patricia had several men dangling like puppets strung from her delicate fingers, but she was determined to punish Grant for divorcing her after discovering her numerous infidelities.

Grant had changed his locks, steaming. *Hell, no wonder Jessie never picked up when he called her cell. She thought he'd lied to her.*

It was lousy timing that he'd been sent to Europe the day after Arvid's call. That case had taken longer than usual and had snowballed right into another theft case. He still hadn't connected with Jessie to set her straight. She probably didn't give a damn, anyway. And even if she did, how could a long-distance relationship work? He slapped himself alongside the head every time he felt tempted to call. But now, he couldn't tamp down the feeling of excitement at the possibility of seeing her.

As the plane shuddered to a stop, Grant stood and helped the elderly woman to his right retrieve her carry-on from the overhead compartment. He grabbed his briefcase and followed the shuffling crowd down the aisle to the exit.

Come on. Come on. Move it.

He mentally shoved people out of the way until it was his turn to politely thank the flight attendant as he left the plane. He

197

stopped at the men's restroom in the terminal, made a pit stop and ran a comb through his blond hair. Then he splashed cold water onto his face to jolt himself awake. Wishing he hadn't needed to haul the big winter coat and boots, neither of which fit into a small carry on, he headed to the luggage carousel to retrieve his checked bag. He stewed until he saw his black luggage jolting its way down the conveyor belt. He grabbed it and unzipped the case to pull out a parka, gloves and snow boots.

Now, dressed for the unseasonably cold and wet weather, he headed to the rental car desk. The grouchy clerk checked his credit card against the one on the reservation and handed him the keys to a Chevy Suburban Premier with four-wheel drive.

"Full tank of gas in her." The man handed Grant a windshield scraper with a brush attachment and pointed vaguely toward the north. "Lot two, sorry it hasn't been plowed. And I 'pologize for you having to clean off the Chevy. I can't help you none." He pointed down behind the counter and Grant leaned over to see what he was indicating. The clerk's leg was in a cast from toe to thigh.

"Not a problem," Grant assured him. "That looks miserable."

"Yeah. Pitched my durn self down the courthouse steps last week, after I went to renew my license. Slick as snot, they were. Oughta sue the city. Least they could do is get some of those big teenagers on community service to shovel them steps and toss some ice melt on 'em."

"I hear you. Thanks."

Grant left, waded through the snow, located the big blue Suburban and went to work. His stomach growled as he brushed off the windows before stepping into the big vehicle and turning on the heater. Pulling out his phone, he checked his mail. The slight delay would give the windshield defroster time to start working. Soon, Grant pulled out of the lot. At the first fast food joint he came to, he pulled through the drive-up window, then parked in their lot to munch his way through an Angus burger. He set his mega-cup of high-octane coffee in one cup holder and placed the large bag of fries in the other before pulling out and hitting the road.

The freeway was clear, and the plow had obviously been through, judging by the high mounds of snow on each side of the highway. Still staring at the road, Grant fumbled into the bag and grabbed several fries, savoring the salty taste. He sipped the high-octane and put the hot cup back into the holder. He knew he was grinning like a kid watching Saturday cartoons.

Cartoons...hell. Why kid himself?

What was playing in his mind were scenes of Jessie O'Bourne. The vision of the redhead standing in her kitchen making sandwiches with the sunlight streaming through the window, weaving gold through her mass of curls. Her slender hands handing him a steaming mug of coffee as her teasing voice challenged him to name old master's paintings whose titles included "morning light". And the bantering tone in her voice calling him "city boy" as they entered the Wild Bull Restaurant. That redneck restaurant with the crazy statue of the huge bull on top of the roof—red swirling lights coming from the eyes. His mouth watered remembering the taste of the elk medallions he'd ordered. Who'd believe they had the best food in the country?

The thought of the restaurant brought up another image, one of Jessie wearing a Wild Bull apron over a torn dress.

Slit up the thigh. Way up.

She stood on stage belting out song after song, tossing her head back and letting that amazing voice pour out. He'd been mesmerized. His hands tightened on the steering wheel as his breath seemed to catch. *Damn. She made his pulse quicken, just by being in the room. Getting involved seemed pure lunacy.* And he'd been sure he'd forget about her once he left Sage Bluff—and her smile—behind. He hadn't. Pictures of her spun in his mind like horses on a carousel. If only he'd grabbed at the golden ring on the carousel and taken a chance. It wasn't too late. Because of this job he was getting just such a chance—a second chance—to make Jessie part of his life.

Must be fate.

A feeling of euphoria came over him. Reaching over, he turned on the radio. He flipped the dial to a country western channel, raised the volume and opened his mouth to sing along. Snow pelted the windshield and the Chevy's cab filled with a rich

199

baritone. On the radio a twangy voice sang about picking up his girl in his brand-new truck. Well, he thought, this isn't a pickup truck, and it might be a rental, but it's got four-wheel drive and a great sound system.

Like that little boy watching cartoons Grant had once been, he thought about what might come next in the story. He liked the beginning, meeting the artist whose paintings he'd collected for several years. The middle—when they'd solved a murder with Arvid's help and found two old masterpieces—was mind-blowing. Then came his least favorite part—where he left without speaking up, without even asking her to give him a shot, left even though he knew Russell Bonham wanted to marry her—wasn't so hot. He cringed. *What if she'd married Russell in the meantime?* Now he had the opportunity to write his own ending.

The cowboy on the radio was "getting a little mud on the tires" and Grant's Suburban was kicking up snow as he drove. He felt happy for the first time in six months.

He was going to see Jessie.

Chapter Thirty-three

Crooked Creek Lodge

While the elderly veteran wended his way toward Jessie, she swished her dirty brushes in the paint solvent and hurriedly stored her tubes of paint in her palette box. She picked up her hand-nailer, a nifty tool used for shooting the small brads that held the canvas in a frame and snapped the wet portrait demo into a custom frame by Graehl Frames of Kalispell, Montana.

Even if it was just a quick demonstration—and a donation to boot—she didn't want her work sold without a quality frame to give it the finishing touch.

In her mind she heard her mother's voice. Jessie was eight. She'd been complaining that the other girls would bring bigger gifts to the birthday party she was attending. "Yours will be the prettiest, Jess girl. Presentation is everything." Her mom had proceeded to show Jessie how to wrap the small gift in shiny foil paper and make an intricate big bow. "See, Sweety? It's all about the package." And so it was.

The small framing job made her think of Tate, and how he'd rescued her frames from the wet weather instead of helping her out of the slush after she'd fallen. The goof. But he was a good-looking goof, and very talented.

As the Gingerbread Man shuffled up to her, she gave him a welcoming smile. She noticed he wore a small hearing aid today.

She'd been correct about the hearing problem she'd suspected earlier.

"How are you today, Miss O'Bourne?"

She wracked her brain for his name. Something about Hades. Maybe Hell. And then she had it. "Ah. I'm good. Mr. Helland, isn't it?"

He nodded.

Thank goodness. I'd hate to slip and say, 'Oh, you're the Gingerbread Man. Right?'

"And how are you, sir? I hope you don't mind if I finish this while we visit." She picked up a Phillips head screw driver and attached the fittings for the picture wire on the back of the frame, threaded the wire through and twisted the ends. The frame job was complete.

"Not at all. I'm fine, just fine. Well, here's the thing. I was hoping you'd honor an old man by visiting some of the art display rooms with me. Perhaps introduce me to a few of the artists?"

Jessie looked surprised. Then she realized what a lonely life the man might lead. She beamed at him. "Of course, Mr. Helland. I'd love to. I don't know most of the artists, either. But let's introduce ourselves. Just let me take my supplies back to my hotel room and check on my cat."

"Of course."

"I also need to take the portrait I just finished to the Yellowstone room—the room the museum is using for their sales gallery. Can you give me—maybe about fifteen minutes total?"

Jessie put her apron into a shoulder bag with her brushes and other paraphernalia, slung it over her shoulder and picked up her palette box, then carefully lifted the wet portrait by the hanging wire.

He slid carefully into a chair and held out a show brochure. "Of course. I'll sit right here and look at the list of artists while you do those tasks, Miss O'Bourne." He tapped the brochure against his knee. "I'll map out our plan of attack, so to speak."

He watched her hurrying figure head toward the door to the hall. Then he looked down at the list of artists and pulled a pen from a shirt pocket. He checked off several names, then tapped the pen on the table and looked thoughtful. Finally, he muttered to himself. "Yes. A good plan of attack."

* * *

Jessie dropped the portrait at the Yellowstone Room and was delighted to hear that they'd sold a small autumn scene, just an 8 x 10 but one of her favorite pieces. As she rode up in the elevator and walked down the hall toward her new room, her thoughts went to Glen Heath and how annoyed he'd been about reducing the price on his pack train sculpture.

He shouldn't have sold it so low if it made him so upset. Then again, maybe he really needed the money. I wonder what he meant when he said his ship was about to come in. Wouldn't it be nice if he caught a good break?

As Jessie turned the corner and approached her door, her thoughts faltered. She could see there was something on the floor. In front of her new room. She approached slowly and swore under her breath. John Deere. Green. The edge of a note peeping out from under the door.

She set her palette box and shoulder bag down. Quickly, she unzipped the bag and drew out her phone. A red bar showed a nearly dead battery. Two percent. She tapped in Arvid's cell number and held her breath. If it didn't connect she'd have to go in and use the room phone.

"Arvid," she barely whispered into the phone. "Can you come upstairs—to 212? There...there's another one in front of the door."

"Aw, poop. I'll be right up. Don't touch it."

"Do you have the Sheriff's number? I left his business card in the room, but I don't want to move the tractor to go in and get the card."

"I'll call Fischer in the elevator."

"Yeeeowwr. Rowwwer. Ick, ick ick." From the other side of the door came banshee-like screeches as Jack realized he could hear Jessie's voice but the door wasn't opening. Jessie interpreted the wails. *"Why aren't you coming in? Where's my chow? Staff? Staff!"*

Oh, good grief, Jessie thought, listening to the unearthly sounds. *Sheriff "I'm scared of cats" Fischer is going to just love this.*

Then she remembered Mr. Helland was waiting for her downstairs and made a quick call to Esther.

"Esther? Are you done playing the piano? How'd you like to meet a lovely gentleman?"

"Oh," Esther said. "Any time. Is my big lug of a husband listening? Are you giving him a bad time? You know, he so deserves it. Tell him I said I like them best if they're short, handsome and Swedish. That'll do it."

Jessie gave a half-hearted laugh. She explained about the new tractor, then filled her in on Mr. Helland, including the Gingerbread Man story. "He's such a nice old guy. And he'll just be sitting there waiting. Will you please go rescue him?"

"Of course. I'd be glad to."

* * *

Esther stacked her sheet music and slipped it into the piano bench. Then she walked to the restaurant and picked up a cardboard tray with two of their specialty cocoas and a large plate of stroopwafels to go.

The elderly gentleman was sitting exactly where Jessie said he'd be. She walked up to him and set the cookies on the table by his chair.

"Hello," she purred. "Did you know that every veteran with the surname of Helland was supposed to receive free cocoa and cookies from a tall, white-haired pianist today?"

He gaped at her. "Uh, no," he said hesitantly.

"Well, I guess it was news to both of us then," she said, smiling. Then she explained, "Jessie O'Bourne sent me. She's unavoidably delayed. I offered to keep you company while you waited for her. May I join you?"

"Oh, I see. Of course." He stood and gallantly waved Esther to the chair across from his.

Esther sat and took a slow sip of heavenly cocoa. "Cornish, isn't it?"

"The hot chocolate?"

"No. Helland. Helland, I believe, is a Cornish name."

His eyes widened. "You're very well informed, Miss..."

"Mrs.," she informed him. "Esther Abrahmsen. Totally Norwegian, I'm afraid. Both myself and my husband." She turned her clear blue gaze on him and lifted the plate, holding the cookies out to him. "And these, according to the restaurant menu," she said with a grin, "are Dutch. Other than red tulips, I believe these are the very best thing to ever come out of Holland. Here," she said, holding out the plate, "Take two."

Helland reached for the stroopwafels and smiled.

Chapter Thirty-four

Crooked Creek Lodge

Upstairs, Sheriff Fischer squatted and took three snapshots of the toy tractor, then scooped it up in a gloved hand and slipped it into a plastic evidence bag. "It's a silly looking little thing to throw off such a huge creep factor, isn't it?" he said in soothing tones to Jessie.

The redhead stood in silence, staring at the note under the door. She was experiencing an unfamiliar feeling. She was chilled. She crossed her arms over her chest. Cold. It was fear, she knew. Bone chilling, soul searing fear. And it was a different kind of fear than she'd so far experienced. When her mom had the heart attack she'd been terrified of loss—of heartache. When she was threatened by a woman with a gun the previous summer, she'd been afraid for her own life. Even then, it was a different type of fear. She could see the gun in the woman's steady hands and the hatred in her eyes. The other woman had substance. Form. The threat was visible.

This danger was from a killer she couldn't see and one who was targeting her for no reason she could fathom. Her lower lip trembled, and she cursed her own weakness.

Get a grip, Red. Don't go all helpless female in front of Arvid and Fischer.

She thought of Benny's vacant eyes looking up from the storage hatch of the motorhome. Wrong thing to think about at just that moment.

Silently she began to recite her mantra of colors. Cobalt blue, cadmium yellow, viridian, burnt umber.... She rested her weight on her right foot, then the left. *Calm down. Calm down. Somehow, this has to be connected with Benny. With the big tractor outside.*

Her mind churned backward, mulling over the newspaper article about the young woman killed while driving the John Deere, trying to seed in the winter wheat. Just doing a good deed for her sick father. Addy Nielson. It was no accident. The girl had been shot by a nameless, faceless killer—from a distance.

Geez. Nowhere is safe. But what the bejeebers does that girl's death have to do with me? Or with the art show?

Jessie's delicate hands balled into fists. The Nielson girl hadn't had a snowball's chance in Hell. And just as suddenly as the fear had swept over her, floods of anger washed it from Jessie's mind. Her hand came up and she fingered a curl of her now-short hair.

* * *

Arvid stood with arms crossed over his chest. He'd been following the play of emotions across Jessie's expressive face and knew the minute she went from afraid to angry, then when her temper hit the high boil. Her eyes flashed. Sparks practically shot from the ends of that red hair like the flames from a gas stove lit by a match.

"You okay, Jess?" he asked.

"It isn't right, Arvid." Her mouth set in a thin line. "It isn't right someone can get away with shooting that girl. Or killing Benny."

"There's more to the story, Miss O'Bourne. Lots more," Sheriff Fischer said grimly. "Well, let's see what the note says." As he reached for the paper, the note began to move, slipping quickly backward under the door until just a tiny corner of white still appeared. Then that fragment disappeared as well.

"What the—" Fischer said.

"The beast," Arvid said with a smirk. "He's a little thief."

"Jack, no." Jessie hissed. "Bad cat. Bad, bad cat." But the scrap of paper slipped under the door and the note was gone.

Fischer visibly paled. He took a step back. "Your cat's in there?"

She nodded.

"Well, do something!" Fischer waved his hand toward the hotel door. "We can't let him ruin it."

She slid her key card into the slot, got the green light and pushed open the door. The tip of an orange tail disappeared under the bed. Jessie dove after him and, grabbing him around the middle, hauled him out. The note hung precariously from the side of his mouth, caught on a tooth. Hugging him to her, she stood and reached for a bag of cat treats near the television and shook several out onto the carpet. Jack's feet began to churn as he squirmed to get down. The note fell to the floor. The tom crouched over his bounty and growled as he ate, looking back toward the door with narrowed eyes focused on Fischer. Jessie bent and reached toward the paper.

"Don't touch it," Arvid and Fischer said in unison. The Sheriff stepped forward, cautiously eyeing Jack, and picked up the note in his gloved hand. He unfolded it, then smoothed it out on the wood surface of the dresser. The block letters were the same as those of the previous notes. The lettering was centered on the paper. The message was short.

YOU WON'T SEE IT COMING

Fischer put it into another clear plastic bag. "Evan Hanson got one this morning, too. Same type of note with absolutely no clues to the writer. Just nowhere to start."

Jessie humphed. "Yeah. Except the lunatic is an artist."

Arvid and Fischer gawked at her. "How do you know that?" Fischer demanded.

Jessie raised her eyebrows in surprise. "The paper and the pencil."

"Go on," Sheriff Fischer said. "What about the paper and pencil?"

Arvid made a rolling motion with his hand.

Jack had finished his treats and was rubbing against Arvid's trouser leg, weaving in and out. In and out. Finally, annoyed at the lack of attention, he stood on his hind feet, stretched to his full length and sunk a claw into the soft flesh behind Arvid's knee.

"Ow! Blast it." Jack flew under the bed, twisted and stuck his head out from under the duvet. His expression was smug.

Jessie twisted an auburn curl around her finger. She tilted her head to the side almost as though listening. "It's been written with a sketching pencil. Probably a 2h or 3h. Either is a very hard lead. Not a regular number-two pencil."

"And the paper?" Arvid asked, rubbing a hand behind his knee. Fischer pulled a small notebook and pen from his pocket and jotted down Jessie's observation.

"Sketching paper. It's probably from a small sketching tablet about 7 x 9 inches. Whoever wrote the note tore half a sheet from a sketching pad that size. There's the ragged edge on one side only, but you can see two full corners and two neat sides, so that's how wide the paper is."

Arvid picked up the implication. "And I'll bet if you look at Evan's note, the torn edges from the two notes fit together like two pieces of a puzzle.

Jessie smiled. "I wouldn't take that bet. I think you nailed it." She looked inquiringly at Fischer. "I have a measuring tape in my demo bag. Do you want it?"

"Yes." Fischer pulled the bag holding the note back out of his jacket pocket.

"Let me shut this door first so His Highness doesn't take the opportunity to duck out and explore the lodge." Jessie pushed the door closed.

Fischer looked apprehensively at the broad orange head peeping out from under the bed. Jack's reptilian yellow eyes stared back at him, unblinking. Then the head retreated. Immediately, where the head had been a second before, an orange tail stuck out six inches and twitched nervously back and forth.

Fischer raised his eyebrows at Jessie. "Now what?"

"Pouting," Arvid guessed.

"Yeah, he's mad because I shut the door," Jessie said. "He'd love to sneak out and explore the halls." She reached into her bag and handed Fischer a small silver purse-sized measuring tape.

He again smoothed the note out on the dresser and measured through the clear bag. "I'll be damned. Seven inches at the bottom. A ragged four and a half inches tall. I'll take this back to the office and see if the pieces fit with the note Evan gave us. Do you notice anything else about the note, Jessie?"

"No. Sorry, that's it."

"Well, it's more than we had before. Thank you."

"I told you she was a lot of help on the murder case last year in Sage Bluff, Sheriff. She notices things I don't see," Arvid remarked. "You might bear that in mind and let her take a look-see at the trail cam video."

"Trail cam?" Jessie's look was inquiring.

They explained.

"I'll think about it," Fischer said. "I hate to get civilians involved."

Jessie glowered at him. "I'm already involved. I'd be glad to watch the video if you change your mind." She looked at her watch, then at Arvid. "I'd better go rescue Esther. There's still about two hours before the quick-draw and I promised the Gingerbread Man that I'd introduce him to some of the artists."

Fischer looked interested. "I'm assuming you mean Joe Helland? How did you meet him?"

"Actually, he met me." She smiled. "He came up to my table in the restaurant when I was having cocoa with a friend and began to talk. He's sure a nice old gentleman."

"Yeah, he is." Fischer looked at Arvid. "Helland was one of Berg Nielson's neighbors. He took those deaths real hard. Addy. Berg. Then Dominic. The old guy looks frail. Much frailer than he was before all that happened, anyhow."

"He seems hard of hearing, too," Jessie said.

"Yeah, but that isn't anything new. He worked with explosives when he was young. He damaged his hearing while he was in the service, working too close to some of the big guns. When he doesn't want to listen to people he turns his hearing aid off."

Arvid grinned. "Man after my own heart."

"He's a heck of a woodcarver," Fischer went on. "His work would outshine most of the sculptors and carvers here. Try to get him to show you some of it."

"I'd love to see his work," Jessie said. "I wonder if he'd be willing to have us visit."

"I doubt it. Helland's never been Mr. Sociability. I'm surprised he wants to walk around the display rooms with you and meet and greet." Fischer looked at Jessie as though he expected her to explain. "It really isn't like him."

She shrugged her shoulders, then picked up her purse, ready to head out. "At the restaurant he came right over and introduced himself. He seems very pleasant to me. Maybe he's lonely."

Fischer shook his head. "I'm just saying that this is something new. Except for his friendship with the Nielsons, he always kept to himself. Not because he's unfriendly, but because of his hearing problem, I think."

"So, this Helland was close to Adele Nielson's family. He's here at the show and the little tractors are showing up?" Arvid had a calculating look in his blue eyes. "You don't think he could be involved with the killer—or worse, *be* the killer, do you?"

Fischer said, "Nah. If he is, I'm a terrible judge of character. And besides, he's too old. He couldn't have bashed Benny on the head, then lifted and shoved him into the motorhome storage area. He wouldn't have the physical strength."

"No," Jessie said, "Besides, there's the sketching pencil. And the paper. I'm telling you, it's an artist."

"You forget Helland is a carver—so he's an artist. Would he be likely to use a sketch pad to block out his pieces?"

Jessie scratched her head. 'Good question, but I'm not sure. He might just use regular cheap newsprint. Or he might make meticulous drawings on good paper before he starts a carving.' She frowned. "And maybe he just plans it in his head and doesn't sketch it out at all. Some sculptors and carvers are absolute geniuses with anything three dimensional."

"Huh," Arvid grunted.

"Well, I'll keep him at the back of my mind, but I doubt very much that he had a hand in any of this mess." Fischer turned and opened the door. "I'll think about having Jessie look at the trail cam feed." He nodded to Jessie and then said to Arvid, "I'll talk to you tomorrow."

* * *

211

Ten minutes later, Jessie found Esther and Helland still visiting companionably. She had trouble thinking of him as anything other than the Gingerbread Man. She certainly couldn't picture him as a killer.

"Did Esther keep you company? I'm so sorry for the wait."

"Excellent company, thank you. I have a new and abiding admiration for the Norwegians," Helland said. "But shall we go? I know you have the Friday quick-draw this evening. And the evening auction." He stood. "I don't want to take your entire afternoon."

"No problem. It will be fun. I'm dying to look around the rooms." Jessie took his arm and gave Esther a little wave. "Thanks, Esther. See you later."

She turned to Helland. "Where would you like to go first? I can introduce you to some of the artists whose work I love, but do you have specific artists you want to meet?"

"Let's visit artists from Crooked Creek first, shall we? I marked four on the list."

"But don't you already know them?"

"Sadly, no. I tend to keep to myself much too much. It's high time I met some of our local artists."

* * *

"I love this old barn painting, Gloria. Is it the one from the south side of town over on Turner Road?" Helland asked the slight brunette. Her work was acrylic, a bit kitschy, and very colorful. The sky in the painting was electric blue, the hill behind the barn a vivid purple and the barn was red, red, red. Jessie could almost feel shock waves pouring out of the frame. *I'm going blind. My retinas are seared.*

She preferred subtler sky tones, but there were many people who loved the bright colors. Mr. Helland was obviously one of those. Art was a personal choice.

"Yes," Gloria said to Helland. "That's the same barn. Let me give you a greeting card of that piece—something I can give you for all the wooden gingerbread men you've given my kids the past three years. You know they're the first thing on our Christmas tree.

My husband is the one who takes the kids trick or treating so I've never put a face to the wonderful man who gives out the gingerbread boys. I'm happy to finally meet you." She produced a 5 x 7 card and slipped it into a plastic sack. She handed the sack to Jessie because Helland, after visiting five other rooms, was now leaning heavily on his cane with both hands. "I knew your wife," Gloria went on. "What a sweet woman. I was working part time in the library and she used to come in to browse the new mysteries. And the romances," she said with a wink.

"Ah, yes." He gave her a lopsided grin. "Of course, she brought the romances home for me," he teased.

Then he asked the same question he had asked in each room.

"By the way. You don't know who drove that big John Deere over—the one displaying the art show banner, do you?"

And got the same answer. "No, sorry."

Interesting, Jessie thought. Very interesting.

* * *

"You have a very easy to read face. I saw you looking at the work in Gloria's room with a slightly disapproving look."

"Oh, no," Jessie said. "I hope she didn't notice. It's just that it was a bit bright for my taste. However, primary colors are popular right now. People buy that style of work. She'll do very well at the show."

"Don't worry, my dear. I don't think she noticed. Bright, was it? I thought so too. But something cheerful can relieve the day to day gloom." He winked. "And I might have fond memories of this particular barn. My wife Shanna and I went to a barn dance and barbecue there once. Shanna passed away some time ago. I'll make a frame for this card she gave me. And hang it in a place of honor. Memories are very important."

Jessie smiled. "Yes, they are."

She guided him into the next room. "I have time to visit several more. The quick-draw isn't until evening. "And I know you'll enjoy this room. It's Glen Heath's. He's a sculptor."

"I'm well acquainted with this gentleman. He's a neighbor." He shuffled into the room, leaned on his cane and extended his hand to shake. "How are you, Wheels?"

"Wheels?" Jessie asked in surprise.

"An old nickname, Jessie." Glen said with a smile. "Sometimes I wish I'd begun using it for my art moniker. Catchier moniker than Glen." Then he nodded to Helland. "Hi, Joe. I think this is the first time I've seen you at the show. You should have a display room. Your wood carvings would put my poor efforts to shame."

"It's my first time at the show, and I'm having a great time."

"You know, I expect an invitation to see your carvings, Mr. Helland," Jessie said. "Glen is the second person to rave about them."

Helland looked pleased. "I'd be delighted to show them to you and your friends, Jessie. And please call me Joe." He turned to Glen and gave him a sympathetic look. "Have they found your stepbrother yet?"

Glen scowled. "No, they haven't. His mother and I are worried sick. At least she's worried when she's having a good day. She doesn't always remember he's missing. She's got early stage Alzheimer's." He looked at Jessie. "It's my younger stepbrother, Harris," he explained. "He started out from Fort Stewart, Georgia, to come home, and never made it. Not a sign of him."

"Oh, I'm so sorry. How awful." Jessie was hit by a sense of loss, remembering her own brother, Kevin, who'd been murdered almost seven years earlier. "How long ago was this, Glen?"

"Over two months. The Army thinks he went AWOL. I know better. That kid was straight as an arrow. He'd never desert."

"I don't even know what to say," Jessie murmured. "I hope they find him."

Glen looked down at his feet. "Thanks. It isn't looking good." He seemed to slump.

Helland was examining a small bronze statue of a cow and calf. "How much is this, Wheels?"

Glen straightened, walked over and read the price tag aloud.

"I'll take it," Helland said. He pulled a wallet from his pocket and handed Glen a credit card. "Would you like to keep it until the end of the Expo and drop it by? I see it's an edition of 20. If you keep it for display, you might sell another one. Besides, I have no good way of carrying it."

"That would be great," Glen said. "I can deliver it at the end of the show. I'll call you before I come to make sure you're at home."

"I'll be honored to have it." Then he began his spiel... "Say, you don't know who hauled over the Nielson's tractor and..."

Jessie had stopped listening. A tall, athletic-looking blond man strolled in through the hall doorway. He spotted her at the same time. A brilliant smile lit his handsome face. She frowned, tossed her head back and gave him the stink-eye. He started toward her and she gave him the double stink-eye. He ignored it, crossed the room in several long strides and scooped her into his arms and hugged her. The conversation between Glen and Helland faded into the distance as her mind went blank. Jessie felt her body go stiff with annoyance.

It was that liar. That louse.

Grant Kennedy.

* * *

"It's so good to see you, Jessie. And look at that cute haircut."

"It isn't good to see you, Mister. You're a liar. And my hair is not cute. Puppies, kittens, babies, and bugs are cute. Grown women are not." She folded her arms across her chest. "Not," she growled, "that I asked your opinion."

Grant grinned. He turned to a gawking Glen Heath and dumbstruck Helland. "I hope you don't mind if I borrow Jessie for a few minutes and straighten out a few things before her redheaded temper causes internal combustion."

"And I am not a cup of sugar you can borrow from a neighbor, you annoying egotistical—"

He grabbed her arm and hustled her out of the art room to the area near the covered pool. "I'm not married, Jessie. I'm not. Arvid called me and said Patricia answered the phone when you called. It was my ex-wife being her usual toxic self. She must have let herself into the condo while I was out. She also changed my answering machine message and caused trouble you wouldn't believe. My own mother called to give me that annoying news. If you'd ever taken one of my numerous calls and let me explain, I could have straightened this out long ago."

Jessie felt her face flame. "Your ex-wife? You really aren't married?" She put her hands to her cheeks. "But why didn't Arvid tell me?"

"He knew I meant to track you down so I could explain in person. You were in Scottsdale at an art show, he told me. I'd planned to fly down. Then I got called on a case the same afternoon and spent months in Europe tracking down some stolen artwork. Arvid probably thought I'd handled the misunderstanding." He looked chagrined. "And I should have."

"But—"

"Jessie, you're talking to a coward. I wanted to tell you what an amazing woman I thought you were when we were both in Sage Bluff trying to track down the missing Moran paintings. I hoped to stay in touch, get to know you so much better. Then, I realized how damnably awkward—almost insurmountable—the distance was between Boston and Santa Fe." He shook his head. "Really. A long-distance relationship seemed pretty crazy."

"It still does, Grant." She gave him a questioning look. "How long were you in Europe? I know with your job it can take some time to follow leads." His appreciation of art, both ancient and contemporary, was one of the things they had in common.

"Three months. We were tracking down a Franz Hals. You'll enjoy how it all came together," he said enthusiastically. "Can I take you to dinner and tell you about it? I know you'll need to paint tonight—Friday night quick-draw and all that—but maybe a late dinner after—"

"So, you were in Europe for three months, Grant?" Jessie interrupted. "And you've been back in the states for over four? But after talking to Arvid, you didn't take time to clear this up. Not in four months."

"You wouldn't answer the phone, Jessie. I—"

"And I guess it's too much to expect a hot shot FBI agent to pick up a pen and...oh, I don't know. Write a sentence or two, stick it in an envelope? Add a stamp?" She waved her hand in the air. "You know, those colorful little square things that move

216

messages from state to state? You can even buy them at the grocery store."

Grant sighed. He rubbed a hand across his forehead. "I'm exhausted. It's been a long day. Can we sit down somewhere and discuss my shortcomings..." Grant's voice had a wariness to it. "...and the United States Postal Service?"

She ignored him. "And exactly what are you doing here? Here, this weekend, at this art show?"

He sounded relieved at the change of subject. "I heard through the grapevine that an Emily Carr painting was going to be in the auction."

"An Emily Carr?" Jessie's eyes widened. "The Canadian painter?" She grew excited, then remembered she was mad at him and continued in a calm tone. "Late eighteen hundred's post-impressionist. Hmmm. Part of a well-known art group called the "Group of Seven." She looked up into Grant's brown eyes. Not exactly brown, she thought. A bit of rich sienna, flecks of a golden ...then she gave herself a mental shake. Rather than think about Grant, she pulled facts about Emily Carr from her memory. "She did totems, geometrics, colorful landscapes. And wasn't she touted as the first woman to give up riding side-saddle?"

"Yes."

"I see." She let a chilliness creep into her tone. "So, what you're saying is that you had a very good reason to come to the Crooked Creek Expo. An important reason. I remember hearing some news about one of her paintings—called "Twisted Staircase" wasn't it?"

Grant nodded.

"Went over three million dollars at auction a few years ago." She twisted a curl around a finger. "Certainly a reason aside from speaking to me to clear up any misconceptions." Her heart thudded. She felt like an idiot. She'd thought maybe he'd come to see her. How gullible could she be? And blast it. He looked better than a hot turkey dinner after a week of cold soup. She felt an almost overwhelming urge to just throw her arms around the man and let the chips fall where they may, pride and long-distance relationship be damned.

"Well…," He looked abashed. "I've wanted an Emily Carr for my collection for some time. But it seemed…." He tugged on an ear as though hoping to pull the correct word out of the lobe. "like a lucky coincidence that one would be up for bid, and that you'd be here, too. Especially since you weren't listed as the guest artist when I bought my airline ticket."

"Oh?" Jessie said coolly. "That was lucky, wasn't it?" Glacial blue eyes met apprehensive brown ones. In Grant's eyes, Jessie imagined a long highway stretching from Santa Fe to Boston. The idea was ridiculous, and obviously she was not important to him. At least, not important enough to make much of an effort. "I hope you're able to win the bid on the Carr painting. It's odd that I didn't notice it in the auction catalog." She made a show of looking at her watch. "I'm afraid duty calls. I have a few other things I need to do before the quick-draw and I want to show the Gingerbread Man several more rooms." She gave him a slight smile. Looking through the doorway into Glen Heath's display room, she saw Helland was still browsing, examining each sculpture with obvious enjoyment. "Have a good time at the show, Grant."

"The what? Gingerbread? Jessie—"

Jessie turned and walked stiffly back into Glen's room, linked her arm through Mr. Helland's, and walked out the opposite door into the hall.

He stood watching her go, arms hanging limply at his sides. Then gave a deep, tired sigh.

A deep voice behind him said, "Well, that was about as smooth talking as if you were speaking English as a second language. Course, it's hard to say much when you got a big foot in your mouth. A big, big foot."

"Were you sitting there listening the whole time we were talking, Arvid?"

"Yeah. Poop. It was a sad performance, too. I could hardly watch. For some reason I thought you big city boys had a better handle on the silver tongue. I wasn't eavesdropping. I'm keeping an eye on Jessie and couldn't help overhearing." He stood and put out a hand. "How are you, Grant? It's good to see you."

218

Grant shook Arvid's huge mitt, then clapped him on the back. "Good to see you, too, Arvid. What do you mean, you're supposed to be watching Jessie?"

"Tell you later. C'mon. And for God's sake, don't let her spot us following her. She's so mad she's ready to go off like a Fourth of July sparkler." He shook his head and snickered. "Hmph. What an idiot."

"Why are you following—" Grant began.

Arvid shushed him. They rounded the corner as Jessie went into the Yellowstone room. Then he asked, "You Swedish, Grant?"

"No, dammit. I'm not Swedish." Grant rubbed his eyes. "I'm just jetlagged. The plane got in late, I had no sleep, and I just finished driving the rest of the way through a bunch of that white stuff you Montanans mistakenly call spring."

Arvid grinned. "I was just checking." He glanced down the hall to see which room Jessie had entered. "You might maybe better call a florist."

"Yeah. I know." Grant rubbed the center of his forehead with a circular motion.

"Flowers. And you know what else? You could drop over at the pet store and pick up a couple catnip toys for the beast. Jack is her weak spot."

"Arvid." Grant's smile was broad. "You're such a genius."

"Ja. Since Jessie didn't take you up on dinner, why don't you have a bite with Esther, Russell and me?"

"Russell? He's up here, too?"

"Uh huh. Don't buy a lottery ticket this week. Your luck stinks like three-day-old fish."

"Russell," Grant grumbled. "Wouldn't you know Russell would show up?"

"They aren't suited, you know. He wouldn't be good for her. Growing up as neighbors in Sage Bluff, he just got in the habit of thinking they belonged together. But ja," Arvid intoned, stepping into the open elevator door. "And I hate to be the bearer of bad news, but there's a good-looking pencil artist here she went out with already."

Grant gave him a dirty look as though it was Arvid's fault. "A fast worker, huh?"

219

"Yuh." The big detective gave him a crooked grin. "Nice guy, too. Jessie invited him to join us last night for dinner. Russell looked like he wanted to poison the guy's chicken fried steak."

"Blast. Roses and catnip it is, Arvid," Grant said in a determined voice.

"Yeah. And now that I think about the way Jessie was laughing at this new guy's jokes, maybe you'd better add a box of chocolates. You know how they say the way to a man's heart is through his stomach? I think the way to a woman's is with chocolate."

Grant's tired eyes held a steely determination. "Roses, and Godiva truffles. And at least two catnip toys for the monster."

Chapter Thirty-five

Jessie waved the Gingerbread Man to the door. "This is the Yellowstone Room, Mr. Helland. It's run by the Crooked Creek Historical Museum. During the show, their staff will promote my paintings along with Cheri Cappello's fine replicas. She makes elk-skin and buckskin Native American war shirt reproductions and parfleche bags. Parfleche bags are dried rawhide pouches. The ones here on display are overflow from a larger exhibit at the museum. All of Cheri's work is historically accurate for the 1800s."

Jessie gestured to a piece near a fringed war shirt. Draped on a wooden stand, it was the shape of a horse head, fabricated with eye-holes. The leather mask was elaborately decorated with beading and the addition of several strands of leather with attached feathers.

"She recently began making the beaded horse masks. Isn't this one magnificent? I can't imagine the time involved."

Helland had been peering at one of the small parfleche "possibles" bags, bags whose use was determined by the user. He bent to examine the leather piece Jessie was pointing out, reading the signage, "Yes, interesting and intricate. In fact, I've never seen anything quite like it. She must have the patience of a saint." He straightened. "But did the Indians actually use such masks for their horses?"

"I'm sure they did. None of Cheri's work is created without extensive amounts of research. She's meticulous about making her work accurately reflect the best quality work that each tribe could have produced and used."

"Amazing."

"That's the word for them, all right. And I know she also does breastplates and pipe bags. They might have a few at the museum. If you get time, you should go see them. It's worth a trip over."

Then Jessie nodded to the left and strolled over to the first four by eight display panel with her oil paintings. "My work is hung on these movable panels and—oh good. They've sold a couple smaller pieces already."

"How can you tell? They aren't marked sold."

"That's what the red dot on the price label means." She pumped a fist. "Whoo hoo! It's exciting that they've found buyers so early in the show."

"Well." He smiled at her excitement. "Congratulations are in order then."

"Thanks." Jessie beamed at him, her smile lighting her face. "It makes me feel fabulous when someone likes my work enough to want it on their own walls."

Helland walked slowly past Jessie's work, exclaiming over several that he liked particularly well. He lingered several minutes before the large painting of O'Bourne's big red barn. Hollyhocks of pink and white blossomed in profusion along the side of the structure. An unreadable expression crossed his face. "Another barn painting. Why, this looks just like the barn over at Nielson's. He was one of my neighbors—actually a good friend. He died last winter, he and his son both," he said gruffly, turning back to the painting. "The barn you painted must've been built by the same builder."

"I'm sorry to hear about your friend," Jessie said, not mentioning that she recognised Nielson's name. "I almost didn't put that painting up for sale. It's one I painted at my dad's place down in Sage Bluff. But I believe that a lot of the barns around Montana and Wyoming were built by the same two men who travelled the Mountain West looking for such jobs. I'd like to see the Nielson's barn, if it looks so much like dad's".

Helland made a noncommittal sound. Then he said, "I still have a set of keys to Berg Nielson's place. I check it several times a week for the executor of Berg's will. I don't think he'd mind if you accompanied me one day. But I'll get permission." He gave a last look at the painting with the barn and peered at the price tag. His eyes widened, then narrowed. "Nice work," he said. "I might have to give that one some thought. Although just a little smaller would be better for my small kitchen." Then he swivelled to look around the room.

Jessie's gaze followed. "They're selling their most popular books about both old masters and contemporary western artists. For instance, Frederick Remington and Charlie Russell—a couple golden oldies—and Howard Terpning and Robert Bateman, two of the contemporary masters."

"I've heard of them all," Helland boasted.

"And do you have grandchildren?" He nodded. "They have children's books on wildlife along with an assortment of artsy T-shirts for children and adults." She lifted a muted brown shirt off the rack and shook it out, showing Helland the front. It showed a Charles M. Russell painting titled *"When Shadows Hint Death"* depicting cowboys on a low ridge above a ravine. The cowboys were watching the play of ominous shadows on the opposite ridge. The shadows warned them of a war party above them.

What a fabulous story and depiction—but depressing, she decided. She refolded it carefully and placed it back on the correct stack. "I plan to come back during the show and buy one of the T-shirts. A cheerful one. Maybe one of the bright ones with the purple horses. It's fun to wear a 'work of art' tee." She thumbed quickly through the stack of shirts, exclaiming over several that sported brightly-coloured, contemporary designs.

He smiled at her indulgently—his expression that of a man weary of watching a woman shop, but too kind to complain—and leaned heavily on his cane. Jessie knew that expression well. Dan O'Bourne, her father, was a master of the unvoiced "Can we go yet?".

She knew exactly which shirt she wanted. It had better be here when she got back to buy it. "Shall we do one more room?" She asked in a cheerful tone. She looked at her artist directory. "Let's go across the hall. There's an artist who does military art. You may find it interesting. It will have to be the last room I visit this afternoon."

They moved on, moving to the back door of the room into the next hall.

As Jessie stepped through the door she saw the artist sitting in a black canvas director's chair watching his customers browse. He looked familiar. Propped on the foot rest of the chair were feet clad in fancy tooled cowboy boots. The man was dressed in a deep blue silk shirt with a western cut. His belt sported a huge silver buckle. He was what the artists called "all duded up" but looked muscular and fit.

She remembered then, that he was the man who said he'd had to dig through couch cushions to find enough change to pay his art room costs. She peered at the artist's name tag on his shirt. It read "Logan Cooper".

"Welcome. Come on in and enjoy the work. Most of my displayed work is prints…copies of the originals." He nodded at Jessie and Helland as a woman walked over clutching a plastic-wrapped print.

"I'll take this one, Logan." She handed the print to him and reached into her purse. "And I'd like one of the books about your experiences in Iraq and Afghanistan. It has a lot of your military sketches in it, doesn't it?"

He nodded. "It's more drawings and paintings than text," he explained. "I was a military artist."

"Really interesting. Will you sign it for me, please? Well, actually for my husband, Jerry Holmes." She smiled at the artist. "I want to give it to him."

"I'd be happy to sign it, but I'm afraid I can't." He held up his right hand and gave the buyer a sardonic look. His hand was missing the index and middle finger. "If you still want both the book and the print that'll be $325."

"I do." She looked at the missing fingers, flustered.

"You can use the small table here to write a check, or I can take a credit card. I can run a card on my smart phone app. It takes me a few minutes, but I manage."

"I'll write a check," she said.

"I'll get your book and bag it for you while you write it out. Thanks so much."

After the woman left, Helland introduced himself. Then he inquired, "I think I've seen you around Crooked Creek, haven't I?"

"You sure have, Mr. Helland. I was raised here. I was sorry to hear about your wife. She was a nice woman."

"Thanks." Helland adjusted his oxygen pack slightly to the right. "Afghanistan and Iraq, huh? Both tough deployments."

"Yes sir, they were."

"Thank you for your service. Did you lose your fingers there? Bomb?" Helland asked.

"Nah. Lost 'em right after I got back. Ironic, isn't it? It was an ATV roll-over."

"That's sure too bad," Helland said. "Really too bad. Were you right-handed?"

"Yeah." Logan growled.

"Say, do you happen to know who parked the John Deere tractor the art show banner is displayed on?"

Logan looked surprised at the change of subject.

"No. I didn't see who it was."

Jessie was looking at the artwork. Then she picked up one of his illustrated books and thumbed through it. "I really like your work."

"Thanks."

"I notice that all your originals are marked NFS." She looked at Helland and told him. "That means the piece is not for sale." Turning back to Logan she asked, "Why are you only selling your prints?"

"Well, yeah. I make a living—not a great one but a living—selling my book and copies of the original paintings and sketches. Both the wildlife and the military prints sell well. In most art shows, you can only display originals on your walls, but they let you sell copies of your original work from a print rack."

"Uh huh. I'm aware of that rule. I do a few shows." Helland looked at Jessie with a slight smile.

"Before the accident, I did well," Logan said. "Now...well, I get by on what I call "pity purchases."

225

"Pity purchases?" Jessie asked in a soft voice. "Are you keeping your originals for something special?"

"Well, yeah. Since I'll never be making new work, I need all my old originals for my display. Otherwise, I couldn't do the shows." He scowled at her.

Jessie looked thoughtful. "So, you aren't making any new work?" Jessie looked incredulous. "None at all? Why not?"

He held up his damaged hand in an angry gesture. "Does it look like I could, lady?" he asked sarcastically. "Don't be ridiculous."

Jessie's eyes flashed. She tapped her head with an index finger. "You create art with your vision and mind, not your hands. It might be awkward. It could take you longer than other artists to get the piece the way you visualize it, but you should still be drawing, still be painting. I have a friend who lost her entire forearm in a grain auger accident, Logan." Jessie reached into her purse and pulled out a business card. "Here's one of the new business cards she sent me. She a watercolorist."

He took it with a sour look. His eyes widened, and he glanced at Jessie. "She's good."

"You bet she is. And she was right-handed. She hadn't painted at all before the accident. Afterward, when she decided to take art lessons, she tried to learn to use her left hand. It wasn't easy. She uses it for most tasks, but when she paints, she still uses her right hand. It's not a hand...it's a hook." She met Logan's eyes. "She holds her brush in that hook. You have a big advantage over her. You could still hold a brush or pencil—maybe not the same way you used to—but you could make it work."

"How do you know?" He glowered at her. "Big words from someone who doesn't have a handicap."

"Maybe I'm out of line. I probably should apologize, but I won't. I won't sell you short. In your work and the book, I see what you can do, and if you keep sitting back—try to get by on what you call the pity sales—then you're selling *yourself* short. Give it a try, Logan."

"Give it a try?" he echoed. "I bet you couldn't draw a lick with three fingers."

"Oh? Because I'll call you on that bet if you want." She reached into her purse again and withdrew one of her own business cards and slapped it on the small table where the last customer wrote the check. She glared at Logan. "We can tape my index and middle finger together and I'll give it a shot. I'll bet you one of my 8x10 originals against one of yours that I can get a decent drawing on my canvas in half an hour, tops. I'll bet you could, too. You have a lot to offer." She glared at him. "Stop feeling sorry for yourself and get on with life."

Helland looked embarrassed. He took one hand off his cane and grabbed Jessie's arm, trying to hurry her from the room.

Logan Cooper stepped backward, a shocked expression on his face. "I—" At that moment a couple came through the door. The artist gave Jessie a dirty look and welcomed the browsers to his room.

Helland gave him a short wave and he and Jessie walked toward the door. As Jessie neared the door she turned, put her hand up with the thumb, fourth and little fingers pinched together, the index and third finger stiff. "Anytime, Cooper." Then she gave him a wink.

After the new buyers left, Logan perched on his director's chair. He stared at his mangled hand, a thoughtful expression on his face.

* * *

"You were very hard on him, Jessie," Helland admonished.

"No. I wasn't. I...I was honest. Okay, also rude. He's being hard on himself being so willing to just curl up and call it quits. You really don't draw or paint with just your hand, Mr. Helland. And that man has a special way of using color, atmosphere, and brush strokes. He has a wonderful grasp of anatomy and perspective and he has interesting stories to tell. Yes, it would take longer and be more difficult, but he could still tell them. He only *thinks* he can't."

Helland was silent.

"I'm sorry if I made you uncomfortable, Mr. Helland." Jessie mumbled.

227

"No. That's okay. Sometimes being chewed out by a pretty woman makes a man think. Maybe you're right. Maybe you're wrong. If you're right, Logan Cooper might man up and next year we'll see some new work. Wouldn't that be terrific?"

"I hope so. Yes, it would be marvelous." Jessie said. She again pinched her thumb together with her fourth and pinky finger. "But just in case he calls me on my bet, I'm going to cheat and practice tonight after dinner. I'll have to ask Esther to tape my fingers together."

A belly laugh erupted from Helland. "You...are a red-headed rascal," he said. "And a shyster." He tapped his cane on the floor and adjusted the strap on his oxygen tank. Then he smiled. "I like that in a woman."

* * *

In the other hallway, several doorways down from the Yellowstone Room, Arvid and Grant stood chatting. Surreptitiously, Arvid had followed Helland and Jessie's circuitous route from room to room.

Grant yawned. Arvid paused in the hall, looking periodically at the door to the Yellowstone Room. Jessie had been in there a mighty long time.

"Did I imagine it, or did you say you're following a certain redhead, Arvid?" Grant asked.

Arvid didn't answer. He moved forward and peered into the room Jessie had last entered.

"Poop," he said. "She's gone. And I'm supposed to be watching her."

"What—"

"There's an elevator at the end of the hall. Let's go see if she went to her room."

Arvid hurried down the hall, Grant almost jogging to keep up. When they reached the elevator, there was a small crowd waiting to get on. The elevator light showed it was currently stopped on the eighth floor. Arvid tapped his foot and glowered at the door. "C'mon. C'mon, you slowpoke," he muttered.

"Arvid, what the heck?"

"Tell you later. Long story," Arvid grumbled.

The doors opened. Grant and Arvid stepped on.
"Second floor, please."

Chapter Thirty-six

After saying goodbye to Helland, Jessie headed to the elevator and pushed the up button. When the elevator doors opened, a little girl with a mop of messy brown hair flew into the space in front of her and began gleefully pressing buttons. A woman with a pudgy baby on her hip, three artists with name tags, and a young couple with two rolling suitcases stepped in behind Jessie. They stood in the expectant posture people assumed when waiting for the movement of the machine to haul them upward. The young couple looked at the bank of glowing lights, showing the selected floors, then at each other. The man looked exasperated. He took the woman's hand and held it between both his own. *Honeymooners,* Jessie thought.

"Lynda Sue, stop that. All these nice people will have to wait for the door to open on every single floor if you push all the buttons." The harried mother had also picked up on the young couple's impatience and gave them an apologetic look.

"But isn't that good for them?" The child pressed the last button. At the look on her mother's face she stepped back and crossed her tiny arms over her chest, chin down, lower lip drooping like melting raspberry gelatin.

"Honey, why on earth would you think it's good for them? They might be in a hurry." Her mother, the woman with the now cooing baby, grabbed Lynda Sue's hand and stepped back into the corner of the elevator. "It isn't polite to make people wait at each

230

floor when nobody needs to get off. Big people have schedules. Schedules means they have things they need or want to do."

"You always say we shouldn't be in so much of a hurry to get what we want."

"Sure," her mother said in annoyance, "but sometimes we need to be on time."

Jessie watched the mother and child. She looked at the baby, a girl. An adorable little girl wrapped in multiple layers of pink fleece, her rosebud of a mouth making suckling motions.

The woman has two daughters. Two. Does she know how lucky she is?

She listened to the chortling coo of the bundled baby and glanced again at the young couple. She felt, rather than heard, a ticking. *Big Ben again.* To her horror, her eyes begin to fill. To stave off tears she silently recited her oil colors.

The elevator stopped on floor two. Nobody moved. The doors shut. Floor number three. The doors opened. Nobody moved. The young couple shuffled their feet impatiently. Lynda Sue's mother glanced around and murmured a low apology. The doors closed once more, and the elevator moved quietly upward.

"See what I mean, honey?" the mother chided. "Because you pushed all the buttons, everybody has to wait."

The little girl grasped a fold of her mother's jeans and looked up at her with eyes like mirror images of her parent's irritated orbs. "But it's so good for them."

"No. It isn't, Honey. Why? Why do you keep saying that?"

"Because when you're busy with the baby, you always tell me that patience is somethin' everybody has to learn, and I'd just darn well better get with the program."

Several people chuckled. Jessie covered her mouth to muffle a burst of laughter. Even Lynda Sue's mother gave a wry smile.

Out of the mouths of babes.

Jessie knuckled her eyes. Right now, finding a husband and having children of her own seemed as likely as elephants trumpeting down the Expo hall.

She thought she'd shoved that dream away a decade before. But when she'd met Grant the previous year, it was like a dim night-light flared to blazing neon. He was what teens would call ...

231

heck, what term *would* they use? She was so long out of that picture she no longer knew what girls would call such a good-looking hunk of male.

Hmmm. She knew what she'd call him. *Hot as jalapeno chili. Handsome in a craggy, rugged kind of way, even though he was a city boy. His intelligence was sharp as a razor blade and his sense of humor stellar.* Jessie smiled ruefully. *A sense of humor buoyed you through rough times like a life-raft over white water. Dad taught me that.*

She'd also call Grant remarkably laid back for an FBI agent, even though she suspected he could be dangerous if the need arose. But above all, she'd call him out of reach. Way, way, way away from her home base of Santa Fe.

She sighed. "Well," her sarcastic inner voice said, "who needs him, anyhow?

On the fourth floor Lynda Sue, her mother and the chortling baby left the elevator along with two artists. Jessie wondered idly what type of work they produced.

Her mind drifted to Tate's graphite drawings. Again, she thought how odd it was that the Gingerbread Man immediately thought Tate was military.

The short hair? No. Something more.

She'd recently purchased a beautifully illustrated copy of *Alice's Adventures in Wonderland* for her nephew. It had always been one of her favorites. When she visited Tate's art display room, she'd felt like Alice looking down the rabbit hole. Like his room was set as the scene of a play. Then, looking at the pseudo-harmless expression on Tate's handsome face she recalled the small poem Alice read in the book.

'How cheerfully he seems to grin,
neatly spread his claws,
And welcome little fishes
in gently smiling jaws!'

Somewhere behind Tate's eyes she sensed a steely resolve. His off-handed attitude toward his own work and ineptitude in putting together the art room seemed odd. After they'd gone to dinner with Esther, Arvid and Russell, she'd gone back to his room and helped him finish setting up.

It was then she noticed that he had no business cards, no brochures. That's bad business, but not weird. And she explained he could get some business cards in a hurry at one of the print shops. One should be given out with every purchase and handed to every customer who showed even a remote interest. At dinner he didn't have any art show horror stories or funny incidents to tell, either. Most artists have a few humdingers. Could it be his first art show?

But of course, there's nothing wrong with that, she thought. *Maybe he just didn't want to admit he was a newbie.*

When the elevator clanked to a stop at the fifth floor, Jessie held the door open while the young couple spilled impatiently out with their luggage. Seeing the long table with the vase and silk bouquet against the wall across from the open elevator door, she realized she'd daydreamed her way to the wrong floor. She and Jack no longer stayed in 510. They were in 212.

Heck. Since I missed my floor, I may as well ride up to the top and back down.

The poster on the elevator wall touted a high-end restaurant and a deck with a dynamite view. Maybe it was worth a quick look before she went down to change.

* * *

Arvid and Grant exited the elevator on the second floor. "I don't know how we lost track of her," Arvid said quietly, "Not that anything could've happened between the lobby and the second floor, but I want to make sure she got to the room okay. As an excuse, I'll say I forgot to invite her to dinner. Then you and I can go have a cup of coffee and I'll fill you in." He knocked on Jessie's door.

Grant gave him a puzzled look.

"Meowr?" came the reply to Arvid's knock.

Grant smiled. "She's got the mouser along."

Arvid nodded and knocked again. A low growl emanated from the other side.

233

"Jessie?" Arvid tapped louder.

A minute later, he pulled his cell phone from his pocket. "She's not here. I'll give her a call and find out where she is. Shoulda done that to start with." He looked down at the black screen. "Shoot." He slapped the phone against his thigh as though he could wake it up. "This battery's dead. Second time this week I needed the blinkin' phone and the battery's dead again. I hate these new-fangled things," he told Grant.

"New-fangled? Arvid, they've been around since 1973. Now, they're 'old-fangled'. My cell is in my hotel room on the charger. I'll go get it and call her."

"See what I mean? Everybody's cellphone is always on a charger. Useless pieces of plastic. But nah, she might not pick up if she sees your number," Arvid smirked, "you bein' such a silver-tongued devil and all." He waved a hand toward the way they'd come. "Let's go back to my room and call from there. In fact, I'll have Esther call her and if Jessie doesn't answer, we'll start back at the lobby and do a redhead hunt."

"How could she disappear between the elevator and her room?"

"That's the million-dollar question." Arvid scowled.

"Okay Arvid, give. *Why* are you so worried about her? What on earth are you following her around for?" Grant's jaw clenched. "What's going on?"

"Someone's been trying to scare Jessie." Arvid's expression hardened to steel. "Or they want to kill her."

* * *

The elevator door opened and shut on the sixth and seventh floors—courtesy of Lynda Sue's handiwork with the elevator buttons. Jessie exited on the eighth. She immediately saw double doors opening into the elegant Copper Plate Restaurant.

A wooden stand held a menu listing the specialties of the house and the wines offered. Jessie's mouth watered at the description of the entrées, especially the braised short-ribs with huckleberry BBQ sauce, and the bacon-wrapped bison tenderloin.

Most of the wines on the list were from the award winning Ten Spoon Winery near Missoula, Montana. By the menu stand, a glass-fronted cabinet displayed the available bottles. She put her hands on her knees, bending to peer into the case and scan the bottles, admiring the clever titles and labels on the wines. They were beautiful, indicative of Montana, imaginative and fun.

"Road Block Red" had an image of a Yellowstone bison bull standing in the middle of the park highway, blocking traffic. It was described as a balance of chocolate, tobacco and spice.

Jessie stood, remembering. She tried the wine last time she went to Missoula. Yes, it had held the promised hint of chocolate. *I think Arvid would like the spiciness and touch of tobacco taste, too.*

"Going to the Sun" Pinot Gris had an image of a backlit Glacier Park mountain goat standing before a craggy range of mountains. According to the blurb, Ten Spoon developed it to honor the mountain goats that leap from peak to peak at the top of the breathtaking Going to the Sun road.

The Pinot Gris, listed as having a delicate floral flavor, sounded like a great gift for Esther. *Before I go downstairs, I'll buy a couple bottles as a thank you gift for switching rooms and ferrying Jack and me back and forth from the Sheriff's Office.*

She pushed through the French doors at the other end of the common area and entered the huge glassed-in sun deck. Not a soul was enjoying the richly decorated seating area with its western-themed overstuffed chairs and loveseats. She looked around. Low tables whose legs and supports were formed by elk antlers faced chairs in front of the welcoming fireplace. A floor to ceiling wall of windows offered a spectacular view. The vista pulled her toward the windows, and she wished immediately for her paints.

Low clouds draped like lace bridal veils over snow-covered hills. Beyond the hills, Jessie could see the far peaks of the Rattlesnake Mountains.

Thick pines wandered down the near hillside like a marching army. Here and there the march was interrupted by the white bark of an aspen tree not yet beginning to leaf, or a charred or blackened pine, a monument to lightning's fury or man's stupidity. Sprinkled

235

here and there were a few brown trees—likely victims of beetle-kill.

In drought conditions the pine bark beetles flourished, and the trees were more susceptible to the insects. Numerous dead trees increased the fire danger. Montana likely rejoiced over the much-needed snowfall.

Minutes passed as Jessie gazed out at the spectacular view, her pity party over her childless unmarried state forgotten as she assessed the scene's potential for plein-air painting.

Where the line of trees began she saw a brown flurry of movement. She peered intently but whatever animal she'd seen disappeared quickly into the trees. *Something small,* Jessie thought, *a small coon or porcupine having to wade through snow too deep for its short body. Nature is a tough taskmaster.*

A bald eagle soared over the trees. Wings outstretched, it flew effortlessly along the top of the mountain. Then it was joined by a second bird. Circling and swooping, they appeared to hover. They'd caught a thermal, an updraft.

A feeling of joy washed over her at the magnificent sight and she raised her arms above her head in exuberance.

"Wow!" She realized she'd said it aloud. She looked around at the empty room, wishing there was someone—anyone—to share the moment. Then, Jessie imagined her mother telling her, "Enjoy each day—never waste it on "might be betters".

Most people never get the chance to see such a fabulous sight. Her mood lifted.

I'm so lucky. Just pull up the big girl britches, Jess, and get on with life.

Her mental tush-kicking completed, she strode back to the restaurant and bought both the *Road Block* and *Going to the Sun* wines. When she was finally back on the second floor, she walked toward her hotel room with trepidation. At room 212, she sagged in relief.

Thank god there's not another of the beastly little tractors and notes waiting at the door. Maybe the lunatic limits himself to one toy and one terrifying message per day. She set the wine down, opened her purse and withdrew her room key.

From inside the room she heard the phone ringing and Jack yowling as though in reply.

Brrring.

"Meowr."

Brrrring.

"Yeowr. Nik nik?"

When he heard the keycard slide into the door lock, his caterwauling grew louder.

"Oh, for cripes sake, Jack. Are you trying to get us booted out of the lodge?" Jessie stepped in and let the door close behind her. The tom wound circles around and between her ankles as she set the wine bottles on the desk and grabbed the phone.

"Jessie?" Esther's voice asked. "I tried your cell, but it must be on the charger."

"Oh, Esther. Hi. Yes, it is. I think they call them cell phones because we're prisoners to the battery charger."

Esther gave her mellow laugh. "That's where ours always seems to be. Of course, it also spends a lot of time forgotten in Arvid's truck—under the seat, in the cubby—or tucked in his fishing gear. I'm always hunting for it. I even found it in the refrigerator once. He says he set it on the shelf, so he could pull out his 'sandwich fixins'."

Jessie laughed.

"Anyway, I just wanted to see if you had everything ready for the quick-draw. Would you like some help carrying things down from your room?"

"Thanks, but I'm well organized for a change. My easel is set up downstairs already, so all I have left to haul downstairs is an art tote. I can manage fine."

"Wonderful. It's going to be so much fun to watch you paint a piece from start to finish. Afterward, would you like to have dinner with Arvid, Russell and me tonight?" She covered the mouthpiece and whispered to the men, "Grant, too, right?".

"Ya, but don't tell her he's coming," Arvid whispered back.

Grant smiled broadly.

"I'd love to," Jessie said. "But before I have dinner, I want to watch the first part of the auction. They sell the quick-draws first and I get nervous waiting for mine to sell. I know I'll enjoy my

237

dinner more after I watch it go. Can I call you after that and see where to meet you?"

"Perfect," Esther said in her cultured tones. "You don't need to call. We plan to go get in line at the Copper Plate restaurant as soon as you sign your name on your painting. That might assure us a table. Just meet us there." She ended the call.

Jessie sat on the bed, taking mental inventory of what she'd set up downstairs at her quick-draw station. She pulled her reference photos from her art tote and stared at them intently, planning her quick-draw strategy. A flutter of nervousness rippled through her stomach when she looked at the photos she'd chosen to work from. It would be a challenge, but she was sure she could make a decent painting in the allotted time. Returning the photos to her bag and setting it aside, she patted her lap, inviting Jack to jump up. He landed with a whump, then nestled into a comfortable position. Immediately his rumbling purr kicked in, soothing Jessie's jangled nerves.

"We have ten minutes of quality time, Butter Tub, before I have to get dressed." She stroked his soft head, planning what to wear. Thank God, she'd hauled her expensive western jackets and boots into the lodge. They would have been pricey to replace. She'd wear a T-shirt, jeans and her leather fringed boots while she did the quick-draw, with the apron the Expo gave each artist for taking part. When she was finished with her painting, she'd add her brown leather jacket with the stylized running horses on the back and the silver concho buttons. That should be dressy enough for the Copper Plate restaurant.

She scratched behind Jack's ears and smoothed the fur on his broad head, all the while telling him what a good boy he was.

There's something comforting about petting a cat. Sometimes I wonder if I take care of Jack—or if he takes care of me.

"I'm getting to be an old cat lady, Butter Tub. No husband, no kids, just a big fat cat with an even bigger attitude." She ruffled his fur. Jack gave her an inscrutable look and yawned, his breath escaping in a waft of tuna kibble.

* * *

238

Esther turned to Arvid. "She's there. She's fine. I have no idea how you two fine specimens of manhood lost a woman between the lobby and elevator." She glared at Grant. "And you...a hot-shot FBI agent."

Arvid gave a sigh of relief and crooked a thumb at Grant. "Yuh. I expected him to be better at tailing someone."

"Hey, I don't even know *why* we were supposed to be tailing Jessie." Grant raked his fingers through his blond hair and rubbed an eye. Then he turned to Esther and explained. "Arvid hasn't told me what's going on. And I'm jetlagged. I think I actually sleepwalked while I followed Arvid around the halls."

"Huh. I thought *I* was following *you*," Arvid joked.

"Good grief." Esther gave Arvid a little shove. "You two clowns go have some coffee. Arvid, fill Grant in on the story. And then find Russell and ask if he's heard anything new. I need to dress."

"We've been evicted, Kemo Sabe." Arvid nodded to Grant. "Let's vamoose."

Chapter Thirty-seven

Quick Draw

"Okay, folks, this is how it works," Max stood on a podium and spoke into the microphone. "A buzzer goes off in ten minutes. Then these artists start their paintings and have an hour—only an hour—to create a wonderful work of art. You get to watch it being made! Then, they'll frame their paintings and we'll auction them off right here! Get your bid numbers now and buy a piece of art! If you don't have a bid number, ask one of the fellows in the bright green vests—the auction gophers—for help"

People milled about, sipping wine and nibbling on hors d' oeuvres. The crowd walked from easel to easel to meet the artists and ask what they planned to paint.

Camille had the quick draw location next to Jessie's. While Max continued his spiel and began introducing each quick draw artist, the two women exchanged glances and rolled their eyes at his banter. Camille again looked gorgeous. She had on a pair of black jeans with a form-fitting soft black sweater and wore high-heeled cowgirl boots decorated with embroidery. Both the sweater and boots had a cactus motif. Her blonde hair was piled on her head, several curls draping loose. She looked stunning. She wished Jessie good luck, donned an artist's apron and sat down at her table, where she would create a colored scratchboard.

Jessie squeezed paint onto her palette. She put her canvas on her easel and got out her reference photos, clamping them onto a support sticking out from the side of her easel. The final painting would be of several cows and a couple of calves standing in the shade of a huge cottonwood tree. She nodded, smiled, and waved to the onlookers when Max came around with the microphone and introduced her, pointing to her easel and reading a shortened biography emphasizing that Jessie was the honored guest artist.

Jessie was setting out her brushes on a small table next to her easel when she felt a quick tap on her shoulder and turned. She gave a squeal and was enveloped in a quick hug.

"Hi, Jessie." Cheri Cappello smiled and gestured to the reference photos. "It's great to see you. I just stopped by to wish you luck on the quick draw. I'll be watching!" She glanced over at Jessie's reference photos. "Neat subject. I'm going to be bidding on yours."

"Thanks. I hope you get it, and I've been hoping we'd get a chance to visit. Are you planning to be around tomorrow?"

"I am. I'd love to visit and get caught up. How about meeting in the hospitality room tomorrow morning? They put on a pretty good breakfast. Can you meet me there about eight?"

"Sure thing. If I beat you there, I'll get us a table. See you then."

Max started the count-down. "Ten!...Nine!...Eight!"

Cheri wiggled her fingers as Max continued the countdown. "You go, girl!"

Jessie poised her brush over her paint.

"One!"

* * *

Jessie's brush flew over the canvas, blocking in the darkest masses of the cottonwood tree and the deepest color on the cows standing under the tree. She wiped her brush and picked up a clean one, swiping it through a glob of ultramarine blue and white with a hint of cadmium orange added to grey down the mixture and began slapping on the sky.

241

Behind the velvet rope strung around the quick finish area, Arvid, Russell and Grant watched the rapidly developing painting. Arvid folded his arms across his chest and shook his head in amazement. Grant lifted his wine glass and sipped thoughtfully, his eyes never leaving the redhead at the easel. Russell stared. A small crowd had gathered behind Jessie's easel, but she didn't sense that she was being watched. Her mind and eye were focused only on her canvas.

For the area near the horizon, where atmosphere filtered out more of the red, Jessie used a large brush loaded with a cool cerulean and worked across the horizon area—then dabbed the same color in a few places on the mass of the cottonwood tree— letting what artists call "sky holes' peep through the leafy area. Jessie stepped back several steps and squinted at her painting, judging the effect before stepping back into place.

She stood still at the easel, humming under her breath for several minutes, staring at the reference photo. In her mind, she was back at the pasture, watching the cows meander under the massive cottonwood. Then she stared at the canvas. The brush began to move again, adding the nuance of green reflected from the grassy pasture to the underbelly of the cow half in the sun, half in the shade—adding a swipe of deep blue across the backs of the cows shaded by the tree, then chose a new brush and flicked on some speckled touches of light where the sun shone through leaves.

Her toe tapped to her soft humming—humming that took the place of the music usually blaring in her studio while she worked. The brush moved faster.

"Fifteen minutes to go," Max bellowed into the microphone. "Fifteen minutes, artists!"

Jessie appraised her painting. Then she flicked the lightest areas of yellows and golds onto the masses of cottonwood leaves.

When she deemed the painting finished, she chose a tiny brush and meticulously signed her name on the bottom right corner, adding a copyright symbol and small QD for "quick draw".

The buzzer sounded, and the crowd cheered and clapped. Arvid told Grant, trying to be heard over the noise, "Man, that turned out great, didn't it?"

Grant nodded.

"I'm going to go find Esther and we'll get in line at the restaurant," Arvid continued. "You two hooligans can help her pack up easel and paints, okay?"

Jessie picked up her frame, put the wet painting into the opening, and tacked it into place with her small hand-nailer. She set it on her easel and removed her apron. She nodded at her small crowd of admirers, giving them a generous smile. When she noticed Grant and Russell, still standing behind the velvet rope, she gave them a little finger wave. Then she looked past them, and her face clouded with apprehension.

Stepping around Russell and Grant, a tall man strode to the velvet rope, lifted it, flung it back over his head and went to Jessie's easel. He slapped a single piece of paper on the table near her paints and gave a whoop. Then, to the consternation of Grant and Russell, the man grabbed Jessie, picked her up in a bear hug and whirled her around before setting her back on the floor.

"Logan Cooper? What the heck?" Jessie squeaked.

"Look at it. Just look." He pointed to the paper and Jessie picked it up with careful fingers.

It was a delicate portrait of a young girl rendered in charcoal. Jessie looked closer. The girl looked familiar. And the sketch was signed 'Cooper'.

"It's…it's just beautiful. And new?"

"You'd better believe it's new, you bossy broad." He waved a hand toward her easel. "I didn't realize when you came into my art room that you were the guest artist. I thought you were about the rudest, dumbest, smart-mouthed woman I'd ever laid eyes on."

"I *was* awfully hard on you." Jessie said. "I'm sorry." She looked again at the portrait. "No, I'm not sorry a whit. This is beautiful work." She picked it up and stared again at the lovely lines. It had a slightly different feel than the older work she'd seen in his room, but it was good.

Now she knew who it was, too. It was the little girl in the elevator—the button pusher. "It's Lynda Sue?" she asked.

"Yeah. It's my daughter." he asked. "Have you met her?"

"I heard her mother talking to her in the elevator." She gestured to the sketch. "How long did it take?"

"Three and a half long hours," he groaned. "For a drawing that used to take me one. But I don't care. I wouldn't have even tried it, if you hadn't blasted me for feeling sorry for myself."

Jessie smiled, then looked behind him and saw Russell and Grant gaping at them. Walking up next to Grant came Lynda Sue and her mother, holding the baby. The woman's face was aglow with happiness. Obviously, she was Logan's wife.

"Well then," Jessie said in a pleased tone. "I don't owe you an 8x10."

"Nope. You've given me my life back." He muttered low, so only Jessie could hear. "Probably saved my marriage, too." He gestured toward his wife. "I think she was darn tired of my bad attitude and my 'poor me' funk." In a normal tone he said, "Thank you, Jessie O'Bourne. Come and pick out any piece of art in my room. It's yours."

Jessie laughed. "Don't make promises you don't mean."

He picked up the drawing. "Oh, I mean it all right. Anything on the wall. Any damn thing. Biggest one in the room if you want. In fact, I wish you'd take a big one because you've given me my life back."

She nodded solemnly. "I'll stop in tomorrow." Blaring from the microphone came Max's voice, urging everyone to "find a seat and get ready to bid."

Jessie watched Logan stride to his young family and take his little girl's hand. He looked back at Jessie and tossed her a casual salute.

One of Max's gophers came over, gave Jessie a quick 'hello' and grabbed the painting from her easel. "Your piece is number seven," he said over his shoulder as he hurried toward the stage. "What's the title?"

"Cows and Cottonwoods."

He gave her a thumbs-up.

A high-pitched whistle filled the hall, and everyone cringed, some putting their hands over their ears. The auctioneer adjusted the pitch and volume on the microphone. He practiced some noisy prattle, a string of numbers, and went on to "Howdy, howdy, howdy folks. We're gonna sell some art!" He swept off his Stetson and put it back on. Now this is how it works," he sing-songed. "You got your auction numbers?"

"Yeah!" The crowd roared.

"You see those tall guys in the black Stetsons?"

"Yeah!"

"They're the spotters. They'll keep track of the bidding. When you bid, if they see you, they'll yell "Go!" and point to you. When the next person bids, they'll point to him and yell," the auctioneer explained.

The velvet rope separating the crowd from the painters was pulled down by two helpers. Tate stepped from the crowd and strode to Jessie's supply table. "Super quick draw painting. The light in it is beautiful," he said, drawing the word out into four long syllables. Then he glanced around. "What can I help with?" He picked up two tubes of paint. "Where do you want your tubes of paint stowed?"

"Art tote, please," Jessie said, gesturing toward the soft sided bag. She snapped the lid tight on her palette box. "I'll have to clean up the palette in the hotel room, I guess." She'd been going to say 'the Hawk' before she remembered it was still in the impound lot near the Sheriff's Office.

"Thanks, Tate." She began loosening the fitting at the back of her easel, preparing to fold it down. "I've got time to carry things up to my room before my piece is auctioned." She loosened the wing nut on the metal leg, folded the easel, and slid it into a carrying bag and set it on the floor.

Grant came and stood at her shoulder. He put out his hand to Tate. "Grant Kennedy."

Tate looked up in surprise but shook Grant's hand and introduced himself. While Tate went back to storing Jessie's paints, Grant picked up the bagged easel. He lifted her small table and waited for her to wrap the dirty brushes in a cloth for cleaning later. Tate picked up her apron.

* * *

Russell stood by glowering at both men. There was nothing left to carry, unless he wanted to sling Jessie over his shoulder and carry

245

the redhead herself. He almost snickered at the reaction that would draw—both from Grant and the new guy.

What kind of name is 'Tate' anyhow? Dumb name. Sounds like an Idaho spud.

Russell jutted his chin forward and glared at the tableau, rubbing a hand across his five o'clock shadow and wondering how best to go about tossing the other men on their keisters and getting Jessie's attention.

He watched her joking with Tate but casting wistful glances at Grant and realized any chance he might have had with Jessie was probably long gone.

If only I'd asked her to marry me without asking her to stay in Sage Bluff and quit the art. Seeing her paint tonight was like seeing her—really seeing her—for the first time.

Tate was folding Jessie's apron with military precision. Russell scowled again. Then he heard a husky voice to his right say, "Don't fret, Sweet Thing. If those two handsome fellows are handling Jessie's clean up, I'll let you help *me* over here."

He turned toward the voice. Camille pushed her chair aside and stood. She put her hands on the small of her back and stretched, rolling her shoulders and accentuating her generous figure. Russell gawked. One blond curl spiraled down next to her cheek. She tossed her head back and blew the curl from her cheek with delectably sensuous lips. Then she untied her apron, dropped it on the chair, and stepped toward Russell. She stood with a hand on one hip and gave him a blatant once-over.

He felt himself move toward her like a heat-seeking missile. With the added height from her high-heeled boots Camille had to look down at him. Involuntarily, his gaze swept from the toe of her extravagant cowgirl boots, up her generous black-clad curves and finally over her lovely face. His eyes met hers.

And there was a blatant challenge in those beguiling blues.

Russell felt his breath catch, felt it whistle through his clenched teeth. He took a step forward.

Chapter Thirty-eight

Arvid and Esther waited in line outside the Copper Plate. While Arvid checked out the menu, Esther quickly texted Jessie, Russell and Grant to tell them the hostess assured them they'd have a table ready within ten minutes.

"Marinated elk tenderloins with a chipotle butter. What the heck is chipotle butter? Buttered meat? Now, that don't make sense," Arvid grumbled, looking at his wife. "Sure we want to eat here? The food sounds awful fancy-schmancy."

Esther ignored him and slapped an emoji into the text to Jessie. It was a toothy dinosaur. Except for the emoji, her text was as readable as a formal letter—all the correct grammar and spelling. "Come quickly if you can," she texted. "Otherwise, Dino here is going to want to head downtown for a chili dog!"

"Crab cakes with a mustard remoulade," Arvid read. "Huh. And you think I'm uncivilized? Even I have enough sense not to put mustard on my fish. On FISH. And what is this remoulade? Sounds French. The only thing they do well is French fries."

Esther sighed.

He continued. "The prices aren't too bad, but are you sure you don't want to go down to Hank's Diner and Dogs? They have the best—"

At that moment the hostess appeared with two menus in hand, ushered them into the Copper Plate and seated them at a table. The round table was elegantly set with real silver, a rose bowl, linen napkins and a pristine white tablecloth. The carved back dining chairs had deep burgundy leather upholstery. Esther sank onto a chair and grinned at Arvid.

"Now then," she said, beaming. "Isn't this lovely?"

Arvid looked at the expression on her face and wisely said nothing. Then, his phone vibrated. He looked at the caller ID. Fischer.

"I have to take this, Esther, but it shouldn't take long. I'll be right outside the door. Order an appetizer, will you?" He got up and whispered to her, waving his hand in the negative. "But not that crab cake and mustard thing." He strode hurriedly to the exit.

"Arvid here." He said. Then he listened and groaned inwardly. Dinner—at least *his* dinner—was going to have to wait.

* * *

"Where's Arvid," Jessie asked, sitting down across from Esther.

"He had to go meet Sheriff Fischer. It seems there's been a development in the case."

Jessie smirked. "Yes, Russell had to leave, too. So, it's just us gals." Esther looked sheepish, but Jessie didn't notice. "But before he went he took a tumble."

"Oh, no!"

"Not that kind of tumble, Esther. He met Camille. And from the spellbound look on his face, he fell hard."

"Camille?"

"Yeah," Jessie said. "Tall blonde. Beautiful and with big...um, curves. Camille is one intimidating woman." Jessie chuckled. "You should have seen Russell's face when she walked over and gave him the come-hither."

"The come-hither? Sounds like something out of a medieval romance novel. What are you reading these days, anyway?" She smiled and pushed her menu toward Jessie. "So, she was flirting with Russell...and you don't mind?"

"Not at all." Jessie picked up the menu and opened it. "At one time, I thought Russell and I would eventually wind up together, but it never happened. It's for the best." She picked up the stemmed water-glass the waiter had delivered and took a sip. Then she snickered. "So here was Russell, standing there. Gob-smacked.

248

Staring at Camille drooling like a basset hound ogling a beefsteak while his phone rang and rang. Finally, Tate said to him, "Hey, buddy—that's your phone." Jessie grinned. "He hated to leave. You wait and see. He'll be back this evening and he'll be extremely uncomfortable. Maybe even embarrassed."

"Embarrassed? Why?"

"Because last year he asked me to marry him and he keeps saying the offer is still good. Like I'm a used car he wants to buy." She grimaced. "Now, he'll have to call me and ask, 'Say, Jessie. Who was that big blonde doing the quick draw?' Camille said they hadn't had a chance to introduce themselves before the Sheriff called."

"Ah. I see." Esther's eyes twinkled. "And last year, Russell thought you should give up your art, stay home in Sage Bluff and do nothing but be a momma hen, didn't he?"

"Uh huh." Jessie laughed. "He never understood my obsession with my art. Now, Camille has blindsided him. Those two are made for each other." She bit her lip and looked thoughtful. "I'm surprised I never thought of it before. But wait until he tries that "no more traveling for art" line on Camille. Man, I'd like to be a flower on the wallpaper during that conversation just to see the fireworks."

"The woman is that self-confident, hmm?"

"Oh, yeah."

Esther lifted her stemmed glass toward Jessie's and they clinked together in a toast.

"And Grant?" Esther asked.

Jessie looked quizzical. "He helped me carry my easel up to the room, but I haven't seen him since."

Esther looked over Jessie's shoulder. "You know that isn't what I was asking. But as a matter of fact, here comes Grant now."

Jessie looked uncomfortable. "You hadn't said he was joining us. In fact, when he and Tate helped carry my things back to my room, Grant never mentioned it, either."

Esther's face was innocent. "Arvid must have invited him." She turned in her seat and gave Grant a finger wave. "Over here, Grant. Come and join us."

"Thanks." Grant pulled back a chair and sat. He had slipped on a dress shirt and blazer since the quick draw. "I'm only here for a short while. I want to keep an eye on the paintings listed at the end of the auction because I'm expecting the Emily Carr to be tossed in at the end. But I have time for appetizers." He pulled Jessie's menu over and opened it, scanning the offerings quickly.

The waiter appeared. Grant waited until the women had ordered, then said, "Think I'll have the sampler plate. And a glass of the *Farm Dog Red*, please."

When the waiter left with their order, Esther asked, "What did you say you're watching in the auction, Grant?"

"I'm watching a valuable Emily Carr—I think."

Both women looked perplexed. "What do you mean 'you think'?" Jessie asked.

"It may not be offered. Either tonight or tomorrow—at the end of the auction—I expect an Emily Carr to come up for bid. It isn't listed anywhere in tonight's auction catalog, but I know it's been consigned. I think our good friend Max will slip it in tonight and bid on it himself. It seems he presents something valuable at the end of nearly every auction. It's always a 'late addition" and never makes the catalog. Toward the end of the auction, he mentions there is just one more piece. No provenance, no image, no estimated value is given. The piece is never auctioned until after most bidders have left."

"You're sure? How would he make that work?" Esther asked.

"Max weights the auction with inexpensive pieces toward the end. Most of the moneyed customers, the knowledgeable bidders, aren't interested in those pieces. They leave, and he can bid on the valuable late listing himself."

"Oh no," Jessie said. "That's so unethical. Are you certain?"

"Well, I know it was consigned by the owner, because she told me so herself. She also gave me a photo of the painting. The Emily Carr is valuable—extremely so. And so far, I haven't seen it hung with the pre-auction display. It isn't listed in the catalog for tonight's auction. Nor for tomorrow."

"That's awful. Keep me posted on what happens." Then Jessie explained about her donated landscape the year before, and her concern that the money it brought was never sent to the humane society.

Grant frowned. "I can help you check on that. What he's doing with the Emily Carr is against his client's wishes and damned unethical, but not illegal. What might have been done with the proceeds from your painting—which I purchased by the way— would be illegal. The Expo promoted the Crooked Creek Humane Society as a recipient of donations and recipient of the proceeds of certain pieces. Yours was one of those total donations. I remember that. If the money didn't get to the society, it needs to be tracked."

Jessie nodded. "I planned to discuss that with him. I just haven't had a minute."

"How about tomorrow morning? I'll make an appointment with him. He can't very well refuse to speak to an FBI agent. Do you want to come along? I'd take you to breakfast first."

Jessie said, "I'm meeting a friend for breakfast, but if you'll make the appointment for about nine, perhaps I could meet you at his office?"

Grant's face fell. "That works."

Sliding a platter of appetizers in front of Grant with a flourish, the waiter said, "Bon appetit!"

Jessie's mouth watered at Grant's appetizer plate—the stuffed mushrooms, parmesan cheese straws, the mini crab cakes, a short bison kebab, and calamari puffs. They looked delicious.

"Help yourself," he said, glancing at Esther and Jessie. And they did.

When the waiter returned with Esther's huckleberry braised short ribs with garlic mashed potatoes, and Jessie's baked stuffed pork chops with roasted cauliflower, Grant glanced at his watch. He reluctantly stood to leave.

"Time to go see if Max has added the Emma Carr. If his pattern holds true, he's more likely to drop it into the auction tonight because this is the slowest auction. Friday's auction always attracts fewer big buyers." He gave Jessie a wink and said, "See you at nine at Max's office on the first floor." He turned to Esther. "Thanks so much for inviting me, Esther. I'm sure dessert will be incredible, and I hate to miss it, but duty calls." And off he went.

Jessie watched him stop briefly at the hostess desk. Her gaze lingered as his broad back disappeared through the exit. Then she swiveled to face Esther. "So," she murmured. "Arvid invited him, did he?"

Chapter Thirty-nine

Crooked Creek Sheriff's Office

"What do you have," Arvid asked Sheriff Fischer.

Fischer looked somber. "First, some remains were discovered not far from Savannah. The military police are nigh certain that the body is that of Harris Freeman, but they're waiting for DNA data to come back. I'm sure you recall that he was the friend of Dominic Nielson who they thought had gone AWOL."

"You wouldn't have called us in on this unless you thought it was tied in with the Nielson or Benny Potter murders," Russell said.

Arvid nodded.

Sheriff Freeman went on. "Right you are. When Dom Nielson died, he had a hand-written, but legal will. He had sent it to Christofferson's law firm before he came home. In it, he left all his worldly possessions to Harris Freeman. So far, no other will has shown up. This is one of those wills servicemen make when they think they might be sent into dicey situations."

"So, explain," Arvid growled. "Let's assume Harris Freeman is the body found near Savannah. Who is now the heir to the Nielson's farm? And what if Harris Freeman is dead? Who inherits both Nielson's and anything else that Harris Freeman owned?"

"Althea Freeman Heath. Leastways, that's what we believe. She's Harris Freeman's mom and Glen Heath's stepmother. Nice old lady. In good health physically but she has good days and bad days with early onset Alzheimer's. Forgetful." Fischer frowned.

253

"She's in an assisted living facility here. I believe everything will go to Glen when she passes away, since Harris is dead, and Althea has a pretty good relationship with her stepson. So, when she dies, Glen Heath will be standing on what farmers around here call the 'top of the heap'. And it's ironic. He'll be the heir to his stepmother's ranch, too, and Glen hates everything to do with farming and ranching. Althea Heath has been paying the Christofferson brothers to care for her property and the livestock. Of course, he could always sell."

"Have you told him about his stepbrother yet?"

"I warned him that it's about a 99% bet that the remains are Harris Freeman's. But that isn't the most interesting thing discovered by the Military Police down there in Georgia."

Arvid and Russell gazed at him expectantly.

Fischer grinned. "When they finally decided to go around to all the car rental agencies again, asking for the rental agreements for a period of three days—records from the day Freeman disappeared and a day before and a day after, guess whose name popped up?"

Arvid gave him a palm out gesture and Russell shrugged.

"Benny Potter's." Sheriff Fischer smiled broadly. "I think we have this one wrapped up. We think Benny went down there and killed Freeman.

"My God. Why would be do that?" Arvid looked puzzled.

"Here's the scenario. Stop me if anything sounds off. Because the whole thing is crazy, but it fits. Last year, Berg Nielson put in a complaint about Benny Potter, who'd been shooting at his outbuildings and his mailbox."

"Well," Russell said, "that isn't really a good reason to kill someone."

"No, it isn't. But we have a little bit of new evidence. According to the head librarian, Benny came into the library frequently when Adele was working and asked her out. She'd tried telling Benny she had a boyfriend, but it didn't discourage him. So instead she told him her dad wouldn't allow her to go out with him. Her dad told her to use that excuse whenever she didn't want to date someone. So, we think he shot at Nielson's tractor and killed Adele, thinking it was Berg out there doing the planting."

"Maybe." Arvid looked grim. "Ya. It might have happened that way."

"After talking with the Binghams," Sheriff Fischer said, "You and Russell both thought Benny might have been shooting at outbuildings that matched the distance from the road to the tractor. I think you're right."

"What about afterwards," Arvid asked. "Do you think the campaign of nasty messages sounds like something Benny would do? Or was he even smart enough to think of it? If he was as slow as folks around here say, that just doesn't add up."

"People tend to surprise you," Fischer said.

"And why would he go down and kill Freeman after both Dominic and his dad died?"

"I think he was worried that Freeman suspected something and that's why he was coming home. And the Art Expo brochure we found in Harris's room—we did what you suggested and fingerprinted good old Benny. The print on that brochure was his."

"So, you think he sent the brochure as a warning? Or do you think he had it with him?" Russell asked.

"He wasn't that bright. He probably simply dropped it there. The motel clerk wasn't sure if he'd gone into Freeman's room or not."

"I don't know." Arvid rubbed his chin. "It sounds a bit far-fetched to me."

"It isn't too far fetched, when you consider how many men go bad over a woman. Dull-witted as he was, he probably thought once he got rid of dear old dad, Adele would go out with him. Adele was quite a looker." Fischer looked sad. "A lovely girl in all ways."

"You think everything snowballed from there—from him shooting the wrong person in the tractor?" Russell looked skeptical. "Then who do you think killed Benny?"

"We brought Evan Hanson in for questioning this morning. We've got good evidence against him."

"Ah, poop," Arvid said in disgust. "Evan? What kind of evidence?"

"He had motive and opportunity. Motive since he was Adele's boyfriend and he likely discovered or suspected that Benny killed

255

her. Opportunity because he was at the Art Expo when Benny died. But the kicker is we had our tech guy look at Evan's laptop. It appears the text asking Evan to go out to the artists' parking lot to meet Jessie was created right on Evan's own computer."

"Geez," Russell said. "I find it hard to believe that Evan isn't smart enough to delete evidence like that. And did you find any boots belonging to Benny that are a good match for those in the infrared camera video?"

"Oh, just about everyone has boots like that. Most guys around here anyhow." Fischer jutted his chin.

"And how do you think Evan discovered that Benny had been Adele's shooter?"

"Not sure. We'll probably find out when we interrogate him. Right now, he's with a lawyer. Dumb kid." He grimaced. "If he'd just let the law handle it, Benny would be the one locked up, not him."

"I don't know about this," Arvid said. He gave Fischer a skeptical look. "I'm not sure it hangs together that well. It just strikes me that you're putting too much certainty on Benny's having killed Adele."

"You can't argue with the facts. Benny Potter rented a black SUV in Savannah and he had no reason to be down there except to kill Harris Freeman."

"Did they find anything else on Freeman's remains?" Russell stood, looking restless.

"Actually, they did," Fischer replied. "Found a letter in his pocket that just said, "I'll pick you up about nine.""

"Do you have a photo of it?" Arvid wanted to know. "I suppose the military police haven't let loose of any evidence?"

"Not yet," Fischer said, "To them it's about Freeman. I guess they aren't concerned with what's been happening here in Crooked Creek."

* * *

The door opened. Deputy Jacob Cramer stood looking apologetic. "Sorry to interrupt, Sheriff." He nodded at Russell and Arvid. "Evan's lawyer says his client is ready for the interview." Jacob

256

rolled his eyes. "Interview, he called it. Not an interrogation. Like it isn't just cut and dried."

"Thanks, Deputy," Fischer said, tossing a glare at the young man. "Be aware it is never cut and dried until a jury says so."

Jacob looked abashed. "Yes, sir." He stepped out, closing the door behind him.

"There's a major flaw in your deductions, too, Sheriff," Arvid rumbled.

"What's that, Arvid?" Fischer asked.

"It's what's been happening to Jessie. Someone dropped one of those tractors and a threatening note outside her door," he rubbed the back of his neck and went on, "after Benny was already dead. And I don't like coincidences. I don't think Benny was responsible for those notes and toy tractors. And Evan got one too, remember."

"Heck, Evan probably did all that himself—leaving the notes and toys both at his own door and at Jessie O'Bourne's, too. Just to cloud the issue."

Russell and Arvid both looked at Fischer. "Nup. I just can't see it. Jessie said Evan has been really nervous. She said Evan blamed himself for Benny's death because he should have been the one to go out to the parking lot. Are you so positive that it was Evan that you're willing to take a chance with Jessie's life?"

"Well—" Fischer began.

"'Cause I'm not," Arvid continued. "Something still smells like rotten trout." He tapped his ballcap against his knee. "What do you think, Russell?"

Russell looked from Arvid's determined face to Sheriff Fischer's annoyed expression. "I think I've got to side with the stubborn Norwegian on this one, Sheriff. Jessie might not be in any danger, but I'd rather keep an eye on her until Evan actually confesses or you arrest someone else who says they're guilty."

"You sure you don't want her to come down and look at the trail cam video? She hit the nail on the head with that art paper." Arvid nodded his head. "Speaking of which, did you look at both Benny's and Evan's homes and find any of that paper?"

"No." Fischer shook his head. "No, we didn't find any of that paper at either place. We didn't have a search warrant for Evan's, but he gave us permission to search anyhow. We haven't searched his vehicle yet, but we'll get to that sometime today. And no, I don't think Jessie O'Bourne should come in and view the video. That paper is probably bought and used by every artist who sketches. And after all...we found Benny in her trailer. She isn't totally in the clear herself."

"Aw, dritt," Arvid growled, giving Fischer a black look. "Let's go, Russ."

Chapter Forty

Cheri Cappello waited by the buffet table when Jessie walked into the buzzing artists' hospitality room the next morning. Her long blond hair fluffed out around her head and she was dressed in western chic that enhanced her willowy form—a fringed leather skirt, embroidered and embellished western shirt and Navajo silver concho belt. A turquoise squash blossom necklace and turquoise earrings put the finishing touches on her outfit. She chatted animatedly with the aproned woman who was sliding a square serving of a baked egg dish onto her plate.

"It's better if you assemble it the night before," the woman said, wiping a hand on her enormous apron. "The flavors mingle. And you can use either breakfast sausage or kielbasa. I call it *Reuben's Roundup Casserole*. I got the recipe from my friend Cecily Reuben. She used to make it for the hired hands at branding time." The big woman gave a belly laugh suitable for a truck driver. "Everybody had trouble getting' hired hands 'cept for Cecily and Bud. I'm pretty sure it was the food."

Cheri thanked the server, then noticed Jessie. "Hi. I grabbed a small table over in the corner. Most of the artists ate in a rush and left to open their display rooms early." She beamed at Jessie. "You're lucky you got here before everything was gone. These artists are like Hoover vacuums. Mostly because this breakfast casserole is delicious. I'm ashamed to admit this is my second helping."

The server smiled broadly at Cheri and slipped a generous serving of the hot dish onto Jessie's plate. The women moved to the next offering, a platter of flaky almond pastry. Jessie helped herself to a piece of the pastry and headed toward the huge coffee urn to get a mug of 'instant wake-up'.

"You're so thin, you can afford thirds," Jessie teased Cheri. She sniffed appreciatively. "And if breakfast tastes as good as it smells, I'll probably be joining you in those extra helpings."

Seated, she picked up her fork and tried a generous forkful of the casserole. *Mmmm.* It was scrumptious. Definitely a recipe she wanted.

"Told you so," Cheri laughed. While they ate, they told stories about their experiences at art shows, playing the usual game of "I can top that'. Jessie won with her story of the unfortunate quick draw in Dallas.

"This drunk kept asking questions while I painted—the quick draw was a pronghorn antelope scene—and I tried to be polite, but it was hard to concentrate."

Cheri listened intently.

Jessie waved her hand around. "So, here he was—this guy with a Budweiser in his hand who was sloshing beer and yelling his questions—even some off-color ones about me—not the painting. When I ignored him, he suddenly staggered right through the roped off area, tripped, and dumped the whole beer onto my skirt and *into* one of my new laredo boots. I had to paint my quick draw smelling like a brewery." She stuck out her tongue. "Phew."

Cheri hooted with laughter.

"Then," Jessie continued, "he was so contrite that when I started to frame the painting for the auction, he staggered over *again* holding a Swiss army knife with the screwdriver attachment opened and wanted to help me frame the piece by screwing the fittings on for the picture wire. I was afraid he was going to slice right through my canvas." Jessie made stabbing motions with her butter knife. "The upshot of the story is that it was one of the best quick draws I ever did," she said. "Because I was so irritated with the drunk that I forgot to be nervous."

Cheri chuckled, again declaring Jessie the hands-down winner, and conversation turned to other art shows and galleries. Cheri told

Jessie about her last show, a great one in Colorado where the people were so friendly and where the décor was hay bales and corral gates. Then, they exchanged information and opinions about the art market in different regions of the United States.

"Arizona and Texas venues sell best for me overall," Jessie said. "I'm not showing in any Montana galleries right now, although I've sent a few pieces to the Crooked Creek auction over the years. This is the first time I've driven up to the Expo with a body of work. But I imagine Montana is a fabulous area for your warshirts, Cheri. How were your sales yesterday?"

"The best," the blonde answered, beaming. "The museum staff knows how to bring in good buyers. I think they sold one of my Lakota warshirts, a horse mask, and at least four of the parfleche bags. Very good for the first day of the show." She pumped her small fist in the air and gave a "yeah, baby". "How about you?"

"I didn't check last night, but in the late afternoon I noticed red dots on two landscapes and a moose painting. So—at least three sales from the room, and the quick finish I did was auctioned last night." Jessie took a sip of the dark coffee and tried not to make a face. The coffee had been sitting on a hot plate long enough to be acrid. She grabbed a creamer and dumped in a generous amount. "The show takes forty percent of the auction price, but the piece went okay, so I can't complain. Well, I could, but it wouldn't do me any good." She took another bite and chewed, then looked at Cheri. "Omigosh. Yum. Did I hear you asking for this casserole recipe? I've got to have it."

Cheri held up her phone. "She knew it by heart, so I recorded it while she recited the ingredients. I also have the almond pastry recipe. It is soooo good."

"Text both of them to me, would you, please?" The word 'text' reminded her of her troubles and she told Cheri about the fake text and Benny's body being hidden in the Hawk.

"I know. I heard about that." She gave Jessie a sympathetic look. "It must have been awful for you. And you must have heard what happened this morning."

Jessie looked up. "No. What?"

"Sheriff Fischer came and took Evan Hanson in for questioning on Benny's murder."

Jessie felt her chest tighten. "Evan? Oh no. They can't possibly think he killed Benny." She thought of the nervous, stammering Evan standing by the elevator—telling her that Benny's death might be his fault. He was devastated thinking that Benny died when he, himself, might have been the target. "Why he's no more a killer than I am." Jessie scratched her head at that. *Or is he? Can anyone kill if the motivation is strong enough? It would have to be pretty strong motivation for me to want to murder someone,* she thought.

"Well, the Sheriff is pretty good," Cheri said. "He must have some kind of evidence if they hauled Evan in for questioning." She smiled at an artist walking by and murmured, "Going back for thirds, are you, Tom? I don't blame you." Then her gaze swung back to Jessie. "I was in the lobby when they brought him out. He looked dumbstruck."

"Did you hear why they thought Evan killed him?"

"No," Cheri said. "But I heard him say it had something to do with Adele Nielson. She's the girl who—"

"Yes, I know who she is. She's the girl who was shot and killed in that tractor. The one they've got the show banner draped over."

"Oh no! I didn't realize that was the same tractor. How macabre," Cheri said. "Yuck. Anyway, it seems that Evan was Adele Nielson's boyfriend. The Sheriff suspects he thought Benny shot her and wanted to get even." She shrugged. "I don't know all the particulars."

"Benny?" Jessie's eyes grew wide. "They think Benny shot her? Now, that's odd." Jessie's appetite deserted her. Instead of getting a second helping, she picked up her plate and set it on the cart with other dirty dishes. As she turned to drop into her chair, her cell buzzed. It was Russell. She muted it and sat, telling Cheri, "It's one of my old flames and I know what he wants. He can stew a few minutes. Besides, don't you hate people who answer the phone when they're visiting with someone else? It's like everyone else is more important than the person they're with."

"I hate that, too. But now I'm curious. An old flame? Is this the guy who proposed to you, but said he only wanted to get married if you gave up your art?"

"Yep. That's Russ."

"Well, let the jerk wait," Cheri said emphatically. Then she asked curiously, "What do you think he wants?"

"He and my friend Arvid have been collaborating with the Crooked Creek Sheriff's Office, so maybe he just wanted to tell me they're questioning Evan. But I think it's more likely he wants some other information."

"About what?"

Jessie gave a wry smile. "He got a mega dose of Camille's fabulous charm at the quick draw yesterday. One minute he was giving me a hang-dog expression because he wasn't getting any attention from me and the next minute—whammo!" Jessie smacked her palms together. "Camille stood up, gave him a sexy look that lit major fireworks and gave him quite an attitude adjustment."

"Oh no! Are you upset?"

Jessie thought about it for a minute. "No. I'm relieved. Last year, I realized Russell and I weren't suited. Maybe he's always known that. I really don't want to marry Russell. But, I do want him to be happy and the sparks weren't only on his side. I think Camille looked very interested. The chemistry was so obvious they might as well have written it in magic marker on their foreheads. The thing is, he got called away by Sheriff Fischer before they even had time to exchange names." Jessie grinned.

"But wasn't there a sign by every quick draw table with the artist's name and room number?"

"Yes, but the volunteers had taken them away by the time Camille did her thing. I'll bet Russell is desperate to find out who she is, and the quickest way to find out is to ask me."

Cheri's melodic laugh rang out. Then she asked, "But Jessie, why would your friend want to tell you about the arrest? Because you found Benny in your motorhome?"

Jessie told her about the toy tractors and the threatening note, and more of the background story of the Nielson family.

"None of that sounds like Evan to me. I really can't imagine him killing someone or threatening an old man. Or you. Especially you. What would he gain by that? And just think about it. Evan isn't very tall. If he was going to kill someone as big as Benny

Potter, he'd have to shoot him or something. It would be difficult to murder someone taller than himself by bashing them over the head."

In her mind's eye, Jessie again saw the dead eyes. She'd been standing by the Hawk when the deputies removed the body. Benny had been a big man. "You're right, Cheri. I can't picture it either."

She looked out the window. Spring had finally descended upon Crooked Creek. A clump of daffodils at the edge of the parking lot showed signs of yellow buds. The clouds drifted by in thick clumps of white against bright blue. The scene looked like the painted backdrop of a play. *A play*, she thought, thinking of Evan's situation. He was being set up. Very cleverly set up. She swung back to face Cheri Cappello.

"I don't think Evan did it, Cheri."

"Neither do I."

"How about Benny? Can you imagine him as a murderer?"

"Maybe. He was—oh, strange. I'm sorry if that sounds unkind. But he was odd. At the same time, I don't think he was intelligent enough to plan the threatening notes to Berg Nielson or to you. Not without making a mistake and getting caught."

"Arvid and Sheriff Fischer keep searching for one killer. But there isn't any reason why there couldn't have been two people in on it." Jessie fussed with the hem of her tee-shirt. Today she wore a pair of her blingy jeans and a deep green pullover sporting an image of Monet's waterlilies. "I just can't figure out why anyone would want to murder all these people. Probably greed. Human nature being what it is, though, it must boil down to money."

Maybe the toy tractors left at her door had nothing to do with the murder. She thought about the phone message she'd left Max, asking to meet with him regarding her donated painting. Could Max be trying to scare her away because he didn't send the money from her landscape to the Humane Society? It seemed like a silly notion. *But…maybe.* She tried to remember the sequence of events.

Had she called Max before or after the first tractor and note appeared? But why would he assume she even knew about the first murder—the shooting of Adele Nielson? No, it was a stretch to think Max was trying to run her off.

264

"Say, Cheri. On a totally different subject, have you ever donated a piece to the auction at this show where the money was to go to a charity?"

"Let me think." Cheri bit into her almond pastry. Her eyes met Jessie's. Then she put the pastry back on her plate and pulled out her phone. "Let me check my file."

"You have that info on your phone?"

"Listen gal...I have everything on my phone. I go to so many shows, and I'm on the road to galleries all the time. I am one organized business woman when it comes to my art."

"Well, now I feel totally inadequate," Jessie laughed. "I'm always glad when I remember to log it all in when I get home. My taxes are a nightmare because I have to dig through all my receipts."

"Shame on you," Cheri said with fake harshness. "Shame." She touched her phone screen. "Okay, here we go. Two years ago, I donated a parfleche bag. I really liked that one and almost kept it. It went for $1400 and it was a total donation to that year's charity, which was a horse rescue." She put her phone away and leveled her gaze at Jessie. "I received a thank you note from the charity and listed it as a tax donation that year."

"My gosh. I'm impressed."

"Yeah, yeah," Cheri chortled. "I should be Secretary of the Treasury. Now give. Why are you asking?"

Jessie recounted what the beautician had told her about the Creekside Humane Society. "She said they never got enough money from the art show to do much with the planned spay/neuter program. My piece alone should have given them money for quite some time. It brought over thirty thousand dollars."

Cheri gave a low whistle. "Wow. Yes, that should've given it a jump start. You might speak to Camille. And to Glen Heath. I believe both gave a small piece last year. So did Bruce Turner." Then she listed four other names she remembered.

"Thanks. I'll try to get around and talk to all of them." Her phone buzzed again, and the blasted little device somehow seemed more insistent than before. Jessie swore it had a life of its own. An ornery little 'biting mosquito' kind of life.

"You should put Russell out of his misery, Jess," Cheri chided. "Then, let's you and I go get some home truths out of Max Watson." She flexed her bicep. "I'm feeling ready for a good rumble."

Both women threw back their heads and laughed. Then Jessie answered Russell's call.

He greeted her with, "Where in Sam Hill have you been? Arvid's fit to be tied."

"Good morning to you, too, Russ. That's strange. I'm looking at the call list and I don't see that Arvid has tried to call." She met Cheri's eyes and saw the twinkle in them. Cheri made a gun out of her index finger and 'fired off' a shot, mouthing a silent 'pow'.

"Uh, I thought he had. I know he wants to talk to you about the arrest Sheriff Fischer made yesterday."

"I heard. Fischer can't be right, Russell—"

"Oh, he nailed him all right. He only took him in for questioning last night but late this morning they searched his vehicle. Evan had three more tractors behind the seat of his pickup, and a couple more prepared notes ready to go. And—a bloody rag. They think he hit Benny and got some blood on his hands. Then tried to wipe it off before he went back into the lodge."

"You're kidding. And he didn't get rid of the rag? I'm flabbergasted."

"Me too. Evan's too short for one thing, and I thought the boots on the video were as big as Arvid's. Although there wasn't much to go by for size comparison and the whole video must have been faked, now that I think about it." Then Jessie heard him mutter to himself. "Now why would Evan bother with the video? That's another weird thing."

"The trail cam video, Russell?"

"Oh." There was a silence on the other end. "Shoot. You know about that. Ask Arvid. I don't think I should have mentioned it. Now that they've made an arrest, it really doesn't concern you."

"Hmmm. Okay. But I already knew about the trail cam video. Since I've still been getting threats the whole case concerns me. But if you say it doesn't, it doesn't."

"Oh, Jess, for Pete's sake. Don't be so stubborn. Fischer wants to keep you out of it since you're just a civilian."

266

Jessie's eyes flashed. "Oh, just a civilian." She drew the word civilian into four long syllables. Cheri covered her mouth to keep from laughing.

"Oh, Jess, don't be difficult."

"Yeah, I'd hate to be a *difficult* civilian." She drew the word out again. "They're the *worst*. But why did they decide to search Evan's pickup, Russell? No, let me guess. An anonymous tip?"

"Yeah. How did—"

"He's being set up. The real killer is still out there."

"Well, talk to—"

"I know, I know. Talk to the big Norwegian."

"Say, Jessie…at the quick draw last night…"

"Gotta go, Russell," she sing-songed. "Talk to you later." Then she ended the call.

"Now girlfriend, that was just plain mean," Cheri said with a wicked grin.

"I know. I know. It really was. But sometimes Russell just gets me hotter than spit on a griddle."

"Well, go tackle Max while you're in that frame of mind," Cheri said. "May as well make good use of that redheaded temper." She looked down at her phone. "I'd come along, but I got a text from a client who'd like to meet me in half an hour. She'd been looking at one of the warshirts. Maybe she'll make a decision, and the talk with good old Max might make me late." She looked regretful. "Sorry not to be there for backup."

"I'll be fine," Jessie said.

"Just keep Russell's 'you're just a civilian' comment in mind, and you will be." Cheri waved at the cheerful volunteer behind the buffet counter and snagged a small piece of almond pastry on the way by. "For extra energy," she called. "See ya, Jessie."

Jessie took a large piece and put it into one of the foam "go boxes" from a stack near the buffet. She wanted to see that trail cam video. The pastry looked like a darn good bribe for Arvid.

Chapter Forty-one

Crooked Creek Lodge – Grant's room

Grant stared at the small Emily Carr painting. It was a highly stylized yellow house surrounded by twisted looking trees in deep blue green. Tilting it toward the lamp he admired the way the light caught the strong brush strokes. It reminded him of Van Gogh's work. And he'd gotten it for a song.

If he could actually add it to his collection with a clear conscience it would be a great addition, but he knew he couldn't. It was too unethical the way Max Watson handled the auctioning of the tiny Old Master. *No image in the catalog. No publicity about the Masterpiece on the Expo website. Placed at the end of the auction.* The list went on. It was the same old story—that which is legal isn't always ethical.

Grant planned to speak to the consignors and see how they wanted to handle the issue. They didn't really have grounds for a lawsuit, but they could probably threaten Max with legal proceedings. If rumors of a threatened lawsuit got out, Max would lose his standing in the art world—along with his job as director. An evil grin flitted across Grant's face. He detested unprincipled, greedy men and enjoyed nothing more than bringing them down to size—metaphorically speaking, since Max was already pocket-sized.

Grant stroked his chin. It was highly likely that Max himself had purchased other pieces by lesser known Old Masters for a song, simply because of the way he presented them at the Expo auction. It was highly *unlikely* that anybody at the auction knew the Emily Carr painting was coming up for bid or had an opportunity to see it before the auction. He and Max had been the only bidders. It reminded Grant of the previous year's auction.

Last year, in the manner of the Emily Carr painting, Max had assigned Jessie's bigger landscape the final lot number. But at least it had been listed in the catalog. Several people bid on the O'Bourne landscape, but they dropped off one by one until it was only Max Watson and himself holding up their paddles. Each time Grant raised his paddle anger flashed across Max's face. *Interesting*, Grant thought. Because he vaguely recalled that Jessie's painting had been listed as a 100 percent donation to the Creekside Humane Society.

Jessie. He'd track Jessie down and ask her if his memory was faulty. He wanted to let her know about his new assignment anyway.

He hummed under his breath. First, he'd tackle the problem at hand. Scrolling through contacts on his phone, he tapped on one. When it connected he said, "Hello, Vincenzo." He listened to three minutes of social niceties from his Italian friend and then looked at his watch. Vincenzo couldn't discuss business until he'd covered all the polite chit chat. Grant grimaced. If he could wrap this up shortly, he still had time to catch Max before any of the afternoon events. He interrupted. "What did you find out?"

The smooth Italian voice on the other end chastised him. "Patience, my friend." Then he told Grant what he wanted to know.

"Yes, I understand. Great work," Grant assured him. "And the Carr painting was auctioned last night...Uh huh. I did win the bid. I think we can handle it separately from the other case. The granddaughter needs that money soon."

Grant listened again, nodding his head in agreement even though the man on the other end of the line couldn't see him.

"Woodcastle, huh? You're a step ahead of me, Vincenzo. I didn't know he was already in town. I'll tackle Max now and keep him talking until Woodcastle gets to the lodge."

Yes, he thought. *I hate grasping, greedy conniving men. But I love bringing them a come-uppance.*

Grant whistled a cheery tune as he left his hotel room and headed down the hall. When he came to the office of the show director, he rapped sharply on the door.

Chapter Forty-two

Crooked Creek Lodge

Jessie strode purposefully down the hall, heading to the room designated as the Expo office during the show. She knocked decisively and heard a relieved voice say, "Please, come in."

When she stepped in, a relieved-looking Max waved her toward a chair. Then he turned to the man whose back was to Jessie and said in a frosty tone, "I'm sorry, Mr. Kennedy. I need to speak to Jessie. You and I will have to continue our conversation later."

Grant stayed seated, giving Max his stern FBI face. Max looked from Jessie to Grant with a look of frustration mixed with something else. With a start, Jessie realized it was fear.

"Hi, Grant," Jessie said. "Shall I come back later?"

"No." He smiled at her and waved her to sit. "Stay. You might have some insight into my discussion with Mr. Watson here."

The color fled Max's face. The skin around his eyes looked pinched.

"Here's the scenario, Jessie. It seems that nearly every year Max has a painting or two that do not make it into the catalogue, nor receive any promotion. They are valuable, but lesser-known Old Masters. They are tacked on at the end of the auction and while Max realizes the value of the pieces, the estimated value is not listed in the catalogue. You know that is not the case on the other valuable auction lots. The value is listed. Yesterday evening, I was able to win the bid on the small Emily Carr."

271

Jessie was about to congratulate Grant, but by his tense body language and the steel in his gaze, she realized this was not the time.

"Often, Max—or a certain other buyer designated as his representative—is the highest bidder on those valuable pieces. Max has been answering inquiries about these paintings stating: 'the piece was acquired for the permanent collection of the Crooked Creek Expo and Gallery'. The sponsor, Cory Stanton, who hired Max to handle the Expo, is in Europe. He pays the operating bills for the show in absentia. In fact, he's been in Norway for six years—except for a recent vacation during which he visited an auction at Christie's Auction house. At this auction he recognized one of the paintings being offered as a small C. M. Russell that Max claimed to have purchased for the permanent collection. That's when he called us."

The show director tapped a pen nervously on the surface of the desk, and his expression had taken on that of a trapped rat.

"Regarding the Emily Carr," Grant continued, "An attorney from Denver, John Hausmann, contracted with Max to handle the sale of this Carr painting," Grant continued. "It was part of the estate of an elderly woman, Mrs. Constance Perkins, who happened to be a dear friend of one of my acquaintances. The estate went to Mrs. Perkin's granddaughter, who expected Max to post ads in Canada—expected him to list the painting on the Expo website and in the national advertisements about the upcoming show and auction. In other words, she asked an attorney to contract with Max to promote the heck out of it…to bring in potential buyers for the painting and receive the absolute best price possible. The attorney advertises that he is knowledgeable about fine art and antiques."

"I did list it. Mostly in Canada," Max insisted. "And in numerous ads. Expensive ads. Of course, you didn't see the ads because they were placed in magazines and newspapers in the Alberta, Canada, area."

"Oh, but I did see your Canadian ads," Grant said. "I wouldn't call two ads 'numerous'. And I noticed your ads gave no provenance for the piece, no estimated value, and say it will be auctioned *Saturday* night. However, it isn't listed in tonight's night's catalogue, either. And you sold it last night. What were you going to do...explain to any buyers who came to bid on it that the advertisements were incorrect? Say, 'Sorry, the painting was sold by accident on Friday night?'"

A sullen glare was Max's answer. Even his rooster-tail haircut drooped.

"Mrs. Perkin's granddaughter hoped to use the proceeds of this one small painting to continue specialized medical training." Grant glanced at Jessie. "She was in Japan at Hamamatsu Medical School when her grandmother passed away. She trusted the attorney, Hausmann, to handle the sale."

"I'm sure he handles many estates, including valuable paintings, and so do I. It's simple to overlook—"

"No. It isn't," Grant said in a cutting tone. "I think it's hard to overlook any painting worth seven figures. And I verified that you did have the painting in plenty of time to photograph it for the catalog."

The show director's face was metamorphosing from pasty white to a purplish hue and he looked at Grant with a malevolent expression.

"And strangely enough," Grant continued, "this same attorney has made a habit of contacting *you* whenever he notices an expensive painting in an estate. Obscure Old Masters continue to sell at lower prices than many Impressionist and Modern Masters in many of the auctions across the United States unless people consign them to Christies or Sotheby's. Only the people who specialize in such pieces know what they're worth. The $43,000 I bid for the Emily Carr is pennies for a painting worth approximately a million five to two million. That is—to use one of Emily Carr's favorite phrases—a whiz bang deal."

"Yeah, yeah. You got a bargain, Kennedy," Max snarled. "I have done nothing illegal. Why don't you take your Emily Carr, be grateful for the bargain basement price, and take a hike?"

Grant reached into a briefcase on the floor by his chair. "I'm afraid I can't do that with a good conscience, Max." He held out his badge. "You see, I'm part of the FBI art theft division. And I'm curious as to why you quit bidding on a painting worth over a million dollars when the bid was still so low. Is it perhaps a copy?

273

The FBI has discovered other discrepancies in your past auctions. Paintings that were bought for a song here and then consigned by your attorney to the better auction houses with their provenance listing. Several of these paintings are now suspected of being forgeries."

"This is a joke, right," Max sputtered. "I haven't consigned any paintings. I've only bought art for the Expo's permanent collection. Someone put you up to this."

"Nope."

"But—"

"I can assure you that it isn't a joke to your attorney friend, Mr. Hausmann. He, unfortunately, has several clients pressing charges for negligence, breach of fiduciary duty and for breach of contract—basically malpractice. Not yet out and out theft, but one of my FBI buddies has been looking at his books and has found some intriguing discrepancies...and a small C. M Russell painting that has been sent to an appraiser."

"Oh, my God," Max blurted out. "But it can't be our little Russell piece. I swear, I have not consigned any artwork anywhere."

Jessie continued to watch the scene play out. She noticed that Grant's eyes sparkled with a mischievous glint. He was enjoying himself. The man was a bit arrogant, brimming with self-confidence and life. Ruggedly good looking. The image of the big man crystalized in her mind as her hand made an almost imperceptible sweeping motion—a dreamy brush stroke with texture and color visible only in the artist's mind. She stared at Grant, the conversation forgotten and only the vision of the man in front of her capturing her attention.

"At this point," The FBI agent said, "I'm not charging you with anything. I don't have any evidence that proves you've done anything illegal. Just unethical. But...the FBI will be auditing *your* books as well as those of *your* attorneys, beginning...," Grant looked at his watch and Jessie's heart did a somersault as his face split in a wide smile. "...in about ten minutes. My letting you off the hook doesn't mean that you won't become collateral damage in the attorney's problems. In fact, I suspect you will. Or perhaps it's the other way around and he will become collateral damage in your activities."

By Max's expression, it was his expectation as well.

"We'll hope for the best, shall we? However, if you don't make this issue right with the Emily Carr, even if the FBI accountant finds nothing—not an iota—amiss, I'll be waiting in the wings. I will make sure that you'll never sell so much as a kindergartner's crayon drawing in future. So, here's what you're going to do. I would like nothing better than to have an Emily Carr hanging on my wall, but we both know the amount I paid for it was ridiculous. Next week, if it is judged to be an original Carr, you will void the sale to me and consign it to Christie's Auction house for my young friend. You will take a small fee for consigning it—a fee equal to the commission the Expo would garner if my purchase was the end of the issue."

Max glowered. "I hardly think that's fair. I don't have anything to do with what John Hausmann does. I didn't do anything wrong. And I have to make a living you know."

Jessie looked at Grant. "Is it my turn yet?"

"Not just yet, Jessie," Grant said. "And, Max?"

"Yeah?" The word was almost guttural.

"I suspect you've been making an *excellent* living. This Emily Carr had better be legit."

Max's eyes avoided Grant's. He shrank into himself until he looked even smaller. "There has to be an explanation."

Grant looked past Max and pointed. "Don't move that small David Johnson waterscape I see hanging behind your desk. It's as luminous and striking as one I saw auctioned at Sotheby's last fall—more so, in fact." Grant stroked his chin. Then he stood, walked around the desk and stared at the painting. "It's remarkably similar. Should I suspect this could actually be the original?" He turned to Jessie. "The Hudson River School Painters, even the second generation like David Johnson, are very popular on the East coast. They draw huge prices there, whereas here in the West, people don't recognize their worth." Looking back to Max, he continued, "I'll be back in to examine it further this evening. Not now. My associate will arrive soon and if I'm here in the way I'll get roped into helping. I have other plans." He gave Jessie a

275

meaningful look. "Agent Woodcastle is bringing an accountant, an art expert, and a search warrant, I believe."

Max sagged, and his face again turned fish-belly white. "But, I've done nothing. Nothing."

"*Now* it's your turn, Jessie." Grant nodded his head and made a sweeping hand gesture toward Max. "Mind if I stick around?"

"Nope. Be my guest. I'll keep it short." She looked at Max. "It's my understanding that the Creekside Humane Society didn't get a good start on their new spay and neuter program last year. And not a shred of a start on the new addition they'd hoped to build onto their clinic. I'll be speaking to them after our meeting here—to see if the check they received from the Expo last year included proceeds from my Glacier Park landscape. The one that sold for $32,250. They had a friend watching the auction, so the shelter had expected to receive those funds since it was announced that my painting was a 100% donation."

Max shook his head. "I wrote the check. I sent the check. It was for nearly fifty thousand dollars. Your accountant friend will be able to verify that. There's been a huge mistake."

"I guess we'll see, Max."

Grant stood and offered a hand to Jessie. She placed her small hand in his large one and stood, looking not at Max but directly into Grant's long-lashed hazel eyes. As he met her eyes, his took on an amber gold cast. He seemed to visibly shake himself and then turned to open the door.

Halfway down the hall, Jessie asked, "Aren't you afraid he'll take off?"

"No," Grant assured her. "As we left, I saw my friend Dillon Woodcastle coming down the hall. He wants first crack at Max's books and he had a capable assistant with him—a woman I've worked with in the past." He shook his head. "It's too late for Max, I'm afraid. He'll be busy with Dillon for some time. And I think he's in water as hot as the geyser at Old Faithful." Grant glanced down at Jessie's take-out box. "So, what's in the box?"

"A bribe for Arvid."

"Ah. Pie?"

"You're close." Her hand tingled—a warm feeling of electricity passing from Grant's fingers to hers. He rubbed his

276

thumb over the back of her hand. The strength of the attraction that accompanied the subsequent tingle was a little frightening. She blinked and resisted the urge to mentally run through her colors. Maybe it was time to take a chance. To live life instead of backing away—being a spectator in her own story. She gave Grant a smile and said, "Almond pastry. Let's go put it in my room and check on His Royal Highness."

"Okay," Grant agreed. "We'll look in on the king of cats…and then?"

"If you have time, I need a ride downtown to the Creekside Humane Society. And after that to the Sheriff's Office, so I can visit Evan Hansen. I won't be long at either place."

"Okay." He squeezed her hand and grinned. "Then I'm your man." Without noticing the look that passed across Jessie's face at that statement, he continued. "Just call me 'Uber'." He grinned. "Not that I mind driving you, but I take it you haven't rented a vehicle yet?"

Jessie scowled. "No, I haven't. I tried. I really tried. I wanted a lovely red Ford F150. You know, that wonderful fire-engine red?" She looked thoughtful. "Actually, it's almost pure cadmium, that brilliant…," she caught herself, paused, and switched gears. She gave a rueful grin with a self-deprecating wave of the hand. "No matter. But the fellow at the car rental place was as chauvinistic as they come. He annoyed me so much that I just couldn't bring myself to hand him my credit card."

"Oh? I take it he didn't want to rent you the pickup?"

"Nah. That was only part of it. The obnoxious jerk. He kept saying it was all wrong for a 'little lady' like me." Jessie blew a raspberry.

"Ah. I can see why he wasn't popular with the ladylike, but modern, redheaded, independent sort of woman," Grant chuckled.

"Yeah. I led him to the row of pickups for rent and he led me right back to the row of cars. Back to the pickups. Back to the row of cars. Esther was with me, and she couldn't seem to make up her mind whether to brain him or bust up laughing After twenty minutes, I was practically seething. And he was even more unpopular when he found the car he thought was 'just perfect for a delicate little lady' like me."

"Uh oh." Grant turned his face away from Jessie to hide his ear to ear smile. "What did this paragon of virtue think you should drive?"

They stepped into the elevator and hit the button.

Jessie's face flamed. "Well, at least he got the color right. It was *red*, but it was hardly even big enough for me and my long legs…let alone roomy enough to have pudgy Jack ride along."

Grant threw an appreciative glance at her legs. "Compact, huh?"

"Weensier."

"And it was…a Toyota? A Prius?"

"Worse." Jessie took her hand back and pinched her thumb and index finger together making a pinching motion. "About the size of a little red wagon. It was one of those dang micro-mini smart cars."

Grant's laughter filled the elevator, turning abruptly into a wheeze. Jessie's elbow had connected.

"Watch it, FBI. We delicate gals pack a colossal punch."

"Don't I know it." Grant stared down at her, his eyes sparkling with good humor. Then they darkened into something else.

She met his gaze and felt herself stumble slightly. Still staring into Grant's eyes, she gave herself a mental slap.

Long distance relationships never work, she reminded herself. She squeezed her eyes shut, then opened them to look again into his, determined to be unaffected. *Flecks of gold in the hazel pupils. Thick blond hair. A slightly crooked nose that only served to make him look rugged. Tall. Darn good-looking, blast him. Enough electricity sizzled between them to power a high-rise.*

She felt herself beginning to pitch down an ever-narrowing tunnel as she gazed at Grant. *A lot of rabbit holes at this crazy art show,* she thought, remembering the heat his grasp had generated earlier. *A rabbit hole. And so help me, I want to slip down it like a kid on a playground slide.*

As though reading her thoughts, Grant gave her a wink.

Jessie hesitated, looking again into those teasing hazel-gold eyes. Then she gave a shake of her head, making the shortened red curls bounce, and reached over to firmly reclaim his big hand, savoring the jolt as his fingers wrapped around hers.

278

Grant rubbed his thumb over the back of her hand.

Tumbling and slithering, Jessie thought. *Down the old rabbit hole. Alice, here I come...*

"It's a crazy question, Grant, but did you ever read *Alice's Adventures in Wonderland* when you were a kid? Do you remember any of the neat quotes from it?"

Grant looked at her in amusement. "We had a choice of novels in our English class, so I read *Lord of the Flies*."

"Ugh. Sorry I asked. I had to read that one, too. It wasn't one of my favorites."

"Just yanking your chain. Sure, I did. Everyone had to read Lewis Carroll. Have we gone from spouting titles of morning and evening paintings like we did last year in Sage bluff, to quotes from the classics?" He thought a minute, then said, "My favorite quote was: 'Why, sometimes I've believed as many as six impossible things before breakfast.'"

"You're on," Jessie said, wracking her brain for a quote. Then she said, "Would you tell me, please, which way I ought to go from here?"

"That depends a good deal on where you want to get to." Grant threw the completed quote right back as easily as lobbing a ball. He stopped walking, let go of her hand and turned Jessie toward him with a serious look. "It depends a good deal on where *you* want to go, too, Jessie O'Bourne. But you and I both know what the *best* quote in the book is." He gestured back to Max's door, where one of the two newly arrived FBI agents was knocking on the door.

Grant grinned and looked at her expectantly. Then, Jessie threw her arms in the air and in unison she and Grant said, "Off with their heads!"

* * *

Up in her room, Jessie scooped kibble into Jack's bowl while the tom purred and wound around Grant's ankles, stopped every other figure-eight to look up at him and make a thrumming sound. Grant reached down and rubbed behind Jack's ears and scratched his back, from his neck to the base of his tail.

279

"I missed you too, Tough Guy," Grant murmured to the tom. "No cats allowed in my Boston condo. It was lonesome, Jackeroo."

Jessie shook the treat bag and Jack's attention swiveled to her. Then he trotted over to see what she held in her hand, standing on hind legs to give it a quick sniff.

"Fickle," Grant said. "And here I thought he was thrilled to see me."

Jessie laughed. "Well, he does like men. And I'm sure he remembers you, but I'm afraid not even you can compete with a salmon snack."

Jack gobbled the treat. Then, Grant and Jessie both forgotten, he ran to the window and leapt to the sill. He looked out the window and gave a muttering grumble.

"What does he want?" Grant asked.

"I don't know." Jessie watched him with concern. "But he's probably just tired of being cooped up."

"Do you want to bring him along? Arvid told me Jack actually walks well on a leash. He was impressed. He says it's amazing."

Jessie continued to watch Jack. The big tom now stood on his hind legs and looked out the window. Then he plopped down on his rump and looked back at Jessie, his gaze fixed on her in an enigmatic stare. He yowled loudly. Finally, with a dismissive 'mrph', he jumped down and walked to his food dish and began to eat.

"Yes. But Arvid doesn't know I have to bribe Jack to get him to walk on his harness—and don't you dare tell him." Jessie shook a warning finger at him.

She walked to the window and looked out, remembering the small animal she'd seen scrabble into the brush while she watched from the deck at the top floor of the lodge. Maybe Jack had seen it from his perch at the window. She'd walk that direction when she took him out for his stroll.

"But thanks for offering to take His Highness along," she told Grant. "I'll take him for a good long walk when we get back. Until then, he'll be okay here. I don't want to take him into the Creekside Humane Society, because it might scare the bejeebers out of him. Poor thing would think he was going to the vet. And I don't want to take him into the Sheriff's Office, because Sheriff Fischer is scared of cats." She smirked. "Or at least of Jack."

Grant burst into laughter. "Well, that's just crazy." He looked over at Jack, who was still wolfing down his food. Jack, as though he sensed someone's gaze on him, gave Grant a determined look and a low rumbling growl as if to remind the big man that the bowl belonged to one rotund tomcat, and he'd best keep his distance. "Hmmm. Well, maybe the Sheriff is a smart man." Jack gave another grumble. "Discerning, even."

Chuckling, Jessie snagged a deep blue sweater from the closet, looked back at the cat, still blissfully chin-deep in kibble, and turned to give Grant a smile as they went out the door, pulling it firmly shut behind them. As the lock clicked into place, they heard a complaint from the other side of the door.

"Mrrrr."

Chapter Forty-three

Downtown Crooked Creek

"Well, I guess that answers that question," Jessie fumed, plunking herself on the seat of Grant's rented SUV. Grant gave her a sympathetic look. They had just left the Creekside Humane Society. The director, Clifford Schultz, said the show manager told him the sale of Jessie's donated piece had fallen through. The CHS had not received any of the $32,250 for which the painting had auctioned.

When Schultz had inquired as to why the sale fell through, he was told that the buyer's check had been returned as "insufficient funds," and the address given was no longer valid.

"Neither the bank on which the check was drawn, nor the Expo staff were able to locate him," Schulz explained. I feel terrible that the piece was the high seller and a 100% donation to the CHS spay and neuter program. Some people are such jerks." At that statement, his eye began to twitch—a nervous tic.

"It's okay, Jessie," Grant assured her. "I'll mention it to our auditor so that the sale isn't overlooked. When the FBI gets finished with Max, the animal shelter will get its money." His eyes blazed and he told her, "I know the buyer personally. I shave his face in the mirror every day and I guarantee his check didn't bounce." He nodded toward his SUV. "Let's head over to the Sheriff's Office and see if we can get in to visit Evan."

* * *

"We'd like to see Evan Hanson," Grant told Sheriff Fischer after introducing himself and showing his badge. "That okay with you?"

"I guess so," Fischer conceded. "It's not like I can argue with the FBI." He turned to Jacob, who'd just walked in, his expression becoming hesitant when he saw Jessie. His eyes grew huge when he was introduced to Grant, obviously the first FBI agent he'd met. "Take Miss O'Bourne and Agent Kennedy down to the jail and let them visit with Evan," Fischer told him. Then he turned to Grant. "I'm assuming you can visit through the bars? You don't want to be let into the cell?"

"Through the bars will be fine," Grant assured him.

"Try to keep it to fifteen minutes." He glanced at the wall clock. "His lawyer will be here in twenty and I hate to keep him waiting. Guy makes me nervous with all his pacing back and forth."

Grant nodded.

Jacob led the way down the hall to the block of six cells Crooked Creek called "the jail". All were empty except two. One held a sleeping drunk who reeked of alcohol and vomit, the smell wafting outward toward Jessie and Grant in nearly visible waves. The other cell held a dejected-looking Evan Hanson. He sat on a narrow cot reading a dog-eared paperback that looked as though it had been there since the fifties. When he saw them, he tossed it aside and hurried to the front of the cell, looking through the bars.

His words came out in a rush, tumbling over one another like pebbles pushed down a swift stream. "Jessie O'Bourne," His face flushed. "I'm so relieved you came. I didn't put those crazy toy tractors and nasty threats outside your hotel room," his voice trembled. "I swear. You've got to believe me." He threw out his hands. "Please listen to me. You could be in terrible trouble. Someone's harassing you and trying to blame it on me—and trying to frame me for Benny Potter's murder. Benny wasn't one of my favorite people, but I didn't kill him."

Grant's deep voice rumbled, "If it isn't you, do you have any idea who might be doing it? Or who killed Benny Potter?" For the

283

third time that day, he reached into his pocket and drew out his badge.

Evan blinked. "FBI? No, but I'm telling you, it sure as hell wasn't me," Evan choked out. "I would never in a hundred years murder anybody. I felt like I wanted to...you know, right after Adele was killed. But even if I'd known then that it was Benny who shot her, I still think I'd have let the law handle it." He stared down at the floor. When he raised his head, his eyes blazed with anger. "And I believe that even more now."

"Why is that?" Jessie and Grant asked, almost in unison.

He waved his hand, gesturing to the tiny cell. "Whoever killed Adele—and Fischer thinks it was Benny—deserves a more miserable punishment than a fast death. To be locked up in a little space like this—well that's a lot worse—and...," he stammered, "and...that's what he deserved."

"Evan," Jessie asked softly, "Do you think Benny was the one sending threatening notes to Berg Nielson? I heard about that." She gave him a sad smile. "And I know Fischer is certain Benny killed Dom Nielson's friend, Harris Freeman."

"Nah," Evan said. "I've done nothing but sit here and think about that. I've been reading the same chapter of this ancient Zane Grey novel over and over. I can't wrap my mind around any of this murder business and I can't concentrate. The words don't even make sense." He grabbed the bars of the cell again and stared at them—intense emotion making his voice tremble. "This whole situation doesn't make sense. But no. I doubt if Benny could even figure out how to book a flight to Savannah, let alone figure out shuttle busses and connecting flights. Benny just wasn't that clever." Evan frowned. "and the Chicago and Denver airports are so busy, he'd probably get lost. Scary, huh? That means someone else has to be in on it."

"I think so, too," Jessie said. "Maybe even two killers. It seems like all a person should have to do is follow the money. Who inherits the Nielson place? And who winds up with Benny's?"

Evan stared at her. "Yeah, follow the money. That isn't much help. But to answer your questions, I don't know. I don't know who inherits Nielson's, but you know what? Benny's place bordered the Nielson ranch. I hadn't even thought of that. He lived in a crappy little shack with his two dogs." He scratched his head, a thoughtful look on his face. "But he has—had—some land. Maybe about 600 acres. He let his land lay fallow—didn't plant crops, let the grass grow tall. Benny was a terrible farmer. And he knew it. So instead of planting the fields, he took a subsidy from a conservation program that used his land for wild birds—pheasants, grouse—some sage hen."

"Do you know who inherits his land?" Grant asked.

"I have no idea," Benny said with a thoughtful expression. "About the only lawyer around here is Richie Christofferson. I'll bet he knows." Looking at Jessie, he said, "What I can't figure out is why you keep getting the notes and little tractors, Jessie. It goes beyond odd all the way to bizarre."

"Me neither, but how about yourself? Why do you think *you've* been getting them, Evan?" Jessie gave him a sympathetic look.

"I think it's because the killer thinks I suspect who he is. But really, I don't." He explained the trail cam video to Grant and Jessie. "There wasn't a good way to judge the size of the boot."

"The video Sheriff Fischer doesn't want me to watch." Jessie explained to Grant.

He nodded and asked, "Work boot or cowboy boot?"

"Just some kind of work boot. They should let you look at it, Jessie. You're used to looking at faint details. Maybe you'd see something they missed."

Then Jessie asked, "Did Benny do any sketching, Evan? Any pencil or charcoal drawing?"

"Not that I know of. Why do you ask?"

"The notes we've been getting are on artists' drawing paper."

"Nobody told me that," he said angrily. "I guess all along Fischer thought I was sending them to myself. That has to be why he hadn't shared that bit of info." He stepped back from the cell bars and rubbed his chin. A line appeared between his brows as he puzzled over Jessie's comment. "So, it's an artist. I wouldn't have thought of that. Well, I'll be."

"Jessie told me about the fake text that got Benny out to the parking lot," Grant said. "Do you have any idea who had access to your computer at the lodge? Someone smart enough to make it appear you sent her that text on the night Benny died?"

"It could have been anyone. My computer sat on the artist registration table almost all day and into the early evening. I was using a data base on it. When I took a break, the volunteers used my computer to log folks in."

"Think on it, Evan, and see if you can narrow down the list of suspects." Grant said. "We were given about fifteen minutes and I know our time is up. We have to go, but first I wanted to ask you about something regarding the Expo auction."

Evan looked puzzled. "The auction?"

"I want to know who designed and sent out the ads to Canada."

"Well, I did." He frowned. "Why do you ask?"

"I'll come to that. Who chose the images for the ads?"

"Again, I did. Max said to use any that I thought would work in the graphics—you know—whatever image would make a strong design."

"He never, at any time, asked you to use the Emily Carr painting that wasn't included in the auction catalogue?"

"No...," Evan said hesitantly. "But I wouldn't have used it anyhow. It just isn't a style most people like. Kind of ugly, in fact, if you ask me."

Jessie and Grant exchanged amused glances.

"Oh, no. I hope the artist isn't a relative of yours or something." He looked embarrassed.

"No," Grant assured him. "Nothing like that."

Jacob came through the door. "Sorry, but Sheriff Fischer said it's time for you to wrap up the visit. Evan's attorney has arrived and is waiting to speak with him."

Jessie nodded and then looked at Evan. "We'll check in with you again soon. Hang in there. Shall I drop you by some newer books? Do you have anybody you'd like us to phone or anything?"

"No, thanks. The Sheriff said he'd bring me some reading material. And I don't really have close friends or nearby relatives. But it's real nice of you to ask," Evan murmured. Then he looked up at Grant. "Take care of Miss O'Bourne. I don't have a clue about how she ties in with all this, but whoever is doing this...I

286

don't think they want to just scare her. I really think someone likes to manipulate and hurt people. She could be a target for any reason this nut can imagine."

They left Evan still staring after them through the bars, a worried frown on his face.

* * *

As they reached Grant's SUV, his face was set in grim lines. When they pulled into the parking lot at the lodge twenty minutes later, his rock-hard expression hadn't changed an iota. His scowl looked as carved in granite as Mount Rushmore.

"You okay?" Jessie asked, studying his strong profile.

"Yeah, I'm fine. It's you we need to worry about. The idea of you being in danger and not knowing where—or who—it might come from makes my temper hit the volcanic stage." The corner of his mouth turned up slightly. "Right now, I might feel better if I could borrow a few of Arvid's choice Norwegian swear words."

Jessie's eyes gleamed and she patted his hand. "I know what you mean. I need to take the Butter Tub for a walk. If you come along, I'll teach you a few of Arvid's best expressions. He's got some that sound so crazy, they'll calm you down in no time. Of course, I don't know what half of them mean. And my pronunciation is so poor I might just be saying 'your socks are an ugly purple. And did you know there's a cow sitting in the cab of your truck?'"

Grant gave a rueful chuckle. "I'd love to come. I don't want to let you out of my sight, but I know my name will be synonymous with one of Arvid's swear words at headquarters if I don't check in with Dillon Woodcastle."

"Oh," Jessie said in a disappointed tone, "I'd almost forgotten."

"I want to check out the David Johnson painting on Max's wall," He smiled at her. "I'm wondering if he—or the attorney who keeps sending work his way—has an excellent forger hiding out somewhere. But before I look at Max's art, I'm going to deliver you to Arvid and Esther—safe and in one piece." Then he grumbled, "Or to Russell, I suppose. If I can't find Arvid I'll have

287

to turn you over to Russell. I can't take you with me because you're a civilian."

There was that blasted word again. *Civilian.* Jessie narrowed her eyes.

Turn me over, huh? Just like I'm a flapjack or something. Or taking a con into custody.

She ached to say something scathing but bit it back. Nevertheless, several crackerjack Arvidisms and a few choice colors flitted through her mind like moths around a porch-light.

Chapter Forty-four

Crooked Creek Lodge

Cheri Cappello was sitting on one of the western-styled sofas in the lobby as Grant and Jessie walked in. "Hi, Jess. You barely missed Arvid. He was just looking for you." She peered curiously at Grant.

"Thanks, Cheri. We'll find him." Jessie gestured toward Grant. "This is my friend, Grant Kennedy...Grant, this is Cheri Cappello, the gal showing all the fabulous beaded warshirts in the Yellowstone Room. Her Native American reproductions are exquisite."

Grant gave Cheri a blazing smile and nodded. "Nice to meet you. Warshirts, huh? Certainly not a common artform. Sounds intriguing. I'll visit the room when I can give your work my full attention."

"If I'm in there, I'll give you a bit of the historical background on each piece. There's signage, but of course it's brief. And I can tell you more than you'll really want to know." She grinned and turned to Jessie. "I thought I'd better tell you that Arvid isn't the only one looking for you. Camille was asking me earlier if I'd seen you. I think she had a question concerning an acquaintance of yours."

"Ah," Jessie said, her eyes twinkling. "Yes, I need to handle that little matter. Let's visit later, Cheri. Right now, I'm on the run." Then she nudged Grant and gave him a wicked smile. "Weren't you going to deliver me to Russell?"

Grant's face darkened. "Let me try Arvid first." He walked a few steps away, pulled out his phone and spoke rapidly when Arvid answered. Jessie heard him say, "And she wants to take Jack for a walk. Okay…okay…uh huh. I'll meet you there."

"Arvid will meet us at your room before I go speak with Woodcastle." He nodded politely again to Cheri and took Jessie by the arm.

Jessie winked at her friend, who chuckled, did an eye roll, then gave her a lash-fluttering dramatic wink in return.

"What's all that about?" Grant asked as they stepped into the elevator.

"That, my dear FBI honcho, is—as our friend Arvid would say—on a need to know basis." Her face wore a smug expression. She imitated the big Norwegian, making her voice gruff and gravelly. "Yuh. A need to know basis. I'll tell you on the first of next month."

Grant looked down at her, crossed his arms over his chest and stood with his feet planted wide apart…the standard FBI tough guy stance. "Won't spill it, huh? I believe I need to up my interrogation game." Then he caught on. "Hey, wait a minute. That's April Fool's Day."

They stepped out of the elevator to see Arvid waiting near Jessie's door.

* * *

"My better half is downstairs practicing again," Arvid told Jessie after Grant left. "You'd think as much as that woman plays the piano she'd burn out on practice—go up in flames—but she doesn't."

"She loves it. Esther is never happier than when she's running her fingers over the piano keys—or writing music." Jessie shook the cat treat bag, and a sleepy-looking orange tom slithered out from under the bed, yawning widely. She tossed him a treat and grabbed the cat harness. His eyes narrowed when he saw the harness, but before he could duck back under the bed, Jessie grabbed him. Jack squirmed and grumped as Jessie fastened the harness around his wide belly, but as soon as it was secure, he started for the door.

"Man, that's a big cat. Tell the truth, Jessie. Did you actually have to buy a dog harness?"

"I most certainly did not." When Arvid stooped to stroke Jack's head, Jessie quickly slid the bag of salmon morsels into the pocket of her light denim jacket.

"That harness has a blue dog bone for a company logo, in case you haven't noticed." Arvid smirked.

"It does not." Jessie punched him lightly on the arm and opened the door. Surreptitiously, she glanced down at the cat harness just to make certain he was yanking her chain.

* * *

Out on the sidewalk, Jack pulled Jessie toward the right, and she allowed him to lead her around the lodge toward the back of the building.

"Are we walking this cat, or is he walking us?" Arvid asked.

Jessie gave him a dirty look and brushed her hair behind her ear. "I wanted to go this way. I'm sure not taking him out near the highway."

Behind the lodge, the terrain sloped upward to the woods with a concrete retaining wall set into the hillside. At the edge of the wall, the ground was leveled and graveled to form a tidy employee parking lot. The sidewalk ended near a huge metal dumpster near a kitchen delivery entrance. As they got closer to the dumpster, Jack began to yowl in emphatic tones.

At the sound of his howls, two women in white aprons came out of the delivery entrance and looked around. One of them, a broad middle-aged woman, nodded at them, then reached into her pocket, pulled out a pack of cigarettes and lit one. The other, a slight Hispanic woman, held a bowl in her hand. She looked uncertainly at Arvid and Jessie.

Jack sniffed the air, feline nose twitching, and his yellow eyes zeroed in on the woman holding the bowl. Then his gaze swung expectantly toward the far trees. His tail twitched.

"Oh," the first woman said, looking at Jack with a smile. "Well, would you look at that big boy—walking on a leash just like my Petey." She lifted her gaze to Jessie. "Petey's my bulldog. Actually, he's a boxer-bulldog mix. Love of my life, that dog." As she took a drag on her cigarette, her eyes took on an expression of contentment. "We heard your cat, and thought it was the stray we've been feeding. It cries at the door, poor lost little thing."

Arvid and Jessie made sympathetic sounds.

"You stayin' here? Don't suppose you want another cat, do you?"

Jessie laughed. "I can hardly deal with the one I have."

Arvid gave a brief, "Nup." His expression, however, was one of deep concern.

"We figure somebody staying at the lodge a few weeks ago lost the poor thing. They're probably several states away by now."

"Have you taken the cat to a vet to see if its chipped? A lot of people chip their cats so that if they get lost, it's easy to find the owner." Jessie reached down and stroked Jack's broad head. "I'd be devastated if I lost Jack. I tried putting a collar on him with my name and phone number, but he gets it off every time. So I had him chipped."

"The little bugger won't let me touch him, but honestly, it didn't occur to me that people would chip a cat." She gestured to the Hispanic woman. "Maybe Luciana here can pick her up, though. I'll suggest it." Chattering away to the Hispanic woman in Spanish, she made hand gestures, waving the lit cigarette wildly to emphasize her words.

The woman, Luciana, shook her head, setting her mouth in a stubborn line.

The only words Jessie caught were 'gato' and 'no'. She glanced at Arvid and realized he was following the conversation perfectly.

"Could of introduced myself, I guess. My name is Fran," the smoker said. Arvid and Jessie nodded and gave her their names.

"And I guess Luciana doesn't want to take the cat to the vet because…well…she's afraid she'd have to pay the vet something. She and her husband, Diego, are strapped for money. He does a lot of odd jobs for the hotel, but he hasn't found regular work. Luciana can't take the cat home because they'd have to buy cat food. It would be more expensive than feeding him table scraps from the kitchen. And they'd have to sneak it into their apartment, since their landlord doesn't allow pets."

"Plus," Arvid said to Jessie, "She's terrified that her grandmother-in-law might eat it."

Fran grinned ruefully, pointing her cigarette at Arvid. "Thought I'd leave that out. Didn't want to offend you."

"Yowr." Jack stiffened, still staring expectantly toward the trees. Jessie followed his gaze. A tabby cat stood on top of the retaining wall, looking their direction.

"That must have been what I saw yesterday from the lodge deck. I'll bet Jack has been watching it from the window. That's why he's spent so much time looking out."

Luciana began a high-pitched calling, and the cat jumped down and disappeared, their view of it blocked by the cars in the parking lot. The Hispanic woman waved her arm in a shooing motion at Jessie and Arvid, indicating they should step back.

"She thinks the cat will be afraid to come and get the food if there are strangers here," Fran explained. "But it hasn't seemed that skittish to me."

Soon, from under a blue Toyota, came a bedraggled looking striped cat. It made a beeline for the bowl Luciana set down for it and began greedily wolfing the scraps, giving worried sidelong glances at Jack and the two strangers. Fran was right, however, and it didn't seem that frightened.

Jessie's heart melted. "Arvid. That cat looks awful. We have to do something."

"Yeah," he said resignedly, "I knew you'd say that." He scratched his chin, thinking. "I'll go pull the truck around. See if you can catch him—or her—and we can drive over to a local vet and see if the cat has a chip. If it doesn't, I 'spose Esther and I can help you find a home for it. We'd need to borrow your cat crate to get it back to Sage Bluff." He turned and strode purposefully back the way they'd come, muttering Norwegian words under his breath. Then he turned around and came back. "Give me your room key, Jess. I'll run upstairs, put the yellow monster in the room and grab your cat crate. Probably the best way to get it to the

293

vet, if you can actually catch it." He held out his hand for her key, pocketed it and scooped Jack up. The big cat hung in his arms like a bag of sand, still looking at the tabby and the bowl of food. Arvid rolled the length of his leash into a manageable wad. "I'll be right back."

"Thanks, Arvid." She beamed at him, and he gave her a casual salute.

As soon as he left, Jessie sat down on the sidewalk a bit closer to Fran and Luciana. "Ask Luciana if she can find just a few more scraps, would you please, Fran? If she can place them in a line from the bowl over to me, maybe I can convince the tabby that I'm not a cat killer."

"Well, okay. But our break ends in ten minutes, so we can only help you for a few minutes longer." She fired off rapid words to the other woman, who hustled back into the lodge kitchen. In record time, Luciana came back out with another bowl of scraps and handed it to Jessie. Then she took a few globs of meat from the bowl and made a path from Jessie to the stray. Muttering in unintelligible Spanish, she gestured wildly and crossed her palms over her heart. Jessie looked inquiringly at Fran.

"She says if you catch her to please let us know later. And she says to thank you for having a good heart. And she says this cat likes chicken. Pollo."

"Pollo," Luciana said emphatically, moving her arms in a flapping chicken motion.

"Got it," Jessie said with a grin. "Pollo it is."

Fran wished Jessie good luck and told her to leave the bowls anywhere and she'd retrieve them on her next break. The women opened the door into the lodge, Luciana tossing a worried glance and a 'gracias' over her shoulder before they disappeared inside.

* * *

By the time Arvid returned with the carrier, the tabby cat was nestled on Jessie's lap as though he belonged there, kneading her lap with small white paws. Jessie's rear ached from sitting on the cold concrete and her back was stiff, but she wore a happy smile.

"We're in luck, Arvid. I'll bet the only reason this cat wouldn't let Fran get close to it is there might be a slight odor of the woman's bulldog clinging to her shoes or slacks. The poor thing is tame, lonesome, and has decided it loves me. Of course, it's actually the chicken I've been doling out that tipped the balance, but I *am* very loveable." She didn't tell him she'd also been doling out salmon treats from the bag in her pocket.

"Of course, you are," he said skeptically. Very slowly, he put the cat carrier down near Jessie. She handed him the bowl just as slowly.

"There's still some chicken in it. Put it inside the crate."

Arvid reached inside and, again in slow motion, placed the bowl toward the back.

"I think the cat will smell it. At least, I hope it—"

Before Jessie could finish her sentence, the cat stood, jumped off her lap and trotted to the carrier to find the rest of the chicken." As soon as it stepped inside, Arvid shut the door and latched it. The tabby chewed, not even bothering to turn around. "Got it," Arvid whispered.

"Well, look at that. It's used to a carrier. This cat must belong to someone who took very good care of it and is probably missing it."

"Yeah, but you know what? This was stupid of me."

"How so, Arvid?"

"Here we are worrying about a darn cat, and I'm supposed to be keeping an eye on you...supposed to be making sure you're safe. And I went off and left you alone without even thinking."

"Oh, calm down. I wasn't even alone when you left."

"Hmph," he grunted. Then he peered into the carrier. "Mighty pretty markings on that cat. Wonder if Esther likes tabbies." He looked again into the crate and wiggled his fingers through the mesh. "Hey, baby," he crooned. "Here, kitty, kitty. Come to Arvid."

Jessie turned her face to hide her grin.

* * *

Twenty minutes later, the vet waved a scanner over the cat's shoulder-blade area and announced. "We're in luck. The cat is microchipped. But of course, that only helps if the owner registered the chip with the proper information. In this case, I'm not sure it matters."

"Why not?" Arvid's voice was belligerent. "It's a perfectly nice cat."

The young vet looked startled. "Well, yes. It certainly is. What I should have said is that I *think* I know whose it is, because several weeks ago we had a call about a missing cat—one of my feline patients. And this little girl looks like the right cat," He picked up the cat and handed it to Jessie. "However, the tabby is a common breed, so don't get your hopes up. The chip registration will make it certain. It's a great practice. Sometimes you find a missing pet with a chip several years after they've been lost."

"Fantastic," Jessie said. "But you said the cat reminded you of one of your patients? One who's been missing?"

"Yes, I think so. But let me have my assistant take a look and see where the chip was registered and check the number. There are several registries. Why they don't standardize them is beyond me."

A few minutes later, he came back with a smile from ear to ear and said, "As I suspected, the tabby belongs to someone we know. This little girl is Moxie. She belongs to Althea Heath, who is in a facility here in town called 'The Foothills Assisted Living'. A staff member calls periodically to see if we've located her cat. She's going to be overjoyed."

"Wait a minute," Arvid said. "I know who you mean, but doesn't she have dementia...or Alzheimer's? How can she care for a pet? Wouldn't it be better to find a new home for it?" He looked at the cat in Jessie's arms with a skeptical expression.

"Are you talking about Glen Heath's step-mother?" Jessie looked dumbfounded.

"Yes." The vet's face became guarded. "But it is my understanding that if the cat were found, Mr. Heath didn't want it."

"Interesting," Jessie said with narrowed eyes.

"The staff member from Foothills said that finding the cat would be a boost to Althea's well-being, and that they'd be glad to care for it. Pets are very beneficial for seniors—in some cases it lowers blood pressure just to pet an animal."

Arvid asked, "Would you like us to take the cat over there? We'd be glad to."

The vet looked at the cat. "That would be fantastic, but if you don't mind waiting just a few minutes, we'll give Moxie a quick check-up and a bath."

"A bath?" Arvid asked.

"She's filthy. I'm sure the Foothills will be happier taking in a well-groomed, clean animal than a filthy-looking one. Although, I have to say, they are wonderful in allowing the elderly to keep their pets. It's hard for people to give up their animals...they're like children to many of the old folks."

Arvid looked bemused. "We'll wait." He pointed to the tabby. "But I'd like to see how you get that cat in a tub of water."

The vet laughed. "Well, come on back. You can help." Giving Arvid a droll look, he said, "This is a medical office." He paused, then said, "We have an excellent supply of bandages and antibiotics."

"Huh," Arvid grunted. "Guess I'll pass."

"But we *will* wait," Jessie said with a chuckle. "And we'll take Moxie to her owner."

She plunked down in a waiting room chair by Arvid as the vet took the tabby and handed her to an assistant.

"I can't imagine Glen saying he wasn't interested in taking care of his step-mother's animal. I'm disappointed in him."

"Don't know him that well," Arvid muttered. "But I know that right now he has a lot on his plate. He's waiting to hear if remains found near Savannah are those of his step-brother, Harris Freeman. I'm not sure how close they were. Maybe not close at all. And maybe he isn't planning on sticking around."

"True," Jessie said.

"I know he's a friend of yours Jessie, and according to Sheriff Fischer, Glen has a solid alibi, but his step-mother isn't well. If something happened to Harris, maybe Glen figured he'd inherit when his step-mom passed away. Didn't he tell you he thought his ship was about to come in?

"Yeah, but Glen just talks that way. Glen's ship is *always* about to come in. He talks a big bluff and he talks big. Everything is always either terrible or fabulous." She waved her hands around to emphasize her words.

"Well, all I can say is that I have a gut feeling that Benny's murder, the Nielson's deaths, and now this possible murder of Harris Freeman—another local who stood to inherit a ranch—might all be connected. And even though they have Evan Hansen in jail for Benny's murder, it doesn't quite tie together. I wouldn't be surprised if they wind up letting him go."

"Have they charged him yet?"

"Nup. And they can only keep him 72 hours before they do. Last I heard they were going over every bit of his pickup, checking fingerprints and looking for any other kind of evidence. Personally, I tend to agree with you that perhaps Evan's being set up by the killer." Arvid looked thoughtful. "Of course, maybe he's just a good actor. Let me tell you, linking the evidence together on these deaths is like trying to tie a bow in a piece of barbed wire. And it's so twisted it makes you wonder if everybody in Crooked Creek is exactly that—crooked. I'd sure like to have you look at that trail cam video and see if you notice anything we missed."

"Push harder on Fischer. If he'll agree to it, I'd be glad to look at it. One thing I feel certain of is that there's more than one person involved."

Arvid stared at her. "Why do you think that?"

She looked embarrassed. "You know me. I always look at everything the way I look at a painting.

"What's that got to do with Benny's murder? Or the Nielson's, or poor Harris Freeman's?" Arvid leaned his elbow on his knee and put his chin on his fist.

"Oh, it's silly. Every painting is made of bits and pieces but should be based on one strong idea. When I paint, I work with a focal area in mind for each painting. If Adele Nielson's death, her father's, her brother's, Harris Freeman's and Benny's murder are all tied together there *should* be one specific goal the killer is working toward. The deaths are all different, though. Almost like haphazard events. But I did learn that Benny owned 600 acres bordering the Nielson's place." Jessie shrugged. "So, the only common thread I can see seems to be land, Arvid."

"This is Montana…lots of people own land. It might mean nothing."

"Maybe. Who inherits Benny's 600 acres?"

"I don't know. So far, Sheriff Fischer is in the dark. Neighbors say he didn't have any close relatives, and no will has turned up yet. I'm not sure what the procedure is. I think it begins with the Montana court system appointing a representative. They'll go through his belongings with a fine-toothed comb to try and locate a will. They'll hunt for debts that need to be paid. They'll open bank boxes, go through correspondence, and that kind of thing. Maybe they put a notice in the paper about the death asking that any creditors contact the executor. I'm not sure how they go about hunting for heirs, but I know it's got to be a can of worms."

"Well, I think it's odd that three properties bordering each other have all had people murdered or at least die in suspicious circumstances." Jessie looked toward the sound of approaching footfalls.

A vet assistant, wearing a pale green lab-coat with the name 'Sheila' embroidered over the left pocket, came through the swinging door holding a sparkling clean tabby who complained loudly. "She's a chatty little thing," she said cheerfully. "Moxie has a clean bill of health and is ready to go see Althea. I called the Foothill Facility and they're expecting you. Were they ever thrilled." Frowning, she said, "I guess Althea is having a pretty bad day. They hope having her cat back will take the edge off. She waved toward the stacked cat food and accoutrements for felines near the check-out desk. "Need a litter box, litter and food? If you asked Glen Heath, he might have those items at Althea's home."

"I think I'll just spring for a new potty box and all the other cat things," Jessie said as she and Arvid stood.

"Nup. They're on me." Arvid pulled out his wallet.

"Let me gather some things together for you."

"And what do we owe for the bath and check-up?"

She gave Arvid an airy wave of the hand. "Not a thing. Dr. Brown says you were good Samaritans to bring her in, and the exam is a freebie. Moxie had lost so much weight that if it hadn't

299

been for the chip, we may not have realized it was her. Althea is going to be overjoyed."

* * *

Twenty minutes later, Jessie gently placed Moxie into Althea Heath's arms and the tabby immediately started to purr. The woman's eyes shone with relief and joy. She looked up at Jessie, then back at the cat. "Please, both of you...sit."

Jessie looked around the pleasant room—the walls covered in brightly colored botanical wall paper, the comfortable loveseat where Arvid seated himself and the small recliner with a soft afghan draped over the arm—the chair in which Althea sat and cuddled her pet. It was a cheerful apartment. She could see into the bedroom through an open door, and the bed was covered with a vivid blue chenille coverlet. The effect was homey.

"Glen used to bring her in to see me before she got lost. Or he would take me out to the farm for a day. He's a good boy, that Glen. I told him Moxie'd be happier on the farm, but I was terribly lonely here. When she ran away, Glen wished I'd just kept her here to begin with. I'm so lucky you found her." A tear slipped down her cheek. "But, maybe she didn't. Run away, I mean. Maybe she rode all the way to town on the engine of his truck. Cats sometimes do that in cold weather, you know, climb up on the engine." She stroked the cats head. "Moxie, you're nothing but skin and bones," she told the rumbling cat.

"She was lucky that some women from the lodge kitchen felt sorry for her and gave her table scraps every day. I can fill the litter box and put out food and water for her before we leave if you like." Jessie said.

"Nonsense." Althea leveled her gaze at Jessie. "I'm having a fairly good day. I can handle it myself. I moved into assisted living knowing that it would eventually be necessary. Instead of waiting, I wanted to make the transition while I still had the ability to make choices. I was getting forgetful enough that I worried about cooking. That kind of thing. You know what Mark Twain reputedly said? 'The reports of my death are greatly exaggerated?' That's actually a misquote. Did you know that? Anyway, reports of my memory loss are greatly exaggerated." She frowned. "That darn Jacob down at the Sheriff's Office came to ask me some questions on a particularly stressful day—a day before I had my medication. I couldn't remember the answer to several of his questions, and now all my old friends think I'm not only mentally incompetent, but at death's door to boot. I used to be a very competent math teacher." Looking into Jessie's sympathetic eyes, she said, "Yes. I've had some very bad days since I heard my son was missing. Anyone would. He disappeared on the way home from an army base in Georgia. I...I can't remember the name of the base." She looked down at Moxie. "Of course, I have some very bad days."

"I'm sorry." Arvid's rumbling tone was sad. "Have they...uh..."

"Yes," she said quickly. "Sheriff Fischer said they are almost certain a body found in Savannah is Harris. I know he'd never go AWOL. So, I am waiting for confirmation. My heart hopes against hope it isn't Harris...then I seesaw and hope it is, so the waiting is over. Because he must be dead. Or he would have contacted his mother."

"Mrs. Heath, I'm helping Sheriff Fischer on Benny Potter's murder. Do you mind my asking a couple questions?"

She looked startled. Then she narrowed her eyes and seemed suddenly quite canny. "I don't mind."

"How well did your son know Benny Potter?"

"Not well. I know they think he went to Savannah and killed Harris. But it doesn't make sense. Not at all." She closed her eyes and when she opened them, they had a vacant look.

"Who will take over the farm if Harris is gone?"

"Our farm?" She looked blankly at Arvid. "Why, my son will take over. He's just in the Army for another year. He's such a good man. And one of his Army friends is coming to meet me." She snuggled her face against the tabby's fur. "And look! He's found my Moxie."

Jessie and Arvid looked at each other. Then Jessie got up, took the litter pan to the bathroom and filled it. She poured dry food into the new dish and put water in the new bowl. When she came out, she grasped Althea's hand and thanked her for a lovely visit.

Althea glowed. "You come again, dear. And bring this big man along." She shrugged. "Hmph. I've forgotten your names. But names are overrated, you know…a rose by any other name and all that."

Arvid nodded to her, his eyes full of compassion. "Yes, Ma'am, they're overrated. You have a lovely rest of the day."

She smiled at him. Then she gave a start. "Roses go in pots. Pots. Benny Potter would not kill my son. You tell the Sheriff I said so. And tell that snotty young Jacob my mind isn't gone yet."

As they left, they heard her tell the cat, "My mind isn't gone, Moxie. It's just doing some major long division and can't figure out the polynomials."

* * *

"I hope that never happens to me—or to Esther. I can't imagine anything worse," Arvid trudged down the hall as though the visit had weighed him down.

Jessie's answer was to wipe her eyes and pull a tissue from her pocket.

A man in a wheel-chair rolled by in the hall, cheerfully greeting Arvid and looking appreciatively at Jessie.

"Well," Arvid said after the old man passed by, "being wheel-chair bound would be hard, too."

"Yes, it would. Life tosses everyone a curve ball as we get older."

"Shoot, if I ever need a wheel-chair, I want one with an extra wide seat and a big engine…maybe studded tires and lawn-mower blades." He made a rolling motion with his big hands. "That would cut my time waiting in the rest home cafeteria line."

"Oh, Arvid, really. 'Cut your time'?" She grimaced.

"No pun intended," he joked. "A wide seat, a drink holder in the arm rest…"

Jessie changed the subject. "I was relieved when she said Glen had been bringing her cat to visit her. I've been fond of him for years, and I hated to think of him not taking care of her cat, or Althea Heath herself. Did you pick up on what she said, Arvid?"

"About the cat or the polynomials?"

302

"Neither. About her son's military friend that was going to come and see her."

"You're right. I wonder if it's true, or just a figment of her imagination."

"I think it's something legitimate that just came to mind as she spoke. We should tell Fischer what she said. He can ask the desk person to call if someone new in town shows up to visit Althea Heath.

"You're right." He pulled out his phone, then stopped in the hall and stared down at it. "Hey, Esther sent a text. We're invited out to Joe Helland's woodshop. Want to go? He included you in the invitation."

"It would have to be tomorrow. I have to paint in the quick draw again this evening at seven and want to look at my reference photos and get set up. But sure. I'd love to see his carvings."

"Huh." Arvid was still reading through his text. "And he included Russell in the invitation. And Grant." He looked up at Jessie with a puzzled expression. "I don't remember introducing him to Russell and Grant, do you?"

"No. But then, I've been busy, and stressed over these darn tractors and notes. And now I'm bummed, too."

"About poor Althea Heath?"

"Yeah. And because I don't even remember what a polynomial is. I'll bet in her prime that woman had a brain that beats mine six ways to Sunday. Deep in her mind, she thinks Benny Potter couldn't have killed her son. I'll bet she's right."

Arvid grunted in agreement. He texted Esther that they wanted to go out to the Gingerbread Man's shop if the invitation could be moved to the next day...then he punched in the numbers for the Sheriff's Office.

Chapter Forty-five

Christofferson's Law Office, Crooked Creek

Tate leaned forward and placed the crumpled notepaper on Richard Christofferson's desk. Looking around the room, he took note of the diplomas hanging in walnut frames on the richly wallpapered walls.

The attorney's hand swept out and pulled the crumpled paper toward him. He reached into his desk drawer and brought out reading glasses. As he read, he ran nervous fingers through his salt and pepper hair.

Tate looked at the family photos on the desk. In them, the attorney stood with his arm around a slender brunette woman and two little boys about seven and nine, posed in front of their parents. *Nice looking little family.* Something he wanted himself, but something that wasn't in the cards right now. He wondered if there'd ever be a time that he could have a family—even with this windfall will that he'd just handed the lawyer. He was committed to the Army for another year.

A pity, too. Now he'd have everything he'd ever dreamed of. Money for nothing. Everything a man could want. He really liked the flame-haired artist, Jessie. If he was going to be around her neck of the woods, he'd make a huge effort to get better acquainted. Give that Grant Kennedy some competition. When he helped Jessie clean up her supplies after the quick draw, and

Kennedy stuck his crooked nose in the mix, he hadn't liked the way the two kept stealing glances at one another.

Oh well.

Maybe he was coming to the attorney's office too soon. Maybe he should have stayed under cover for a while longer. Then he saw the framed quote hanging behind Christofferson's desk area and he brightened. The attorney's choice of décor gave him hope.

"Discretion is the perfection of reason, and a guide to us in all the duties of life..."
- Sir Walter Scott

Hopefully this small-town attorney knew the meaning of discretion. Tate made up his mind to give him the benefit of the doubt.

"It's the original will, sir, and I hope you'll keep it quiet for a while. I imagine you received the faxed copy of the handwritten will that Dominic Nielson, Harris Freeman and I all signed. This original was witnessed by a couple of the Army officers we knew." Tate was somber. "The three of us were good friends." He cleared his throat, which was suddenly tight. "Like brothers. We went through a lot together during our time in the army. I was from Hawaii, not raised around here like Dom and Harris, but it didn't matter. We watched each other's backs."

Christofferson looked up from the paper and nodded. "Go on."

"When Dom died, Harris and I were determined to find out exactly what happened here in Crooked Creek. Harris bought a ticket home, but I don't think he even got out of Savannah." His voice caught. "My superior called me today. This morning, a Georgia farmer and his son were out squirrel hunting, and they found the remains of a man. In the woods about twenty miles out of Savannah. The local police and the military police had been working together to find Harris. Papers found in his pockets make it pretty certain it's him, but he wasn't wearing his dog tags. The tags weren't in his luggage left at the hotel, either. Because of the deterioration of the body and the fact that critters had been at it...well, the MPs at the base are waiting for DNA confirmation. There was a phone on the body, but it had to be sent to a data recovery wizard."

"I'm sorry to hear," Christofferson said, his tone sympathetic. "His mother is in an assisted living facility here in Crooked Creek. I hope her dementia will be somewhat of a barrier between her and such a blow." He looked down again at the paper in his hand. "For a few of these old folks, sometimes it's a blessing not to realize what's happening. I sure hope I never get to that point, though." He looked again at the paper Tate had given him. "You realize that when Althea was told she was developing Alzheimer's, she put everything into Harris's name. Everything. Not even her stepson knows that at this point." He looked up. "It's a considerable amount. It does stipulate that her health care and assisted living expenses are to be paid—any expenses incurred that are not covered by her insurance, that is—and it stipulates a nice bequest to her stepson." He looked down at the paper again. "A handwritten will, witnessed by two army officers. This may be remarkably distressing to the stepson, even though he hates farming." He looked up at Tate. "You're an MP, correct?"

Tate nodded in the affirmative.

"Interesting. I think it is alright for me to tell you that I received another copy of this in the mail two months ago—from Harris Freeman. I have not made this public because there is not, at this time, valid proof he is deceased. And you realize it will need to be verified. Then it will have to go through probate. That often takes several months." He flipped the pen he was holding end over end in his fingers. "It was determined that Dom passed away after his father had already died. The sequence of deaths determines that the Nielson place and all monies, including life insurance, went from Berg, then to Dom, then to Harris Freeman and now to you. It's a large bequest."

"I know," Tate said sadly. He cleared his throat. "I never visited out here, but I had suspected as much."

Christofferson gave Tate a pointed look. "Don't be offended, not that you'd tell me, but I don't suppose you killed Harris Freeman yourself? You're actually the best suspect. You had motive. You were in Georgia. You knew his plans."

"No. I'm not offended. If I didn't know I hadn't killed a good friend so that I could inherit a ranch—two ranches, actually—I would even suspect myself. Nielson's is certainly a nice place. I drove by yesterday, just to take a look from the road. I'll need to make some arrangements for its management and for that of the Freeman ranch. I haven't been by the house there, yet, but I understand the two properties share a common border. Do I recall Harris saying that your brothers did some farm management?"

"Yes, they do."

"I may need to contact them and ask if they have time to handle a few more acres." Tate leaned forward. "However, the inheritance isn't the only reason I'm here. I came out to find out what happened to the Nielson family. What can you tell me? Who had reason to kill Dom's sister? Who would want to drive the old man half-crazy with worry until he was so paranoid he shot his own son? And how does it tie in with Harris Freeman's murder? Because he had to have been murdered."

"I really don't know. And I've given it a lot of thought. The logical suspect for Harris' murder would have been Wheels—sorry, that's Glen Heath—Harris's stepbrother. The two were never close. He probably never knew that Harris would inherit from Dom, but he probably thought with Harris gone that he'd inherit the ranch. But Glen is a nice fellow, and he wasn't even in town for most of the problems with Berg Nielson. I heard that he was totally cleared by Sheriff Fischer with an iron clad alibi. When Addie was killed, and Berg began receiving the threatening notes, Glen was recuperating from some miserable surgery. Gallbladder? Gallstones? I can't recall."

"Well, if you think of anything, no matter how small, please call me." He handed Christofferson a card with his cell phone number. "Until I'm satisfied the Sheriff's Office identified the correct killer—or killers—for each and every one of those deaths, I'm staying put."

Christofferson looked startled. "I've heard of no arrest."

"They couldn't make an arrest because the suspect is dead. His name is Benny Potter."

Christofferson stared in bewilderment. Then he shook his head. His eyes met Tate's. "No." Christofferson said the single word again, with even more conviction. "No. Not Benny."

"You don't think so, huh? Do you know that Potter went all the way down to Savannah and rented an SUV? And that was the vehicle the motel clerk saw Harris get into the day he died. It's pretty cut and dried. But I agree with you. I've been checking on this Benny. Everyone I asked, 'Did you know this poor guy who got killed?' said he wasn't very bright. I don't think he was capable of the planning. So, my job here is not done."

"No." The attorney said again emphatically. "You're right." Then he sighed and shook his head. "Since it's been proven that he went to Georgia, *maybe* he's the one who killed Harris Freeman—although I can't imagine why—but I went to school with Benny Potter. He barely graduated. He could never plan something like the campaign mounted against Berg Nielson." He tapped a pen on his desk, a thoughtful expression on his face. "I imagine the Sheriff would love to think that Benny did this. He'd like to think the matter was settled, too—that people are safe now. But no. Benny was a bit slow mentally. However, he was also gullible."

"Gullible in what way?" Tate demanded.

Christofferson stopped tapping the pen and leaned back in his leather office chair. His face was furrowed in thought. Then he spoke. "From junior-high school on, Benny was always being taken advantage of by boys who talked him into doing their dirty work. Want to have a dead chicken put in someone's school locker? Pay Benny five bucks. Want chewing gum stuck in your ex-girlfriend's hair or a rival's new car keyed? A dead catfish slid under the backseat of a teacher's car? Pretend to be his friend and ask Benny." He gazed out the window. "Young people are cruel. It was pitiful."

"So, you think someone else—someone pretty damn vicious by the sound of the nasty notes sent to a harmless old man—pulled Benny's strings?"

"Yes. I do. Do I understand that you plan to stick around until you figure out who the puppeteer is?" The lawyer's tone was sharp.

Tate leaned forward again. His eyes were hard. He answered the lawyer in the lawyer's own clipped tones. "Yes. I am. And I'm going to find a way for the law to hang him from his own strings."

"Well, here's what I suggest. There's an old fellow in town who knew more about the Nielson family than you'd be able to find out anywhere else. He's been acting as a caretaker. I can't give you a key to Nielson's place yet. That will have to wait until the will is verified, but the old man has one. Get him to show you around. I'll give him a call and tell him to expect you. And I'll tell him not to mention you're looking into the murders. Or that you'll be inheriting."

Tate nodded. "Thanks."

The lawyer yanked a post-it-note from a stack on his desk and scribbled a name and address. "Don't let his appearance fool you." Christofferson smiled at Tate. "Lately, he seems about half a birthday candle from dead, but he's a healthy old codger and tough as an old railroad spike. He tells me he's been trying to check into the deaths, but so far hasn't had a lot of success." He handed Tate the contact information. "Joe Helland. Around here they call him the Gingerbread Man."

Tate raised his eyebrows. Then he thought about the old vet who'd lingered at the table while he and Jessie O'Bourne were drinking cocoa. Jessie had brought the old guy into his art room, too, with the man lugging an oxygen pack and appearing exhausted.

He looked at Christofferson and grinned. "I may have already made this fine gentleman's acquaintance."

Christofferson nodded. "He expected someone from the army to come looking for Harris Freeman." His eyes grew serious. "And Tate?"

"Yes?" Tate noted the grim expression on the lawyer's face.

"Like I said, the stepbrother is going to be a might upset that he isn't the primary heir. But the law is the law. Right now, it is assumed that Mrs. Althea Heath will inherit, and I'll let people assume so for a bit. When Berg first wrote his will, he had several minor bequests he asked Dom to honor. I can go over them with you in detail later. You could choose to honor those as well. It might make you a tad more popular in the community."

Tate nodded.

"And I'm assuming you do plan to check in with the Sheriff's office?"

"Tomorrow."

309

"They aren't a bunch of rubes, you know. If you actually did have anything to do with Harris's death, they'll eventually find out."

"Nothing to worry about, sir." Tate flashed an impish grin. "I'm innocent as the proverbial newborn babe. I'll visit this fine Sheriff's Office tomorrow, as promised. But today I'll go speak with Mr. Helland."

Christofferson harrumphed. "I don't suspect Glen had anything to do with the Nielson's deaths, either. Or his own step-brother's. But someone has gone to a lot of trouble and planning—it could have nothing—or everything—to do with the property you inherited. Watch your back."

Tate tossed him a quick salute and turned to go.

After he left, Christofferson reached into a drawer and pulled out a thin file folder. He opened it and read through it once more, checking each bequest Berg Nielson had listed, and evaluating the wording to see how binding the bequests were. Then he sat for a time, forming circles with the tip of his index finger on the stack of papers. Thinking.

Chapter Forty-six

The Gingerbread Man

Tate looked up at Joe Helland in amazement as the old man climbed off the top rung of the steep rickety ladder and hoisted himself onto the floor of Nielson's barn loft like a man half his age. "For God's sake, be careful," he called up, fussing. "And don't think I'm coming up. I hate heights. And that beat up ladder doesn't look like it would even hold my weight."

"That's fine," Helland rumbled down.

Tate heard a low muttered 'little wuss' but pretended he hadn't caught it.

"I just want to check and see what's left up here. Berg used it for storage and he has some big steamer trunks up here. They should be fairly secure. But I want to make certain the mice aren't getting in. They can squeeze into a quarter of an inch hole if they feel motivated. Berg used to have a couple barn cats to keep after them. One of the neighbors gave them a home after he died, so all you've got left to keep the mice down is the King. Watch out for him." Joe Helland scurried down the ladder, stepped down onto the dirt floor of the barn and wiped the palm of his hands on his jeans.

"The King?" Tate asked. "Nielson had a cat named after Elvis?"

Helland looked blank, then chuckled. "No...he isn't named after Elvis."

311

"King Tut?" Tate looked at Helland with expectation. "Martin Luther King?"

"Nah," Joe said. "Named after a card. The King of Diamonds—probably around here somewhere." He waved his hand, indicating the interior of the barn. "Unless he's still hibernating. But they usually come out of hibernation in March or April if it hits sixty degrees out."

"Cats don't hibernate."

"Right you are. It isn't a cat. It's a big rattler. Diamondback."

"A snake?" Tate took a step backward. "You're joking, right?"

"Nope. Berg took the shotgun out several times to try and get rid of it last fall, but I don't believe he ever got him. I've seen a few mice in the loose haystack over there, and I know they'd attract him like a magnet." He gestured to a large pile of hay in the corner from which a pitchfork protruded. "I'd planned to move the hay out this spring. Don't suppose you want to take care of that while you're here?"

Tate pulled a face and laughed good naturedly. "Nossirree. Good story, though." He waved his hand above his head in an airy manner. "Go ahead and make fun of the new Hawaiian kid on the block. I can take it."

Helland looked at him. "No story. I'm dead serious. Be careful if you come out here by yourself and walk around. See that small cabinet on the wall? It has a few things in it Berg used to keep when he had horses or new lambs. Veterinarian type stuff. But let me just check if there's also a snake-bite kit. He used to keep one here because of old King." He walked over and opened the cupboard door, rummaging around in the supplies. "Nope. Not there anymore. Might be that he put it in the house." He strolled toward the open barn door. "Do you want to see any more?"

"Yes. I meant to ask you to show me approximately where Berg had the trail cam placed over by the house. The one he told you about?"

"Sorry. I never saw it. Probably somewhere near the front door because the notes were almost always left at night. Evan Hansen loaned the camera to him. I know that young man. He was sure sweet on Adele. When she died, Evan took Berg under his wing. He brought over meals—big dinners Berg could use for several days at a time. He was pretty disgusted about the video cam though…said Berg moved it and the only thing it captured on film was someone's feet. Not much you can tell from that. When you go in to talk to Sheriff Fischer, you can ask him about it."

Tate glanced at the lonesome-looking house. "I will. I suppose I'd better head back. I have a room-sitter watching my art display."

"How's that going for you? You actually interested in art? Or are those sketches even yours?"

"Oh, they're mine all right. Old ones I did before I joined the Army. And it's going well. I've actually sold enough to cover my framing and the show-room fee. It's amazing. I've always loved drawing. Getting to try my hand at doing an art show make me rethink a military career. And I like meeting the people who come to the show."

Helland grunted. "It's a good cover story, too. Why do you think someone at the art show is involved with the Nielson's deaths? And I suppose if what you are telling me about Harris is true, whoever was responsible for Adele Nielson's death and Berg's notes is probably involved with Harris Freeman's death—if he is indeed dead—as well. You know, that almost has to be Harris's body they found near Savannah.

"Yeah, I feel certain it's him." Tate peered around the barn warily—obviously looking for a snake.

As they stepped through the barn door into the sunlight, Joe Helland was glad he was walking in front, so Tate couldn't see his wide smile.

"I saw several of the notes Dom's dad had received," Tate said to Helland's back. "When Dom and Harris invited me to their barracks to collaborate on the crazy will Christofferson told you about, we all looked at the notes. Harris got an odd look on his face and said, 'I've seen that type of paper before.' When we pressed him to tell us more about it, he mentioned the Crooked Creek Art Expo and said he'd probably just seen it in some of the work at the show. He told us that if he remembered anything solid, he'd tell us.' And when he disappeared, there was an Expo brochure on the nightstand in his motel room."

Tate reached into his jacket pocket and pulled out a folded piece of paper. "I took this to an art store in Savannah. It's a corner off one of the notes. I draw myself, but I don't use this particular paper. There are about five local artists in the show who are displaying sketches or prints. Four men and a woman. I checked the website listing for the Expo and thought if I came to the show as one of the artists, I'd have more opportunity to talk to all of them and to their acquaintances. Basically, I was at a loss. It was all I could think of to try, mostly because of the Expo brochure found in Harris's hotel room."

"Find anything out?"

"Not much. One of the women artists had drawings done on this type of paper, and two of the men did as well. They were all out of towners. I can't find any association whatsoever with Sage Bluff or Dom. I discovered that this type of art paper isn't sold in the downtown art supply store. Of course, with the way e-commerce has taken over, it can be purchased online from anywhere in the world. And anyone who paints usually does a lot of drawing, too…but they don't necessarily display the sketches at every show. It could be any artist in the show—or any artist not in the show, for that matter."

Helland nodded in agreement. Abruptly, he changed the subject. "So…what do you think of your inheritance?"

"I wish I didn't have another year to go in the Army. I'd love to come back to Crooked Creek and learn to run this place. And the Freeman ranch, too. I need to do something with that right away, because I owe it to Harris to take care of his mother and give something to his stepbrother. How do you think I should go about that?"

"Well, there's a piece of property nearer town. It isn't connected to the rest of the acreage. It's cut off from the Freeman place by a road and about 400 acres of Gunderson's wheat fields. I know Pop Gunderson has been wanting to buy that acreage for years. You could deed that and the farmhouse at Freeman's place to Glen Heath. He could sell both the land and farmhouse to Gunderson if he was of a mind to. Frankly, it would be more than Glen deserves. He never did a thing for Althea until this past year when he came home, so in my mind she doesn't owe him anything. And neither do you. He wasn't that nice to her before he needed a resting spot to recuperate from bad health."

Tate looked at Helland. "Is that right? But he came home when he got sick, right?"

"Actually, he came home one other time that summer, I think. Then again when he got sick."

"Was he ever one of Benny Potter's good friends?"

"Not that I know of."

"Just thought I'd ask."

"You're stretching. I see where you're going with that thought, but Glen would have to plan miles ahead to inherit not only Nielson's farm, but also Harris Freeman's ranch. It's a big leap. First, he'd have to know that his stepbrother Harris was Dom Nielson's heir."

"That's not so far-fetched. Harris might have let that slip. He might have mentioned it in a letter to his mom and perhaps Althea then told her stepson."

Helland said, "But even if Wheels—sorry, I always think of Glen as Wheels—knew that, he'd have to plan on all three Nielsons, his own stepbrother, Harris, and Althea Heath, his stepmother, to all die before he'd benefit in any way. That's a long, convoluted chain of events."

"Stranger things have happened."

"Yes, but luckily for Glen, he has a solid alibi."

"Yes, it sure is." But in his mind, he wondered if it was solid as granite or solid as the oatmeal mush served in the mess hall.

Chapter Forty-seven

Crooked Creek Lodge

Jessie walked into her hotel room to find a very disgruntled Jack. She knew why he was annoyed. His walk was cut short. He'd watched another cat eat meat scraps, while he wasn't given any. And now...Jessie smelled of this other feline. She grinned at him. "Her name was Moxie. She was gorgeous, especially after her bath. And you didn't need her food, Big Fella." She leaned toward him. "But you were such a good boy to lead us around back to find her."

He narrowed his eyes. One canine tooth overlapped his lower lip, giving him a sardonic expression.

She straightened, hung her sweater in the closet, then walked over and bent to stroke his head. He responded by whipping around, turning his back to her and sat flicking his tail. He offered her a view of a broad orange rump and flattened ears. Then he stalked off, crawled under the bed and disappeared except for the tip of a flicking tail.

"Well, you ornery little demon." Jessie put her hands on her hips and laughed. "You can sulk until I'm dressed, but I'll bet you forget all about being mad when it's dinner time."

She reached down and touched the exposed tail making it twitch angrily. Then she undressed and hopped in the shower, humming a snatch of Esther's newest music. Letting the water stream over her, she stopped humming and thought about Althea Heath. And how short life could seem. For no reason she cared to

316

admit, she began thinking of quotes from classic novels. And a pair of laughing hazel eyes. From that thought of Grant, she remembered the angry look in Russell's blue eyes at the last quick draw, watching Grant and Tate help her with her supplies and clean up—before Camille had worked her magic on him. She needed to give him the blonde's name. She toweled off and wrapped the thick hotel robe around herself and walked out to grab her phone. Frowning, she saw that she had at least four messages from Russell.

And I'll bet all of them are asking 'who was the blonde?'.

Pictures of Russell flashed across her mind. Her favorite memory of him was watching him banter with her mother in the kitchen at Sage Creek. In her mind, there was Russell, helping Hanna O'Bourne squeeze lemons for lemonade. Russell, playing ball with her brother, Kevin. Russell, casting a fly rod with Dan O'Bourne down at the river. Russell offering her burnt pizza the night he introduced her to K.D. for the first time, saying 'I cooked'.

Do I love him? Yes. But no longer in that way, she thought. *He's more like a good friend. Or even a brother.* And *his* life and *his* happiness are stuck in the bleachers watching while the game is played, too. She tapped in his number and almost cringed when he answered. Her heart hammered.

"Where on earth have you been?"

"Long story." She took a deep breath, then said lightly. "Russell, I think I'll always love you—"

She heard a slight gasp and hurried ahead. "But like a brother—a member of our family. Always. You and I are never going to be a couple. But we'll always be family."

"Oh, Jessie. I—"

"Just listen. You know that gorgeous big blonde at the quick draw?"

"Uh, yeah."

"Camille Johnson. Room 145. And you know what, Russ?"

"What, Jessie?"

"Life is short. Too short. You and I love each other—we do—but not the way it takes to make a life together. There's not that spark. I saw that spark when you and Camille just looked at each

317

other. Take a walk down to room 145. Camille isn't part of the quick finish tonight, so she'll have her art room open until the auction starts. And I can give you a heads up."

"Dammit, Jessie, I—"

"It's okay, Russ. We're good. Solid. I just want to tell you that Camille is never, ever going to give up her art. Not her art, not her art shows. Not for anyone. The thought of suggesting she might had better not so much as cross your mind. Accept that."

"I learned that lesson already, Jess." His voice had a slightly sad sound. "It was a hard one." In a brighter tone, he said, "145, huh?"

"Yep." Jessie ended the call. She sat on the bed watching the numbers on the desk clock flip from minute to minute, feeling melancholy seep into her bones.

Maybe I'll open the bottle of wine I bought for Esther.

Then she gave a rueful smile.

Nah.

She sang a couple of lines from "Margaritaville". Later, she'd text Cheri Cappello a wicked looking emoji—maybe one of those little happy-faced devils—and let her know she'd finally put Russell out of his misery.

A paw hooked out from under the bed and tapped her ankle. She jumped. Then Jessie untied the sash of the hotel robe and dangled it near her foot. The paw reached out again and swiped at it.

"Missed by a mile, Butter Tub. You can do better than that. You're getting slow, Orange Boy."

She tossed it out a foot from the bed and dragged it across the carpet, wriggling it to mimic a slithery snake. Jack's head popped out from under the bed, eyes riveted on his prey.

The game was on.

* * *

Esther handed Arvid the phone. "It's Sheriff Fischer." He mouthed his thanks.

"Yes?" Arvid took a notebook and pen from the desk. "You don't say…So you released Evan…Very interesting. And no

318

matches, but both sets were different." His expression changed to one of surprise. "Yes. I'll ask her...okay, for tomorrow."

He sat on the bed and tapped his chin with the edge of the phone.

"What is it?" Esther's voice was full of concern.

"They released Evan Hansen. He kept telling Fischer he was being set up and now the Sheriff believes him. It's probably true. The forensics fellow lifted prints from Hansen's pickup door handle and another one from the top of one of those little toy tractors. None of them match Hansen's own prints."

"But that doesn't really make sense. If someone was planting evidence in his truck, surely they'd have enough sense to wear gloves, so they didn't leave prints." She watched his face. "Don't you think so?"

"I do. But it poses some interesting questions. The prints were nice and clear—good index finger prints—and they don't match each other. They're from two different people. And neither one was found in the state Biometric Identification System, which automatically checks fingerprints from crime scenes and suspects against a database."

Esther ran a brush through her short hair. "What do you think this means for the investigation? And for Jessie?"

"I want to give it some thought. There's a couple ideas butting heads in the old noggin, but I want to let 'em fight it out a bit. And I think we need to call a meeting of the minds. Grant, Russell, Jessie...mebbe get together tomorrow and brainstorm."

"And me, Arvid."

"And you, love of my life."

Her hand stilled, stopping in the middle of finger-combing her short hair, adding some shine solution. She smirked at him.

"Now you're laying it on thick. You want something."

"Me?" Arvid answered her reflection with his chin resting on his fist.

"Yes, you. You're as transparent as glass."

"Huh. I don't think I'm that bad." He yawned. "But I was just wondering something. Wanted to pick your brain."

"Okay. Shoot."

"What in Hades is a polynomial?"

319

Jessie slipped the T-shirt over her head. Deep turquoise, it showed an image of a bucking bronc from a painting by C. M. Russell. She pulled on fresh jeans, her best boots and a leather fringed vest. Then she added sterling silver earrings hand-stamped with a Navajo design. Fluffing her curls and finishing with a spritz of perfume, she pronounced herself ready to rumble. Opening her tote bag, she drew out the reference photos she planned to use for the evening quick draw.

Staring at the pictures, trying to plan the drawing and color palette, she had difficulty concentrating. Something bothered her about the visit to the jail to see Evan Hansen. She couldn't put her finger on it, but something hovered at the back of her mind. Finally, she gave up and called Arvid to tell him she was ready to go. He had insisted he and Esther would escort her down to the restaurant for a snack before they walked to the Expo quick draw area.

"It's just silly," she told Jack. "I'm a big gal. And I can certainly take care of myself."

He opened his mouth in a silent meow that became a wide yawn, showing sharp incisors.

As he snapped his mouth closed, she heard a buzzing on her phone and picked it up to see a text from her dad. She gave a loud whoop, sending Jack scurrying under the bed. Dan O'Bourne and Marty were coming up to the quick draw—in fact, they were already on their way—and they were driving separate vehicles, so they could bring her old red pickup to Crooked Creek so she'd have transportation.

She gave a small fist pump.

Yes! Thank God for Dad. Besides, she loved that old pickup, commonly called Fred, even thought it was a gas guzzler. *Good old Fred, the Ford.* She was glad she'd found a good shipping company, too, as she could never haul all the artwork back to Santa Fe in Fred. And she didn't want to shop for a new motorhome until she got back to Santa Fe—after the insurance company reimbursed her for the lost Greyhawk.

A knock sounded at the door. Jessie took a quick look in the mirror and grabbed the tote bag. Then she remembered that the three musketeers—Arvid, Grant and Russell—had given instructions to check the peep hole before opening the door, even if she was expecting one of them. She peered through it and took a step back. Outside her door stood Tate Kamaka. And she could see—even through the peephole—that he was wearing an army uniform. As she stared through the tiny window wondering what to do, she heard a loud WHUMP, and Tate disappeared from view. From the hall came more loud grunts and yelling and Jessie swung the door open to see Arvid on the floor, Tate flattened beneath him like road-kill, yelling, "Get off! Get off me! What the hell's the matter with you!"

"I'm gonna give you about two seconds to explain, buddy." Arvid's voice was not loud. It was the low threatening growl of an annoyed grizzly.

"What the—"

"Two seconds to explain that toy tractor you had in your hand, you miserable piece of—"

Tate stilled. Then he wheezed, "The toy tractor? I can't breathe, you crazy—"

"Yup." Arvid pushed harder on the small of Tate's back. "The toy."

"It was on the floor by Jessie's door. On top of an envelope. I picked them up before I knocked on the door. Why—"

"Jess, you didn't plan to let him in, did you?" He gave the redhead a look that said he hoped her brain was in working order.

"Of course not," she said emphatically. "And don't look so skeptical. My brain can still work long division." She gave Tate a look with blue eyes as cold as chips of glacial ice. "So, what's going on?"

"I have no idea what's going on or what you're talking about, but let me get out my wallet," Tate's voice was choked. "I can explain. Can we step into Jessie's room and get out of the hall?"

* * *

321

"So, that's my story. I've been snooping around trying to find out anything that might shed light on Harris's murder, and the Nielson's girl, Adele. Besides, the way Berg Nielson was harassed, I think that could have been intentionally set up to cause him to have a heart attack from the stress. It was tragic that he shot Dom. But perhaps cunningly planned."

"You could be right," Arvid said. "I've seen some pretty odd scenarios. It's a stretch, though."

"I need to go see Glen Heath and inform his that his step-brother has been positively identified," Tate said. "You seem to know Glen quite well, Jessie. I thought it might help if you came with me to give Glen a little emotional support. Although I know that he and Harris weren't close, he *was* family."

Jessie nodded. "I could come. But Camille Johnson knows him much better. Let me go ask her instead, Tate."

"Nup. Let's both go, Jessie. I don't want you wandering around the hotel by yourself." Arvid had explained the toy tractors to Tate and had told him about the threatening notes.

"Good idea, Arvid." He nodded to Jessie. "We don't want anything happening to our favorite redhead."

"I understand his step-mom has some health issues, and I wanted to ask Glen to come with me when I go to see her—to help cushion the blow."

From under the bed came a rumbling meow.

Tate squatted down and peered under. He grinned and straightened.

"Am I finally making the acquaintance of His Highness, Jack Dempsey?" he asked Jessie.

"Yep. But today he's being more of a royal pain." She went to the closet, pulled out the cat kibble and poured a bit into his dish. An orange head peeked out from under the bed, followed by the rest of the huge tom. He looked at Jessie, gave Tate a disdainful once-over, laying a tattered ear back, and then began chomping the kibble, stopping to peer at Tate periodically and to rumble an inquiring growl.

Tate gave a broad smile. "An apt name for him, Jessie. He acts like he has staff and doesn't put up with insubordination."

"Yeah, yeah, I'm cat staff." Jessie sighed. "Let's go get Camille. Russell's down there, too. He can watch her room while you and Camille go speak to Glen."

"Russell's down in Camille's room?" Arvid gawked at Jessie. "Our Russell?"

"Yep, and I think he'd better get accustomed to handling an art display room," she said airily. "After you, gentlemen." She waved a hand toward the door. "Unless you need a couple aspirin after being stomped on by my big Norsky friend here, Tate?"

He inhaled deeply and put a hand on the small of his back, wincing. "No. I'm good."

Chapter Forty-eight

Helland's Woodshop – next morning

"It's like a wonderland." Jessie turned in a full circle. "I don't know where to look first." She picked up a small chunky carving of a fat robin resting on a partial branch. "All the carved pieces are so life-like. Coming here is like visiting a small museum. Thanks for inviting us."

Arvid was squatting down to look at the front of a large chest. The front was a relief carving of several bison and calves.

"At least half of the animals were carved by my grandfather," Helland explained. "I can't bear to give them away. Silly of me, I guess. I know a lot of people who would enjoy them." Helland leaned on a cane and waved his hand around the room. "My granddad, God rest his soul, started working with wood during the Depression. People were kinder back then, nicer to each other. I guess it boils down to not being as selfish. Times were hard, and most folks were down and out, but they still tried to help each other. Whenever someone did the family an act of kindness, Gramps carved them something. It was all he had to give—a gift of his talent—of himself. He never tried to sell his woodcarvings. Their new owner's name was written down in a little notebook he used before he put the first nick into the wood using an old pocket knife. He carved chunks of Russian olive—wood salvaged from the older trees out in the field windbreak. A lot of farmers in those days planted Russian olives in long rows to block the wind—keep the topsoil from blowing away."

"Dad did that, too," Jessie said. "I painted out at the fields. The olives had that wonderful grey green foliage. Some of my best plein-air paintings came from there." She was staring at Helland.

The old man chuckled and shook his head. "Well, I used to cuss those trees. They were old. Whenever a wind storm came through Dad would have me and my little brother help him haul the broken limbs to a stack behind the barn. We always left some downed wood for the birds. It's good cover for the pheasant and grouse in the winter. Rabbits, too." Gramps was in a wheel-chair by then, but he wanted most of the wood salvaged." He grimaced. Tom and I used to complain to dad, 'there's enough wood piled up to last Grandpa 'til Armageddon', but Dad was adamant. Most people who lived during the Great Depression were careful about letting anything go to waste. My memory of Gramps is of him whittling, whittling, whittling. It was sure a shame when his hands became too arthritic.

"I'm well acquainted with Russian olive," Russell said, shaking his head. "I used to snag my jeans, my shirt sleeves and my skin, on the big thorns when I hunted pheasants in O'Bourne's windbreak. I didn't know there was any good use for those vicious trees."

Helland wheezed with laughter. "Those awful thorns. Aren't they wicked? Nasty. That's why I hated hauling the wood back. But Gramps never had any money to buy wood when he carved pieces for those he deemed "worthy acquaintances" during the Depression. Even though most people consider it a trash tree, the wood grain is gorgeous. In the middle east, most of the nativity sets they sell are made from olive wood."

He picked up a small carved cottontail rabbit and ran his thumb along the smooth back of the wooden animal. "The Russian olive trees here in America are likely a cousin to those olive trees in the Middle East. There, they get good fat eating olives. The olives on these aren't edible. Well, except for wildlife—think deer and such browse on the trees, and certain birds get a benefit from the fruits." He handed the rabbit to Arvid. "This is the first thing I ever carved. I gave it to my mother, and when she passed on, I couldn't bear to part with it. It's crude, but she loved it and I remember her long fingers stroking across the animal when she was stressed. It was like a worry stone."

Arvid held the small carving in his hand, turned it over in his meaty palm and studied it. "Crude?" He shook his head. "Nup. It's gorgeous." He waved a finger over the carving, angling it toward Jessie. "Look how the swirls in the wood help shape the curve of the rabbit's round body. He handed it to her."

Jessie gazed at it in appreciation, becoming momentarily lost in the whorls and graceful lines of the wood...then passed the chubby bunny to Grant. She looked at the old man in admiration. "Your first work of art...It's wonderful. You inherited your grandfather's eye." Her eyes sparkled. "It's an unusual talent to be able to see into the wood. Looking at the grain and whittling it into something only your mind can visualize."

"You do the same thing with your drawings and paintings, Jessie. You paint more than what your eyes can see. A lot of your painting comes from an inner vision separate from eyesight."

"It does." Jessie nodded. "Carving must be the same. What about the large pieces? Especially the gorgeous swans in the corner?" She walked over to the carving and studied it. It was of two adult birds, almost life-sized. The base was carved to appear as a bit of shoreline, with water rippling to the edge. One bird rested contentedly on the base as if nesting, head cocked toward its companion. The second swan was little more than a graceful suggestion. "This will be magnificent." Her voice lowered almost to a whisper as she stared intently at the piece of wood. "Absolutely breath-taking."

"I haven't had the heart to finish that one. Those tundra swans were started for Berg Nielson's wife, Vi. She died before I could give it to her."

"What kind of wood is that?" Grant asked. He spoke to the old man, but his eyes kept glancing back to Jessie.

"Black walnut. It's the only wood I ever bought for carving instead of creating furniture. Actually, it's the only wood I ever bought, instead of scrounged." He scratched the back of his head and sighed. "When my wife had cancer, Vi Nielson came over every day to help me take care of her. Every blessed day until Shanna died. The two women were like sisters. Vi's good nature and sweet caring attitude helped my wife get through each day— even the real bad ones.

When Shanna was so sick she probably didn't know Vi was here, Vi still came. Held her hand, talked to her. Read her stories we weren't even sure she heard." He heaved another sigh. "How can a person hope to repay such kindness? My wife lay in bed, longing to get out of this world. Out of pain." He ran the tip of his index finger on the curve of the swan base, stroking the length of the ripple carved into the walnut. "I'd hear Vi tell her, 'It's okay, Shanna. Your job here is done. Just stretch your wings, honey. Can you feel those wings in your soul? Stretch them out and up like a swan's. Let them lift you up and carry you away."

He swallowed. "Shanna would go calm and get such a peaceful look on her face. Then one day. . . well, I guess she just stretched those wings." He cleared his throat and looked at the swans with a resigned expression. "The Nielsons had a walnut buffet in their dining room. I wanted this to match it. The shape and wingspan needed something thicker than the Russian olive I had available. Like I said before, I lost interest in working on the swans after Vi passed. Heart attack, it was. Sometimes I think I was about as brokenhearted as Berg when that woman passed on."

Arvid surreptitiously wiped at his eyes. Esther pulled a tissue from her purse and passed it to him.

"And what will you do with the swan carving now? Once it's finished, I mean?" Grant asked. "Because I'm assuming that someday you'll complete it."

"Maybe. Now, I want it to go to the person clever enough to find the bastard that drove Berg crazy. Crazy enough to shoot his own son." He glanced at Jessie, "Pardon my bad language. My dad said only someone with a lousy vocabulary needed to swear, but that's the only word to describe someone who'd torment a good man like Nielson."

Helland cleared his throat and went on in a voice sharp as a butcher knife, "I'm glad Vi was spared living through the hell of what happened to her family. You've probably heard the story by

327

now of the Nielson's girl. Addy was a sweet person. I hope someone can find out who killed her—and Berg. He may have died from the heart attack, but it was the horror of realizing he'd shot his own son that caused it. Someone planned that, I think." His face grew hard. "And Dominic's death was unnecessary. He had good Army training. Bless that boy. He could have saved himself if he hadn't been working to clear the lane, so an ambulance could get to the house...maybe save his father."

"So, what you're saying is that you don't believe it was actually Benny Potter. You want to be the one to find the real killer," Jessie said. "It's what you plan to do to repay Vi Nielson, isn't it? That's why you've been walking the art rooms with me, visiting with the artists. You think like I do. The killer is an artist at that show."

He coughed. Then pointed at his chest. "Yeah. I don't think Benny had the smarts to pull those murders together...someone else planned it. Sadly, an old man like me can't do much to find a killer, even if I wanted to." He looked at her with a guileless expression and changed the subject. "And I enjoyed meeting those artists with you. I always wondered what it would be like to make a living by doing something creative—something you loved. To do nothing to pay the bills but plan your next elaborate carving or sculpture. Or in your case, a painting." He sighed. "It bothers me that Sheriff Fischer has about closed the case on the Nielson family. And probably will soon on Harris Freeman's murder, too. He'll think the military should handle it. But I'm just too old. I have to leave the sleuthing to the experts like Sheriff Fischer. I wish—"

"Hogwash." Jessie said. "You old fraud."

"Jessie," Russell said. "What the heck? For God's sake. You—"

Jessie didn't take her eyes from Helland. "Your carvings are wonderful. Phenomenal, actually. But you didn't bring us here to see them. You wanted an opportunity to take a good look at us and see if we measure up somehow." She placed the side of a fist against her chin and stared at Helland. "Let's see...Esther and Grant fit in, too. You're a cagey, devious old devil. And not nearly so infirm as you pretend." Her hand dropped to her side and she leveled her gaze at Helland. "So, what's up?"

Arvid looked stunned at her rudeness. Grant, who'd been watching Jessie's face and wondering at the calculating look in her lovely blue eyes, looked merely curious. His focus swung from Helland to Jessie and back to Helland.

"Don't get me wrong," Jessie said to the room in general. She waved her hand toward Helland. "I *like* this cagey, devious old son-of-a-gun. He reminds me of Dad." She chuckled. "I'll bet he already has a good list of suspects. But, he wants to hear our take on the people we've talked to...the way we think the puzzle pieces fit."

Russell reached toward her. "Knock it off, Jess. Why—"

"No," Esther's polished voice cut in. "Jessie is right." She turned to the carver. "Mr. Helland...may I call you Joe?"

He nodded.

"So." She crossed her arms and tapped her toe on the wooden floor. "What's up, Joe?"

Helland looked from Esther to Jessie and gave a slight shake. Then he smiled. He straightened and stretched. He stood as erect as a forty-year old and seemed four inches taller than before. His eyes sparkled as ten years seemed to fall away. "What gave me away, ladies?"

Esther and Jessie both pointed at the portable oxygen pack.

"Well, for starters," Jessie accused, "you forgot to turn that on."

Chapter Forty-nine

Tate sat in his art display room, making conversation with other artists wandering through and judging the interest of people looking at each sketch. *Are they serious buyers or tire kickers?* It was a welcome pastime that let him avoid thinking about the sad chore of telling Althea and Glen Heath about the positive identification of Harris Freeman's body. He had even made a morning sale. At the recommendation of Jessie O'Bourne, he had raised his prices, so the sale of a framed piece was now a serious chunk of change.

A middle-aged man in blue cargo shorts and a too-tight tee shirt took a price tag from a drawing and began walking toward Tate. Tate smiled at him and stood, while thinking,

Oh no. Does he want a price break? How much would be reasonable?

"I'll take this one." The man handed the price tag and a credit card to Tate. He breathed a sigh of relief. It had been a last-minute decision to get an account for processing a credit card or PayPal payment.

Do people ever use cash anymore? It's becoming a plastic society.

When he handed the bubble wrapped drawing to the happy buyer, he felt like an old pro.

I know what that barn is good for at the Nielson place, he thought. *It would be a fabulous artist's studio. If I didn't have a year left in the Army, I'd renovate it. Lights, a bathroom, a big*

sink. Maybe old plank flooring. Then he stopped short. *Wow. Yes, it would be a knock 'em dead studio. It really would.* And he'd heard the big guy, Glen Heath, talking in the hospitality room, blowing steam, saying 'pretty soon I'll have a wonderful sculpting studio. My ship's going to come in.' *Was Glen thinking he'd inherit the Nielson place, too? If he knew Harris originally had a signed will with Dom, he might think he was the heir, not just to Althea's ranch, but to the Nielson property as well.*

Glen had no way of knowing that Dom, Harris and I made a new will. Legit. Witnessed and all. Everyone discounts the idea that Benny killed Adele Nielson. Could he have been set up to take the fall for Harris's death, too?

Tate pulled his phone out of his pocket and made a call. "Hey, Drew. Do you have that list of names from the rental agency in Savannah? I want you to include people who leased any kind of vehicle up to three days prior to Harris's disappearance. Yes, any kind of vehicle...not just dark SUVs. And I want you to check the same dates for the major airport car rental services. Try Atlanta's first. Start with the big airports and work your way to the small ones." He listened to the voice on the other end, then said. "Stop ranting. Here's what I need. There are only several names I need you to check. Shouldn't take each rental agency more than a few minutes because they can pull up a reservation by name...No, I'm in a hurry...I want it like last Christmas."

An hour later, Tate again pulled out the scissors, tape, and bubble wrap. His smile was wide and sincere as he handed the sketch of a herd of pronghorn antelope to the buyer. "Thank you, Ma'am. Best wishes to your husband on his birthday. I hope he enjoys my work. I put a business card in with the wrapped sketch."

Again, he was glad of Jessie's suggestion. *Thank you, Quicky Print. Mahalo.*

His phone rang.

Chapter Fifty

"I can't believe Fischer finally asked me to look at the trail cam video. But if you and Russell didn't see anything worthwhile, there's probably nothing I can spot."

"You never know. Another pair of eyes don't hurt."

Jessie watched out the window as they went through the town of Crooked Creek, passing Hank's Diner and Dogs, a quilt shop, several small galleries and the Creekside Medical Center. "And can you believe that Joe Helland, trying to sleuth on his own? He's going to take me over to the Nielson's, by the way."

"What for?"

"I want to take reference pictures of the old barn. We had quite a discussion on barns when I took him around the art rooms. He commissioned a small one, an 11x14. According to him, it's a fabulous old structure. Barn paintings sell well, so I'll do a quick study for the Gingerbread Man and several for my galleries."

Arvid made a left turn, heading into the Sheriff's Office parking area.

"Funny how nicknames stick, ain't it?"

"Yes, it is. Did you ever have one, Arvid?"

"Nah...my own name seemed funny enough to the kids. "'Course, I was big. Grew earlier than most of the runty boys in my school." He chuckled. "The girls grew early, too...ever notice how in junior high school most of the girls reach their mature height, but the boys are shrimpy?" Then he grew serious. "Helland

332

seems very competent, but he's no spring chicken. Can you take someone along—Esther maybe—or your friend Cheri Cappello?"

"I guess I could. I'll ask. Esther may have practice, but Cheri can probably make it."

..*

Jessie looked at the video image and her heart sank. "Freeze it right there, Sheriff." She stared at the video frame, hating to speak. Her throat was tight.

"You see something, don't you," Arvid asked.

"Yes. I do. She moved her hand and pointed to the screen. "Blow it up...see that?"

"That dirty spot?" Fischer asked.

"No, it isn't dirt. It's darker because it's a cleaner spot, an area where a metal logo used to be. We don't ever see the left boot in the video. We only see the right."

"What makes you think it isn't just a spatter of mud?"

"Because I took a ride with Glen Heath two days ago. And I recognize the boot."

"Oh, do tell," Fischer said. "You recognize the boot? I find that hard to believe."

Jessie glared at him. "It's a Harley Davison Motorcycle boot, and on the left one, he still had the metal logo. On the right, the metal logo was missing."

"If Jess says she recognizes it, she recognizes it," Arvid growled.

"Glen Heath." Fischer's voice was flat. "I didn't want it to be Glen. It means he isn't at all the man I thought he was. He's a cold-hearted vicious killer. He'd have to be, to threaten an old man...to kill Adele. And the sad thing is, I can't figure out why. Why would he do such a thing?"

"And how can we prove it? No jury is going to believe Jessie identified a specific boot from this lousy footage."

"I didn't want it to be Glen, either. But I should have thought about it before," Jessie said sadly. "Sculptors use drawing paper as much as any artist. They sketch out ideas for each new piece, sometimes doing very detailed drawings before they ever start.

333

And the 3D quality of the little tractors would appeal to a sculptor as well. What I don't understand is why he targeted me at this show. We were friends."

"We can get a warrant and check his house for the drawing tablet. If we can find it, it may still have the matching page in it— the one from the last threatening note."

"Go for it," Arvid said. "I'll grab Russell and we'll help you search."

"Do we have any idea where Glen is right now?" Fischer asked. "Perhaps working his display room at the art Expo?"

"No. Tate came and picked him up. He wanted Glen to go with him when he informed Althea Heath that her son's body had been positively identified. I'm sure that after they did that, Glen would head back to the Expo. In fact, they've probably been back for an hour or more."

Fischer snorted. "That M.P. should have come in right away and introduced himself. I'm not happy about that."

"Well," Arvid said. "I hear you. But instead of wasting time worrying about that, if you can grab a warrant right now, we can go over to the house while Glen is otherwise occupied. Maybe we can find that tablet and match the paper to Berg Nielson's, Evan's, and Jessie's threatening notes. Then we have strong grounds to bring him in for questioning. But we'll sure have to dig into his alibi for the time Adele Nielson was shot. There has to something fishy with that alibi."

Jessie stood listening, a tear slowly trickling down her cheek.

"Right now, even if we find the tablet, what can we arrest him for? All we have on him is harassing folks. Not murder. He might have a motive for killing Harris since he probably expected to inherit the ranch—but we know Benny went to Savannah and he looks good for that murder. And what about a motive for Adele?"

Jacob knocked on the door. "Sheriff, Richard Christofferson is here and would like to speak to you. And a Tate Kamaka called for an appointment for this afternoon."

"Ask him to come in, Jacob."

"What kind of name is Kamaka, anyway? That's a new one on me."

"Hawaiian. And give Miss O'Bourne here a ride back to the Crooked Creek Lodge, will you?"

"Sure." Jacob stared at Jessie. A slow flush crept up his face, and she realized he was thinking about the skunked Hawk. She flashed him a brilliant smile. It was hard to be that young.

"Jessie," Sheriff Fischer said grasping her hand in a firm handshake, "Thank you. Thank you very much. And I'm sure I don't need to tell you to keep our information under your hat."

She gave him a nod.

..*

Jessie looked out the window as she drove, deep in a funk.

So, it was Glen of all people. Who would have suspected that he was such a scumbag? Man, life throws you some curves. I just can't picture him as a killer—to be someone who makes a living creating things, but then turns around and takes a life. She felt her eyes grow moist. *More than one life.*

"You okay, Jessie?" Cheri looked concerned. "You seem sort of down."

Jessie tried to smile. "No, I'm good. Just tired, I guess. Have you been out this way before?"

"Quite a few times. I used to buy porcupine quills from a lady out this way. You know, to use on my warshirts. I never asked where they came from. Ugh. I imagine road kill. But after I clean them thoroughly and soak them in hot soapy water, they're lovely." She pointed to the west. "There are some abandoned cabins over to the North. But next to them, there's an old blue trailer house. That was hers."

"I see it."

"It's practically falling apart. The door's missing and the windows are filled with pressed board. Probably has animals living in it now. Just driving past those old cabins when my friend Amanda lived out here was like moving backwards through time fifty years at a stretch." Cheri chuckled. "Amanda was a lot like you, Jessie. She wasn't afraid of being on her own, and she'd haul that trailer up to Glacier Park and paint for a week or two at a time. Just like you do in the Hawk."

335

Or used to, Jessie thought. *My poor Hawk. At least Dad brought me the old Ford.*

She thought back to the night before as she did her quick draw of the cows, standing under a big cottonwood tree. Her dad kept suggesting she change a few colors. 'Why is the cow so blue?' And is that little one a yearling? His wife, Marty, finally threw her hands in the air and said, "Let your daughter paint, for Pete's sake, Dan. It's what she does.' *Still. Too bad they couldn't stay for a day or two. And as soon as the insurance money materializes, I'm ordering a new Greyhawk...same beautiful interior...same upholstery.* She tried to keep track of what Cheri was saying.

"She'd take all four of her cats along. They were good company, she said, and that way her daughter didn't have to pet sit. Amanda passed away a couple years ago. I miss her."

"What happened to her cats?" Jessie's mind went to Jack.

"Her daughter took all four. Said it wasn't right to split them up, they'd been part of a family for so long." Cheri looked at Jessie and grinned. "Her dachshund wasn't real pleased."

Jessie felt her mood improving. There were good, generous people in the world. "This is Helland's lane." She pulled in, parked, and got out to knock on the door. She beckoned to Cheri when Joe answered. "Come on...you need to take a look at his carvings before we go out to see the Nielson's barn."

Chapter Fifty-one

Althea Heath's ranch

"Bet Evan will be relieved if Glen is arrested," Fischer commented as he opened another drawer in Glen's bedroom. "He's been getting the threatening notes just like Jessie. And he kept asking us to look harder at Glen."

They'd been through the shop—where it appeared Glen did most of his sculpting—and found nothing. Then they decided to go through the bedroom.

"Did he now? That's real interesting, because my gut keeps telling me we're missing something. Why would Evan suspect Glen of anything? He knows Benny went to Savannah and probably killed Harris. So far as anyone knows, Glen had a rock-solid alibi. At least for Adele's shooting." Arvid was looking through a stack of magazines, gloves covering his hands. And then he saw it. "Here it is."

Russell and Fischer both scurried over to see.

"We'll see if we hit pay dirt." Arvid lifted the cover of the tablet carefully. The page on top was torn in half. The remaining half—at first glance—was a possible match for one of the notes Fischer had in the evidence files. "We're going to have to take him in for questioning. Not until we see if the torn edges of this tablet match up with those of a threatening note, though."

337

"And we'll need to see if his fingerprints match the ones on Evan's truck door handle." Russell looked glum. "This is going to be hard on both Jessie and Camille."

"Not to mention his step-mom," Arvid grumbled. "If she's having a good day, she'll know things have gone south." He thought about Althea and her polynomials. She'd likely been having fewer and fewer good days, and nobody deserved this. If Glen was behind the harassment of Berg Nielson, he probably had something to do with his step-brother's murder, too, even though Benny was the prime candidate for that. "Poor woman."

"You said it," Russell agreed.

"It just seems to me that everything started with Adele Nielson's murder and everything else may have snowballed from there. And I gotta say…sometimes a horse just don't need zebra stripes."

"Do you mean, 'when you hear hoofbeats, think *horses*, not *zebras?*'," Fischer asked.

"That's exactly it." Arvid looked at Russell and Fischer. "This all began with Adele and you said Evan was her boyfriend. Or fiancée. Are you sure things were happy between them?"

"So far as we know." Fischer slipped the tablet into a clear evidence bag and labeled it. "Let's head back to the office. I could really use a cup of coffee. And if it isn't too much of a standard joke on cops of all kinds, a donut."

* * *

Back in the Sheriff's car, Arvid asked, "Did you look for any connection between Glen Heath and Evan? I mean, besides the obvious one of both being involved in the Expo?"

"We looked, and we found one. But it's tenuous. They both took a class in marketing and promotion at the college in Bozeman about three years ago."

"Promotion, huh? Well, the notes to the old man that made him increasingly more paranoid seem a lot like promotion. Like advertising. When you see the same message over and over, supposedly it sinks in deeper each time. But don't it seem that the best person to send a text from Evan's laptop was actually Evan?

338

And he could certainly pretend to get the notes. Maybe he sent them to Jessie just to make his own more believable."

"Now you sound like young Jacob. He thought Berg Nielson had a screw loose and was pretending to get the notes just to get attention." Fischer looked amused. "Do you really think Evan made it appear that someone was setting him up, but he was actually organizing everything behind the scenes? No. If that was the case, he had no idea how long he'd be locked up. Or if he'd ever be released."

"Mebbe," Arvid replied in a matter of fact tone. "But if he had enough faith in our finding out the boots in the video were Glen's, he might be enough of a showman to pull it off. I've watched him in action at the art show the past couple years. Evan's a good actor. He works a crowd. And I think we need to find out what happened to the first toy tractor Jessie turned in at the check-in desk at the lodge. Did anybody check to see if it was still there? Because the young man behind the desk must've handled it. Heck, several people behind the desk probably picked it up and fiddled with it."

Fischer was looking at his phone. "I'll find out if it's still there."

"Best person to put the bag of tractors and old notes into Evans pickup is Evan himself. Easiest thing in the world to call in the anonymous tip to your office." Arvid stroked his chin.

"Maybe using a throwaway phone," Russell said. "Yeah. He could have done all that...but why?"

"I don't know." Arvid sighed. "But it all started with Adele and he's the only one who had any ties to the young woman. But...it doesn't explain Glen's boots on the video, either."

Fischer ended his call. "Good call, Arvid. The first toy tractor disappeared, all right. The kid at the check-in desk thought the child who lost it must've claimed it. I'll send Jacob over there to fingerprint him. Then we'll see if we have a match for the print on the toy tractor cab."

"Even if they match," Russell griped. "We still have the other set of prints on the pickup door handle to account for."

"I like your analogy of trying to tie a bow in a length of barbed wire." Fischer said. "And here's something else to muddy the water. We know Benny went to Savannah. But maybe he was met at the airport by someone who knows the area. Say, an Army M.P.?"

"Tate? You're talking about Tate? What does Tate have to do with it?"

"I forgot to tell you. You'll love it. The reason Christofferson came to see me today was to let me know Tate Kamaka was an army buddy of both Dom Nielson and Harris Freeman. He's the heir."

Arvid and Russell stared. Finally, Arvid asked, "THE heir? You're saying the heir to both ranches?"

"In a nutshell. Tate knew both wills were in his favor. He claims he came to town to see the ranches and try to find out what happened to Harris. But, being in Georgia when Harris disappeared, he had means and opportunity. He inherits the whole kit and caboodle—the land, the money. Everything except a few miscellaneous bequests." Fischer looked frustrated.

"I just can't see how he could orchestrate any of this from Georgia," Arvid grumbled. "No matter how smart he is. And I do think he's smart."

"Yeah," Russell said. "It almost has to be someone from Crooked Creek. And with Glen's boots on the video and finding this tablet here, it's got to be Glen. He's probably the one that dumped that stuff in Evan's truck."

"I think we should have a meeting of the minds before we arrest him. We need to sit down. Go over all the options." Fischer rubbed his eye. "Can we have that friend of yours—the FBI fellow—sit in?"

"I'll ask him."

"Who's keeping an eye on Jessie?" Russell asked.

"Aw, she's fine. She's with Joe Helland and Cheri Cappello. Cheri wants to see Helland's carvings, and Jessie wants to go over to the Nielson place, so she can take photos of the barn."

"Nielson's? She's going to Nielson's?" Both Russell and Fischer wore dumfounded expressions.

"Yeah. Helland has been acting as sort of a caretaker over the place, and he commissioned Jessie to do a small painting of the barn for him." Arvid looked out the window at the passing scenery. The winter wheat was barely up. One pasture held a mixed herd of horses, including an Appaloosa and foal. Fischer drove the speed limit, tapping his finger on the wheel.

"I don't like it," he said. "It makes me nervous. Wasn't it you. Arvid, who said the murders must be connected but to figure it out is like trying to tie a bow in barbed wire? You got that right. Tate should be done speaking to Althea Heath at the assisted living facility by now. He probably took Glen back to the expo. But we don't know that. And we don't have any idea where Evan is. The killer could be any one of the three. Or it could be any two of them. Geez. They're all on the loose and all we have in hand is this tablet. Was anyone around when you asked Jessie O'Bourne to come in and view the trail cam footage? Did anyone hear she was going to be looking at boots?"

Arvid closed his eyes and thought. *He had told Russell. And Camille was in the room. Could she have heard? And if so, would she have told Glen?"*

Arvid and Russell both looked at Fischer with concern, then said in unison, "Step on it, will you?"

Russell pulled his phone from his pocket and tapped in Jessie's number. In the old red pickup, Jessie's phone emitted a shrill trill. And then trilled and trilled.

Chapter Fifty-two

Crooked Creek Lodge

Grant glared at Woodcastle. "What do you mean, so far the books look great?"

"I mean, so far the books look great." Woodcastle gave him a dirty look right back. "Unless you find something fishy with the paintings—like one that's been copied and sold as an original—then Max Watson is in the clear. Granted, the way he handled the sales of these high dollar items has been unethical, but not illegal. Not actionable."

"I just feel like there's something wrong here. Get someone in to look at the paintings in his office and at his home." Grant slouched against Max's big desk and thumped the side of his hand on the wooden surface. "Look a bit harder at the books, too, will you?"

"Of course, I'm going to look harder." Woodcastle slumped and sighed. "I've barely started. Just with the barest scratch on the surface. I'll be here all week, Grant. You don't finish an audit like this in one day. But I will say that, as a favor to you, I verified with the bank that the money for Jessie O'Bourne's $32,500 painting went right to the Creekside Veterinary Clinic as it was supposed to."

"Well, I'll be. Curiouser and curiouser."

"Really? I'm doing all of this work and you're going to come in guns blazing and quote Alice in Wonderland at me?"

"Guns blazing?"

"Well, okay," Woodcastle conceded. "Eyes blazing. How's that?"

"I'll only let you malign me like that because you're so good at your job." Grant stood with his head tipped back, thinking. Then, he stood and said, "Places to go, crooks to catch. See you later."

Chapter Fifty-three

Creekside Humane Society

"Good morning. How may I help you? Are you here to choose a new forever pet?" The young woman behind the desk at the Creekside Humane Society looked hopeful.

"Sorry, no. My name is Grant Kennedy and I was in yesterday to speak to the director, Clifford Schultz. I need to speak to him again on a matter of some importance. Is he available?"

"Why, no. I'm afraid he isn't in this morning."

"Can you tell me when he might return?"

"Well," she glanced toward the back of the office and spoke hesitantly, "I don't know. I think that Mr. Schultz had an out of town family emergency, and he and his wife aren't sure when they will return. It was unexpected. They left yesterday afternoon."

"I see. Is there someone in charge in his absence?"

"One of the vets is in today…Dr. Sullivan. She would be the person in charge."

"Then I'd like to speak to Dr. Sullivan, if I may."

"I'll see if she can come out. This is her surgery morning." She bustled down the short hallway and through a swinging door. She was back in under a minute with a tall dark-haired woman wearing a pink lab coat and a harried expression.

"I'm Dr. Sullivan. May I help you?"

"Yes, I'm afraid you can. What I need to discuss might be better said in private."

She looked startled, glanced at her receptionist and then beckoned Grant into the nearest examination room. They stepped in and she closed the door.

"I'm in between patients and don't have much time. What's this about?"

"My name is Grant Kennedy. I was here yesterday to see Clifford Schultz." He showed her his badge.

"FBI? Is this a joke?"

He waved his hands palm out in a self-deprecating gesture. "Dr. Sullivan, you'd be surprised how often I am asked that question, but no, I'm afraid it isn't a joke. Not to alarm you, but while handling another issue in Crooked Creek, it's come to the FBI's notice that you likely have a problem here at the Creekside Humane Society."

"What kind of problem?" She traded her harried expression for a skeptical one.

"Financial." He handed her a business card. "I don't believe your director had an out of town family emergency, nor do I believe he plans to return. And it would be wise to inform your CHS board—if there are members of the board other than the absent Clifford Schultz—that it would be prudent to conduct an immediate financial audit."

"Schultz? It sounds as though you think he may have defrauded the society."

"We know of at least $32,000 that was donated to CHS and evidently did not get deposited into your accounts. According to Schultz, he had been told the check had not been viable, but that seems not to be the case. There may be other ...inaccuracies if it is the director who has the access to the bank accounts and books. Of course, people are innocent until proven guilty, but I wanted to share our concerns."

"Why that scumbag!"

"We would like to speak to him. Do you have any ideas on where Mr. Schultz would go?"

"Not a clue. But I do know he is a firm believer in chipping his pets, Agent Kennedy. And he is very attached to his dog, which

345

is an escape artist—digging under the fence, bolting out the door when Schultz gets his mail. That type of thing. Once Schultz feels he has found a new place to stay, he will probably update the location data on his corgi. I don't think he will expect anyone to be monitoring a change in the information, but I am assuming that the FBI could do that."

"That's a great idea, Dr.," Grant smiled wickedly, "And yes, we could make that happen."

"Then finding him is just a matter of time. Either he'll update the data, or the dog will get loose and someone will pick him up and take him to a vet to see if he's chipped. When they inquire, you'll be able to see where the inquiry came from. Let me get you the chip number and write down the dog's name so that you have it. If I can't find it in our records, I seem to remember that he wrote it down and put it in his desk drawer the day he had Porgy chipped."

"Oh, he didn't."

"I'm afraid so." Her expression was rueful.

"Porgy the corgi?"

She nodded.

"Man, someone should arrest him just for that."

Grant's phone vibrated, and he pulled it from his pocket to glance at the screen. *Woodcastle*. He looked at the vet, gestured to the phone and said, "Please excuse me for just a minute, Dr. Sullivan.'

She nodded.

"Kennedy speaking," Grant said. "You have something?" He listened to Woodcastle's response and, as the other man spoke, Grant's smile grew wider and wider.

Chapter Fifty-four

Nielson's Barn

Sunlight burnished Jessie's red hair into flaming curls as she walked around the picturesque old barn, looking through the Nikon viewfinder and snapping photos. After issuing dire warnings to watch for a snake that Helland described as about the size of Cincinnati—the King, he'd called it—he and Cheri unlatched the huge double barndoor, slid it open and disappeared inside.

Jessie skimmed through the reference photos, deleted several that were out of focus, then walked back to the spot where she'd taken them and did re-takes. Finally, she turned off the camera and walked into the barn, the dim light filtering through cracks in the old barnwood and tossing patterns onto the walls in fascinating stripes being the only illumination. Before her were two horse stalls and a pile of loose hay with a pitchfork sticking out of it. The smell of alfalfa hung thick in the air.

What a neat old place.

Helland and Cheri had climbed the rickety looking wooden ladder leading to the loft. Jessie could hear Cheri exclaiming about vintage leather bridles that were hung on the walls of the loft, and the neat antique trunks.

"You should come up and see this, Jessie," she yelled down. "One of them is a gorgeous old steamer trunk. I saw one almost like it in an antique store in Denver."

Helland had forgotten to check for roof leaks the last time he'd been to the ranch, so he was doing due diligence, muttering to himself about one corner where damage appeared to have allowed rain or melting snow into the barn.

Jessie stood still. It hit her what bothered her about the visit to see Evan in jail. He had said that 'Benny wouldn't have known how to book flights, and that the Denver and Chicago airports were crazy busy'. She had flown to Savannah before and remembered there was a direct flight from Billings. Had Benny flown through Chicago one direction and Denver the other? If he had, how would Evan know that?

Unless Evan had booked the flight. Could he have coerced Benny into going to Savannah, but also gone himself? On a different flight? He could've killed Harris Freemen and then got rid of Benny so that he'd be blamed for the murder after his death. And for Adele's. Dead men can't defend themselves.

She needed to call Arvid or Sheriff Fischer and tell him about Evan's comment. She patted her pocket. She'd left the phone in the pickup.

I'll call as soon as we're done here.

Jessie looked at a curious form covered by a dusty green tarp and wandered over to it, wondering if it would be horribly nosy to take a quick peek. After all, it wasn't Joe Helland's ranch, even though he'd gotten permission to bring her out to take pictures. That didn't mean she could snoop around. Hannah O'Bourne had taught her better.

Still, she wondered what was under the tarp. She lifted a corner. Then uncovered half the object. It was a bike. Not a bike— a vintage motorcycle. What she thought was called a 'strap tank', according to the old magazine in Glen's art room. She yanked on the tarp and tossed it to the side. A strap tank Harley. Old…very old. She'd seen one very similar to it in the motorcycle magazine in Glen's art room. In the article she saw, the 1907 Strap Tank Harley had sold for over $700,000. Her hand flew to her mouth. *Glen. Glen would know how valuable this Harley was. And many men would think it worth killing for.*

"Hey!" She shrieked up at the loft. "Hey! I found something. Come down."

348

"Be down in a minute. And it looks like someone's coming, Jessie. Looks like maybe Glen." Cheri sounded cheerful.

"Yeah. That's just Glen. He's pulling in."

"Cheri, call 911!"

"What the heck? Why?"

"It's Glen. Glen's the killer. Call right now. Stay up there and be quiet! He won't know you're up there."

But I've got nowhere to go...

She looked around in desperation. Should she cover the bike and try to bluff her way out? She spotted the pitchfork and moved toward the pile of hay. A pitchfork would be a good weapon.

Blast. I hate sharp things. I should just carry my gun when I think I might get into a dangerous spot.

A pickup door slammed.

"Hello? You in there, Jessie?" A silhouette of Glen's large form appeared in the wide doorway. "Oh, there you are. What the heck are you doing out here?"

"Hi, Glen." She hoped he didn't notice the slight tremor I her voice. "I know I shouldn't be such a snoop. But I got a commission to paint this barn and came out to take reference photos. After that, I just couldn't resist looking around." She waved her arm in a sweeping motion. "It has so much atmosphere, doesn't it?"

"Well, yeah. But who gave you permission to come out here?" He stepped into the interior and walked toward Jessie.

"Joe Helland. He's the caretaker at the moment. He's the one who wants the barn painting, too." Jessie was pleased to hear that her voice was now steady. "I stopped to see his carvings and he mentioned the barn. Thought I'd come right over and get my photos. Strike while the iron is hot, so to speak."

Geez, now I'm babbling. Get a grip O'Bourne.

"Oh, Joe Helland. That's all right, then." He looked relieved. "I thought you were trespassing or something. I didn't want you to get in trouble. Of course, now that I'm here, I guess if we get caught trespassing I'll be in the next cell." He laughed at his joke.

"What are *you* doing out here, Glen?'

"Oh, I saw your red truck and I wanted to stop and thank you, Jessie.'

349

Her mouth fell open. "Excuse me? Thank me for what, exactly?" She tried to think.

"Well, for finding my step-mom's cat. It's been a horrible week for Althea. Actually, for both of us. But finding Moxie and taking her out to her . . .it made things a little more bearable for her. That cat is like her child."

Jessie relaxed a little. "Oh, I was glad to do it."

"You can imagine how awful I felt when the cat disappeared. I think I was just gone too much. To a motorcycle rally in Oregon, for one thing. But one of the neighborhood teenagers was supposed to come and check on Moxie and accidentally let her outside. I never saw her again until you found her."

"Poor thing. But all's well that ends well, right?" She edged toward the pitchfork.

"What the hell?" He was looking at the motorcycle.

"What?" Jessie started. What?"

Bluff. Stay Calm.

"Will you look at this? Oh, man! This thing must be old!" He circled the motorcycle, then reverently caressed a handlebar. "A strap tank Harley. Wow. I've never even seen one." He squatted and looked at the tires. "This thing belongs in a museum."

Jessie felt confused. Glen sounded sincere. As though the bike was a complete surprise. Maybe he was innocent.

"Or Nielson could have sold it for good money. Someone left an old magazine in my art room. There was an article in there that said a strap tank model sold for over $600,000."

"$715,000. Artists aren't that good at remembering numbers," came a voice from the doorway.

Jessie knew the voice. "Hello, Evan. I imagine it was you who left the magazine in Glen's room. A bit of window-dressing?"

"You're a good guesser, Jessie. Adele wasn't supposed to tell anyone about it, but one day I was helping her with chores and I took a look under the tarp. Imagine my surprise. The strap tank used to belong to Dom's grandfather. And now it's going to belong to me." He raised the gun that he'd been holding at his side and looked at Glen. "In fact, you're going to help me load it in the back of my pickup and cover it—probably we can use the same tarp. I'm going to salvage something out of this ridiculous mess."

350

"What mess? What are you talking about?" Glen didn't turn his head. He continued to examine the Harley.

"He means all the deaths that have happened since last fall. He's been involved in all of them." Jessie gestured toward the bike "Was this what it was all about? This old hunk of metal?"

At the ice in Jessie's voice, Glen glanced up at her, startled, and then he stood. "Jessie?"

Jessie's voice was scornful. She waved her hand toward the motorcycle again. "For this, he killed Adele. And Benny. And planted all the notes to harass Berg Nielson. He probably killed Harris, too."

"Dear God!" Glen sputtered. He had finally focused on the smaller man, and the gun.

"Here's what he probably did." Jessie didn't dare look up at the loft. She hoped Cheri had called the Sheriff's Office. And she prayed that Cheri and the Gingerbread Man would stay quiet in the loft, no matter what. *I need to stall.* "He left a day or so before Benny, then threw the blame on him by manipulating him into going to Savannah...probably asked him to deliver something to Harris...maybe just an empty envelope, or one with an Expo brochure in it that Benny had actually touched." Jessie bit her lip. "Yes. That would get his fingerprints on the brochure. Benny thought he was delivering something important, and Harris was alive and fine when Benny left to head home. After he'd gone, Evan killed Harris and then returned home by flying out of an airport some distance from Savannah," Jessie said.

"How did you figure that out, Jessie?"

"When we visited you in jail, you talked about Benny not being smart enough to find his way around the big airports like Denver and O'Hare. Most people wouldn't know where you'd have a layover on the way to Georgia unless they checked flights. You must have booked your own flight through Denver one way and Chicago the other. I'll bet Benny didn't suspect he'd been gulled until he'd heard a man's body had been found near Savannah. He must have panicked, thinking he'd be blamed and not knowing you'd been the one to kill Harris. The poor guy was trying to find homes for his dogs, because he planned to leave town. But instead, you decided you had to get rid of him."

351

"You think you're so smart, Jessie. And yes, I could always talk Benny into doing anything I wanted. Ever since grade school. Of course, it wasn't all about the bike. It was about the land. Adele and I were supposed to get married. Her dad didn't like me and talked her out of it. I figured if I got rid of Berg, she'd lean on me. She'd come around. Instead, she spoiled everything by taking her dad's place on the tractor that day. So, I had to do some quick thinking. I had to find someone to take the fall for Adele's death. Dom told her in a letter about him and Harris making wills. I decided I'd make it look like Glen wanted to inherit and hurried things along. It was like building a jigsaw puzzle from scratch. I thought I'd have to find a way to put Dom out of the picture myself. It was pure luck that Berg shot Dom and his own heart gave out. Man, I should have gone to Vegas that week. I'd have made a killing." He gave an ugly laugh. "Poor choice of words."

Jessie heard a faint rustling in the loose hay behind her. *Mouse?* Near the pitchfork. Was she blocking Evan's view of the pitchfork? *I think I am.* Then she heard a slithering sound. *Oh, God. It's the King.* Jessie froze.

"Get behind me, Jessie," Glen said quietly.

"No! Stay right where you are. It doesn't matter how big a man you are when I'm the one with the gun, Glen. Don't be stupid. It was gullible of you that night to deliver Berg's dinner for me. While you were gone, I switched the drawing tablet I used to write my note on with one in your studio. You really should get away from that country mentality of leaving your doors unlocked. I'd been leaving Berg threatening notes for a month by then and I offered to set up the trail cam to catch who was harassing him. I only got your boots on the video because Berg moved the camera, but if you hadn't lost the Harley emblem on the boot that showed best, it would have been easy to identify. Of course, I wouldn't 'remember' about the trail camera until after Harris was dead. But it would have pointed the Sheriff right to you. Jacob at the Sheriff's Office let slip that Jessie watched the video and identified your boot anyhow—just this morning. From a faint mark."

Glen looked at Evan. "You were bothering that poor old man? Why?"

"Promotion, Glen. You tell someone something ten times and they start to believe it. I hoped he'd either have a heart attack or shoot someone out of paranoia when someone—anyone—came to the house. I was angry that I killed Adele by mistake."

"I hope you didn't think I'd terrorize an old man," Glen said to Jessie. "We've known each other for years."

"Of course not," Jessie fibbed. She forced her gaze back to Evan, even though the slithering sound was getting more obvious. She reached her hand behind her back. *Where exactly is the pitchfork handle?*

"You had it all figured out, didn't you?" Jessie said in a scathing tone. "And I'll bet you borrowed Benny's truck and drove around shooting at outbuildings to make people think Benny was a loose cannon. You borrowed his truck whenever you went shooting, didn't you."

"Sure. Ten times, Jessie. And this is the type of place where a person is identified by their truck…folks see an old blue pickup going by and someone in it is wearing a cap like Benny's, so it must be Benny. Folks already thought he had a screw loose. I just gave their attitude some reinforcement. It's promotion. It's all promotion. Glen knows. He's taken the class—just like me."

"I'm nothing like you, Evan. Nothing. I'm not a common criminal, and I'm sure no killer." He took a step to the side to try to put his body between Evan and Jessie.

"Get back over there." Evan waved the gun at him until Glen took a half-step back. "And I'm not a common criminal, either. Circumstances warranted action, and I took action. Most men are too weak."

"It's obvious you sent Benny out to my motorhome. The text was just window-dressing in case someone heard you. Why did you leave me the threatening notes, Evan? And the toy tractors?"

Glen looked surprised. It was obvious he hadn't known.

"Hey, a damsel in distress makes every man around stand up and focus on her problem. You were a pretty woman, and you were handy. While the Sheriff was looking into that, he didn't take time to check airlines to see if anyone besides Benny went to Savannah. I speak fluent Spanish. There's a fellow doing odd jobs around the lodge, and I told him I was leaving you love notes. I asked if he'd deliver them each day for ten bucks. I told him to take the rest out to my pickup. I snagged the one off the check-in desk, too, just to confuse things a bit.'

"And parking the big tractor at the lodge was as a warning to Benny?"

"I'm a showman, Jessie. It made a huge statement, didn't it?"

"Why—," Glen began.

"It's enough explanation. Let's move the old Harley out to my truck. That baby's going to reside in an old outbuilding of Benny's for a while." He gave Jessie a condescending look. "I'll bet that's one thing you didn't know. Benny didn't have much, but he had a house, 600 valuable acres, and no family. I sympathized with him. Told him since we were both without brothers, we should make a will leaving each other our worldly goods like Dom and Harris had done. So that I could take care of his dogs, legal like, if anything ever happened to him. When I shot Adele by accident, I lost any hope of ever getting this place. But I'll salvage something—600 acres and a motorcycle worth about a million dollars by the time I sell it."

"You'll get caught, Evan." Glen's voice was harsh. "And no motorcycle is worth jail time. Or murder."

Evan looked smug. "This one is. Besides, I had to find a patsy to take the fall for Adele's death."

"Tell it like it is, Evan. You mean Adele's murder," Glen growled. "Not death—murder."

Jessie listened intently, judging the slight rattle. In her mind, she practiced a long brushstroke beginning from directly behind her to the man with the gun. The pitchfork would be the brush. *Ochre*, she thought. *A long yellow-gold stroke.*

One chance.

She judged the slithering sound. *It was almost perfectly aligned, she thought, with the pitchfork.* She took a deep breath.

Soon.

"Now, Jessie!" Cheri's voice came from the loft. Evan's gaze flew upward toward the sound as Jessie whirled, grabbed the pitchfork, scooped the wriggling load of hay and flung it. Through the air flew the King of Diamonds, the largest diamondback rattler Jessie had ever seen. Its mouth opened wide as it hit, one large

354

fang piercing Evan's cheek. The gun catapulted into the air as he screamed and clawed at the snake, pulled it off his face and launched it backward through the open door. Its body whipped back and forth as it propelled itself from the barn.

Glen tackled Evan, landing with a sickening thump.

"Get off me! I've been bit—"

"Holy moly! Would you look at that?" Arvid's voice boomed through the open door. "Dritt, that's the biggest snake I've ever seen. Did you see it?"

Helland and Cheri hustled down the ladder as Russell and Fischer hurried into the gloom of the barn.

"Jessie, are you okay?" Russell pulled her in and hugged her hard. Then he let her go, stepped back and looked at her intently.

"She's delightful," Glen said. "Girl has the best follow through I've ever seen. Swoosh. Just delightful."

"I'm fine." Jessie gestured to Evan. "But I think Evan needs to be treated for snake bite."

Fischer was pulling out cuffs.

Jessie walked to Cheri and wrapped her in a bear hug. "Thank you, thank you. If it hadn't been for you, I'd have waited too long to take the chance."

"You're welcome." Cheri grinned. "It was quite a sight."

"Damndest thing I ever saw," Helland said. "And I have everything Evan said on my phone here."

"You got all that from up in the loft?" Jessie gave him an incredulous look.

"I'm a bit hard of hearing, so this phone here is amplified. Cheri did that new texting thing to 911, while I crept to the edge of the loft, so I could record the situation. We wouldn't have let him hurt Jessie or Glen." He patted the pocket on the vest he wore. "I was planning to shoot him." "Beretta Pico. It's a .380 caliber, but only weighs eleven and a half ounces, so it's easy for an old guy like me to carry." Helland noticed the look on Sheriff Fischer's face. "And yes, before you ask, I do have my concealed carry permit. But Cheri thought she knew what Jessie was planning and whispered that if I shot Evan, Jessie might move. And if she moved forward—even an inch—that snake would strike. So, Cheri watched the movement of the snake under the layer of hay and yelled when she thought the rattler was exactly parallel to Jessie."

Fischer slapped him on the back. "You rock, Joe."

Arvid peered down at Evan. "Let's get him to the hospital. Looks like only one puncture mark, but it's swelling fast. We need to hurry."

"Joe, come along." Fischer was abrupt. "Bring your phone."

* * *

As they hurried Evan into the Sheriff's Chevy Tahoe, a car screamed into the yard and two men bolted out. Russell had called Grant and Tate while enroute to the barn. Out the side window, he saw the big blond man run toward the barn—and to Jessie—and felt a momentary pang of loss. The feel of Jessie in his arms just a few minutes before had felt like coming home after years of wandering in the desert. He wondered if it would ever be that way with Camille. Yeah, there were sparks. But with Jessie there were deep embers—the kind that glowed throughout a lifetime and never diminished. Jessie said they were family. He sighed. The O'Bourne's had been the only real family, the only caring family he'd ever known. He loved Jessie, but now that he'd felt that special spark with Camille, he wanted it. The blasted redhead was right again. Russell squeezed his eyes shut...rubbing them with an index finger. He wondered if Grant had told Jessie yet that he'd turned Max's investigation totally over to Woodcastle—who was now beginning to find discrepancies in Max's books—and to an FBI art appraiser. The appraiser had determined the painting in Max's office needed to be 'further examined'. Russell opened his eyes and sighed. Jessie would be happy to hear that Grant's next assignment would be in the Santa Fe area, investigating a huge turquoise jewelry theft. A feeling of jealousy washed over him, then dissipated. He grinned.

And then he wondered what was happening in room 145.

Chapter Fifty-five

Jessie's studio – Santa Fe, New Mexico

Jessie was downing a cup of dark roast Kona coffee from a bag of ground beans and working a crossword puzzle when the delivery truck backed into her drive. She saw two men jump out and manhandle a large wooden crate toward her front patio. Before they reached it, she opened the door and stepped out. They set the box down and one hefty fellow pulled a sheet of paperwork off the crate. "I'll need your signature on this, ma'am."

"Excuse me. I'm not expecting anything."

"Are you...." He looked down at the invoice, "Miss Jessie O'Bourne?" He held it out to her.

"Yes." Jessie looked at the sheet. It was indeed her address. There was no return address. It was just a form asking for proof of delivery. She signed with the pen he held out to her. Then she motioned them inside and supervised as they carried the heavy box indoors and placed the box on the floor of the studio.

Later, Jessie twisted the screw on the last corner of the heavy plywood crate, pulled it from the wood and dropped it into a metal dish. Inside, the box was loaded with foam packing nested around a second container of lightweight wood, a box closed with buckled leather straps. Another box, she mused. It had red arrows pointing upward, as had the outer container, and the standard "this side up" warning.

Curiouser and curiouser, as Grant would say. A lot of expense in shipping and no return address.

She grunted as she tried to lift the box out, complaining to the curious tomcat watching the process. "My gosh, it's heavy as lead. Someone sent me a set of weights. Maybe anvils, Jack. Hmm…Somehow, this smaller box must be attached to the outer container." Indeed, it was. After removing the foam packing she could see support braces on the underside of the interior box and suspected those braces were wood-glued or screwed to the outer container.

Jack ignored her, busily batting at a piece of packing foam. He whacked it and charged, his tail puffed out, claws skittering across the floor. He snagged it with a claw and tossed the piece in the air, then smacked it toward the wall and let it carom off before pouncing again.

Jessie watched his antics and smiled, then turned back to her project and puzzled at the inside carton. Finally, she left the inner box in place, still attached to the outer, and undid the leather straps. The last clasp let go with a snap. Inside, lay another cocoon of thick foam. It was a type of insulating foam that she'd seem blown around objects to form a mold so that the object could then be cast in bronze. It was slit down the center and the two halves duct taped together.

On top of the shaped foam lay a manila envelope. Jessie slit it open and pulled out a wooden gingerbread boy, a thin sheet of paper and a photograph. She stared at the image of a smiling family. Turning it over, she saw the names scrawled on the back.

Berg and Vi Nielson, Dominic and Adele…in happy times.

On the sheet of white paper were just a few words.

> *Jessie,*
> *May you always stretch your wings and fly*
> *above trouble in grace and beauty. Heartfelt*
> *and eternal thanks from an old whittler,*
> *Joe Helland*

Jessie felt her eyes fill. She set the photo and letter aside. She caught the edge of the thick foam and peeled it back. Her breath caught when she saw the whorls of dark walnut.

"Oh Joe, you didn't," she whispered.

Sweeping aside the rest of the packing, she stared at the carved base, the walnut mimicking the ripples of water lapping at the swans' nesting place. The carving had been painstakingly rubbed to a rich, mellow sheen.

The swan that had been unfinished in Helland's studio now stood solidly on wide webbed feet and stretched to its full height, its breast puffed out and its graceful neck extended, bill opened as if calling. The head was slightly tipped upward and in the brown head were luminous black eyes.

The wings were flung gracefully outward and up—substantial, exquisitely feathered. They lifted gloriously, triumphantly, upward toward the freedom of the sky.

ABOUT THE AUTHOR

MARY ANN CHERRY

Award winning mystery author, Mary Ann Cherry, is a professional artist much like her book heroine, Jessie O'Bourne, and was raised in rural Montana in an area similar to the fictitious town of Sage Bluff within her first novel. Cherry now lives in rural Idaho with her husband and several pudgy cats.

When Cherry isn't writing, she travels to art shows, where she exhibits her paintings professionally and takes part in "quick draws", producing a painting in about an hour's time from start to finish. Her work is in the permanent collection of several art museums, and she is a Master Signature and Emeritus member of the Women Artists of the West.

Usually, you can find her painting in her home studio or writing at a desk situated on an upper floor landing—one that affords a lovely view of a grassy yard and lush golden willow tree during the summer and the flower beds that are not getting weeded while she is putting down words. Luckily, the view is only frost covered branches and snow during those cold Idaho winters. Wherever she is working, the coffee pot is always on and the brew is of the good strong Norwegian variety that holds up the spoon.

Information on current writing projects can be found on Cherry's website: www.maryanncherry.net

If you missed the first novel of the Jessie O'Bourne series, be sure to read DEATH on CANVAS.

DEATH on CANVAS

The first novel of the Jessie O'Bourne mystery series finds the artist working with her Norwegian friend, Sheriff's Deputy Arvid Abrahmsen, on a desperate search for a killer and two missing Thomas Moran masterpieces worth millions. The paintings connect the cold case murder of Jessie's great aunt Kate with the present-day murder of a Native American grad student Jessie discovers in the O'Bourne family hayfield—a girl who whispers before she dies that her attacker was a cop.

The colorful writing in this award-winning novel offers the reader a glimpse into the mind of an artist and a view of the picturesque setting of rural Montana. Lovers of the mystery genre will enjoy the twists and turns in this who-done-it and laugh at the humorous interludes afforded by Arvid Abrahmsen and Jack Dempsey, Jessie's disreputable orange tomcat (appropriately named for a 1920's professional boxer).

With Jessie's biological clock (A.K.A. Big Ben) ticking away, the romance reader will also find themselves evaluating acting Sheriff Russell Bonham and hunky FBI art theft agent, Grant Kennedy, as suitable mates for their favorite artist.

Made in the USA
Middletown, DE
26 December 2023

46818739R00205